Requiem for a Patriot

David J Oldman

GW00492663

First published by Endeavour Media Ltd in 2018.

Table of Contents

1

Sunday, January 5th 1947

A stiff east wind was blowing, cold enough to take your breath away and – if the Met Office was to be believed – coming straight out of Siberia. I had heard it said that once over the Urals there is nothing to stop a Russian wind blowing our way; other sources have it that these days wind is one of the few things still able to get out.

I didn't know much about that, but standing on the cliff with snow whipping out of an opaque sky, Russian wind or not, it felt keen enough to cut. Like a razor drawn across skin.

I'd been cold before, in the winter of 1944-45 in the Italian Abruzzo traipsing through the mountains looking for any of our POWs who had managed to evade the Germans. And for any men still alive from those we had parachuted into the Apennines to assist the partisans. Ever since, I've been able to recall the sound of ice cracking underfoot on those isolated wooded trails; how the snow had looked lowering on the slopes above us.

Now though, gazing out on the turbid North Sea, I was beginning to reassess my definition of cold.

Below me, the figure on the beach was becoming blurred by the falling snow. He had been out there for more than an hour moving like a wraith against the foreshore, and I had begun to doubt whether he was there to keep a rendezvous at all. I was starting to wonder if he had any better idea what he was doing there than I did.

His progress seemed aimless. He'd walk a few yards then stop to stare out across that rough and dreary sea. I suppose I began daydreaming. Thinking of Italy again and of warmer times in Sicily and Naples. Whatever I was doing I wasn't paying enough attention. By the time I came to my senses the blurred shadow had stripped off his overcoat and was taking off his jacket. Before I knew it he was down to his shirt and trousers, pulling off his shoes.

I yelled at him but that Siberian wind snatched the words out of my mouth. I started down towards him – there was no path – sliding and skidding through the mud of the crumbling under-cliff and hollering at the top of my voice.

He was in the water by the time I reached the beach and even if he could hear me I knew he wasn't going to stop. As I got to the shoreline I saw something that might have been his head bob momentarily above the waves. Then it was gone. After that there was nothing but snow, the grey sea and the chopping swell.

I had begun to unbutton my own coat although the impulse to follow him into the water didn't live long – no longer than I imagined he would live in that freezing sea. Besides, I wasn't ready to die yet. If that time ever came I was pretty sure I wouldn't do it by drowning myself in icy water. I'd have sooner taken the razor.

So I buttoned up my raincoat again – a thin, cheap affair that couldn't have kept out a summer breeze – and went through the pockets of the clothes he had left in a neat pile on the beach.

There wasn't much to find. He carried no wallet or identification, just a packet of cigarettes and matches and two keys – one with a fob to his room back in the small hotel in Riseborough a couple of miles along the coast; the other, though similar, might have been to anything.

I lit one of his cigarettes, cupping the match against the wind, then pocketed the keys. I thought how much warmer his coat looked than the one I was wearing. Mine was part of the nondescript apparel Watchers were instructed to wear: an old raincoat worn over a shabby suit and topped by a trilby hat. I had had to borrow the raincoat although the shabby suit was my own. I'd left the trilby in my room – it was either that or be forever chasing the thing down the street each time the wind took it off.

Looking again at the decent coat on the stony beach, now half-covered by the settling snow, I thought how the man was past any need of it. But the war was over – after a fashion – and I didn't suppose the taking of souvenirs was met with the same blind eye which had once been turned to that sort of thing. His shoes too, I noticed, were of good quality: Oxford brogues from a Bond Street retailer. Being a size smaller than the muddy pair on my feet, though, they were hardly a temptation at all.

I finished his cigarette and scanned the empty shoreline and the sea once more, watching the current and the waves running obliquely to the beach before that Russian wind. There was no sign of him although I supposed the coastguard might know where he was likely to wash up. I would have to call my office before I spoke to the coastguard though. Before I spoke to anyone for that matter. Reticence being a virtue in my business. So I left the clothes where they lay and walked along the beach until I found an easier path back up to the top of the cliff.

****

'You'll have to work the weekend, I'm afraid,' Bryce had said. 'His ticket is booked for Friday afternoon so you'd better go down in the morning. Will that be a problem?'

If it was going to get me out from behind my desk, I would have been as happy watching paint dry at the Service's new Leconfield offices. As it turned out, though, by Sunday morning I was beginning to think that watching the paint might have been the more exciting option.

The man's name was Joseph Wolff. Harry Hunter who ran the Watchers out of B6 at the St James's Street headquarters was short-handed and Abel Bryce asked me if I fancied a day or two away.

'Be unobtrusive and observe. Just act naturally. We're a little concerned about him and we don't want him to know we're keeping an eye on him.'

The way Bryce put it the job sounded quite paternal.

I was merely to watch. If it looked as if Wolff was about to return to London, I was to telephone ahead to the office. Bryce would be on call; if not someone else would.

They didn't tell me anything about him although Bryce gave me a thin file to read on the train down.

Wolff was an Oxford academic. According the file he had spent the war on some sort of unspecified government work. He had no family – there had been a wife before the war who had died of tuberculosis, and a younger brother who'd been killed on active service. No one else. After the war he'd gone back to what they call "the groves of academe".

I had always thought how very appealing the phrase sounded, conjuring up, as it does, pictures of leafy bowers and wood nymphs and a ceaseless supply of decent wine. Judging by what Wolff had done I didn't suppose it had been much like that at all.

****

He arrived at Riseborough late on Friday. I was there waiting for him. He had been shadowed on the train, I'd been given to understand, although I never saw the Watcher who'd come down with him. After Wolff checked into the hotel he stayed in his room for the rest of the evening. He barely left it the next day.

7

In the absence of any other reason for watching him, I assumed Wolff was there to make contact with someone. Consequently, I spent most of Friday evening in the residents' lounge where I could see the front door. Saturday was much the same. I read the papers and now and then, just for variety, loitered in the café across the road from where I could still see the hotel door. But Wolff didn't leave and no one else arrived. The only time I got a glimpse of him was when he came down for meals. Not that he ate much, just picked at his food while staring listlessly at nothing in particular. Then he'd go back to his room again.

It was Sunday morning before he left the hotel.

As he wasn't carrying his suitcase or heading towards the railway station, I assumed he wasn't going back to Oxford. I also assumed that this was to be the pre-arranged rendezvous.

Had I known exactly who it was he planned to meet, I might have tried to get in his way.

****

Back at the hotel I let myself into Wolff's room. The air inside was cold enough to make my breath condensate and I saw ice had formed on the inside of the window panes. The chambermaid had been in – the bed was made and a fire laid in the grate although it hadn't been lit.

No one was wasting coal on empty rooms that winter.

As I stepped into the room I had to resist the temptation to clap my hands and stamp my feet. The old saying "as cold as charity" came to mind and I remembered a magazine cartoon I'd once seen depicting charity as a hungry waif dressed in skimpy rags. I imagined her at that moment, kneeling at the grate where she'd be trying to put a light to the fire if only she'd had Wolff's box of matches.

The cold aside, the room looked in good order. The maid had been through although, judging by the neat way Wolff had left his clothes folded on the beach, I doubted she'd been left with much to do. There certainly weren't any untidy clothes lying around, nor any carelessly discarded papers or magazines.

I found his wallet on the table and beside it a note that began:

'This betrayal of trust is more than I am willing to accept. I have decided ...'

It ended there and I found nothing else in the room to suggest the nature of the betrayal of trust, or exactly what Wolff had decided. He didn't seem to have left a diary or a journal, not on the table nor in the drawers of the bedside bureau. I went through everything else again; through the wardrobe and through Wolff's luggage. In an elasticated pocket in the lid of the suitcase I found a letter. The envelope was addressed to Wolff but not to his college, merely to: *Mr Wolff, Oxford University, Oxford.* The letter inside was written on a single sheet in large childish handwriting:

'*Dear Mr Wolff,*

I have your name from my sister Oksana. She is friend to your brother who tells her you are at university Oxford. I cannot find my sister and would much like to speak to you of her. I am now at home of above address. Please write.

Katja Tereshchenko.'

The address she had given at the top of the letter was on West Road, Riseborough.

I read the letter again then went through the room methodically. I checked for envelopes taped beneath drawers; even looked for loose floorboards and gaps behind the skirting boards and architraves. Without any reason to think he would, I searched for any of the myriad of places where Wolff might have secreted something. After almost an hour, the name Katja Tereshchenko was still all I had for my trouble.

Downstairs, while the receptionist was busy with a guest, I leaned over the desk and left Wolff's room key along with my own next to another already lying there.

The receptionist looked across and smiled, said, 'Thank you Mr Tennant.'

I raised a hand and went out.

There was a public telephone in the hall for the convenience of the guests but I wanted somewhere more private. I walked down the road to a call box I'd noticed on the corner. I asked the operator for a trunk call to London then waited until the phone rang back, getting stiff and cold and feeling like a corpse in an upended glazed coffin. The operator told me how much money to insert and once through I asked for Bryce, feeding the box to keep the connection as I waited another age for him to come to the phone.

When he finally came on I kept it circumspect.

'This is Harry. Our friend went swimming this morning.'

'Swimming?'

'The kind of dip you don't come back from.'

9

Bryce remained silent for a moment. Then he asked, 'Did he meet anyone?'

'No. And his room's clean. He'd begun a note but didn't finish it.'

'You've got it?'

'Yes.'

'And there was nothing else?'

'A letter from someone called Katja Tereshchenko.'

He was silent again and I wondered if he recognised the name.

'No other papers of any sort?' he eventually asked.

'None. Shall I raise the hue and cry?'

'No, I don't think so, Harry. Leave that to someone else. You come back to town. We'll talk then. Bring the note and the letter.'

Someone would raise the alarm soon enough although I doubted if anyone was going to stumble on Wolff's clothes before the snow covered them. But he'd be missed at the hotel before long and I supposed his body would wash up somewhere along the coast in a day or two anyway.

2

Sunday, January 5th 1947

The only train to Norwich for a London connection that afternoon left me in Riseborough with four hours to kill and little of interest with which to kill them.

I'd been told the place had been a port of some importance back in the Middle Ages, but there wasn't any evidence of it now. Sometime in the 14th century a storm had washed half the town into the sea and then the river and the harbour had silted up. After that the North Sea had taken to nibbling at the coastline – an indication that once your luck starts running bad, nature has a tendency to put the boot in. More storms swallowed much of what was left of the town and many of those still living there finally abandoned the rest. There had apparently been a modest revival in Victoria's time when it became fashionable to bathe in salt water, but the North Sea being what it is, the town never really became one of the fashionable resorts. And, if Wolff was anything to go by, sea bathing in Riseborough had its drawbacks.

In January the town looked a desolate spot. What attractions it might boast during the summer were now firmly closed. A few bedraggled pedestrians had braved the weather, disconsolate individuals looking like vagrants in search of a bread line. I supposed them to be residents of a refugee home just outside the town I'd been told about, out for an afternoon ramble and gawp into the shops along the high street. But being a Sunday they were closed too.

I thought I'd kill some of the time waiting for my train over a pot of tea in the café across from the hotel where I had watched for Wolff. Perched on the cliff edge, the café had reputedly once possessed a nine-hole pitch and putt course in a rear garden. Until another storm had reduced this to six holes and left a bigger hazard than most golfers could comfortably contemplate. Crossing the road though, I saw a sign on the door announcing they were closed on Sundays as well.

It had gone 12 so a pub further along the seafront should have just opened and I walked on, head bent into the blustery wind with snow settling on my raincoat and already an inch deep on the road.

The pub was called The Dragoon Guard and featured a series of prints on its walls harking back to the days when soldiers were not only expected to die in the service of their country but to do it wearing fancy dress. I'd dropped in there on Friday before Wolff arrived, familiarising myself with the town. The barman turned out to be the sort who didn't need his nails pulled to make him talk and he'd been the one who had supplied me with the potted history of the town. I told him I was a salesman travelling in stationery and office supplies. He told me I'd find it difficult to make a sale in Riseborough. Even so he took it upon himself to suggest one or two places I might try.

There were a few customers already huddled over half-pints in the bar when I walked in, refugees from the refugee home by the look of them. According to the barman they were for the most part east Europeans – Poles, Hungarians and Czechoslovaks; displaced souls who for various reasons had washed up in East Anglia. When they weren't shuffling around the town looking in shop windows, I had noticed them wrapped in scarves and shawls sitting out on the cliff in an odd circular shelter that resembled a shrunken bandstand. Where perhaps, sitting in an easterly gale was for them some small remembrance of home.

Katja Tereshchenko, the name I'd found on the letter in Wolff's suitcase, didn't sound particularly Polish or Hungarian but it was east European and it seemed reasonable to assume the writer was the reason Wolff had come to Riseborough. He hadn't visited the home while I'd been watching him although he may have been expecting Tereshchenko to contact him.

After a few words with the barman to confirm his opinion I'd find business slow, I brought the conversation round to his customers and the refugee home.

'That's old Tibor,' the barman said, gesturing at the more grizzled of the two men sitting at a table. 'Speaks more English than most of them but that's not saying much.'

My easternmost language was the smattering of German I'd picked up in Berlin. Given the events of the last few years, I didn't suppose any refugee would be keen to be reminded of it, so instead of trying to talk to them I asked the barman about the home.

'A Miss Patterson runs the place, but you'll be wasting your time trying to sell her anything. Being a charity they're more interested in donations than spending money.'

I told him I'd give it a try anyway, drank up and left.

Following Wolff along West Road that morning, I recalled he had stopped outside a large building set back from the road and, for a moment, had thought he might be thinking of going in. As he hadn't, I'd not taken much notice of the place. Now, standing outside again, the redbrick monstrosity looming out of the snow, I saw the sign advertising itself as a "Residential Home".

It had once been an hotel according to the barman, then a school before finally becoming a home for refugees. In a changing world, I supposed that was as good as anything to be. Just what a refugee home was doing in an out-of-the-way place like Riseborough, though, was anyone's guess. Perhaps that was the point.

The place couldn't have been much to look at new and now the only architectural feature of note was a rusty fire escape that zigzagged down its facade like an articulated snake, frozen to the brickwork by the sudden drop in temperature.

The draughty entrance hall made the place feel as welcoming as a penal institution, the chipped tiles and scratched paintwork not quite cheered by a once colourful but now threadbare carpet. An old poster on the wall paradoxically advertised the attractions of a south coast resort.

At the end of the hall a nameplate on a door pointed me to Miss Patterson's office and, despite it being a Sunday, to Miss Patterson too.

I knocked and walked in.

An old paraffin heater standing against the wall was throwing out thick fumes; some battered chairs beside it provided a soft landing for any visitor who might succumb to them. The heater may have taken the edge off the cold, although I soon began to regret having thrown my old gas mask away.

Miss Patterson got up from her desk, a stately matron who cruised towards me with the effortless purpose of a dreadnought, double chin as solid as steel plating and eyes narrowed like a pair of twelve-inch guns seeking their range.

'Miss Patterson?' I asked, trying not to breathe too deeply. 'I'm so sorry to trouble you on a weekend.'

I took out the identification I used to carry while at my old army intelligence unit. It didn't signify much so I held it only briefly in front of her face before saying: 'Harold Tennant. Office for Strategic Planning – Department for Displaced Persons.'

She looked puzzled, as well she might.

'I don't think I'm familiar with—'

'We're based mostly on the continent,' I explained quickly before she was able to tell me what she was familiar with. 'That's where the vast majority of the people we deal with are found … ' I let the sentence trail so she might infer the rest. 'We're trying to trace someone by the name of Katja Tereshchenko and were hoping—'

'Goodness!' Miss Patterson exclaimed with a suddenness that set her superstructure quivering. 'Now you're the second person in two days who's asked me about poor Katja.'

I did my best to look no more than mildly surprised. It was difficult to imagine it had been anyone other than Wolff who had been asking and, if he had already seen her, it would explain why he had stopped outside the home that morning but not gone in.

'A gentleman,' Miss Patterson said. 'Friday evening, after dinner.'

'Friday?'

'The office was closed, of course, but he seemed rather insistent. Now what did he say his name was …? The name of an animal, I remember.' Miss Patterson's forehead creased with the effort.

If it had been Friday, Wolff must have called in straight from the railway station while I'd been waiting for him at the hotel. The Watcher from B6 was supposed to shadow him on the train and from the station to the hotel and I should have been told if Wolff had stopped anywhere between. Unless the Watcher hadn't known – hadn't bothered to track Wolff all the way from the station.

'Wolf,' Miss Patterson finally announced. 'That was his name.'

I asked her if the "Wolf" in question had told her why he was looking for Katja Tereshchenko.

'No he didn't,' she said. 'I asked, naturally. But when I told him that Katja was no longer with us he became most distressed. Very distracted indeed. To be honest, I'm not at all sure he knew quite what he was saying. Something about her brother, I think, but he wasn't making much sense. I'm afraid I understood very little of what he said.'

'So Miss Tereshchenko no longer lives here?'

'They came for her a day or two before Christmas. She really wasn't fit to travel. A weak heart, poor thing. She was never very strong and after what she had been through …'

'Who exactly was it that came for her?'

Miss Patterson's gun-muzzle eyes widened as if she expected me to know already.

'The men from the bureau for resettlement. Surely you're aware of the programme if you work for displaced persons, Mr Tennant?'

I smiled apologetically. 'You know what it's like, Miss Patterson. Sometimes the left hand doesn't always know what the right hand is doing …'

She raised her chin, giving the impression she always knew exactly what both her hands were doing.

'I wasn't here at the time,' she said. 'Had I been, I would have told them that Katja should be given more time to regain her strength. But my staff tell me the men were quite adamant that there could be no delay. All the arrangements had been made apparently.'

'Arrangements?'

'To re-home her.' She fixed me squarely with her twelve-inch gaze. 'I sometimes think we lose sight of the fact that these are human beings we are dealing with, not just names and numbers on a list.'

'I quite agree,' I sympathised. 'And where exactly would Miss Tereshchenko's new home be? Her name suggests …'

'She was Ukrainian, of course,' said Miss Patterson firmly. 'But I think that is hardly likely. I'm afraid I have no idea where she might presently be. They provided us with no forwarding address.'

'She has family somewhere?'

'Well, that's the thing, Mr Tennant. I understood there was no one left except her sister. Her sister is why she came to England, after all. Although, as I told you, Mr Wolff did say something about a brother.'

'Do you have any other Ukrainians here that she was perhaps friendly with?'

'Not anymore,' Miss Patterson said. 'Most of our guests are from Poland or Hungary. We do have a few Czechs but no Ukrainians. There was only poor Katja. We used to have some Russian guests although they were all re-homed a year or two ago as you probably know. They had been with us for years. Refugees from their revolution. Old friends. Then most of our residents are quite elderly, of course. Katja was an exception. But that was

15

due to her health, you understand. That's why I never referred her when she arrived. And it had been some time since the other men were here.'

'The other men?'

'The ones who came for our Russians. Two years ago was it? It must have been. My how time flies ...'

'Doesn't it?' I agreed. 'And were these men interested in Katja Tereshchenko at that time as well?'

'No. Katja wasn't with us then. They did leave me a contact number should we take in any more Russians or Ukrainians, but under the circumstances ... Katja was in no fit state to travel, which was why I felt compelled to write to them when I found they had come for her. I do hope I did the right thing.'

'I'm sure you did,' I said.

'Even though she *was* Ukrainian, I thought it an unkindness to take her from us in her state of health. And she certainly had nowhere else to go. She told me the rest of her family were dead. That's what seemed so cruel to me. Katja having walked all the way across Europe – a girl alone and suffering.'

'So she came here originally looking for her sister.'

'Not *here*,' said Miss Patterson. 'England. She had heard that her sister was in Yorkshire and came to find her.'

'And did she find her?'

'I'm afraid she was too late,' Miss Patterson replied sombrely.

'She had died?'

'No. She had left.'

'Where did *she* go?'

'I am afraid Katja was never able to find out. So sad.'

I commiserated for a moment then asked, 'Can you tell me anything more about her? About Katja?'

'Not much more than I have, I'm afraid.' She regarded me expectantly. 'Perhaps you can tell me what your interest in Katja is exactly, Mr Tennant?'

'Well I don't have the details,' I said. 'I'm just a small cog in a large machine, if you understand me. Tereshchenko is one of the names on my list. My task is to make first contact if possible. We try to put people back in touch with their families if at all possible. But she told you they were all dead?'

'Yes. Killed in the war except for her sister.'

'Would her name have been Oksana?'

'I believe it was,' Miss Patterson replied.

'And do you think Oksana was why Mr Wolff was looking for Katja? The sister who came to England?'

'Well, I really couldn't say. As I've already told you, he mentioned a brother … To be honest, though, he was less than coherent. Is it possible one of Katja's brothers survived?' Miss Patterson sighed with some feeling. 'She was so sure her family were all dead. And it was all so quick. They arrived without warning one morning and simply took her away.'

'It's always possible a brother survived,' I said. 'We do have Tereshchenkos on our list. And Mr Wolff gave no indication as to why he had come to see Katja?'

'None.'

I thanked her and told her we'd be in touch if we learned any more. Then I walked back to the hotel.

The biting wind was as cold as it had been when I watched Wolff wade into the sea, but I was happy to be out in it, out of the home. Outside there were no paraffin fumes, no odour of over-boiled vegetables and unwashed clothes, no reek of disillusion and hopelessness. I couldn't help thinking that even if, like Katja Tereshchenko, the inmates of Miss Patterson's home for refugees had escaped their fractured homelands with their lives, they still had little else. Wolff had obviously come to Riseborough to talk to Katja Tereshchenko about her sister Oksana; possibly about her brother, more probably about his own. Whichever it had been he had obviously learned no more than I had.

It was always possible there was more to be learned about his motives in his Oxford rooms and I assumed Bryce would have someone examine them. But as for me and Riseborough, there didn't seem much else I could do.

****

Snow was beginning to drift with the wind and at the station I found my train had been delayed. I missed my connection at Norwich and by the time I finally reached London the Tube had closed and there were no buses running. Stumping up for a cab, I endured a frustrating crawl through icy streets, the meter turning quicker than the taxi's wheels.

I was living in a Broadley Street mansion block, just off the Edgware Road north of the Marylebone Road. Although the flat was too big for me and more than I could comfortably afford, I had taken the place not only because my old Clerkenwell rooms in Cowcross Street had been scheduled for demolition, but also in the expectation that my wife and I would be living together again. That plan had fallen apart quicker than my Cowcross Street flat had when, the previous summer, my wife Penny had asked for a divorce. By the time this happened, however, I had already signed the lease on the flat and spent some money on redecoration.

In the event Penny and I were still married. She was the one who wanted the divorce yet still expected me to supply the grounds – as well as the room and the girl and the witness. And a photographer as well for all I knew. I had tried to contact her several times since the autumn, either to make her change her mind or, failing that, to arrange things to her satisfaction. Contradictorily, though, she refused to speak to me or to answer my letters. For the time being I had given up trying.

What with everything else that had happened back in the summer, I'd had little stomach to begin the search again for somewhere else to live. So I had moved in, regardless of whether I'd be able to afford to keep the place up. As it happened, not long afterwards they'd pulled the Clerkenwell building down and so, whether I liked that or not, there was no going back.

Given the shortage of decent accommodation in London I suppose it would have been no great problem to sub-let. But after living in Cowcross Street – two cramped rooms and cracks in the walls almost as big as some of the ravines I'd seen in the Apennines – I had been looking forward to a little comfort. Also, given the present weather, I was congratulating myself upon the fact I wouldn't have to spend the winter in Cowcross Street, with no gas for heating or cooking, and with water pipes that froze up at the first sight of a snowflake.

My new flat boasted the luxury of a gas fire and I'd been patting myself on the back since the cold spell began. I felt even smugger when the shortage of coal resulted in a run on electric heaters. Now though, to everyone's dissatisfaction, as well as cuts in the electricity supply they were talking about reducing the gas pressure, too.

And that wasn't the half of it. Everyone was grumbling about how, since the end of the war, rather than goods becoming more plentiful as people had expected, just about everything anyone needed to make life tolerable seemed to be getting harder to find. The shine was beginning to rub off of our Labour government. Bread had been rationed since the previous summer – something to which the wartime government had never had to resort – and what with ever-more stringent cuts seemingly introduced daily, people were beginning to ask just why we had fought the war at all.

As far as I was concerned, I had fought it so I could have a gas fire and, closing the door behind me, I wasted no time in lighting the thing.

Even so, it was still a while before the room warmed up sufficiently for me to take the cheap raincoat and trilby hat off.

When it did and I started looking for something to eat, I discovered I hadn't had the foresight to leave much in the larder before catching the train to Riseborough. But I ate what I found then, once the temperature in the room pushed above freezing, took off my coat and began my report on Wolff.

I vacillated for a while about mentioning the fact that Wolff had called into the refugee home straight from the station, since that had been before I took over the surveillance. The fact should have been recorded in the report of the B Division Watcher who had been detailed to follow Wolff on the train. But that was to assume whoever it was had followed Wolff to Miss Patterson's refugee home. As the Watcher hadn't informed me of Wolff's visit, I suspected he hadn't trailed him from the station to the hotel. In the end I decided to leave that detail out. And, having decided to do that, it seemed judicious also to leave out the fact I'd spoken to Miss Patterson myself – at least until I had consulted Bryce about the matter. So, all that finally went into my report was a description of what I had actually seen Wolff do at the hotel, his subsequent suicide and the details of my search of his room.

The consequence of which was that I made no mention at all of either the refugee home or of Katja Tereshchenko.

3

Monday, January 6th 1947

The news on the radio the next morning was mostly about the weather. The blizzard that had hit eastern England while I was shadowing Wolff was still blowing. Electricity supplies had been cut and travel on the railways and roads thrown into chaos. Anyone with a suspicious nature might have started wondering if the Siberian wind was yet one more ploy "Uncle Joe" Stalin had dreamed up to demoralise us.

Outside, the streets were already under several inches of frozen snow and turning black with London soot. Any traffic still moving was creeping along no faster than the pedestrians, and most of them were picking their way on the icy pavements as if expecting glaciers to open up beneath their feet at any moment.

As it was obvious I was going to have trouble getting into work, I didn't hurry. I had another cup of tea on the strength of having saved on my ration while holidaying in Riseborough, then swapped the Watcher's raincoat for my old army greatcoat and joined the rest of the arctic explorers on the street.

I managed to hop on a bus going my way although, after a while, we had to part company when it skidded into an abandoned vehicle. I elected to walk the rest of the way, cutting through Hyde Park and over the frozen Serpentine to Prince's Gate and the offices where I was currently working on our damaged Registry files.

At the beginning of the war the card index and filing system known as the Registry which had been in use with the Service through the 1920s and 1930s had been moved for safety from its base at the Mayfair Headquarters to Wormwood Scrubs Prison. With the heavy air raids at the time it had been thought that a prison would be a more secure home for the Service's files. As an added insurance against possible loss, a microfilm record of the Registry was made before the move. Once completed, the whole of the Service's filing system and records were shipped across town and into the old prison laundry at the Scrubs.

I suppose it had seemed a good idea at the time.

Unfortunately, the laundry had a glass roof and in 1940 that proved inadequate in keeping out an incendiary bomb. The fire and subsequent hosing down the files received reduced the Registry to little more than a black and sodden mess. It was an embarrassing situation but not thought an irretrievable one; not, that is, until it was discovered that the meticulously constructed microfilm record proved illegible. All of which left the Registry in Wormwood Scrubs not only a black and sodden mess but an *irreplaceable* black and sodden mess.

What could be salvaged was sealed in moisture-proof bags and given to the girls who worked in Registry – referred rather sardonically within the Service as the Registry Queens – to piece together and reconstruct. By the time I arrived six years later, most of the work had been done. All that remained were a few intractable gaps, those missing portions of files so damaged that it almost took the forensic skills of a pathologist to piece them together.

Regardless of ability that was the sort of work they liked to give new boys like me.

****

One of the first things I learned on arrival was that the Service was soon to move into new headquarters in Leconfield House, situated on the corner of South Audley Street and Curzon Street. A systems analyst named Potter had been employed to put the Registry on a more up-to-date and secure footing and he was already in the process of installing the revamped Service's records at the new offices. It wasn't ready yet but like everybody else I'd been given the tour shortly after I joined.

Potter – neat and tidy, grey and meticulous – had seemed more than pleased to show me over his domain, taking me around to the muted accompaniment of drilling and hammering overhead. He said the place was being soundproofed, which brought to mind a joke I'd once been told about the OGPU in Russia never soundproofing their basement cells on the basis that being able to hear prisoners screaming under interrogation encouraged the rest of the staff to toe the Party line.

Not a very funny joke, I admit, and I could only assume we did things in a more gentlemanly fashion in London.

Potter conducted me around the new Registry like a proud father showing off his newborn child. Or perhaps not a child. It wasn't easy to picture Potter procreating and, on reflection, it was more like being shown his new car. Second-hand, of course, as a man like Potter would only have had second-hand. Although it had to be said there was nothing second-hand about the Registry.

Covering the whole of the ground floor it put me in mind of library stacks without the books. The aisles were wide with tracks to accommodate the trolleys on which the files were to be moved. As this would be manually, I could only wonder how the Registry Queens would take to their new roles as pit-ponies.

'They will be held under three categories in the main,' Potter explained, talking about the files not the Registry Queens. 'Personal Files in buff folders in alphabetical order; Subject Files on organisations of interest, operations or events and the like; and the duck-egg blue List File which will contain material gathered during investigations which is not obviously accommodated in either of the first two categories. Needless to say all will be meticulously cross-referenced.'

'Needless,' I echoed.

'We use card indexes to locate the file required, adopting the punched-hole method so it can be conducted mechanically.'

Potter began to show me the method which involved master cards and needles that fitted the punched holes, but my mind was already wandering.

I pointed through the empty stacks to recesses set in the walls. 'What are those?'

'Lifts,' said Potter. 'That's how we will transport the files to the offices above when they're needed. Far quicker than staff carrying them up by hand.'

'And when a particular file is requested?'

'It will be signed on and off as now, although I am refining the process. A request form will have to be filled in. Any request will need to be approved by a member of the Registry staff. With records of requests tabulated, naturally.'

'Naturally.'

I reflected on how different the filing system had been in my old office where we'd investigated war crimes. There, if you needed a file, my corporal Jack Hibbert would turn standing piles of paper on their heads until it was found.

'So,' I recapitulated, 'all files will be accessible through the request forms.'

'Not all,' said Potter. 'Not all. There will be the Y-Boxes.'

'Y-Boxes ...'

'Where we will keep our most sensitive material.'

'In what way sensitive? Isn't it all sensitive?'

Potter bristled.

'Certainly. But the Y-Boxes will contain information not regarded as suitable for general dissemination.'

'What, like the names of informers say?'

'Spies ...' said Potter, '... suspected spies; defectors from the other side; those who *might* defect given the right inducement ... those from our side who have defected or are under suspicion as possible defectors ... associates and family of, and those connected to—'

'Sounds like they need to be big boxes these Y-Boxes,' I said.

'I've designed the system to accommodate any future need for expansion,' Potter replied.

Which, given the way things were heading, I thought was probably just as well.

'And how does one access this sensitive material, if necessary?'

'Only through the officer in control of the particular case. And ultimately through the Director General himself.'

Impressive, I thought to myself as I left, and once up and running difficult to get into.

Although in the meantime, the old Registry was back in Mayfair, still working out of the St James's Street Headquarters. But not me. I'd been allocated an office in the basement of some makeshift premises in Kensington. Where the damaged files in the moisture-proof bags were kept.

****

It was midmorning by the time I reached the office. Half the staff still weren't in so no one had missed me anyway. Down in my cold and clammy dungeon cell I found things to be much as I had left them the previous week and, as soon as I sat down, one of the girls brought me a cup of ersatz coffee and the same bag of blackened paper I had been going through before I left. I smoked a cigarette, looked at the bag and finally took out what was left of the file.

Its burnt pages had stuck together where they had been dowsed by the fire hoses. By now they had stiffened into the consistency of cardboard. I began prising them apart with tweezers in the recommended manner, releasing as I did little flakes of charred paper that floated around the office in the cold air.

It was after lunch when Abel Bryce finally put his head around the door.

'Everything all right?'

I was attempting to pry two sheets of brittle paper apart and, startled, I dropped the tweezers and the paper on to my desk where it broke in several pieces.

Bryce glanced at the shattered file.

'Any trouble getting back?'

I dusted off my hands. 'Train was delayed. I was lucky they were still running.'

Bryce perched on the edge of my desk, ran a finger through debris then examined the resultant smudge on his skin.

'I suppose Wolff meant to do it?'

'He wasn't wearing a swimming costume, if that's what you mean. And no one helped him in.'

I took my report out of my briefcase and handed it to him along with the suicide note Wolff had begun. I remembered the few words Wolff had written: '*This betrayal of trust is more than I am willing to accept. I have decided ...*' I asked Bryce what he thought Wolff might have meant.

'I've no idea, Harry,' he said, leafing through my report. 'He probably didn't know himself. Curious he went all the way to Riseborough to drown himself. If that's what he meant to do, he could have done it in the Isis.'

'He would have had to break the ice first,' I suggested.

Bryce gave me one of his wintry smiles.

I asked if Wolff had met anyone on the train.

'Not according to Hooper. He sat by himself and went straight to the hotel.'

'Hooper?'

'The Watcher who followed him down.'

I told him about Katja Tereshchenko and the home for refugees.

'I imagine that was why he went to Riseborough.' I passed him the letter from Katja Tereshchenko. 'I found it in his suitcase.'

Bryce read the letter. 'You found nothing else?'

I was about to tell him about the second key I'd taken from Wolff's jacket on the beach. But before I could, Bryce said: 'Have we got anything on this Katja Tereshchenko?'

'I'm hardly in a position to know,' I said. 'Isn't that your department? I thought it worth asking about her in the refugee home while I was there though.'

'What kind of refugees?'

'Poles and Hungarians mostly.'

'Russians?'

'There were some, apparently. Émigrés … from the revolution. The woman who runs the place, a Miss Patterson, told me they'd been re-homed a couple of years ago.'

'And Katja Tereshchenko?'

'She was Ukrainian.'

'And you say Wolff attempted to contact her?'

'Yes, but straight from the train. Before he came to the hotel. He was too late though.'

'In what way late?'

'Katja Tereshchenko wasn't there. A couple of men from some resettlement bureau came for her before Christmas. She was in bad health, apparently, but they insisted.'

'So Wolff never saw her?'

'Not on this visit.'

'Tereshchenko? Ukrainian, you say?'

'According to Miss Patterson. She said she didn't know much about her, only that her family was dead and that she'd had a bad time of it before she arrived. There was the sister she mentioned in the letter. Up north somewhere, apparently, but she couldn't find her. It might be worth talking to the other residents if you're interested. There aren't any Ukrainians left now but some of the others there might have got to know her.'

Bryce folded the letter in two and tucked it into the breast pocket of his jacket.

'Would you like me to follow it up?'

He stood up. 'No, Harry, I don't think so. I'll see if we've got anything on Tereshchenko or this refugee home. Now Wolff's dead it's probably not of any consequence.' He glanced down at my desk and the bag of musty paper. 'How are you getting on? Making progress?'

'I've not unearthed any pre-war spy rings if that's what you mean.'

Bryce smiled again but his heart didn't seem to be in it.

'Tedious work, I know. But top floor regard it as important.'

I felt like asking in what way. The Registry Queens had reconstructed the majority of the system from the damaged files and illegible microfilm years ago. Now it was being put into far more accessible form at Leconfield House, all that was left were a few burnt files, so fragile they usually fell to pieces as soon as they were touched. As far as I could see none of it was of much value at all.

'Watching Wolff made a pleasant change,' I ventured.

'Well,' Bryce said, nibbling at the bait, 'we may soon have something else for you.'

'More Watching? Are the Russians sending over more men than B6 can cope with?'

'As a matter of fact,' Bryce said, 'at the moment it's not the Russians who are stretching our resources.'

I laughed. 'Yanks playing up?'

That didn't even rate a wintry smile.

'A little closer to home than that.' He leaned over the desk as if even in a Service's basement he was afraid of being overheard. 'We've had a tip that Irgun and the Stern Gang are planning something here.'

Before I could ask planning what, one of the girls came in to see if we wanted tea. Bryce declined but gave her a smile that was anything but wintry.

He turned back to me.

'Everything all right otherwise, Harry? Have you put in your expenses for your weekend away?'

It was the first thing I'd done. Working in Administration as I did, I had a pretty good idea of how long it would take until I'd be reimbursed. I suspected my not being an official Watcher would be the sort of anomaly that was going to require all sorts of checks and counter-signatures in place before Accounts would be sufficiently satisfied to part with the few pounds I was out of pocket.

'And how's the family?' Bryce asked unexpectedly.

I wasn't quite sure which family he was referring to. There was my wife and my in-laws, and then there was my mother and my brother. The two didn't interlink except through Penny, although I was pretty much *persona non grata* with both camps. I only ever heard news if something was required of me, or one of them felt the need to vent some personal acrimony.

'I don't hear anything much of them,' I told him. 'Not after that Pellisier business last summer.'

Bryce tried to look sympathetic. 'No? A bad show, you getting caught up in all that.'

Which I thought was a bit rich since Bryce had been the one to kick it all off in the first place and had then deliberately drawn me into it because of my family connections.

'Well,' he added, tucking my report under his arm and adopting that innocent look he sometimes assumed. 'Perhaps they'll come around.' He nodded at me from the door, as if to suggest it might all be for the best anyway. 'Good work, Harry. I'll talk to you later in the week.'

4

Thursday, January 9th 1947

By midweek the weather had warmed up sufficiently to shroud London in fog. The snow and ice on the streets had turned into a grey slush. Much of the rest of the country remained under snow, though, some isolated villages in Cumberland still cut off. The railways hadn't yet got back to normal either, which wasn't helping as far as coal supplies went. At the beginning of the year the mines had been formally taken into State ownership, only most of the talk now wasn't about how the industry would be on a sounder footing but about how Emmanuel Shinwell, the Minister for Fuel and Industry, had allowed the country's stocks of coal to run dangerously low.

It wasn't worrying me as I still had my gas fire. I'd spent the last few evenings huddled over it while combing through the papers for any mention of a missing Oxford academic or of a body washing up on the east coast. I didn't find either and it was Thursday before Bryce turned up and I learned anything new.

I assumed that by then he would have spoken to Hooper about not following Wolff to the hotel although, if he had, he never mentioned the fact. I wondered, too, if anyone else had been sent down to Riseborough to speak to Miss Patterson.

'Turn up anything on that Tereshchenko girl?' I asked as he walked into my basement office.

'The Ukrainian refugee? No, nothing.'

'What about Wolff's place? He had rooms in Oxford didn't he? Did you find what you were looking for?'

Bryce raised a sceptical eyebrow. 'And what would that be, Harry?'

'Whatever it was you thought I might find in his room at the hotel?'

He didn't reply and looked instead at the mess on my desk that was the file I was currently working on. Seeing the slight expression of distaste on his face I asked: 'Given any thought to finding me something else to do?'

'I'll let you know when we do, Harry,' he said, then added almost casually, 'The body washed ashore, by the way. About five miles along the coast.'

'You managed to get a positive ID, I assume?'

'From his dental records. Did you think there might be some doubt?'

'No. I saw him go in. Even Captain Webb wasn't going to swim his way out of that sea.'

He frowned and I said: 'The channel swimmer. There will be an inquest, I suppose?'

'Early next week. Nothing you need worry about.'

'No?'

'You weren't there if you recall.'

'No, of course not. So what now?'

'He's dead. They'll close the file. I'm told the matter was only ancillary to another issue anyway. Not of any great importance.'

'Important enough for Wolff to drown himself,' I suggested.

'If that's why he did it.'

'Well, whatever the reason, isn't anyone curious why?'

Bryce smiled, a little patronisingly I thought.

'Not as curious as you, Harry. That's *their* decision.' He started for the door then turned back. 'You did your part.'

'Did I? When the man I'm supposed to be watching drowns himself?'

'Could you have stopped him?'

'If I'd been closer, perhaps. I would have thought that if we were so concerned about him it might have been an idea for someone to have a word. It seems a cavalier way to treat a man who spent the war doing government work.'

Bryce looked unimpressed. 'Most of us did that one way or another. I would have thought getting through it alive was reward enough.'

That seemed a cold-blooded point of view to me, as if after everything we'd been through we just ought to pick up the old threads again and stop complaining. And even if Wolff had got through it alive he hadn't stayed that way for long.

'What was it about anyway?' I asked. 'If it was of no importance, it can hardly hurt to tell me can it?'

I got the wintry smile again.

'It always hurts to tell, Harry. You know what they're like upstairs. Maybe he'd just been jilted. I wouldn't worry about it if I were you. Case closed.'

I might have reminded him that I had no idea what they were like upstairs; told him that Wolff had been married before the war and that his wife had died. His brother, too. Bryce would know that, though, and besides, it was all beginning to sound like a good reason for drowning yourself. A self-tied end to the matter and that was that.

'Forget it,' Bryce said again. 'Case closed.'

But Bryce hadn't watched Wolff wade into the North Sea, I had. And it wasn't a sight I was finding easy to forget.

****

At the end of the day I bagged up the file I was working on and took it upstairs and along the corridor to Magdalena Marshall's office to lock away for the night.

Somewhere in her late twenties, Magdalena Marshall was a coolly efficient woman who had been with the Service through the war and was – in effect if not officially – the person who ran the section of Administration to which I'd been appended.

On being introduced to her I'd thought Magdalena was a lot of name for anyone to carry about but I was told her father was a bishop – one of the tub-thumping, Old Testament kind – and the name, after all, had a biblical derivation. It crossed my mind he may have subscribed to the doctrine of predestination, but if so had saddled his daughter with a burden she was going to have to spend *this* life living down.

I'd heard that her friends called her Mags for short but if they did it was the shortest thing about her. She stood over six foot in heels and looked down on most of the men in the building – and not simply because of her height. Needless to say I never called her Mags. She was Miss Marshall to me and she was good enough to call me Mr Tennant.

Also needless to say, her family gave her the kind of provenance shared by most of the girls who worked for the Service. The recruitment policy of the first director, Vernon Kell, had been so deeply ingrained you could now hardly walk down the corridor without bumping into a debutante or find a socialite or two running around the office. Kell's reasoning, formed before the First War, was apparently based upon the supposition that, along with their provenance and because of it, came unquestioned loyalty to the country. Even if some of them weren't too bright.

Whether the girls had learned on the job or the powers that be had become more picky, I couldn't tell. By the time I joined, though, it was plain that most of the girls working there were as sharp or sharper than the men they worked for. Not that that meant they'd ever be more than clerks and typists, of course; Service policy apparently reserved the status of "officer" to employees of the male gender only.

There had been occasional exceptions although Magdalena Marshall wasn't among them. Nevertheless it was generally acknowledged that, to all intents and purposes, she ran the department; if you ever wanted anything, it was quicker to go through Magdalena than the man who was the titular head.

As I walked into her office she looked up and gazed through dark-rimmed glasses at me, giving me the feeling as usual of being a specimen under observation. Since she was sitting behind her desk she had a slightly less formidable air and I was able to maintain at least the fiction of a height advantage.

I placed the moisture-proof bag on her desk.

'All finished, Mr Tennant?' she asked.

Her voice had a throaty purr that I found at odds with her otherwise austere appearance, as if she was operating under false pretences. Under its spell I had once suggested that she call me Harry. But only that once. Closer acquaintance soon led me to believe that I had already joined those men upon whom she looked down.

'As much as I can get out of this one, Miss Marshall,' I admitted, handing her the separate sheet of paper on which I'd detailed the few meagre words I had been able to decipher.

She glanced through the disjointed phrases I'd noted without commenting.

'Not much progress today,' I added, trying not to sound too apologetic.

'Mr Bryce called in, I believe.'

I smiled. 'I can hardly blame Mr Bryce for the lack of progress. He merely wanted to tie up a few loose ends from that business I was engaged on over the weekend.'

I had half-expected, in fact, that Bryce had to come to see me because I hadn't included in my report the fact that Hooper, the Watcher, hadn't followed Wolff all the way to the hotel. Now, standing in front of Magdalena Marshall and thinking about it, I had an idea of saving him the trouble.

Working in Administration I had discovered it wasn't particularly difficult to get hold of employees' details. Access to confidential files held in Registry might be restricted to those with authorisation – and accompanied, no doubt, by sundry forms filled in and signed in triplicate – but the mundane information held in our personnel files was another matter. And along with such details as dates of birth, pay grades and pension entitlement, staff home addresses were listed.

The bag of papers I had been working on that afternoon was the same file I had been trying to decipher before Bryce had asked me to shadow Wolff. I was finding it intractable not only because of the damage but because it was boring. It held information compiled before the war on some left-wing journalist named Thompson. I had no idea what interest the Service had in him, although it was always possible that all the interesting bits had been burned beyond recovery. All I had ever managed to elicit were a few tedious details about Thompson's household accounts and the fact he was occasionally sleeping with one of the typists from his newspaper.

I watched Magdalena sort through the contents of the bag and made a suggestion.

'Of course,' I said, 'it might help if I had some sort of context as far as some of these difficult files go.'

She peered up at me over the top of her glasses.

'Context? In what way, Mr Tennant?'

I had already decided there was something mournful about Magdalena Marshall's eyes. Spending the war pouring over files in badly-lit offices was enough to ruin anyone's eyesight, I suppose, but as far as Magdalena was concerned I thought there might be more to it. In idle moments I'd taken to wondering if perhaps she had lost someone close to her during the war. Although on reflection and more prosaically, I supposed having a bishop for a father was probably sufficient to squeeze the joy out of anyone's childhood.

'Well,' I explained, catching myself just in time from committing the impertinence of perching on the edge of her desk. 'From what I can glean this fellow Thompson was some sort of left-wing journalist. So it seems logical to assume we would hold files on some of his associates. If that's the case, it might be helpful if I could have sight of them. To cross-reference, I mean. You can often infer quite a bit that's left unsaid when you have more than the single point of reference.' I smiled again, adding, 'Otherwise one finds oneself merely guessing.'

She blinked myopically as if my syntax suggested I might be the one operating under false pretences.

'You have done this sort of thing before, I understand.'

She slipped the sheets of blackened paper back into the bag.

'What, grub around burnt files?' I asked, sounding more like myself.

'Cross-reference subjects to build a larger picture,' she offered, rather more elegantly.

As this was shaping up to be the longest conversation I'd ever had with Magdalena Marshall, I began to flatter myself that she might have made enquiries about me. She soon quashed the notion.

'Mr Bryce told us you had a background in Military Intelligence.'

'I used to run a small war crimes investigation unit for the Army,' I admitted, trying to sound self-deprecating while at the same time letting her know I hadn't always been an office dogsbody.

Magdalena sat back in her chair a little, as if she was seriously considering my suggestion.

'I see no reason why you shouldn't have access to files you believe to be relevant,' she finally said. 'Of course, you will have to submit to me the names of the individuals whose files you wish to consult. I will then relay your request in the usual way.'

'Of course, Miss Marshall,' I assured her. Then, having got my foot in the door, ventured, 'This file on Thompson, for example, it only covers the years up to the fire in Wormwood Scrubs of course. Assuming he's not dead, would it be possible to see anything more recent we hold on him?'

She stood up, gathering the bag and rising an inch above me.

'We do have a new file on Mr Thompson. He isn't dead. He recently joined the government as an advisor to the Ministry of Transport.'

Amazed, I said: 'Thompson's in the government and we're still keeping a file on him? Is that ethical, Miss Marshall?'

She fixed her sorrowful gaze on me again.

'The Service has never claimed to be in the business of ethics, Mr Tennant.'

5

Friday, January 10th 1947

Patience not being a virtue I have ever been blessed with, I decided to test the matter of accessing the Registry files the next morning. I wasn't interested in the journalist Thompson, of course, and since he was on the government's payroll thought it might be best to steer clear of him anyway. The file I had been working on before his on a man named Jenner had been equally problematic, however, and I thought I might use him as a stalking horse. I drew up a shortlist of names and took it upstairs to Magdalena Marshall's office.

'I thought I might go back to Jenner,' I announced after knocking on her door. 'There were a lot of gaps that sight of some other Registry files might help. I've drawn up a list. I give it to you, is that right?'

She clasped her hands together on the desk. 'That's the procedure, Mr Tennant.'

I put the list in front of her and she pulled a ledger from a drawer.

'And this is in connection with the Jenner file?'

'Yes.'

I had actually taken the names from another file as well as Jenner's and had put Joseph Wolff's name in the centre of the list in the, perhaps naïve, hope it might pass unnoticed.

'Do they bring me the file or do I have to fetch them myself?'

'They will courier them here once they've been logged.'

'And apart from the Registry log and your record, does a copy of my request go to Abel Bryce?'

Her pencilled eyebrows lifted a millimetre or two.

'Mr Bryce is B Branch. *Not* Establishments and Administration.'

'Yes, but since he was the one who arranged for me to work on the files I thought he might want to oversee what I was doing.'

It might have been my imagination but I thought Magdalena Marshall squared her shoulders.

'Our department head, Mr Harrison, oversees the work done here, Mr Tennant. Not B Branch.'

Which I thought was pretty far-sighted of Harrison as we barely saw the man from one week to the next. But I nodded sagely and returned to my basement, not exactly whistling but feeling pretty smug about the way things had turned out.

The system appeared efficient enough but didn't seem beyond being exploitable; something I doubted would shortly be the case once Potter got his hands of the Registry files.

I would have much preferred to trawl through the Registry for Wolff's file myself but having it brought to me was the next best thing. And the best part was that neither Bryce nor B Branch would need to know I'd seen it – an interpretation of the phrase "need to know" I'm sure they had never intended.

****

It was quite late in the afternoon before the courier arrived with the files and Magdalena brought them to my office herself.

'I'll need to lock them away tonight for the weekend,' she said handing them to me. 'I trust you won't be too long.'

'I'll just have a quick look through now,' I assured her, 'and get down to it properly on Monday.'

It was going to be a novel experience working with paper that didn't leave me looking as if I'd just swept the chimney. As I undid the string that tied the bundle together I congratulated myself on my cleverness.

Pride before a fall, as they say, or perhaps it should be smugness before a pratfall. Everything I had asked for was there except the file on Joseph Wolff.

Instead of a file on Joseph Wolff I had one on a Joe Wolf, a union organiser in the Durham mines back in the 1930s. I went through it anyway, on the wildly implausible off-chance that my man had been a miner before turning academic. Or, less implausibly, that Joseph Wolff's papers had found their way into Joe Wolf's file by accident.

But they hadn't.

The only thing Joe had in common with Joseph was that he was dead too, killed at Dunkirk having been conscripted in 1939.

I took the file back to Magdalena Marshall's office.

'They've given me the wrong Wolff,' I said, any incipient jokes about barking up the wrong tree or sheep's clothing stillborn in the face of Magdalena's unreceptive expression. 'This one was a union organiser.'

'And your Wolff?' she asked, reaching for her phone.

35

'An Oxford professor.' I spelt the name out again.

I waited while she telephoned the St James's Street office and had a brief conversation.

'They are going to call Leconfield House,' she said once she had replaced the receiver. 'Some files have already been transferred. They'll get back to me.'

I was going to hang around for some idle chit-chat while we waited but Magdalena, obviously with better things to do, dismissed me with a casual, 'I'll let you know what they say, Mr Tennant.'

Put firmly in my place – back in the basement – I went through the other files just to pass the time. Although it was Wolff's I was primarily interested in, I hadn't picked the other names out of totally thin air. Most had some bearing on the damaged files I was deciphering and, while they may not have been of great use to me, I had always found poking around in other people's lives of interest – even as described in the Service's unremittingly dry and tediously mundane style.

It kept me occupied, though, which was just as well as it was over an hour before Magdalena Marshall reappeared at my door. Already well past the time we generally packed up and made our way home, she was decent enough not to mention the fact.

'No Joseph Wolff fitting your description, I'm afraid,' she said. 'In fact there are no other Wolffs on file at all – Wolff with two "f"s, that is. I did ask that they check alternative variations of the name; the spelling of some of our clerks leaves something to be desired, I'm afraid. And we do have two files under Woolf – one "f" and double "o".'

'Joseph?'

'No, Virginia and Leonard.'

She seemed perfectly serious.

'Are you pulling my leg, Miss Marshall?'

'Certainly not, Mr Tennant.'

'But Virginia and Leonard Woolf are the writer and her husband.'

'Quite so.'

I was still not convinced she wasn't having a joke at my expense – as out of character for Magdalena Marshall as that seemed – and was about to ask why we should keep files on the Woolfs. By now, though, I was beginning to acquire an understanding of the nature of the organisation for which I was working. Since neither of the Woolfs had been above poking the occasional literary stick at the establishment when it suited them, I realised that might be sufficient for someone "upstairs" to order them placed under surveillance.

Virginia was now dead, of course – and a suicide by drowning coincidentally. I had no idea what had happened to her husband, Leonard.

'If you found a mention of a Joseph Wolff's name in someone else's file,' Magdalena suggested, 'it might be that he was not deemed important enough to warrant having one of his own opened.'

'But there must be one,' I persisted.

'And why would that be?' she asked evenly.

Since the files I'd requested were supposedly in connection with those files I was working on, I could hardly say there must be a file on Wolff because I'd been sent to Riseborough the previous weekend to watch him. After all, I'd submitted a report on how he'd drowned himself. If there was no file where was that? And where was the one Hooper, the Watcher, would have been required to write?

'Not even a Samuel?' I asked, remembering the notes I'd been given to read on the train to Riseborough. And where were they?

'Who is Samuel?'

'Wolff's brother.'

She shook her head, setting her hair dancing.

'Is it possible,' I asked, the thought just occurring to me, 'that Wolff's file has been given a security grade above my clearance? Could it be in one of Mister Potter's Y-Boxes?'

'Possible,' Magdalena allowed. 'Although if that was the case I would have been informed. We don't expect our staff to work in the dark.'

Talking to her in the depths of my basement office I was prepared to give her an argument about working in the dark, both physically and metaphorically, although that wasn't quite the point at hand.

'I happen to know that Joseph Wolff is dead,' I said. 'Would a file have been destroyed under those circumstances?'

'We do not destroy our files, Mr Tennant,' she replied, as though the very suggestion was a sacrilege. 'Not under any circumstances.'

No, I thought, they'd rather have the Luftwaffe do it for them. Anyway, I had Joe Wolf's file and he was dead. It seemed once they had you, they had you for life – the present and the after.

I thanked her for her trouble and said I hoped I hadn't kept her late. She took the files away again for locking in the safe and I lit a cigarette and put my feet up on the desk. It was the position I liked to adopt on the rare occasions I needed to think something through.

There *had* been a file on Wolff because Bryce had told me it had been closed. And the reports Hooper and I had written must be stored somewhere along with the information Bryce had given me for the train. So either Magdalena was wrong in her assumption that files were never destroyed, or someone had become aware of my interest in Wolff and had chosen to keep me in ignorance.

And in ignorance was just where I felt I was. I barely knew any more about Wolff just then than I had the morning I'd watched him drown. It seemed to me that if I was going to learn anything else I would have to find a new tack, approach the problem from a different direction.

6

Friday, January 10th 1947

Joining the Service hadn't been my own idea. I'd got into a mess the previous summer – one not entirely of my own making – and Bryce and a man called Gifford from Special Branch who I'd known briefly before the war had cleared it up. They had disposed of an awkward body for me, leaving them with something to hold over me and leaving me with the distinct impression I was under an obligation.

When Bryce suggested I join the Service, though, the decision wasn't one that kept me awake at night deliberating. I was out of work at the time; my military career had come to an abrupt end when the war crimes unit I was heading was closed from under me and I had been summarily demobbed from the army.

Even so, I had expected more of the job. If nothing else it had promised a change of pace, an alternative to what I had been doing, which was mainly trawling through dusty files, cross-referencing the names of bit-players and the roles they had assumed in a bigger drama. Instead, I found myself trawling through another organisation's files. And these were worse than merely dusty.

Yet it was the boredom that irked more than anything.

In the event, I saw little of Bryce and nothing at all of Gifford. The Special Branch man, for all I knew, was busy spending his days clearing away awkward bodies for other people. Bryce was employed in B Division – Intelligence – a decidedly sharper end of the business than the dull environment in which I had been placed. That was A Division – Establishments and Administration – and, damaged files apart, the work appeared to consist mostly of the kind of tedious office duties I had done my best to avoid in the office from which I'd come.

There were compensations. Most of the staff with whom I came into contact were female. If they were no longer quite the bevy of debutantes with whom Vernon Kell, the first director, had reputedly liked to surround himself (most of those, I suspected, were sequestered over in the St James's Headquarters) they were in the main girls still out of a drawer somewhat higher in society's bureau that the one from which I issued. Copies, in fact, of the kind of girl I had married.

I had lost my footing there, though, and now found it somewhat ironic that the nearest thing to hand by way of companionship was a sort of ersatz simulation of my wife. A poor imitation, if you will, like the coffee and powdered eggs that in our straightened circumstances was all we were currently allowed. Like living a life on ration.

****

Hooper lived in Pimlico, down one of those narrow streets that back on to the bus station. Buses were running again through the slush and I found one going to Victoria and climbed on to the top deck. Much of the street lighting was still only working intermittently and the dark streets below me were still scarred by the German air raids after almost two years of peace. The snow that remained helped mask the ugly reality of the bombsites to some degree and, turning a corner, the bus would occasionally present a scene more like an urban Christmas card than a devastated city. But Christmas had come and gone and the ugliness under the snow was just waiting for the thaw.

Hooper's apartment block looked grey and inhospitable, like an inflated concrete bunker that had been abandoned now peace had been declared. He lived on the second floor back, which gave him a view of the bus station. Handy for a Watcher who wanted to keep his eye in, I suppose.

I rang the bell and waited, not knowing what to expect.

Along with the debs, most of those staffing the upper echelons of the Service were drawn from society's higher ranks – the superior end of the middle-classes, old established families, and not a few with aristocratic connections. Watchers, on the other hand, were drawn from the other end of the spectrum: lower-middle and working class fodder. More fitting, I suppose, for a type expected to hang around in draughty doorways and hop on passing omnibuses in pursuit of their quarry.

Hooper, when he opened the door and peered at me uncertainly, looked designed to fit the bill.

'Tennant,' I said, showing him my Service ID. 'A Division. You went down to Riseborough with Joseph Wolff. I was waiting at the hotel.'

He glanced down the corridor and I half-expected him to tell me to keep my voice down.

'Tennant,' he said, once satisfied I was alone. 'Right. What's up?'

Despite his name there was nothing spherical about Hooper at all. Thin and angular with a patchy stubble already shading his jaw, he was dressed in a cardigan and trousers. But for the raincoat and trilby, he looked as though he was ready for an assignment at a moment's notice. He had long bony wrists and hands one could imagine crawling around independently of the rest of him, like large white spiders.

I was still standing in the corridor. 'Have you got a minute?'

He shrugged and stepped aside. 'Does the office know you're here?'

'B6? No. This is just a loose end, that's all.'

I followed him into his sitting room. It was shabby, the frayed curtains drawn across the window unable to keep out the lights of the bus depot. The radio was playing – the Light Programme's *Up and Doing* – music and jokes – and I wondered if he was waiting for quarter-to-seven when *Dick Barton Special Agent* came on. A bottle of brown ale stood on the mantelpiece over the fire – more smoke than fire – and an empty glass rested precariously on the arm of a worn chair. Hooper wrapped one of his spidery hands round it and placed it beside the bottle.

'Sit down,' he said. 'What's the problem? I heard he drowned himself. Has he washed up yet?'

I sat in the twin of the chair Hooper dropped into.

'He didn't talk to anyone on the train, did he?'

Hooper reached for a packet of Woodbines and lit one. 'Not a soul.' He puffed a lungful of pale smoke at the darker stuff going up the chimney.

'And when he got off?'

'He headed straight for the hotel. I put it all in my report if you care to read it.'

'I'm in A Division. I don't get to read those,' I told him, having decided to keep to myself the fact that his report along with my own had gone missing. 'Bryce asked me to stand in at Riseborough. You were short-handed, he said.'

'We're always short-handed. There's only about a dozen-and-a-half of us. How they expect to cover all the work they keep giving us I don't know.'

'Is that why you didn't follow Wolff all the way to the hotel? Had another job to get back to?'

He looked at me sharply. 'What do you mean?'

'There's a refugee home in Riseborough. Wolff called there before he checked into the hotel.'

'I never saw him,' he said.

'That's what I'm saying. You would have if you'd followed him to the hotel.'

Hooper shifted in his chair. 'He was almost there. I only had a few minutes between trains so I went back to the station. I would have had a three-hour wait if I'd missed it. Did he go there again? Is that how you knew?'

'No. After he killed himself I found a note with a Ukrainian name on it in his room. I thought it worth talking to the woman who runs the home. She told me he'd called in Friday afternoon.'

'Well there you are,' he said. Whatever that was supposed to mean. 'No harm done. I suppose you put it in your report?'

'That you didn't follow him? No. I thought I'd better talk to you first.'

Hooper stood up and poured himself some more beer.

'You know what it's like, old man,' he said, his voice assuming a wheedling edge. 'Bloody cold it was and I didn't fancy hanging round that railway station for three hours. Who's this Ukrainian anyway? Did Wolff talk to him?'

'Her. And no, she left the home before Christmas. Wolff couldn't have seen her.'

'There you are then,' he said again.

'What did they tell you about Wolff?'

He shrugged his bony shoulders once more. 'What do they ever tell you? Follow your target and keep your eyes open.'

'You don't know why we were interested in Wolff then?'

'Don't know and don't want to know,' he replied curtly. 'Not my business. I do as I'm told and don't ask questions. They told me the man at the hotel was new so if you take my advice, Tennant, in the future you'll do the same. You're in A Division and they won't thank you for asking questions about B's business. Take my word for it. I've found in this business it pays to keep your head down and do as you're told. You'll learn.'

I left him to his brown ale and his woodbine, wondering if I really wanted to learn Hooper's business.

Monday, January 13th 1947

First thing Monday morning I found a message from Bryce on my desk asking me to meet him in the coffee room of the Travellers Club in Pall Mall at ten-thirty. Even though I had plenty of time it seemed hardly worth taking my coat off, so I turned around and went back upstairs, stopping by Magdalena Marshall's office as I passed. At some point I was going to have to tell her I no longer wanted the files that had been couriered over on Friday and needed to come up with a good excuse.

For now I just said: 'Bryce wants to see me. I'm not sure when I'll be back.'

She looked unsurprised and sadder than ever, regarding me from her desk with those doleful eyes.

'He's asked me to begin arranging things in the meantime,' she said.

'The meantime?'

'The files have begun to arrive.'

More moisture-proof bags, I assumed. I said goodbye to her then made my way out the building and across the road to the Prince of Wales Gate and South Carriage Drive. We'd had gales and rain over the weekend and, although a cold wind was still blowing, there was no longer any ice to make walking on the pavements difficult. I decided to stretch my legs.

I could have caught the Tube at Knightsbridge to Pall Mall, but the station was almost halfway there anyway and I'd then still have to change for either St James's Park or Charing Cross and have as long a walk the other end. So hoofing it seemed just as quick – through Hyde Park then Green Park, walking past the St James's Street headquarters where I would have thought it might have been easier to meet Bryce in the first place.

The Travellers Club was number 106 Pall Mall. I'd never been inside before – never been inside any of London's gentlemen's clubs except the Army and Navy – and then, to judge by the staff's attitude, only on sufferance. I was aware though that the Travellers, London's oldest club, had a cachet all of its own. It catered for members deemed "travellers and diplomats" which made me wonder what it took to be put up. I'd been all over north Africa, from Cairo up through Italy to Austria and Germany, but I didn't suppose that would count as travelling. Any more than my working for an organisation that routinely spied on foreign diplomats – some of them members probably – would get me in from the diplomatic angle. But they let me through the door when I asked, Bryce having left instructions at the desk, and escorted me upstairs to what they called the Coffee Room.

Like many similar establishments in this part of town the place had suffered some damage in the air raids that hadn't yet been repaired. Some of the antique wall panelling had taken a knock and a few doorways were still boarded up. But the staff appeared unperturbed by it all so I summoned what *sang-froid* I could still manage, finding after my walk in the wind that I had no trouble at all with the *froid*.

The Coffee Room turned out to be the dining room. Rows of long tables had already been set for lunch although peppered here and there I saw a few members were actually drinking coffee.

Bryce was waiting for me in one corner talking to a man at the next table. Bryce stood as I approached and the other man went back to reading *The Times*.

'Thank you for coming, Harry.' We shook hands and he raised a finger to one of the waiters who was doing just that at a discreet distance. 'Have some coffee. You'll find they still have the real thing here.'

We sat down and Bryce made small-talk while I thought it a pity he hadn't invited me for lunch instead as they probably served real food as well.

'We've been thinking,' Bryce said. 'How do you feel about tackling something new?'

I wasn't sure who the "we" were; whether the pronoun covered the whole of the Security Service or if Bryce meant merely himself and perhaps the man at the next table. Bryce had made no effort to keep his voice down and the other man – well turned out, I noticed, but balding above rather pleasant features – was well within earshot, even if he didn't seem to be taking any notice of us.

'If it'll get me away from those old files,' I said, 'I'm up for anything.'

'Still filing, I'm afraid,' Bryce replied with a smile. 'I think you'll find the work more interesting though. At least the information you'll be dealing with will be current. We want you to help assemble and collate the material we're gathering on the Zionist threat.'

'What you were talking about the other day?' I said. I glanced at the man at the other table, still a little uncomfortable at the way Bryce was discussing Service business within his earshot. The bald man seemed unconcerned, though, turning the page of his morning paper as if we weren't there.

'I told you we've been getting reports that Irgun or the Stern Gang – probably both – are planning an attack of some sort here.'

Our coffee arrived and Bryce at least stopped talking long enough for it to be served. The waiter stepped away and Bryce spooned sugar into his cup from a bowl overflowing with more of the stuff than I remember seeing since Hitler walked into the Sudetenland.

'We don't know as much about them as we'd like,' Bryce confessed. 'Which is rather amiss of us since the British have the mandate in Palestine. A report last August intimated that one of the groups was planning to send five terrorist cells to London. In their words, "to beat the dog in his own kennel". Their plan, it seems, is to operate like the IRA.'

'That'll concentrate Henry Gifford's mind,' I joked. 'How good are they?'

Bryce didn't seem amused. 'Good enough to worry us. We know they don't make idle threats. It was the Stern Gang that assassinated Moyne in November 1944. And it was Irgun who were responsible for blowing up the King David Hotel last July.'

I knew about the King David Hotel but didn't know Moyne.

'Lord Moyne,' said Bryce. 'He was British Minister of State in the Middle East. There were several attempts to kill the High Commissioner for Palestine, Sir Ronald MacMichael, as well. Now it seems they're after the Foreign Secretary.'

'Ernie Bevin?' I said. 'What an earth for? I thought Bevin was a supporter of a Jewish state.'

Bryce's expression turned sardonic. 'So he was until Attlee made him Foreign Secretary. You heard what he said at the Labour Party conference last year, I assume.'

I had no idea at all what Bevin had said. I never paid any attention to party conferences.

'I'm not much of one for politics,' I admitted.

'You don't have to have opinions in the Service, Harry,' Bryce said in a rather schoolmasterish tone. 'But you do need to know how things stand.'

'And how do they stand?'

'President Truman wants Attlee to allow one hundred thousand Jews into Palestine immediately.'

'All right. How many does the government currently admit?'

'Fifteen hundred a month. And this, remember, despite Labour having opposed a limit when in opposition.'

'That's the exigencies of power, I suppose.'

'Whatever it is,' Bryce said, 'it isn't helped by Bevin joking at the Labour conference that the only reason the Americans want us to allow mass Jewish immigration is so that they won't all go to New York instead.'

I smiled. 'Well at least we now know the Stern Gang and the rest of them don't have a sense of humour.'

Bryce regarded me sourly. 'I think any sense of humour they once had went up in smoke in the chimneys of Auschwitz. One thing we know for certain is that the leader of the Irgun, a man named Menachem Begin, has disappeared from his usual haunts. SIS think he might be in Paris and heading this way. They also think he might have had plastic surgery to alter his appearance.'

He took two photographs out of his briefcase and laid them on the table in front of me.

'This is all we have on him at the moment and we're far from sure how good a likeness they are.'

In both photos the man had adopted a hunched position, his head and unshaven chin pushed slightly forward, lending something simian to his appearance. His face had full downturned lips and round eyes that stared straight back at me.

'Ugly customer,' I said. 'If it were me, I'd consider plastic surgery even if Special Branch wasn't on my tail.'

Bryce ignored me and pointed to the less prepossessing of the two photographs. 'Gifford thinks this one was taken from Begin's military ID card.'

'And now he might not look anything like it.'

'Plastic surgery can only do so much, Harry. The point is, catching him from a visual sighting isn't very likely. Our best bet is tracking him down through any possible associates he has here. Watching them and waiting for him to turn up.'

'And how do we know who his associates are?'

'By collating all the information we're gathering on Jewish organisations. That's why we want you. You've had experience with this sort of thing.'

'Have I?'

'Your war crimes unit. I gather your work involved tracking suspects through witness statements and interrogation reports … gathering and collating any relevant information.'

'In part,' I admitted, 'but I had a staff to help me. I couldn't handle everything myself. I only assessed what they brought me.'

'We don't expect you to do this on your own, Harry. We're assigning Magdalena Marshall and two of her girls to assist you. You've met Magdalena, of course?'

Now I knew why she had looked at me so dejectedly earlier that morning.

'The files I've been examining come through her office,' I said. 'You've already told her she'll be working with me, I take it?'

'Oh yes,' said Bryce. 'She's been fully briefed. It's the sort of work Magdalena has done before so she'll be able to instruct you in anything you're not familiar with.'

The bald man at the other table had put his copy of *The Times* down and was looking at me with an expression so bland I could read nothing in it. I met his gaze for a moment then glanced back at Bryce. His expression, by contrast, was seriously earnest.

'This is important work, Harry,' he said.

'Of course. When do you want me to start?'

'I had the relevant files sent over this morning.'

****

'These are the HOWs,' Magdalena announced without preamble as I walked into the new office. It held two desks and a long table on which she had placed several stacks of printed paper.

'HOWs?'

'Home Office mail and telephone intercept warrants.'

'Phone taps.'

'And post. These …' she said, indicating one of the other piles, '… are ISPAL and SIME.'

'Don't tell me. Let me guess …'

'Intercepted Jewish cipher traffic from Palestine,' she went on regardless. 'SIME is Security Intelligence Middle East.'

'Okay,' I said. 'Whose phones are we tapping?'

'Mr Bryce didn't explain?'

'He wasn't specific.'

I might have imagined her shoulders slumped. What I didn't imagine was her manner. It suggested she assumed I was along as the token male. Like Harrison, I was a fig leaf that masked the fact that women ran the everyday work of the Service.

'Very well,' she said briskly, as though accepting the inevitable. 'The phones and post being intercepted belong to Zionist organisations and certain suspect individuals. The Jewish Agency and the Jewish Legion are established organisations and mainstream in their policies. The United Zionist Revisionists and the United Zionist Youth Organisation are both rather more extreme.'

'And the individuals?'

She picked a file off the table. 'Currently we are intercepting the telephone calls and the post of Harry Isaac Presman, Leo Bella and Samuel Landman.'

'And who are they exactly?'

'You'll find all relevant biographical information in the individual HOW file. These were compiled when the application for the warrants were submitted.'

'I'm sorry if you're going to find this awkward,' I said.

She blinked those eyes at me. 'Awkward, Mr Tennant? In what way?'

'Having to work with me on this.'

'Why should I find it awkward?'

'Well,' I said, beginning to wish I'd kept my mouth shut, 'I'm still feeling my way around here and we haven't exactly hit it off, have we?'

She seemed genuinely surprised. 'Is there any need for us to "hit it off" as you put it? If we're working together?'

She was standing by the table with her arms crossed, completely self-contained.

I tried again. 'What I meant was, it's going to be a lot of extra work for you. Seeing as I don't know my HOW from my SIME, I mean.'

'I'm sure you'll pick it up in no time, Mr Tennant. Given your previous experience with this sort of thing.'

I gave her a rueful smile. 'I'm not sure people have understood the exact nature of the unit I ran. I had a staff that handled all this clerical stuff.'

'And we have Geraldine and Lily,' Magdalena said. 'They'll be working in the adjoining office.' She indicated the door to her right. 'They'll be handling our copying and typing, any fetching and carrying needed … all the kind of jobs I imagine your previous staff used to perform for you.'

I opened the door to the next office and saw two girls working at typewriters. They looked up, smiled at me brightly, and said in unison, 'Good morning.'

'It seems as if everything's been arranged,' I said to Magdalena as I closed the door again. It was obvious she was still not happy about the arrangement. 'When were you told about it?'

'Thursday, when Mr Bryce came to see you. He asked me not to mention it until he'd spoken to you.'

'In case they decided I wasn't up to it?'

'I really couldn't say, Mr Tennant,' she replied impassively.

'If we are going to work together I'd rather you stopped addressing me as "Mr Tennant". Call me Harry, please.'

'I'm not sure such familiarity would be appropriate,' she said.

'I assume it will be appropriate for me to call Lily and Geraldine by their Christian names?'

'Of course. They are your juniors.'

'Quite, Miss Marshall,' I said, having made my point. 'Quite.'

8

Friday, January 17th 1947

The work, I found, was hardly less boring than trying to recover information from the damaged files had been. And while much of the SIME and ISPAL material came to us in the form of smudged carbon copies – something which took me back immediately to the previous year which I'd spent with my Intelligence unit sorting through carbon copies of interrogation reports – it turned out to be a cleaner operation than picking my way through the Registry's burnt offerings had been. Inky fingers aside.

One important difference was that the intercepts and taps Bryce sent our way were at least up to date. Many were less than twenty-four hours old by the time they landed on our desks. In the main, I was to be on the lookout for any mention of the Lehi terrorist, Menachem Begin; for any reference no matter how veiled that might suggest he had made his way to Britain.

Mostly, though, the bulk of material gathered on the particular organisations we were watching proved to be as tedious as the sort of work undertaken in any office – mundane in the extreme, no matter if it be business or bureaucratic. And against expectations, the telephone and mail intercepts turned out to be even more unrewarding, reminding me that it wasn't just myself who was leading an unexciting life.

****

By the end of the first week Magdalena and I had come to a working arrangement that suited us both. Almost always in the office before me, Magdalena would gather the SIME and ISPAL security intercepts, the transcripts and copies that had been made of the previous day's Home Office Warrant telephone taps and postal intercepts, sign for each of them and arrange them in appropriate piles on the long table. In order that we both became familiar across the range of the material we were reading and collating – the individuals under surveillance and their contacts – we alternated the work: one day Magdalena would read the HOW transcripts and the next day I would. In between we had the SIME and ISPAL intercepts sent from the Middle East to comb through.

After the first day or two I found I was having to ask fewer questions of her and from then on, sometimes for long periods, we often worked in silence.

The material, being for the most part innocuous, made tedious reading although now and then something of interest would turn up. Someone would get careless and drop an unguarded comment or name, or, conversely, some passages would appear too guarded in the language used. Anything of note which couldn't be filed immediately in the relevant Personal Files or the Subject Files that the Registry kept on organisations, we referred to Lily and Geraldine who placed them in Potter's duck-egg blue List Files. Anything of immediate interest was copied by one of the girls and sent by courier to the St James's Street HQ.

In the meantime I immersed myself in riveting questions such as that posed by characters like Chaim Polonsky from the Jewish Legion, who incessantly complained to an acquaintance about the difficulty he was currently experiencing due to the shortages in buying gefilte fish in London.

The routine proved undemanding and I soon discovered that reading other people's post and eavesdropping on their telephone conversations quickly became, like pornography, tediously boring after the first initial thrill. Far from corrupting, the biggest danger to the reader was the temptation to skim through the material without absorbing its content; to risk missing, amid the infinite tedium, something of note.

So it was at the end of the week when I almost overlooked the first hint of something suspicious that crossed my desk.

I was reading a transcript of a telephone conversation Leo Bella had had the previous evening with a man he referred to simply as Jacob and had almost come to the end of it before I realised the conversation had turned cryptic. Several times during their exchange Bella referred to certain "material" – something he had been expecting to take delivery of which was late in arriving. Jacob offered excuses – the weather, the state of the roads, the difficulty of getting the "material" to Bella in time for an unspecified purpose.

It was really only the fact that the word "material" was used in reference to something otherwise not actually named that alerted me to the fact the conversation was suspect. Had Bella called the subject of the conversation tins of spam, I don't suppose I would have thought twice about it. But he didn't. He called it *"material"*.

Our file on Leo Bella described him as a Jewish businessman of Russian origin, presently stateless. I reread the biographical information we'd collected on him and flipped back through some of the earlier intercepts gathered. Despite suspicions that Bella had links to a Paris-based terrorist organisation that included members of the Irgun Zvai Leumi and the Stern Gang, nothing we had so far assembled came close to substantiating the fact.

'I don't know if this might be worth sending over to Abel Bryce,' I said to Magdalena. 'It seems a little suspicious to me.'

I passed her the transcript and Bella's file.

She read both. 'Mr Bryce may well have already been alerted,' she said, 'but another copy won't hurt. You had better include it in your weekly report.'

'My what?'

'Your weekly report to Mr Bryce.'

'When am I expected to do that?'

'Fridays. He did tell you, didn't he?'

'No,' I said. 'It's Friday today.'

'Well,' she replied caustically, 'at least you know which day of the week it is.'

She took the transcript in question into the adjoining room for one of the girls to copy while I, put firmly in my place in my chair, lit a cigarette and wondered what sort of report Bryce expected from me.

When Magdalena returned she frowned at my cigarette and asked, 'Anything else from Bella?'

The transcripts in front of me had already been sorted by telephone number and individual subscriber and there was nothing else from Bella's telephone. I crushed out the cigarette and looked through the postal intercepts.

'No, that was the only call he seems to have received. Nothing outwards. He must have had a quiet night.'

'Or a busy one if he went out,' she suggested.

'Are we watching him?'

Geraldine came back in with the typed copy of Bella's conversation and handed it to Magdalena. She put it in front of me.

'You'll have to ask Mr Bryce that when you give him your report,' she said, glancing at the clock on the wall. It was already mid-afternoon. 'I suggest you start writing it now.'

I stared at the copy of the transcript for several minutes then surrendered to the inevitable. I asked Magdalena exactly what sort of report Bryce would be expecting.

Instead of huffing and muttering as I had supposed, Magdalena surprised me when she told me to draw my chair up next to hers while she told me what to do.

Within the hour Magdalena collated our week's output, tabulated and summarised our findings, and expressed it all in clear and unambiguous language. Sitting next to her, I watched entranced by her efficiency – and her eau-de-Cologne – until she broke the spell by collecting the papers together and squaring the edges on the desk. She handed them to me.

'Give it to Geraldine to type up. She's neater than Lily.'

I did as she suggested.

'Do you think you can manage that next week?' she asked when I returned from the girls' office.

'I think so, Miss Marshall,' I said. 'I'm sure I will.'

And, as soon as Geraldine came back in with the fair copy, I grabbed my hat and coat and left the office, musing upon how strange were the way things sometimes turned out.

And how much more pleasant had been the scent Magdalena was wearing than the air of tension which had been present in the office all week. Tinged, as it had seemed to me, with the redolence of gefilte fish.

****

The snow of the previous week was still giving problems in the north although in London it had largely thawed, the weather turning milder with blustery winds and sleety rain. It remained cold and in the dusk of late afternoon the lights of St James's Street glistened on the wet road. I was looking down on it through the window of Abel Bryce's second-floor office while he sat at his desk reading through my – or perhaps I should say Magdalena's – report.

It was a small office and a small desk and there was nothing on it besides the report except for an open file. A photograph of a man in a rumpled pinstripe jacket was attached; his tie was askew and he hadn't had the benefit of a razor for a few days by the look of him. The photo was upside down from where I had been standing earlier and it was difficult to make out much more than the name of Lev Aaronavich at the top of the page. It was a Jewish or Russian name – possibly both – and it was then that it occurred to me that Joseph Wolff might also be a Jewish name.

I'd not given him a great deal of thought that week what with the new work I'd been given and it struck me that it was almost two weeks since I'd watched him drown. I still had the second key I'd found in his jacket pocket, having forgotten to mention it to Bryce in the aftermath of the suicide and later too embarrassed by the fact to bring it up again.

I might have said something then had Bryce not broken my train of thought.

'Very comprehensive, Harry. Well done.'

I turned from the window. 'Magdalena Marshall gave me a lot of help with it. She's still showing me the ropes.'

Bryce nodded. 'I thought I recognised her style.'

'No line on Menachem Begin as yet but I thought the transcript of the Leo Bella tap might be something.'

'It might be innocuous,' said Bryce, 'but "material" could be a coded reference for explosives or guns.'

'For a person, perhaps? Begin?'

Bryce smiled tightly. 'Who knows. We'll certainly follow it up. All the indications are that the extremist groups want to bring their terror tactics to Britain. Not a pleasant thought given what they did at the King David.'

The previous summer when the King David Hotel in Jerusalem had been bombed I'd had other things on my mind. The atrocity had been all over the papers, of course, and although I'd read about it, that was about as much as I knew of the business. The rights and wrongs of the British mandate in Palestine or the views of the opposing sides hadn't meant much to me at the time – apart from prompting me to thank my lucky stars I'd not been sent there whilst in the army. The colossal loss of life in the explosion – women and local people among the dead, not just British army personnel – had seemed to even those sympathetic to Jewish emigration to put the extremist groups beyond the pale. No one was saying the Jews hadn't been through a lot and that there was an enormous amount of goodwill towards them after what had happened in the Nazi camps, but any more attacks of that sort – especially in Britain – would soon exhaust any fellow-feeling they might have counted on among the British public.

Personally, I saw no reason at all why they shouldn't have their own homeland in Palestine; but then I wasn't one of the Arabs currently living there.

Once the bombing of the King David Hotel dropped out of the news it dropped out of my consciousness too. I'd not given it another thought until

Bryce first intimated there was a terrorist threat from the Irgun and the Stern Gang. Now I had, I was starting to wonder if there might not be a Zionist angle to the business with Wolff.

I spent an hour or so with Bryce while he filled me in on what was happening on the ground in Palestine, details I wasn't getting from the ISPAL and SIME traffic. Until then, aside from what I'd gathered courtesy of newspapers and cinema newsreels, I had no real inkling of just how vicious the fighting had become. Acts of random violence against innocent people, simply because of where they were and what they were, had become almost routine; violence committed not only by Jews but by Arabs and the occupying British as well. It was having a deleterious effect on the morale of those trying to enforce the mandate and leading to the opinion the British would be better off out of it completely.

By six-thirty with a head full of current horrors, I was glad to get out of his office. And, when I ran into Brian Ogilvy who suggested a drink on the way home, I was only too happy to agree.

Like Abel Bryce, Ogilvy worked in B Branch. I'd been introduced to him along with a dozen other officers while familiarising myself with the Security Service's set-up during my first tour of the St James's Street HQ. The names of most of those I'd met had gone out of my head since, but I did remember Ogilvy. That was partly due to his urbanity and charm, which seemed to go deeper than the sort of patina that money and social breeding can bestow. But mostly it was because he represented that class which supplied many of the Service's Intelligence officers. He was a "Right Honourable" or something of the kind which, I soon discovered, was the other – male – side of Kell's coin in employing debs. They were "our kind of people" as the saying went, and if intelligence – without the capital "I" – wasn't rated quite as highly as who one's people might be, it was just an indication that, in many ways, Intelligence was still an amateur sport.

I had only met Ogilvy the once and so had formed no opinion of his intelligence. But I had been given to understand that he was highly thought of and had been filched after the war from under the noses of SIS – our sister intelligence organisation. I didn't suppose for a minute there had been a skeleton in Ogilvy's cupboard (or a corpse on *his* floor) that had obliged him to join, and assumed that his recruitment had been voluntary. Even so, I didn't hold it against him.

I ran into him as I was leaving the building.

'Harry, isn't it?' he said, extending a hand. 'Brian Ogilvy. Bryce introduced us. I'm glad I ran into you. Fancy a quick one or do you have to get straight home?'

'No, I'm in no hurry,' I said, wondering if the invitation was purely social.

All afternoon I had been half-expecting Bryce to ask me why I'd requested Joseph Wolff's file and, when he hadn't, thought I'd got away with it. Now having been collared by Ogilvy I wasn't so sure.

'I was talking to Bryce,' he said. 'He told me they'd taken you off those old files.'

We walked for a hundred yards or so before turning into a narrow street.

Ogilvy was a member of a drinking club not far from the St James's Street HQ, a place favoured by many Service staff. Any evening, I'd heard, you could find a half-dozen of them down there, knocking back scotch or swilling beer, apparently anaesthetising themselves against having either no one to go home to, or someone to go home to they'd just as soon not. Bryce had introduced me to the place along with a warning to guard my tongue and an injunction while there not to talk shop. I'd been in once or twice since, when I had a member to sign me in and when the fact of my having no one to go home to had overcome my aversion to the boys' club atmosphere.

As for "shop", I'd heard precious little else talked. What the club staff thought of it, I couldn't say. I supposed that working there would be an ideal position for a foreign agent although that must have occurred to everyone. So perhaps it was all simply some intricate game of double-bluff.

The club was in the basement of what had once been a gentlemen's outfitters. It was the kind of place that could be found in any Mayfair street although a bomb had closed this one leaving the basement intact.

Ogilvy signed me in and we walked up to the bar. A couple of men with vaguely familiar faces greeted him.

'You've met Harry Tennant?' Ogilvy asked. 'From Prince's Gate?'

'What brings you over this way, Harry?' one asked as we shook hands. 'Don't tell me you've caught us fiddling our expenses.'

We all laughed.

'Brian suggested a quick one before I went back to my cold flat,' I explained.

'Harry's a grass widower,' said Ogilvy.

'Occupational hazard,' the other one warned.

'For a secret service,' I suggested, 'there's not much you can keep to yourself, is there?'

They all guffawed again.

'How did you manage it, Harry?' asked the first. 'I've been trying to send my wife down to the country but she won't have any of it.'

'She knows what you'll be up to as soon as she's gone,' said the second.

Ogilvy had a scotch. I had a gin and French. The others declined a refill, one looking at his watch and feigning surprise at the time.

'She'll be standing by the door with the rolling pin,' warned his companion.

'That's why I always stop by for a couple before going home,' said the first. 'Numbs the pain.'

Everyone laughed again and they drank up and said goodnight. Ogilvy indicated a vacant table.

It had gone seven and the club was busy. Old drinkers left and new drinkers arrived. A blue haze of smoke hung in the air, stirring only when the door opened. I looked at the faces around us and found Ogilvy was looking at mine.

'Men with no homes to go to? Is that what you're thinking?'

'I'm new,' I told him. 'I'm in no position to judge.'

Ogilvy smiled and asked how the new work suited me.

'Pleased to get away from those old files, I shouldn't wonder. It beats me why they don't dump the lot. It's all pre-war stuff, mostly redundant. Time we realised there's a new world out there. New enemies to worry about.'

'The work certainly makes a change,' I said non-commitally.

'And Magdalena? How are you two getting on? We're all very fond of her at St James's Street, you know.'

I could detect no hint of prurience in his tone but I couldn't help thinking that it was there all the same.

'Well enough,' I said.

'Just well enough?'

Perhaps I should have changed the subject but decided there might not be a better opportunity to ask.

'I might be oversensitive,' I said, 'but I thought I detected a note of resentment when I arrived. Not just Magdalena Marshall, but among some of the others, too.'

'The girls?' Ogilvy laughed. 'Office politics, Harry. Don't let it worry you.'

'Politics? In what way?'

Ogilvy sipped his scotch. 'I imagine they regard you as having been parachuted in over their heads. They were probably hoping Magdalena would be made an officer. All the girls look up to her you know.'

'And was I? Parachuted in?'

'We don't have any female officers,' Ogilvy explained. 'We haven't since Jane Archer left. You've probably heard of her. Able woman but too critical of Jasper Harker, Kell's successor as DG. He had no choice but sack her. Petrie, of course, who took over from Harker, made it all but impossible for a woman to be promoted to officer grade at all. And our present DG, rightly or wrongly, seems to believe it to be purely a male preserve. As with a few of the others, Magdalena does the work of an officer. No question. But it's generally felt that anyone heading up a department – if in name only – should be a man.'

'But I don't head the department,' I said. 'That's Harrison.'

'Nominally,' Ogilvy allowed. 'He's due to retire soon.'

'And I'm not an officer,' I pointed out.

'You're a man though,' he said, signalling the waiter for another round. 'I wouldn't let it worry you, Harry. Magdalena might come across as rather reserved at first, but she'll come round. They always do.'

I felt a little uncomfortable discussing Magdalena with someone I barely knew but all the same couldn't help asking:

'Did she lose someone in the war?'

Ogilvy took a cigarette out of a gold case, tapped the end and lit it with a Dunhill lighter.

'The story I heard,' he said, 'was that she was engaged to a pilot in the RAF who was shot down in the Battle of Britain.' He grinned. 'Then if you tot up the number of dead pilots for every time you hear that story we would have lost the bloody war.'

'You're probably right,' I agreed.

'I heard you had a change of scene a couple of weeks ago,' he said, changing tack abruptly. 'Bryce told me Hunter co-opted you?'

'That's right,' I said. And on the assumption it was indeed Wolff's file that Ogilvy had wanted to talk to me about after all, decided to make no secret of the fact. 'Bryce asked me to keep an eye on some Oxford academic in East Anglia.'

'Drowned himself, I heard,' said Ogilvy.

'Yes.'

'Any idea why?'

'I haven't a clue,' I admitted. 'I wasn't given the details.'

And having given Ogilvy the perfect opportunity to bring up the fact I'd requested Wolff's file, it was almost a disappointment when he didn't.

'I did wonder,' I said, 'if the fellow might have something to do with this Jewish threat. Since Bryce put me on him.'

'Oh, a Jew was he?' Ogilvy said. 'Not my department, old man. They're all running around like headless chickens over Palestine at the moment. Taking their eye off the ball in my opinion.'

'Which ball would that be?'

'The bloody Bolshevik ball,' said Ogilvy.

'I thought they called themselves communists these days.'

'I'm old school,' he said. 'And at least with the Bolshies you knew who you were dealing with. The bloody Jews have got the Irgun and the Lehi, the Stern Gang and the Haganah Bet and God knows who else.'

For someone who said it wasn't his department it struck me that Ogilvy seemed to know a lot about it.

'As far as I can tell they're all one and the same,' he went on. 'In my opinion it's a pity they've waited until now to pick up the gun. If the Jews had been half as militant against Jerry as they are against us, Adolf might have found he'd bitten off more than he could chew and thought twice about invading Russia.'

Perhaps it was obvious I wasn't following his train of thought.

'*Then*, Harry,' he explained, 'we might not have half of Europe under Uncle Joe's thumb. Right? So, your man was mixed up with that lot, was he?'

'I've no idea,' I said. And, to pre-empt him, added, 'I requested his file, as a matter of fact. Just to see if there was a connection to what I'm working on.'

'And was there?'

'I don't know. I was told there wasn't a file on Wolff.'

'Chap's name was Wolff, was it?'

'Joseph.'

'And no file?'

'Nothing on him at all.'

He waved his cigarette in a dismissive circle. 'All sorts of stuff has been transferred to the new HQ and they've probably misplaced the thing. Don't care to admit as much. These days no one seems to know where anything is. I shouldn't be surprised if it doesn't turn up over there.'

'I did check with Potter at Leconfield House,' I said.

'In that case,' Ogilvy replied, tapping the side of his nose, 'it might be "need to know".'

'You're probably right,' I said again, happy to leave it at that.

We had a third drink, compared notes on our respective war service, then left.

At the end of the street on the other side of the road I spotted a stooped figure in a trilby, walking along the pavement with a shorter middle-aged woman. It was the man who had been sitting at the other table in the Coffee Room when I visited Bryce at the Travellers Club.

'You don't happen to know who that is?' I asked Ogilvy, indicating the couple.

'You mean you haven't met?' He sounded surprised. 'That's Guy Liddell. The head of B Branch. The woman with him is his secretary. I'm surprised you've not been introduced. He'll be on his way to the Travellers Club. He usually dines there.'

'Another man with no one to go home to?' I asked, as we turned in the other direction.

'Not anymore,' Ogilvy said. 'His wife, Calypso, ran off to America with her half-brother during the war. There was a big fuss at the time over custody of the children.'

'Calypso? That's an eccentric name.'

'One of the Baring banking family,' he said, as if that were an explanation. 'And if you think her name's eccentric, you should to meet the lady herself.'

9

Friday, January 17th 1947

Riding the Tube back to my flat and getting a chance to look through that morning's edition of *The Times* for the first time that day, I found an article on page four that reminded me of Miss Patterson's refugee home and her Russian émigrés. It was a short report on the execution of several Russian generals in Moscow after being found guilty of fighting for the Germans in the war. They were Cossacks, apparently, who during the Russian civil war in the 1920s had fought on the White side against the Bolsheviks. In 1939, caught between the devil and the deep blue sea, they had backed the wrong horse. It was difficult not to believe they would have lost their money no matter who they'd backed as, by all accounts, Stalin had a long memory.

I tried putting myself in their shoes, wondering what I might have done under the circumstances. But of course I couldn't. I'd been safe and sound – at least until I'd been shipped out to North Africa – and couldn't begin to understand what they must have felt as Hitler's Panzers powered their way into the Russian homeland. Perhaps if Hitler had triumphed, like Miss Patterson's Russians they too would have found a new home. It has been said that with the Germans at the gates of Leningrad and Moscow Stalin was about to run. He might even, like Hitler when he'd found there was no way out, have put a gun to his head. He didn't and more's the pity many of us thought. Then it was always possible that even with Stalin dead it wouldn't have made any difference.

As in any pantomime there is always another villain waiting in the wings for his cue to step out on to the stage.

It all made me think again about what Brian Ogilvy had said about communism and our taking our eye off the ball. I couldn't see that protecting ourselves against the threat of Jewish terrorism meant we were ignoring Russia, but I supposed it all depended upon one's opinion. The further Right one's stance, the closer – paradoxically – the threat from the Left loomed. Perhaps with a Labour government in power it was why some of those in the Service thought it politic to keep files on some members of that government.

Personally I had never held any strong political opinions. In the police force, where'd I'd been before I joined up, it hadn't been the sort of thing they encouraged. And although in the army they didn't mind you thinking for yourself occasionally, one soon learned that what they really wanted you to do was to do as you were told. No one actually expected you to have opinions of your own. Which is fair enough, I suppose, as the military is at the beck and call of whichever government happens to be in power; and those in it are obliged to follow orders regardless of what the individual might think of them. Again, fair enough, assuming the orders came from someone standing higher up rank's ladder than you do. After all, sitting down to mull over the pros and cons before deciding whether or not to obey or disobey an order is hardly conducive to the successful outcome of a military campaign. Routs are another matter.

I don't think I ever met a communist until I arrived in Berlin and came up against the Red Army soldiers while patrolling the various sectors of the city. Even then I never formed any definite opinion of them beyond an inclination never to trust one. But then I wouldn't have trusted a Yank or a Tommy either, particularly if the matter involved money, or a woman, or alcohol.

Like thousands of other servicemen, though, I had voted in the last election. Still overseas, I had sent in my postal vote in the expectation that someone would count it. I had voted Labour, not because I didn't appreciate the great effort Churchill and the wartime administration had put in defeating Nazi Germany, but because I couldn't see that after everything the country had gone through there was any way we could return to the status quo that had existed before the war. Whatever one's opinion was of Churchill, the truth was that he hadn't done it alone. There'd been Attlee and Eden, Herbert Morrison and Beaverbrook, and Ernie Bevin among others …

And primarily the "others" had been *us*: the ones carrying the guns and flying the planes and manning the ships; not to forget the ones in the munitions' factories and on the farms and down the mines … the men and women in civil defence … The list is endless. And it had seemed to me that to cast a vote for Churchill was to vote, not just for him, but for all the old gang who had let us drift into the unholy mess until it was almost too late in the first place.

At least, if not a vote for *them*, for their sons or their younger brothers; for the Old Boys' club ... the squirearchy ... for vested interest ... capital and finance.

In short, people like my father-in-law.

Not the best example to offer, perhaps, as Reggie Forster was still serving a prison sentence for what he'd got up to during the war. Although despite that he still seemed to me to exemplify the type of person who was running the country. That my wife's father had had his membership of the Old Boys' club withdrawn didn't seem to make much difference.

All the same, back in London and out of the army, a civil servant of sorts and one serving the Labour government I had voted for, I was coming to realise that things had taken on a different perspective. For one thing, expectations had been raised that had yet still not been met. There were plenty of plans – for a national health service and for nationalising key industries and the like – but from anyone's standpoint things seemed to be getting worse instead of better. We may not have succumbed to the Nazi tyranny (Churchill's phrases still sprang to mind even if he was no longer there to voice them) but having knocked the German monster down we had discovered there was another standing just beyond him. The fact that Stalin had *always* been there, not as obviously flashy as Hitler with his torchlight parades and gaudy military uniforms and ranting speeches, didn't mean he wasn't was just as murderous. To say now, as some were, that he was worse than Hitler seemed to me an attempt to compare the incomparable. But were we to believe we had only just discovered how murderous he was?

It sometimes seemed that was what we were now being asked to believe. And if so, we must have all been suffering from collective amnesia since 1941 when the Russian-German pact fell apart. Good old Uncle Joe had then become our ally and the uncomfortable truth was that we wouldn't have defeated the German axis without him. Yet to my mind it left us standing on very shaky ground indeed – almost as if, now we had cured ourselves of amnesia, we had in its place developed an acute case of paranoia.

What this all had to do with the Security Service being nominally apolitical, I wasn't sure. During the war I supposed the Service, like the military, had been allowed a certain amount of leeway in their actions. It had been necessary if we were to win. So perhaps I was being naïve in assuming that, along with the peace, government organs would resume taking a more ethical approach in their behaviour.

Then again, perhaps I was being naïve in assuming that they ever had.

****

The block in which I lived had been built in the 1920s as service flats although the economic collapse before the war had mostly done for that concept. Except for those up-market locations that could command a higher rent – and a better class of tenant. The place was a step up for me though after Cowcross Street, and while not as large as some of the flats in the block it had all the room I could use. The more spacious apartments on the upper floors had been subdivided into smaller units and the service element – maid service, a laundry and a small restaurant – all formerly situated on the ground floor and in the basement where the staff used to have quarters and where the kitchens had been located, had also been turned into flats.

Three girls rented the basement apartment. I often ran into one or another of them in the foyer where the postman left all the residents' mail for us to sort through ourselves. It was how I knew two of the girls were sisters, Frances and Muriel Southerby, and that the name of the third girl was Carol Newcombe. They were all smart dressers with, I assumed, jobs in town and I found them friendly whenever we met. Well, excepting one of the sisters perhaps. The two had similar features although where in one this resulted in modish good looks, in the other the same arrangement seemed almost to approach caricature. If, on canvas, Frances was a Renoir, then Muriel would be a Toulouse-Lautrec.

Carol Newcombe was, by contrast, no more than blandly pretty and seemed overshadowed by her friends although she did possess – as far as I could tell given the weather and the bundles of clothing everyone was obliged to wear – a very trim figure.

I got another chance to admire it when I saw her sorting through the mail in the foyer as I walked in. She looked up and said: 'Hello. Someone was just asking after you. He went upstairs.'

'Anyone we know?' I asked.

She smiled. 'And who do *we* know, exactly?'

'Good point. He didn't look like a debt collector, did he?'

'What do debt collectors look like?'

'If he turns out to be one,' I said, 'I'll send him down to the basement so you can get a good look at him. For future reference.'

'I think,' Carol Newcombe replied with a knowing smile, 'you'd better keep your debt collector to yourself, Mr Tennant. Don't you?'

I grinned and said goodbye. Then I followed my visitor up the stairs.

Of all the people I might have expected – and as if my thinking about my father-in-law and pantomime villains on the Tube were some sort of sorcerous incantation – on taking a turn on the stairs I found myself faced with the latter: brother George, standing in front of me as though he had been propelled on to my stage through a hidden trapdoor.

'George,' I said. Which might not have been original but at least was a start.

He offered me a diffident smile that didn't live on his face long and he gestured up the stairs.

'I left a note under your door.'

I edged past him and he followed me back up. The note beneath my door read:

'Called by but you were out.
Your brother, George.'

It certainly stated the facts but, like George himself, left much to be desired by way of explanation. I glanced at him although got nothing more in return than a slightly less assertive version of the earlier smile.

'Come on in,' I said. 'What are you doing here? Mother send you with a message for me?'

When I'd seen George for the first time on coming back home I had found it oddly difficult to adjust to the way my brother looked. I'd gone down to Gloucestershire to see Penny just as soon as I had been able to manage it and, since she was living with my mother and brother, it meant I would inevitably have to see them as well. I had got on with George well enough growing up. He was a year or so younger than me and I suppose I bossed him around a bit. Back then he was what was known as a "sickly child", always coming down with one complaint or another, mollycoddled by my mother and the centre of her attention. Which had been another bone of contention between us. But seeing him for the first time in almost five years I had been astonished by the change in him. Poor eyesight and a weak chest had kept him out of the army but he'd done his stint in the land army and it had been the making of him. Still not quite as tall as I was, he had filled out, looked weathered, tough and hard. I had been impressed until I found the change hadn't extended any further than his neck. Up top he was still the same diffident and muddled old George.

'No, something else,' he said, his expression turning obdurate.

That might have disconcerted me had I not remembered he always looked that way when doing something he didn't really want to do in the first place.

'You should have written,' I said.

'But you never reply.'

That was true and, even if it hadn't been, I wasn't going to argue the toss so I asked if he wanted something to drink. I'd used up my tea ration and didn't have any cider or whatever it was farmers were supposed to drink so, since the off-licence at the pub was open, offered to fetch a couple of bottles of beer if he wanted.

He said no and sat himself down on my settee, frowning and looking at his calloused hands as if he had recently discovered them growing out the sleeves of his coat.

'It's Penny, I suppose,' I said. 'I know she wants me to arrange a divorce, but it's not that easy.'

That wasn't strictly true but I didn't suppose George would know that. He had had a sheltered upbringing – mother had made sure of that – and probably didn't know much about the seamier side of life. Apart from watching bulls and heifers, that is.

I could have approached one of my old pre-war associates in the police. They could have doubtless pointed me at the right shady operative in Brighton or Clacton who could arrange the matter over a weekend that wouldn't be quite as dirty as the write-ups in the *News of the World* always made it sound.

'It's Mr Forster ...' George began, and I thought how Reggie would like being addressed in that way – a prospective son-in-law showing him due deference. Or at least the deference Reggie Forster would have assumed was his due. Not the way his presently real son-in-law addressed him, as Reggie, and mostly because I'd known it irritated him.

'What?' I said. 'Are they letting him out already? One old boy doing another a good turn, I suppose.'

'... he's dead,' George finished.

'Dead?'

'It was his heart.'

I'd never been entirely convinced Reggie Forster had had one but didn't think it was the time to bring that up.

'In prison?'

'In the prison hospital. There was some talk of transferring him out but he died. The day before yesterday.'

'How's Penny taking it?'

'Oh,' said George, 'upset, of course. We all are.'

George made it sound like a sad but inevitable loss. Like having had to move a once good milker now past its prime on to the abattoir.

'She blames you, naturally,' he added in much the same tone.

'*Me*? Reggie Forster over-indulges all his life, never putting one foot in front of another if he can find someone to do it for him, and it's *my* fault he has a heart attack?'

'That he was in prison, I mean,' said George. 'Penny says we could have taken better care of him if he hadn't been there.'

I didn't doubt she blamed me but the injustice of it still rankled.

'The fact he was in prison,' I said, 'was nobody's fault but his own. As his wife knows better than anyone. *I* had nothing to do with it.'

'Yes, but if it hadn't been for you no one would have found out.'

'For God's sake, George,' I shouted. 'It was *treason.*'

'There's no need to raise your voice,' he said. 'I understand you did what you felt you had to do. I've told Mother as much. But one has to be prepared to accept the consequences. You appreciate that, Harry, don't you?'

What I was beginning to appreciate was that I was well out of it.

'So when's the funeral?'

A look of concern passed over his face. 'A week Tuesday. You're not thinking of coming are you?'

It was tempting, if only to see the look on Penny's mother's face. But she'd probably get hysterical and that wouldn't do anyone any good.

'I'll stay away,' I assured him. 'But tell Penny I'm sorry, will you? Tell her I'll write.' I knew I wouldn't and George knew I wouldn't but it was the sort of thing one is expected to say. 'Where are you staying? Do you need a bed for the night?'

'No,' he said, getting up and looking a little sheepish. 'That's quite all right. We're going back down tonight. The reason I came up was to see our solicitor. Old Jenkins? You remember him? Something Mother wanted.'

He didn't elaborate and, as I walked him to the door, I didn't ask. I vaguely remembered old Jenkins and wondered whether our mother was cutting me out of her will. Assuming I'd still been in it. What hung in the air a little more pregnantly was the sentence, "*We're going back down tonight*." George and Penny had been staying with her mother, I assumed, but I didn't ask about that either. I no longer wanted to know.

10

Saturday, January 18th 1947

Wolff's rooms lay on the north staircase of his college. Although it was a Saturday I found the college busy, Hilary Term having begun the previous week. The weather remained blustery and wet but the place was full of students, passing in and out of the college and leaving muddy footprints in the grass across the quadrangle in spite of the signs.

The fact that undergraduate education had been interrupted by the war was evidenced by the number of older students. Some would be resuming their studies after war service but there were others who had taken up the grant offered to servicemen who wished to pursue degree courses. I'd come up by train and I suppose I must have looked like one of those eager to improve himself as no one looked twice at me as I walked past the porter's lodge and up the stairs.

Edging by two young men clattering down the narrow stairway, I climbed to the second floor, the key I'd found in Wolff's abandoned jacket on the beach near Riseborough in my hand. I was hoping it would fit the door to his rooms. According to what scant information I'd been given on Wolff, he had lived down one of Oxford's leafy roads until his wife died. After that he had given up the house they had rented and returned to college rooms.

Halfway along the landing I came to a nameplate on a door that read "Professor Wolff", and I pushed the key into the lock and found that it turned.

Stepping in and closing the door behind me I saw the rooms looked comfortable enough if lacking a woman's touch. But perhaps that's how it seemed to someone who knew Wolff's story. Bookshelves lined most of the walls, filled with densely erudite volumes on mathematics and statistical analysis to judge from their titles. I looked for something lighter – modern novels or whodunits – but it seemed as far as his reading went Wolff hadn't had a lighter side. There were a few pictures hanging where the shelves allowed the space – some charcoal sketches of what might have been 19th century Oxford, and a framed playbill from a Bristol theatre.

On the mantel stood two photographs, one of a wan young woman and another of a youthful Wolff in army uniform. He was smiling cheerfully, having no idea what the future held it seemed. A small alcove provided a kitchenette where he might brew tea or perhaps toast a slice of bread, but I saw no cooking utensils and assumed Wolff was in the habit of taking his meals in college.

I stood by a worn armchair in the middle of the room for a minute or two looking around before I disturbed anything. Everything looked in place but the telltale signs of book spines unaligned, of dust disturbed where an ornament had been moved, of a cushion in a chair left askew, told me someone had been there before me.

The police would have already visited the college but I doubted it had been them who had searched Wolff's rooms. In my experience premises turned over by the police were generally left looking like a scrap yard. I had always assumed it was the vandal in them – a streak of vindictiveness that often inhabits the detective. By contrast, this search had the air of having been conducted with cool objectivity. Had I not known Wolff for the tidy man he had been, I might not have noticed anyone had been there at all.

It left me feeling redundant. I didn't suppose I was going to find anything a professional would miss so I contented myself with a cursory look around, as if at the very least I might absorb something of the essence of Wolff from where he had spent his days. A thin sheaf of papers lay on his desk as though they may have been the last thing he had worked on, a single sheet fixed to the top by a paperclip. It was covered with pencilled notes in a hand I recognised from the aborted note I found in the Riseborough hotel room. Beneath, as best as I could make out, was some sort of mathematical paper – lines of densely written exposition in another hand, interspersed by algebraic formulae.

I looked through it but it was all Greek to me and I came away no wiser.

In Wolff's bedroom wardrobe I found clothes of the same quality as those he had left on the beach. They hung in rows, now as redundant as I was. On the bedside table there were more photographs – two of the woman I'd seen on the mantel. His dead wife I assumed, staring unsmiling at the camera, pale and hollow-cheeked as if already carrying the tuberculosis that killed her. In another photograph Wolff stood next to the young man in uniform I'd seen in the sitting room and who had I taken for Wolff himself. He was certainly a younger version of Wolff, although more handsome than the man I'd watched drown. He had had a brother, I remembered, and when I found several more photographs of the same man in a desk drawer – one of him regaled in robes complete with long wispy hair and a beaked prosthetic nose – I went back to the theatre playbill I'd seen on the wall. It was a Bristol repertory company production of *The Merchant of Venice* and heading the cast as Shylock was Samuel Wolff.

I spent a few minutes more going through the desk and looking again at some of Joseph Wolff's books, hoping to establish some connection between his Oxford life and his suicide. But I came to no conclusion. In the end I replaced the books where I found them, took one last look around and left.

I had just turned the key in the lock again when a door across the hall opened and a man's face appeared.

'I say,' he said, 'you haven't got a key to the Prof's room by any chance, have you?'

Since I was holding the thing in plain view there didn't seem much point in trying to deny the fact.

'Police,' I said, trying not to look furtive and ready to show him my Security Service badge if I really had to. 'Did you know Professor Wolff?'

He stepped out into the corridor. He was young and wiry with a once-decent face now marred by a scar pulling his left cheek into a crooked smile. It nearly gave him the appearance of being amused.

I suppose I was staring at it because he touched the scar lightly with his fingertips.

'Shrapnel. Lucky it didn't take my head off.'

'Bomb?' I asked, morbidly curious.

'No, Panzer shell actually.'

'Artillery?'

'Tank corps.'

I offered my hand. 'Bloody infantry. Well, mostly.'

He shook my hand, his own fingers stiff like a bird's talon.

'And now the police?' he said.

'I was in before it started,' I explained.

'Stick to what you know?'

'Something like that.'

'Michael Wright,' he said. 'I'm one of Professor Wolff's students. *Was* one, I suppose I mean.'

'You heard he died then.'

'Yes, it was all over college. Nice chap. A bit eccentric but that's usually the way with mathematicians. I daresay I'll get a bit odd if I stick with it.'

'So Wolff was a mathematician?'

'Number theory.'

'Oh?' I replied, none the wiser.

'What they used to call arithmetic.'

That didn't help much either but I knew better than to pursue the matter.

'You do have a key to his room, don't you?' he asked again.

'We're just taking another look around,' I told him.

'We heard it was a swimming accident although I can't see how. The Prof couldn't swim. And I can't see him paddling in the North Sea in this weather, can you? He was eccentric but he wasn't stupid.'

'I couldn't say,' I said.

'And he didn't have a dog, either, as far as I know.'

'A dog?'

'A statistically significant number of people drown trying to rescue their dogs from water.'

'Is that a fact?'

'Apparently.'

'I don't know anything about a dog,' I said, standing a little more erect. If I was going to play the policeman I thought I'd better look the part. 'You wanted to know if I had a key to his room?'

'It's just that I gave him a paper I'd written a couple of days before he went – where was it he went?'

'Riseborough,' I said. 'East Anglia.'

'Of course,' Wright said, 'the North Sea.' He stroked his scar again as though the wound might help his memory. 'The thing is, I need it back. The college has found us a replacement tutor and he insists I submit it to him. But the porter says he can't let anyone into the Prof's rooms until the police give him the say-so.'

I put the key back in the lock and opened the door.

'Decent of you,' he said and went straight to Wolff's desk and picked up the sheaf of papers I'd been looking at. 'This is it. Looks like the Prof made some notes. I hope he thought it good enough. Even Whithers wouldn't quibble if Wolff thought it passed muster.'

'Whithers?'

'He's the chap the college has assigned us,' Wright said. 'Only a post-grad although he knows his stuff …'

I heard a '*but*' and asked.

Wright pursed his lips so that even the crooked smile lost its air of amusement.

'I'm probably not being fair,' he said. 'It's just the fellow's younger than I am and he ... I mean he didn't—'

'What, serve in the war?'

He smiled sheepishly. 'Yes. I suppose that is what I mean. There's quite a few of us here who have come back ... you know, picking up where we left off ... For some reason that doesn't go down too well with fellows like Whithers. It's not as though we purposely make anything of it. Making a point of talking about it in front of them, that sort of thing. Well, not consciously, anyway. But I don't think they *understand*. What it was like, if you know what I mean.'

I said I did. After all, I'd seen a lot of it: husbands coming back to wives who didn't understand; men who couldn't understand why they were unable to find a job because civilians had filled them in their absence; civilians who couldn't understand why they lost their job because servicemen came back to claim them again ...

I'd been through something like it myself with my brother George. Mostly, though, I'd been through it with Penny; the experience made worse by my failure to understand that in my absence she had probably had a tougher time of it than I had.

Michael Wright was still standing by Wolff's desk, his paper on number theory or whatever it was clutched in his hand. And thinking of Wolff I said: 'You have to try to remember that those back here didn't have it so easy either. What with the air raids and rationing. At least we usually got to eat regularly. And it's not as though they weren't doing war work, too. Your professor, for instance. Wasn't he doing some sort of government work?'

'I suppose you're right,' he replied, not answering directly. He glanced at his watch. 'Well, thanks for letting me in, anyway. I was just off for a pint down the pub when I saw you. Now I'll probably need one before reading what the old Prof made of this.' He waved his paper in the air.

'That sounds like a good idea,' I said. 'Do you know a decent pub around here?'

He looked surprised. Perhaps he hadn't heard that policemen drink.

'I usually go to The Eagle and Child in St Giles Street. You tend to get a literary crowd in there but they're usually decent enough to keep to themselves. And they do serve a good pint.'

'Fine,' I said.

Wright grabbed a coat from his room, leaving his paper there while I locked Wolff's room once again.

There was a gusty wind blowing through Oxford's streets but The Eagle and Child was close by, an old and narrow building already busy with the Saturday lunchtime crowd. We bought two pints at the bar and found a table in a small room at the back.

Rather than rush him about Wolff, I asked where he had been wounded.

'Normandy,' he said, laboriously rolling a cigarette with tobacco from a tin after declining one of mine.

As it happens, I'd learnt a thing or two the previous summer about the fighting in Normandy, how tanks had found difficulty operating in the *bocage* until they crossed the River Orne near Caen into open country. I was able to hold up my end of the conversation while Wright told me how two other men in his tank had been killed and he'd been shipped back home. I told him something about North Africa and Italy and we were on our second pint before I brought the conversation round to Joseph Wolff once more.

'I suppose the work he did meant he wasn't conscripted,' I said. 'He was of an age after all, wasn't he? He couldn't have been more than thirty-seven or thirty-eight when the war started.'

Wright frowned. 'I didn't know him then, of course. And he'd already left Oxford when I came up. But I think he must have been a little older than that. I know he served in the Great War – at least during the last year of it. He always used to say it was the making of him.'

'Oh? In what way?'

'In forming his attitudes, I think he meant. He had no time for militarism or totalitarian regimes, you see. Seen too much of what that sort of thing can do. The kind of thing we had all too much of in the '30s.'

'He was left-wing, then?'

Wright fingered his scar again. 'No, I wouldn't say particularly so. Certainly not an apologist for Russia, if that's what you're suggesting. You'll always find some of those in universities, of course. What do they call them … "fellow travellers"? But not the Prof. He knew something about Russia, by all accounts. He didn't have much time for Stalin and the communists.'

'Did you know his brother?'

Wright shook his head. 'Only what the Prof told me.'

'His brother's death hit him hard, I imagine,' I suggested.

'Naturally,' said Wright. 'Although by the time I came back up he appeared to have come to terms with it. He certainly seemed proud of his brother. That's why he often talked about him I suppose.'

'Wasn't he an actor?'

'Before the war. I'd never heard of him but to hear the Prof speak you'd think Sam Wolff had been one of England's finest.'

'Did he ever speak of the work he did during the war? I asked.

'No, not a word. I got the impression it must have been hush-hush.' He laughed. 'Whatever it was it must have had something to do with figures, though. The poor old Prof didn't know much else. His field was prime numbers although they probably had him compiling statistics. Politicians and bureaucrats love their statistics.'

'And you say he was here when you came back?'

'Yes. I received an early medical discharge so was able to get a jump on some of the other fellows. The Prof was already here when I arrived. Happy to get back to his work, he told me.'

'Happy?'

'Content, I suppose I mean. It wasn't always easy to tell with the Prof. He usually seemed cheerful enough. Until towards the end of Michaelmas, anyway.'

'Last term?'

'Yes. Something must have happened. I wasn't the only one who noticed it. He became preoccupied. Withdrawn, almost.'

'Woman trouble perhaps,' I suggested.

Wright chuckled. 'That never occurred to us. The Prof never seemed the type. Although one can never tell ...'

'There were no rumours, then?'

'About a woman? No. None that I heard anyway.'

'And you've no idea what it might have been about?'

'No. I recall he'd been away for a week because it had given me time to work through a particularly knotty problem the Prof had set us. Then when he came back he hardly seemed to care how we'd tackled the thing. I thought he might be depressed or something ... The anniversary of his brother's death was coming up, I think. Though I don't recall it had upset him the previous year.'

'The Michaelmas term in '45, you mean?'

'Yes. His brother had been killed in November 1944, I think it was. But as I say, that was before I came up.'

'But the depression was clear when he returned from his week away?' I persisted.

'Depression might be a bit strong a word for it. The Prof wasn't moping about, or sitting staring into space. He was constantly busy but not busy with what he was supposed to be doing, if you see what I mean. He was preoccupied with something else.'

'Any idea what it might have been?'

'None. That's why I thought it might be because of Sam.'

He looked across the table at me, the earnestness in his face detracting from the appearance of good humour his wound had left.

'As a matter of fact,' he said, 'when I heard he'd drowned I did wonder if he hadn't done it deliberately. But do people kill themselves because their brother's dead?'

He seemed to be expecting an answer. Speaking personally, I wouldn't have been inclined to kill myself if George had died. But I supposed that Wolff had been closer to his brother than I was to mine. After all, I had no photographs of George decorating *my* mantel.

'And I suppose he never said anything to you about it?' I asked, evading the question.

'No, nothing. Actually, at the beginning of Hilary I thought he was back to his usual self. Still preoccupied but more his old self, if you know what I mean. I do know he was keen to get away that weekend.'

'To Riseborough.'

'Yes.'

'He didn't say why he was going down there did he?'

'No, but it must have been important to him. His mind certainly wasn't on his work. He was late marking papers which is why he kept that paper of mine longer than he should. I turned up for a tutorial the afternoon before he left only to find he'd forgotten all about it. Uncharacteristic, really.'

'But he didn't seem morose to you before he went?'

'No, not the way he had been anyway.'

I pumped him a little longer but learned nothing more. Wright was friendly and talkative but I thought he had already told me as much as he knew. Finally, probably tired of my questions, he drained his pint and collected up his tobacco tin.

'I'd better be getting back and see what the poor old Prof made of that paper of mine before I submit it to Whithers.'

I wasn't sure how his arithmetic was going to add up after a couple of pints of beer and suggested that, if he found Wolff hadn't cared for his paper, he could always ditch his assessment.

'Let Whithers make up his own mind,' I said.

'I suppose so,' Wright replied gloomily. 'But if Wolff thought it was rubbish I can't see Whithers giving it his seal of approval.'

I walked back to the college with him, using the excuse that I'd inadvertently left my notebook in Wolff's room. Unlocking the door once more, I went through the desk again, examining the photographs I'd found earlier of Wolff's brother, Samuel. I slipped two into my pocket – one of Samuel in army uniform and the other a posed studio portrait of the kind actors and their agents put around when canvassing work.

Having taken them, I went over Joseph Wolff's books once more. I pulled out two or three on statistics and skimmed through a few pages. Had I understood any of it, I might have come away with an idea of how statistically likely it was that Wolff might drown himself. But in the end, lacking any insight, I put everything back the way I'd found it and locked the door behind me for the last time.

For a moment I considered dropping the key back through the window of the porter's lodge, the way I had left Wolff's room key at the hotel reception desk. But if it turned up unexpectedly I thought it might cause a few ripples. That was just the sort of thing likely to start an over-sensitive nose like Henry Gifford's twitching.

I'd already been told that the case was closed and would be expected to accept the fact. I didn't think it would do me any good to have someone at work discover I was still curious about Joseph Wolff.

Or the manner of his death.

11

Saturday, January 18th 1947

By late afternoon I was back at the flat and decided to telephone Jack Hibbert, my old corporal at the war crimes unit. I waited a while as it was the first full season of football we'd had since before the war and the pools had started again, too. The results were always announced on the wireless Saturday teatime and although the weather had played havoc with the fixtures I knew Jack would be listening, marking his coupon.

Having started buying and selling with a friend out of a van, Jack was now in business for himself and had a yard in Tooting near the cemetery. I waited till six then phoned. He answered straight away and when I said I needed to see him he suggested a pub near his yard.

'I've got to go out anyway,' he said, 'but make it seven and I'll have an hour.'

I took the Northern Line at Charing Cross and rode the Tube to Collier's Wood. Too far south of the City to sustain a lot of bomb damage, Tooting hadn't been much to look at anyway. Away from the High Road, walking down Cavendish Road to Clarendon and Devonshire, I found the aristocratic names hadn't rubbed off on the area. Shops and small factories, lock-ups and yards at least gave the area a bustle that some of the more devastated parts of London might have envied. The pub was in Crusoe Road and I thought things might pick up when I got to Pitcairn – named, I assumed, for the island where the Bounty mutineers had ended up. By the time I reached the pub, though, there was still no sign of any tropical paradise.

I had just sat down when Jack walked in. Dressed in a suit – and not the cheap demob issue that made everyone look as if they'd just stepped off the pages of the same clothing catalogue – I hardly recognised him. The landlord addressed him by name and he had a few words with one of the other customers before bringing his drink to my table. Not his habitual drink, a pint, I noticed but a short.

I grinned at him. 'You didn't have to dress up for me, Jack. Or are you taking the old lady out tonight?'

'Nah,' he said as we shook hands before he ostentatiously checked his watch. 'I'm meeting an associate at eight-thirty.'

Jack used to have mates; I supposed now the fact he had associates was a measure of how far up in the world he'd come.

'Saturday night?'

His face had assumed the old lugubrious expression I remembered from sharing an office with him for several months.

'Just a bit of business over a few drinks.'

'Wining and dining? You must be doing all right.'

'Can't complain,' he said.

'Still buying and selling?'

'Army surplus. And not just army. The stuff they're getting rid of …' He shook his head. 'Pity they couldn't have been as free with it a few years ago when we needed it.'

I wondered if it was still black market.

'What kind of stuff?'

'You name it,' he said, pushing his glasses up his nose with a finger and leaning across the table. 'Anything you want. Most stuff's for sale although arms can be a bit difficult. Even them, though …'

'When I decide to start an insurrection I'll know where to come,' I said.

'Clothing …' he went on, '… camping equipment, tents …'

'I would have thought people had had enough of camping out.'

'Now, yes,' he said. 'But in five, ten years, who knows? I've rented the space. I can wait. Camping could be the coming thing.'

'Boy scouts?'

He shrugged. 'I know where I can lay my hands on a couple of Bren gun carriers.'

'You're joking,' I said. 'Carriers are a sore point with me, remember?'

'I can get you a Spitfire for fifty quid,' he said.

I choked on my beer. Now he was just bragging. 'What would I do with a Spitfire?'

'You could learn to fly,' Jack suggested. 'Or scrap. Not much in the fuselage and wings but the engines are good.'

'I just hope we don't have another war,' I said. 'If they're in this much of a hurry to get rid of everything.'

He knocked back his drink. 'Well, you'll know more about that than me.'

Jack knew I'd had dealings the previous summer with Henry Gifford from Special Branch and, after our unit had been wound up and we'd been demobbed, I'd told him I'd been offered a job by Abel Bryce. I hadn't said anything about the Security Service, but Jack had a habit of being a step or two ahead of most people and a knack of knowing things without being told. It was what had made him such a useful man about the office.

I just smiled. Jack took another tack.

'Seriously,' he said, 'there's money to be made. My problem is raising capital. If you've any spare cash, Harry, I can guarantee you a good return. Not much risk, either.'

'If I had any spare cash,' I said, 'I might be working for myself like you.'

Jack checked his watch again so I got to the point.

'I was wondering if you've kept up with any of your old contacts.'

He raised his eyebrows. 'That depends which ones you're talking about.'

'Army.'

Jack had had all sorts of connections when he'd been my corporal, working them whenever we needed to find something or somebody and didn't have the time for normal channels.

'I still know a few people,' he admitted. 'It's how I'm able to lay my hands on army surplus. You looking for something?'

'Information mainly,' I told him.

'Can't you do that through your lot?'

'My lot? No.'

'Is it kosher?'

'It's kosher,' I said. 'I didn't think that made much difference to you.'

'Of course it makes a difference,' he replied, sounding affronted. 'Especially if it puts me in Dutch with the wrong people. Like your lot.'

'It's all above board,' I assured him.

He gave me a doubtful look. 'Got a name?'

'A name, but that's just about all. Apart from this.' I took the photograph of Wolff's brother in his army uniform out of my pocket and passed it across the table. Given that Joseph Wolff had been employed on government work during the war, I thought that making enquiries about him might start bells ringing. So I decided to approach things obliquely and find out what I could about his brother.

'The name is Samuel Wolff,' I said. 'He died on active service, probably November '44, but I don't know where. He was some sort of actor before the war and had an elder brother called Joseph who was an Oxford don.'

'And you can't ask him?'

'He's dead, too.'

Jack peered at the photo. He lifted his glasses and brought it closer, then dropped the glasses back on his nose and squinted at it again.

'What's that, do you think?'

He pointed to the insignia on Wolff's tunic arm. Not full-on, it was difficult to make out. There was a dark patch with what might have been a cross within it, and some sort of design within that.

'I don't know,' I said.

'Could be FSS.'

'Field Security Service?' I looked closer but still couldn't make it out.

FSS were Intelligence Corps, small units that had been attached to Divisions in just about every theatre of the war. The prided themselves on being "first in and last out", part military police, part security guards, part investigative agents. They had done much the same sort of work as Jack and I had, during and after the war as the Allies had moved into enemy-held territory. Securing ports and airfields, command centres and the Nazi concentration camps, FSS had been in the forefront of rooting out the lesser war criminals.

'You think?' I said.

'Won't be so easy to track down if he was FSS.' He pulled on an earlobe and grimaced as if to demonstrate the difficulty. 'Tell you what, though, there's someone who might be able to help if I can't find out the usual way. The bloke I'm seeing this evening. His name's Sydney Stanley and he's got a lot better contacts than I have. But he might need a sweetener. You don't get 'owt for nowt these days, as Stan used to say.'

'How much?' I asked, reluctantly reaching for my wallet.

'No,' said Jack. 'Not money. Not what you and me can afford anyway. Besides, I thought you were pleading poverty?' He picked up the photograph again. 'Can I keep this for now?'

I didn't care much for the sound of someone who might not want money in return for a favour, but these days Jack knew all sorts.

'Okay,' I said. 'But just the same, be discreet.'

'My middle name,' said Jack.

'Be casual about it, will you? The fewer who know about this the better?'

He eyed me suspiciously. 'All right. If you say it's kosher. Mum's the word.'

'How is Stan, anyway?' I asked. 'Heard from him lately?'

Stan Woodruff had been one of my team in the Intelligence unit. A sergeant and an ex-boxer, he'd moved up to Burnley to go into the building business when he got out of the army.

'He's thinking of coming back down,' Jack said. 'Argument with his brother. You know what family can be like.'

I knew. And Jack knew I knew.

'I could put some work his way,' he said. 'But don't know whether to suggest it.'

'They don't come straighter than Stan,' I told him.

'Yeah, that's what I was thinking,' said Jack, as if that might be the problem.

We spent a few more minutes reminiscing then Jack said he had to go.

I couldn't give him my office number but the Service had installed a phone in my flat in case I needed to be on call. And since it was the Service, I didn't even have to put up with a party line. I wrote the number on the back of Sam Wolff's photo and Jack said he'd get back to me if he got anything.

****

In the event I didn't have to wait long. Jack called back on Monday evening, the telephone ringing while I was trying to make a stew of my leftovers. I took the spoon out of what was beginning to look like a mess of potage, and turned the gas down.

Jack got straight to the point as if he had better things to do that evening than talk to me.

'Your Samuel Wolff,' he said. 'He was lost on the *Scythia* off Murmansk in '44. That's all I've got.'

'Murmansk? So what's that, Atlantic convoys? I thought the uniform was FSS, not navy.'

'Maybe he was dressed up for a concert party,' Jack suggested. 'You said he was an actor.'

'Be serious. What was the *Scythia*? Convoy protection or merchant marine? Torpedoed, I assume?'

'I told you, that's all I've got. No one's giving me anything else.'

'If Samuel Wolff *was* FSS,' I said, 'does that mean it might have been some sort of Intelligence-led operation? What does it look like to you?'

'Nothing the British army did ever looked intelligence-led to me,' Jack said.

'I'm serious.'

'So am I. Maybe he was FSS, maybe he wasn't. But you know as well as I do that most of what they did was routine army bullshit. Guarding docks and the like ... General security detail. All so much KP duty ...'

'Yes, but what are they doing on Atlantic convoys?'

'Honest Harry,' he insisted, 'it's all I can get. You can try the Lloyds Register or the shipping list if you like, but if you ask me, your best bet is to find someone who crewed her. Assuming anyone survived.'

'And how am I supposed to do that?'

'Beats me,' said Jack.

'What about this friend of yours ... Stanley Sydney? Can't he get any more? I thought you said he had contacts in the right places?'

'It's Sydney Stanley,' Jack said. 'And it was Sid who got the name of the ship and that it was Murmansk. My usual people couldn't give me a dickybird.'

'Maybe your mate Sid isn't as well connected as he makes out,' I suggested.

'Oh, he's connected all right,' Jack shot back.

'Yeah? Who to exactly?'

'Sid is how I get to hear about the bigger government surplus contracts I tender for.'

'Tender? I thought you got your contracts by slipping banknotes in people's pockets.'

'Ways and means,' said Jack.

'And how does this Sydney Stanley hear about the contracts?'

'Because he's the sort of man who knows people ... if you know what I mean. The kind of man who can get things done where others can't.'

'You mean he's a fixer.'

'If you like.'

'In my experience fixers don't come cheap. I told you last time, I haven't got the money for—'

'It's not going to cost you anything,' Jack cut in.

'Everything costs someone something,' I said. 'Owt for nowt, remember? So why would this Stanley help me if he doesn't want money?'

'As a favour to me,' said Jack. 'You know how it works – you scratch my back, I'll scratch yours. No big deal. All he needs to do is ask the right person the right question.'

It all sounded like wishful thinking to my mind.

'Have you told him about me?' I asked.

'Yeah. But only that you're my old CO.'

'Not who I work for?'

'How do I know who you work for, Harry?' asked Jack. 'Anyway, Sid's all right. He's probably tighter with your lot than you are. Politicians and businessmen? You know what I mean … Where the money is. He doesn't usually bother with this sort of thing. You're lucky he took the trouble to get what he did.'

'Right,' I said. 'I'll light a candle next time I'm in church.'

'Sid's a busy man,' Jack went on. 'He's got bigger fish to fry than your tiddlers. Sid swims with the big fish.'

'Let's hope he doesn't get gaffed then,' I said. 'It wouldn't do you any good getting caught up in his net.'

'I told you,' he protested, 'I'm all above board these days.'

'Of course you are, Jack.'

'I don't see what you're so pissed off about. It didn't cost you anything, did it? Sid did it as a favour to me. Anyway, I've had an idea. It'll be a long shot so don't get your hopes up.'

'What idea?'

'Give me a ring the end of the week and I'll let you know if anything comes of it,' Jack said.

'All right. How's Thursday? And thanks for trying,' I said. 'I appreciate it even if it doesn't always seem like it.'

'Sure, Harry,' he replied. 'I know. Wasn't I always pulling your fat out the fire when I was your lowly corporal?'

I smiled as I put the phone down, wondering why all NCOs suffered from the same delusion of having the best interests of their officers at heart.

My potage had stuck to the bottom of the saucepan. But I was too hungry to throw it away so ate it straight from the pan, trying to ignore its charcoal-baked flavour.

I turned the wireless on but there was nothing I wanted to listen to and toyed with the idea of walking down the Edgware Road to see what was playing at the cinema. It had turned cold again with the wind back in the east and I thought it would be warmer in the picture-house than in my flat. I didn't relish the walk there and back, though, so in the end I washed out a couple of shirts in the sink while listening to what the wireless had to offer – a *Father Brown* story followed by Charlie Chester in *Stand Easy*.

I hung the shirts over a chair to dry, hoping they might be fit to wear by the end of the week before what few clean shirts I had left ran out.

12

Friday, January 24th 1947

I waited until Thursday before I rang Jack again. By then the cold weather had returned with a vengeance and everyone was walking around with pinched faces and red noses and wrapped up tighter than Egyptian mummies. Much of the country was covered in snow again and we'd even had several inches in London.

My weekly report to Bryce was due the following day and I'd been scratching around our files searching for something to pad out what little I had to say. The ISPAL and SIME intercepts were still arriving but if the content meant anything to those collecting it they weren't sharing the fact with us. We still had nothing on Menachem Begin's whereabouts and our taps on Bella, Presman and Landman were producing nothing worth looking twice at.

I spent my time going back over material we'd already assessed, exercising the muscles of my thumbs with more twiddling than was good for them. So, when on Thursday afternoon Magdalena stepped out of the office on the pretext of chasing up some of her girls down the corridor, I took the opportunity to telephone Jack.

When the receiver at the other end was finally picked up, the ringing in my ear was replaced by a ringing in my head that sounded like someone was taking a sledgehammer to metal.

'Harry? I'd thought you'd call earlier.'

Jack was yelling to make himself heard above the racket.

'Does that mean you've got something for me?'

'What?'

'What on earth are you doing there?' I shouted.

'Beating swords into ploughshares,' Jack said as the noise suddenly stopped.

'Sounds to me there'd be more money in it if you did it the other way around.'

'You go with the market,' he said.

'If you say so. Have you got anything?'

'As a matter of fact I have. I found someone who knew your Wolff before the war.'

'Which one?'

'Which one what?'

'Which Wolff?'

There was no one in the office but I found I was covering the mouthpiece and whispering anyway.

'The geezer in the photo you gave me of course,' he said. 'The actor. That's what gave me the idea. I put an ad in the trade paper for anyone who knew him. Got a tickle yesterday. Said she knew Sam Wolff in Paris.'

'She?'

'They come in all shapes and sizes, Harry.'

'What was he doing in Paris?'

'How the hell should I know. You'll have to talk to her.'

'All right. Where do I find her?'

'I haven't arranged that yet,' he said. 'You want to meet me tomorrow?. Evening's out. Can you manage lunchtime?'

'It's going to be awkward getting to Tooting,' I said. 'I've got to be in Pall Mall in the afternoon.'

'Pall Mall?' he repeated. I could almost hear his eyebrows rising. Then he suggested one o'clock in a pub we both knew in Wardour Street. 'You can do your hobnobbing on the way back,' he said.

Just then Magdalena walked in and, adopting a businesslike tone, I said, 'That sounds acceptable,' down the line and put the receiver down.

I smiled at her. 'My report for Bryce,' I said before she could ask. 'It's going to look a bit thin. Any ideas?'

We spent the rest of the afternoon padding out my report and the next morning, after checking that nothing of importance had come in overnight, I ran it past Magdalena then asked Geraldine to type it up for me.

At twelve-thirty I said to Magdalena, 'I'll grab a bite out and run it over early. You know how Bryce likes to go into every little detail. Can you manage if I don't get back?'

She replied without looking up from her desk or with the least trace of irony.

'I'm sure we can. I'll see you Monday. Enjoy your weekend.'

I reciprocated, grabbed the report and my coat and scarf and hurried downstairs to the bus stop. A number nine took me to Piccadilly Circus and I walked the rest of the way to the pub. It had only just gone one o'clock but I found Jack already at the bar paying for a pint. He bought another for me and we took a table away from the door.

'So who's this woman who knew Samuel Wolff in Paris?' I asked as we sat down.

'First things first,' Jack said. 'My mate Sid managed to get a bit more on him after all.'

'Go on,' I said.

Stringing it out, Jack took a mouthful of beer and wiped a hand across his lips.

'Well, he was FSS as we thought. And it turns out the *Scythia* was a troopship.'

'A troopship? What was he doing on a troopship? I didn't know we sent troops to Murmansk in '44. What were we doing, invading Russia again?'

'Again?'

'The 1918 intervention.'

'Before my time,' Jack said. 'And apparently the *Scythia* wasn't torpedoed. It didn't go down at all. It turns out Samuel Wolff was the only casualty. Lost at sea.'

'Lost? How do you mean?'

'He went overboard presumably.'

'What's that,' I asked, thinking of his brother, 'an accident or suicide?'

'They didn't say. Maybe they didn't want to admit it was suicide.' He shrugged. 'Put it down as killed in action to spare the family's feelings. Maybe that's why they were being cagey about it all.'

'It can hardly matter now,' I said. 'His brother's dead and there's no other family as far as I know. Can't you press them harder?'

Jack shook his head then adjusted his glasses. 'We're not in Jekyll's unit anymore, Harry. These are Sid's contacts, not mine. I can't lean on them like I used to for you. If they don't want to tell, we ain't going to make them. Simple as that.'

'Sorry,' I said. 'I suppose I just got used to you being able to find out everything I needed to know.'

'Are you sure you can't get anything out of your lot?' he asked. 'I thought that was the sort of business you were in now.'

'I can't just nose around in anything that takes my fancy,' I said. 'I do have particular duties.'

'Must put a crimp in the way you operate,' said Jack. 'Sid suggested he make a few enquiries about the brother. Approach it from a different direction.'

Since that was what I was already doing but couldn't say as much to Jack, I didn't think it was a very good idea.

'No,' I told him. 'I didn't like to say anything before but the brother was doing government work during the war and he might be a bit sensitive. You don't want to draw attention to yourself by asking about him.'

Jack put his glass down with a bang, slopping beer over the table.

'Thanks a lot, Harry. You might have told me this before I started putting ads about his brother in the paper.'

'I can't imagine anyone's interested in Samuel Wolff,' I said, wishing he'd keep his voice down. 'Who's this woman who answered your ad, anyway? You haven't told me anything about her yet.'

'Ah,' said Jack. 'To be honest the ad wasn't exactly my idea. It was Sid's. He's the one who suggested the theatrical papers. He wants to meet you, too.'

'Meet me? What for?'

'He likes to know the people he does business with.'

'We're hardly doing business,' I said.

Jack glanced at me sourly. 'Look, he's doing me a favour. If it's going to be a problem …'

'No, it's not that,' I said. 'When does he want to meet? It's going to have to be after work. It's awkward getting away during office hours.'

'It's not that complicated,' Jack said. 'He's over there.'

And he turned in his chair and waved to a man standing at the bar. He was short and stocky, wearing a charcoal-grey coat over a narrow pinstripe suit. I'd noticed him out the corner of my eye earlier when I'd caught him looking our way.

The man smiled and walked over.

I thought it a bit odd but then Jack had always known a lot of odd people.

'Sid,' said Jack, 'this is Harry. My old CO.'

I stood up and shook his hand. It was soft and pudgy. Sydney Stanley drew up a chair and sat down.

'Nice to meet you, Harry,' he said.

His accent was north London although it seemed to lay on a bedrock of somewhere else … East European if I had to guess. He had a round, jovial face contradicted by a sharp nose and a pair of watchful eyes.

'So, Harry,' he said, leaning towards me. 'When Jack tells me you need some information I said no problem. Then this particular individual turns out was FSS. As we know that makes him Intelligence.' He waggled a hand over the table. 'Can be a problem but I happen to know a man who might be able to help. Even so, it might be a dicky business – know what I mean? So I says to Jack, best if I meet you in person before I ask too many questions. Just so I'm happy everything's on the up-and-up.'

'I just needed some background,' I said. 'If it turns out he was doing anything sensitive, I don't necessarily have to know the details.'

'Understood,' said Stanley, shrugging. 'Maybe it's something secret ... Why should we know? Not our business. You keep a clean nose – people trust you. You know what I mean, Harry? My contact said this bloke maybe drowns himself, maybe just falls overboard ... Jack says he had a brother but you can't ask him because he's dead too?'

'That's right,' I said, thinking I ought to start rowing back on the whole thing. 'But we don't have to bother about him. This is really not much more than curiosity on my part.'

Across the table, Jack's face assumed a deadpan.

Stanley smiled in a conspiratorial way. 'Understood,' he said. 'Curiosity ... don't underestimate it. A man can go a long way on curiosity.'

'I appreciate you going to all this trouble,' I said.

'It's no trouble,' Stanley said with a shrug.

'Unfortunately,' I said, thinking I better make the situation clear, 'as I told Jack, I'm not in any position to offer you much in return for your help.'

Sydney raised his hands in mock surprise.

'Harry, have I asked? No trouble, believe me. This is between friends. I do you a favour. Jack maybe does me a favour. Maybe sometime *you* do me a favour. Maybe sometime you can introduce me to someone I need to know.' He took a business card from his pocket and slid it across the table. 'That's what it's all about, Harry.' He smiled and shrugged again. 'Contacts. That's how the world operates. Am I right, Jack? It's the oil that lubricates business.'

'Greases the wheels,' Jack said more prosaically.

'One hand washes the other,' Sydney offered.

I looked at my watch. I had to get to Pall Mall and had heard enough proverbs for one day. I picked up Stanley's card and put it in my pocket. We shook hands again and I told him he could contact me through Jack if he learned any more. Jack said he'd ring me about the woman who'd known Wolff once he could fix up a meeting.

I walked out of the pub into a sleeting rain. Pulling up my coat collar, I thought that the only proverb really worth a damn was the one about one swallow not making a summer. Even so, just then, one swallow would have done nicely.

****

Abel Bryce wasn't in his office. I hung around a while but when he still didn't turn up I scribbled a note to him and left my report on his desk. I thought about dropping by to see what Brian Ogilvy was up to then decided against it. It was snowing and I didn't want to end up in Ogilvy's drinking club again. If Jack was going to get back to me that evening about the woman who'd known Sam Wolff, I didn't want to risk missing the call.

****

Hindsight is a wonderful thing although the big drawback with it is you don't know anything about it in advance. That's why, riding the Tube to Edgware, I gave no thought at all to the metaphysics of time and place – how chance can set one on a particular path which, under other circumstances, one would never have taken. But then we spend all our lives without the benefit of hindsight, even when some things have that look of predetermination about them.

Perhaps if I'd called in on Brian Ogilvy that afternoon instead of going back to my flat things might have turned out differently. Perhaps not. History and events have their own weight and momentum, pushing one along whether one cares for the direction or not. As it was I went straight home and ran into Carol Newcombe, one of the girls who lived in the basement flat.

The compacted snow on the roads and pavements had turned to ice and, as I came around the corner towards the flat, I found Carol sprawled on the pavement by the front door. She was trying to get up but seemed to have turned her ankle and wasn't able to put any weight on it.

She looked up at me, obviously needing help but trying to maintain as much dignity as anyone can while sprawled in the gutter like a discarded marionette.

'I think I've sprained my ankle,' she said.

I knelt down to take a look. She had two of them, both shapely, although the sprained one was already beginning to swell. I put my hand on it and she winced.

'Put your arm around me,' I said.

She wrapped her arm around my neck and I hauled her upright. She hopped as I helped her to the small flight of steps leading down to her basement front door.

'They'll be slippery,' I warned her. 'Be careful.'

I might have suggested I carry her down if I hadn't thought we both might end up in a tangle at the bottom of the steps. The idea did have its attractions although she had probably already lost as much dignity that evening as she cared to.

We managed to reach her door and she rummaged in her handbag for a key. Once inside, I guided her down a dark hall and into the sitting room, lowering her on to a settee.

'You ought to get some ice on that ankle,' I suggested. 'It'll help keep the swelling down.'

She glanced up at me. 'Where am I going to get ice? Oh ...' she said.

I found the kitchen and a tea towel, went back outside and snapped off a row of icicles hanging from a windowsill. I broke them up a bit and wrapped them in the tea towel. In the sitting room Carol Newcombe was stretched out on the settee, leg up on a pillow and skirt riding above her knee. She saw me looking and tugged it down.

I put the tea towel against her ankle and wrapped it up with my scarf. It felt almost as cold in the flat as it had outside and I suggested I light the fire.

'I think the gas meter's empty,' she said. 'It was Frances's turn but none of us had any change. When the gas ran out last night we just went to bed.'

'Best place,' I said.

She eyed me as if I'd made an indecent proposal.

I sorted through the change in my pocket and found a shilling.

'You shouldn't ...' she said.

'Where's the meter?'

'Under the stairs.'

I found the cupboard, stumbling into some brooms and a dustpan in the dark. There was money in the electricity meter, though, as the light came on when I flicked the switch and I pushed my shilling into the gas meter and turned the dial until the coin dropped. Back in the drawing room I lit the fire.

'I'll make you a cup of tea,' I said.

'Please, don't bother. The others will be back soon.'

'No bother. Best thing for shock. I know where the kitchen is.'

Unlike the cupboard under the stairs, everything in the kitchen cupboards was neat and tidy. Clean, too; at least, cleaner than my kitchen. A window over the sink, just below pavement level, gave a view of the street and passers-by from the knee down. I pulled the curtain, lit the gas and put the kettle on to boil.

I found the tea in a cheap tin caddy with a packet of powdered milk beside it. I couldn't find any sugar and popped my head back around the sitting room door.

'Sugar?'

'I don't take it. If you're making one for yourself I'm afraid our ration's gone. Frances again.'

While I was waiting for the kettle to boil I nosed around a little more. Some of the tins and packets in the cupboards had been labelled with the girls' names and I saw Muriel had a tin of cocoa to herself. It had been years since I'd tasted cocoa and I was tempted to filch a cup. But I remembered the aroma was quite distinctive and was hesitant about being caught taking a liberty. At least, a liberty with cocoa. I didn't want to get off on the wrong foot with any of the girls – even if at that moment Carol didn't have a choice of foot.

The kettle boiled and I made the tea, putting everything on a tray I found on the kitchen table. I carried it back to the sitting room. This time Carol was demurely composed, skirt below the knee.

'You're on the second floor, aren't you, Mr Tennant?' she asked.

'It's Harry,' I said as I poured the tea. 'You'll need to stay off that ankle for a couple of days. Will that be a problem where you work?'

She shook her head. 'I don't work Saturdays. Anyway, Solly won't mind. I'm only there helping Mu out.'

'Who's Solly?'

'Solly Epstein? The theatrical agent? Mu's his assistant and Frances is one of his clients. You must have heard of him.'

I'd never heard of any Solly Epstein, but I supposed the theatrical world thought themselves the centre of the universe.

'Is Frances an actress?'

'Yes. She's just finished a run in a West End play, as a matter of fact. Not a big part but she got a mention in one of the reviews.'

'And what are you? Are you in the business as well?'

'I'm a dancer,' she said. 'But I like to eat regularly. Mu was looking for someone to help her in the office and Solly didn't mind.'

'You'd better tell your boyfriend they'll be no dancing for few days,' I told her, nodding at her ankle.

'What makes you think I've got a boyfriend?'

We heard the front door open which saved me from coming up with some clunky compliment. A moment later one of the two sisters she shared with came in. She looked at Carol then at me then at the tea tray. It was Muriel, Solly's assistant, rather than Frances, the actress who didn't have the money to feed the meter. Not as pretty as her sister, Muriel was tall and had brown, mousy hair. Bobbed short it framed an almost cruel face.

'Hello Mu,' Carol smiled at her. 'It's Mr Tennant ... from upstairs—'

'Harry,' I said again.

Then Muriel saw the tea towel on Carol's ankle.

'Darling,' she said. 'What on earth's happened?'

'I slipped on the ice.'

Muriel knelt beside her and stroked the swollen ankle. I watched, thinking I could have done that myself.

'It's not broken,' I said.

Muriel glanced up, her expression suggesting that if it had been it would probably have been my fault.

'If it's no better in a couple of days,' I advised, 'she ought to see a doctor.'

Muriel continued fussing and I said I'd better leave.

Carol laid a hand on Muriel's arm. 'Mu darling, be a sweet and give Harry a shilling, will you? He put one in the meter.'

'Don't worry,' I said. 'I drank your tea. And any time you need any sugar ... I hardly use it. Number eight, second floor.'

On the doorstep I ran into Frances with the sweet tooth. Brunette and willowy, she was alike enough to her sister to make me wonder if cruelty ran in the family.

'Carol slipped on the ice,' I explained then left the three of them to it.

Up in the entrance foyer I found a letter from Penny waiting for me. I took it upstairs and dropped it on my kitchen table while I lit the gas fire. Then I thought I'd probably need something in my stomach before I read what Penny had to say so made a spam sandwich with the last of my bread.

The trouble Penny and I had the previous summer had left a simmering resentment in its wake and it had taken until Christmas before she had finally broken her silence. That letter had been a litany of complaint. I thought this time she might want to tell me why George had come up to town the previous week, but she didn't. Rather than mention George she made a list of the hardships they were suffering in Gloucestershire because of the weather: the snow had been so deep no one had been able to get out of their village; the train services had been disrupted and nothing had been moving on the roads; on top of that their water pipes had frozen.

I wondered if she wasn't working herself up to admitting she missed London and wanted to come back. I assumed that now her father had died she might move back in with her mother. But her mother had been living with her sister, Penny's Aunt Julia, and perhaps the thought of the three of them together was too much even for Penny. As it turned out, she was only writing to say that because of the bad weather they were all coming up to town early for her father's funeral. She didn't express any hope to see me there, instead ended the letter with one anticipating that I might have finally begun putting the wheels of our divorce in motion.

I still hadn't, of course, despite George's appearance last Friday. Since she expected me to provide grounds, a named correspondent and evidence that would stand up in court, I did think briefly of writing back and telling her about the girls in the basement. I could promise that as soon as I'd talked one of them into bed, I'd be able to provide her with her evidence. But beyond the pleasure I'd derive from irritating her, I couldn't see that it would materially help matters.

My usual course of action was not to reply at all – just leave her letter in view where I might flagellate myself with its presence for a few days before attempting to telephone. But whenever I did that, Penny always refused to speak to me and all I'd achieve would be to give my mother the opportunity to berate me over my conduct. My mother's tongue may not have been as cutting as a flagellant's whip, although it ran it a close second. Sufficient punishment, one might think, to salve my piteous conscience for not writing.

On this occasion, though, I didn't have time to deliberate long over the letter as the phone rang and Jack said: 'Half-past twelve tomorrow. The ABC tearooms on Tottenham Court Road. Do you know it?'

I said I could find it and asked if he'd be there.

Jack laughed. 'What for? Don't tell me you need a chaperone.'

'How will I know her then?'

'You're to be carrying a copy of the *Evening News*,' he said.

'Where am I going to get an *Evening News* before twelve-thirty?'

'Nip out and get one now,' he suggested. 'She's a looker so I don't suppose you'll miss her.'

'You've met her?'

'Very briefly. Just to check her out. And Sid's got a date for you,' he added.

'I thought you'd just fixed me up with one.'

'Funny,' said Jack. 'Not that sort of date. The *Scythia* left Liverpool for Murmansk on October 31st, '44. Your man Wolff went missing the second week in November. They supposedly didn't miss him until after the ship embarked again. If you can believe that,' he added sardonically. 'Anyway, Sid says getting the details wasn't easy.'

'If it was easy,' I said, 'I wouldn't have needed Sid.'

'That ain't my fault,' Jack said. 'Twelve-thirty, don't forget,' and rang off.

13

Saturday, January 25th 1947

The ABC tearooms weren't as fashionable as the Lyons establishments and, unlike the Lyons shops which had all been undergoing refurbishment since the end of the war, the ABCs hadn't changed at all. They looked a bit tired and worn, although you could have stuck that label on any of us. The ABCs still had waitresses while the Lyons Nippies had gone. Now Lyons tearooms were becoming self-service cafeterias, American-style. The ABCs looked old-fashioned by comparison.

I did some grocery shopping in the morning, doling out my ration stamps like a reluctant miser, making sure I was five minutes late at the ABC so that the woman would be looking for me rather than the other way around.

The place might have been unfashionable but it was still busy. Most of the tables were taken and I walked up and down between them, my copy of yesterday's *Evening News* in my hand as instructed. I didn't spot her right away, having dismissed a girl sitting at the end of the room as far too young to be the woman I was meeting.

But I didn't see anyone else with an *Evening News* and, as Jack had said, she was looker.

She watched me as I approached, holding up her own copy of the paper like a flag on coronation day. Petite and pale, she had a tangle of dark hair crammed under a small hat she'd pinned at an angle. I stopped and she looked up at me with startled eyes, like a fawn who has just been told about wolves. Her full lips held the hint of a pout, suggesting that disappointment was never far away. Her tongue passed nervously over them before she spoke.

'Are you the one?'

'Sydney sent me,' I said, since it had been Stanley's idea about the advertisement in the first place.

She stared back at me blankly.

'Or was it Jack?' I tried.

'Mr Hibbert?'

I pulled out the chair opposite her. Her eyes weren't as big nor as mournful as Magdalena Marshall's although despite her obvious nervousness they held a spark I'd noticed Magdalena's lacked.

'I'm Harry,' I said.

She offered me a small gloved hand. 'My name is Elizabeth,' she said. 'Lizzie … Lizzie Lazarus. It is all right to meet here like this?'

'Of course,' I said, wondering why it shouldn't be.

She had slipped her coat on to the back of her chair, revealing a trim figure in a dark green tailored dress, tight under her breasts and snug, I imagined, over her hips. Her accent sounded French. She may not have dropped her aitches or stressed her sibilants, like the clichéd French maids Frances perhaps played in West End farces, but the way she had said "Lizzie" and "Lazarus" had still possessed a hint of air escaping a balloon. It wasn't a French surname as far as I knew – the only Lazarus I'd heard of was in the Bible although I could imagine the right sort of look from this one might possibly raise something other than the dead.

'I was told the meeting was to be private because of your work,' she said.

'Who told you that, Mr Hibbert or Sydney Stanley?'

She frowned at me. 'Who is this Sydney Stanley? It is Mr Hibbert who tells me the meeting with you is to be private.'

'So you met Jack?'

'Very quickly. And we speak on the telephone.'

'You answered an advert, is that right?'

She unfolded her *Evening News*. Inside was a copy of *The Stage*, the theatrical newspaper. It was open at the classified ads and she passed it across the table and pointed one out. At the bottom of the page, in print so small I wondered how she had managed to spot it at all, were two brief lines:

"WANTED – ANYONE WHO KNEW LATE ACTOR SAMUEL WOLFF. INFORMATION NEEDED FOR POSSIBLE MEMOIR."

The telephone number that followed was Jack's.

A waitress arrived and I ordered a pot of tea and some cake. When we were alone again I asked Lizzie Lazarus how she had come across the advert.

'Because I am an actress,' she said. 'I read this paper to find work. They make a list of auditions for the plays.' Lizzie Lazarus shrugged her slim shoulders and pouted. 'It is not easy for a girl with an accent to find good parts. They want you only to play the domestic servant or maybe a street-girl.'

'It must be difficult,' I sympathised.

'I look for work and I see this.' She tapped the ad with a crimson fingernail. 'I used to know a man called Samuel Wolff who was an actor so I telephone the number. This is the man you wish to talk about, no? You write his biography?'

'Not exactly,' I said.

'Oh? Someone else writes the book?'

'There is no book,' I confessed. 'But I am interested in Samuel Wolff ... if it's the same man. You say you knew him in Paris? But this must have been before the war.'

She held my gaze. 'You are thinking I am not old enough?'

I had been. If she had known Sam Wolff in Paris before the war she couldn't even have been in her teens. Despite the makeup and the way she wore her hair she barely looked twenty now.

'How old were you?'

'I was ten. Perhaps I was eleven.'

'Then how was it you knew him?'

'Because he was a friend of my mother. She was a poet. She knew many artistic people.'

'Artistic?'

'Literary people. Theatrical.'

'When was this exactly?'

She placed a small black handbag on the table, unclasped it and took out a photograph.

'Nineteen thirty-seven.'

The photo was creased from handling and was of a dark young girl who was staring intensely at the camera. Under heavy brows, a pair of piercing eyes bore into me.

'This is my mother.'

I could see the resemblance. 'She's a striking woman.'

'This was taken in 1924. Before she knew Samuel Wolff, of course.'

'Were they good friends?' I asked.

'They were lovers,' she replied coolly. 'My mother had many lovers.'

The waitress returned with our tea and cake, sparing me the need to come up with a reply. I poured the tea and passed her a slice of cake.

'Your mother ...' I began.

'She is dead,' Lizzie Lazarus said. 'She was in the Resistance and was shot by the Milice. You have heard of these men?'

The Milice were a far-right French militia. The names of some members had cropped up while I was with the war crimes unit. They had worked for Petain's regime in Vichy, using torture and assassination against the Resistance. A mixture of hardline fascists, petty criminals and men avoiding forced labour in Germany, they were, by and large, an unsavoury bunch. I'd even heard it said that the Gestapo thought twice about employing some of them.

'That must have been difficult for you,' I said.

'Of course.'

'So you knew Samuel Wolff because he was a friend of your mother's. Do you remember much about him?'

'I remember that he was very good-looking,' she said. 'And he was nice to me. He used to buy me presents when he came to our apartment.'

'Did you know him long?'

'No. He left before the war started.'

'What was he doing in France?'

'He was touring with a theatre company, I think. My mother met a lot of this sort of people.'

It was obvious I wasn't going to get anything of use out of Lizzie Lazarus about Samuel Wolff let alone his brother, but I asked anyway.

'I don't suppose you remember him ever talking about his brother? His name was Joseph Wolff.'

She pretended to give it some thought. 'No, I don't remember anything about his brother,' she said eventually, munching on her cake. 'Is this the one who did secret work in the war? Mr Hibbert said that was why you are discreet and we have to meet carrying an evening newspaper.'

I could see I needed to have a word with Jack.

'I think Mr Hibbert should be in your business,' I told her. 'He's something of a dramatist himself.'

'You make a joke?'

'There is nothing secret,' I assured her. 'Samuel Wolff was killed in the war. I'm just trying to find out the details, that's all.'

'Mr Hibbert told me Samuel died in the war. I did not know he was dead until I saw the advertisement. So sad.'

'I don't suppose your mother heard from him after he left Paris?'

'No. I do not think so. But if you would like me to ask her friends …? I am still in touch with some of them.'

'Thank you, Miss Lazarus, but—'

'Please, call me Lizzie …'

'Lizzie then … Thank you, but I doubt if they would know anything.'

'Maybe because Samuel did work like his brother?' she asked. 'What you call hush-hush?'

'Probably not,' I said smiling at her. 'Even so, it would probably be better if you didn't mention I'd been asking about him to anyone else.'

'I understand,' she said, lowering her voice. 'The war has ended but there are still some things in France it is better not to talk about. I know this is true. I was in the Resistance with my mother.'

I didn't believe that for a minute. 'Surely you couldn't have been old enough,' I said.

'Oh yes,' she replied pertly. 'Even a young girl can be useful when the enemy occupies your country. I have the Croix de Guerre and a medal from General Patton himself. So I know how to be careful, Harry.'

Now I knew she was telling stories.

'You must have been very brave,' I said.

The pout became more pronounced. 'Now you play with me.'

'Not at all,' I said, pushing my plate and piece of cake towards her. She looked as though she could do with a square meal. She glanced at me doubtfully and I nodded, then changed the subject while her mouth was full. I asked about her career.

Dropping crumbs from those full lips she explained how she had worked in Paris but thought she might find better opportunities in London.

'But it isn't easy for a girl on her own,' she said. 'When you do not know many people in the business.'

I sympathised again. I said I'd heard it was difficult because a girl who lived in my building had had to take work between engagements. I told her she was working for Solly Epstein, the theatrical agent.

Lizzie Lazarus's eyes widened. 'You know Solly Epstein?'

'You've heard of him?'

'But of course. Mr Epstein is one of the biggest agents in London. I have tried, naturally, but if he would just see me … I am sure he could find me work.'

The unspoken implication hung over the table like the aroma of tea.

'I've not actually met him myself,' I said.

'But you know a girl who works for him,' she said.

'Well, yes. In a way …'

'It would be too much to ask for you to mention me, Harry. I know …'

I was beginning to wish I hadn't brought the subject up. She was looking at me with her doe eyes and I realised I'd talked myself into a corner.

'I could ask,' I said. 'But I can't promise anything.'

'Oh, Harry,' she said, gripping my hand in her crimson talons. 'I would be so grateful.' She began rummaging in her bag again and came out with pen and paper.

'This is my telephone number,' she said, writing it down. 'Please do not be worried if a man answers. We have a line that is shared. It is nothing more.' She smiled across the table in a meaningful way. 'And if I can do more to help you about Samuel Wolff, please, ask me.'

I promised I'd call her. We finished our tea and cake then I helped her on with her coat. Outside, I watched as she walked down the frozen street, handbag tucked beneath one arm and hips swaying slightly beneath her coat.

****

When I got back to the flat and before going up, I thought I'd drop down to the basement and see how Carol Newcombe's ankle was mending. I had been thinking about asking her out for a drink. Or even a meal if she felt up to it. Being considered to be an erring husband by my wife, I thought it was time I began to err.

Flowers for the invalid might have been a nice touch had there been any to be bought. But it was the wrong time of year for flowers and even the early daffodils sometimes brought in from the Scilly Islands were, according to the papers, presently under several inches of snow. I daresay the fields were a pretty sight. At any rate, prettier than the snow in London. Scraped from the pavements and roads, it lay piled in filthy mounds in the gutters, black with soot and embedded with litter.

To my surprise, Carol answered the door herself. The ankle was bandaged and she was leaning on a stick.

'I came down to see how your ankle is,' I said. 'You shouldn't have got up. Are the others out?'

'Frances is out. Mu's in the bath. Come in,' she said. 'I can't leave you freezing on the doorstep after you rescued me yesterday.'

I followed her into the sitting room.

'Mu says I should keep warm so we've got everything on. It's only a sprain, the doctor said. I'll be fine in a couple of days.'

'Good. As a matter of fact I was going to ask if you fancied going out for a drink or something one evening?'

'That's sweet of you, Harry.'

'I don't suppose you're up to it tonight.'

'I can't tonight,' she said. 'There's a party at Miriam's. Mu says I shouldn't go but it would be a shame to miss it.'

'Some other time then,' I said.

Her eyes brightened and she put a hand on my arm.

'Why don't you come with us?'

'To the party?'

'Miriam won't mind. It's always open house when she has a party. Really.'

'Who's Miriam?'

'Solly's partner at the agency.'

'Will he be there?'

'I should think so. He usually drops by for a drink.'

'They'll all be theatrical types, I suppose.'

'No. Miriam knows all sorts of people.'

If there were going to be actors at the party I thought it possible one of them might have known Samuel Wolff. Maybe even Solly Epstein had himself. It was a long shot, though, and I was beginning to think Sam Wolff was a dead end anyway. After all, even if I did manage to learn more about him it wouldn't necessarily help me as far as his brother went. Not tell me why Joseph Wolff had killed himself.

At that moment the door opened. Muriel, flushed from her bath with her robe hanging open and naked beneath, walked in. She saw me, scowled and pulled it together.

'Harry dropped by to see how my ankle was, Mu,' Carol said. 'Wasn't that sweet?'

'Very sweet,' Muriel replied tonelessly.

'I've asked him to the party tonight. Miriam won't mind, will she?'

Muriel glared at me. 'You won't know anyone there.'

'Oh, you won't mind, Harry,' said Carol. 'You'll know us.'

'Perhaps he has someone he'd like to bring,' Muriel suggested. 'Do you have a girlfriend?'

Of your own, the implication seemed to be as I was beginning to see which way the wind was blowing.

'Well, as a matter of fact,' I said, thinking of Lizzie Lazarus and the half-promise I'd made her about Solly Epstein, 'there is someone. I've only just met her and I don't think she knows many people in London. She's an actress. French, actually.'

'What sort of actress would that be?' Muriel asked acidly.

I ignored her and turned back to Carol. 'If you think it would be all right for me to bring her.'

'Why not? She might meet someone useful. That's how it's done.'

'The more the merrier,' said Muriel.

'Only if it's all right,' I said.

'Frances's boyfriend is picking us up at eight,' Carol said. 'He's got a car.'

'Let me have the address and I'll see you there,' I said.

'Pop down for a drink before we go,' she suggested. 'There's some of the scotch left, isn't there Mu? You drink scotch, don't you, Harry?'

Carol wrote down the address and I said I'd see them that evening. Upstairs, I asked the operator for the number Lizzie Lazarus had given me and, once past the man who shared her telephone, I told her about the party.

'Will Mr Epstein be there?'

'So I'm told.'

'Oh Harry,' she said, 'but I have just remembered I have an appointment tonight I cannot break. I could still come but it would not be until later. Ten? Would ten be all right?'

I said I couldn't see any reason why it shouldn't be.

'I'll tell Epstein about you before you get there,' I said. 'The flat's in Hampstead. Will you be able to find it or would you rather we meet somewhere?'

'I will find it,' she assured me. 'Ten tonight, yes?'

****

The flat was in a block the Belsize Park end of Hampstead. I had no reason to wait until ten so at seven-thirty I went down to the basement for the drink Carol had promised. A swotty-looking young man named Bertram who turned out to be Frances's boyfriend was there and by the way they were all behaving it was obvious they were already a couple of drinks ahead of me. When I said my friend wouldn't be coming until later, Carol insisted I go with them.

After another drink we all trooped up on to the frozen pavement and crammed into Bertram's tiny Austin Seven, Frances riding up front with Bertram and with me squeezed in between Carol and Muriel. Carol didn't seem to mind the squash, her body emanating enough heat for me to consider suggesting she might come upstairs on cold nights as an alternative energy source; Muriel, though, was taking pains to wedge herself against the far door. After a couple of scotches, I was happy to allow her the excuse of not wanting to crease the tailored suit she was wearing – one of a far better cut, I couldn't help noticing, than the shabby affair I had on. It gave her an androgynous air, I thought, a million miles from the party frocks Carol and Frances wore. Frances looked particularly alluring in a sparkly cocktail dress that glittered like her eyes.

In Hampstead Bertram pulled up in Lawn Road outside a large block of flats, three or four stories high and built in the modernist style. It had once been painted white as far as I could tell under the patchy streetlight although now, after six years of war and austerity, had been left like the rest of us looking a little shabby. You could hear the gramophone music playing from the road outside, a jazzy dance band that seemed at odds with the freezing February weather. We clambered out of the car and smoothed ourselves down, then trooped up the stairs to a first-floor flat already groaning under the press of party-goers.

The three girls began greeting people by name and were instantly swallowed by the crowd. I tagged on behind Bertram to a small kitchen where an array of already half-empty bottles stood by the sink. Bertram fixed drinks for the girls while I rinsed out a glass for myself and turned up a bottle of vodka hiding behind an unfamiliar Russian label. I poured a shot and looked for a mixer. There wasn't one so I drank it neat and found I was being watched by a girl with glazed eyes wearing a derby hat with a feather stuck in the crown.

'Should I know you?' she asked.

I said I doubted it and told her I'd come with Bertram and the girls.

Her glassy eyes narrowed. 'Don't know any Bertram.'

'Muriel and Carol,' I said. 'They work for Solly?'

'Oh, Solly!'

'Is he here?'

She waved her glass carelessly towards the lounge, slopping whatever had been in it on to the floor.

'Over there somewhere.'

I edged past her into the next room in search of anyone I thought could be called Solly and saw a short and portly man who looked like my idea of a theatrical agent. Puffing on a cigarette while his gaze roamed the room, he was half-listening to a tall woman in a fox stole who had to bend down to get her mouth anywhere near his ear. His eyes caught mine in passing for an instant and stopped long enough for me to recognise the expression of boredom in them before they wandered on.

A man drifted past me into the kitchen and I pointed at the portly man and asked if that was Solly Epstein.

'Don't you know him?'

'We haven't met.'

The man filled his lungs with air and bellowed over the music. 'Solly! Come and meet ...'

'Harry,' I said.

'Harry!' he bellowed again.

Solly looked up and started towards us, leaving the tall woman in the fox stole stooped over an empty space.

By the time Solly reached me the man who'd called him had moved on so I stuck out my hand and said: 'Harry Tennant. I came with Carol and Muriel.'

'Muriel's here? Now maybe I can go home. What do you think? Harry, was it?'

I didn't know what to think.

'Love, eh?' said Solly. 'Never easy is it?'

I said I supposed it wasn't.

Solly jerked his chin across the room to where Muriel was deep in conversation with a middle-aged, white-faced woman whose heavily mascaraed eyes were giving her a startled look.

'Drinks too much,' said Solly.

'Who does, Muriel?'

'Muriel? No, Miriam.'

'That's Miriam, is it? It's her flat and party?'

'You boys are all the same.' said Solly. 'A party's a party, right?'

I didn't know what he meant but agreed anyway.

'There's the triangle,' said Solly as Carol limped up to the two women. 'It was something before the war. You should have seen it.'

'The triangle?'

'The triangle?' Solly repeated querulously. 'The flats, the flats!'

'Oh, the flats.'

'The talent,' said Solly. 'All sorts.'

'I bet.'

'Moore and Mondrian ...'

'The painter?'

'Who do you think, Mondrian the butcher? Of course the painter. Moore the sculptor ... George Orwell and Walter Gropius ...'

'Now there's a pair,' I said. 'What about Sam Wolff? He ever come here?'

Solly's fleshy brow creased. 'Wolff?'

'Sam Wolff, the actor. You didn't know him?'

'Wolfitt, sure.'

'No, this was Wolff. Played Shylock at Bristol. In '38, I think it was.'

'Ask Miriam,' said Solly who appeared to be tiring of the conversation. 'She deals with the provincial companies.'

I glanced over at Miriam who was now looking decidedly teary, her mascara on the verge of painting her cheeks like a tarmacked road. A passing girl grabbed Solly and steered him away. I circulated, found the kitchen had been restocked and tried some gin before attaching myself to a conversation on the theatre to which I found I had nothing to add. I saw Frances dancing with a man who wasn't Bertram, and a good deal closer than seemed necessary, then I looked at my watch and saw I still had an hour before Lizzie was due. I decided I might as well start asking around about Samuel Wolff again.

'Sammy Wolff?' said a gauntly tall man named Corbett, still hanging on to traces of matinée idol looks that must have been quite striking thirty years earlier. He was the only guest I'd canvassed who vaguely remembered Wolff.

'If it's the same Sammy Wolff,' he added discouragingly.

'Shylock? Bristol '38' I said.

'Manchester,' he replied doubtfully. 'I played Bassanio, if memory serves. But of course I was younger then. After that I opened in a new play at The Ambassador.'

'Bristol?'

'Drury Lane, dear boy. Of course, it wasn't long after that they closed the theatres. The next thing I knew I was playing an officer in the Scots Guards.' Corbett smiled wryly, pleased by his joke.

'Wolff joined the FSS.'

Corbett stared at me blankly.

'His brother was something at Oxford,' I persisted.

'Repertory?'

'The university.'

Like Solly he seemed to lose interest, and after one last stab at it so did I. I had another drink then found a chair in a corner and after while closed my eyes. The dance band came to me filtered through the general hubbub and I suppose I fell asleep because when I opened my eyes again it seemed that many of the guests had gone. So had the gin bottle but in return I had a headache and a crick in my neck. The music had been turned down and so had the lights and the few couples still dancing were shuffling around the floor locked in tight embraces. Miriam was sitting on a sofa watching a couple and as I followed her gaze I saw that it was Carol dancing, despite her ankle, with Muriel. Carol looked drunk and was hanging on to Muriel to stop herself falling over.

I might have got up and cut in if I hadn't remembered I'd realised which way the wind was blowing. Then a glance at my watch told me it was getting on for eleven o'clock and I'd forgotten all about Lizzie Lazarus.

I found my coat in a bedroom, prised it out from under a drunk and went downstairs, hoping I wouldn't find her frozen on the doorstep.

14

Saturday, January 25th 1947

The night was still and as cold as an arctic icecap. The few streetlamps still working threw an insipid light that seemed to deepen shadow rather than illuminate anything. The music from the party upstairs was now muted and the cars I'd noticed parked haphazardly in front of the flats when we arrived had thinned, as if those who'd come in them had heard of a better party down the road. In the lights of a passing car I saw a couple leaning against one vehicle, about as close as two people can get without taking a lesson in anatomy, and I wondered why they didn't get inside until I noticed the windows were steamed up and supposed they were having to wait their turn. There was no sign of Lizzie and, trying not to look like a voyeur, I lit a cigarette and decided to give her another fifteen minutes before I started wondering what the best way to get home might be.

Across the road there were two men in a parked car who didn't seem to be doing anything but it might have just been that they'd smoked their quota of second-hand cigarettes for the evening and had come out for a lungful of fresh air.

I walked up and down for ten minutes to keep from freezing and at eleven-fifteen I assumed Lizzie had either come and gone again or had changed her mind. I flicked my cigarette butt into a snow bank, ready to give the evening up as a bad job, and had just turned towards the door again when a car approached and stopped outside the flats. It was a taxi and, as it stopped under one of the streetlights, I saw Lizzie climb out, swathed in a fur coat that looked somewhat more expensive than the threadbare garment she'd been wearing at the ABC tearooms. She paid the driver, saw me and waved, tottering over on heels high enough to give anyone vertigo.

'I am late, Harry,' she said breathlessly as if I hadn't seen her get out of a taxi and she'd run all the way there. A wash of perfume drifted on the cold air as she leaned forward and kissed my cheek in the French style. 'Tell me you have not been waiting for me. Not in the cold.'

She looked as though she hoped I had and when I said I'd just come out she pouted with disappointment.

'Nice coat,' I said trying to claim back lost ground. 'You'll put everyone else to shame.'

She pulled the collar tight to her neck. 'Shame? Why shame?'

'A figure of speech,' I said.

'What is a figure of speech? Pah, English! It makes no sense.'

'It's still a nice coat,' I said.

'I keep it for my best,' she said. 'For the … the *impression*, you know?'

'You'll impress them all right,' I assured her. 'Compared to you, everyone else looks like they're dressed in last year's curtains.'

She smiled, all white teeth in the darkness. 'You pull my limb … I say this correct?'

'Any time you want it pulled,' I said. 'You look ravishing.'

Her eyes widened, pupils flaring.

'I think you are what they call a wolf, Harry,' she said, slipping an arm through mine.

'You're wearing the fur,' I told her.

'Is Monsieur Epstein here?'

'He was. His partner is. It's her flat. Come on up and I'll introduce you.'

In the entrance hall where there was more light she stopped and turned to face me.

'I look well enough?'

'If I was a wolf,' I said, 'I'd eat you.'

Upstairs despite the crowd having thinned the cigarette smoke was thicker than a London fog. One of Hutch's recordings was on the gramophone and an occasional shriek of laughter pierced the song like antiphonic counterpoint. Things had livened up again and several couples had surrendered to the rhythm, throwing themselves at each other with enough abandon to test the floor joists. I hoped the people downstairs had been invited. If not, that they'd gone away for the weekend.

Miriam was standing by the door, surveying her guests like a prison warder. As we approached she looked at us, her eyes wasting little time on me before settling on Lizzie.

'That's Miriam,' I said into Lizzie's ear. 'She's Solly Epstein's partner.'

'She looks frightful,' Lizzie said, clutching my arm tightly.

'I think you mean frightening,' I said. 'I'm told she's very affectionate.'

'You came with Carol,' Miriam said to me as we reached her, making it sound like a felony. 'Who is this?'

I introduced them. 'Lizzie is an actress,' I told Miriam.

'Really?' Miriam said, brightening. 'How interesting.' She put an arm around Lizzie and guided her towards another room. 'Come my dear. We'll find you somewhere to leave your gorgeous coat and you can tell me all about the work you've done.'

Lizzie glanced back at me nervously and I nodded encouragingly at her. She'd told me she'd been in the Resistance so I didn't suppose Miriam would turn out any worse than the Gestapo. I went back to the kitchen wondering if there was anything left to drink.

A drunk was fumbling at the gramophone by the door, trying to change the record although only succeeding in putting the same song on again. I found a little gin left but still nothing to mix it with. Nor any ice unless I wanted to go back outside with an ice pick. I did find Muriel and Carol standing by a hole in the wall that turned out to be a dumb waiter. They had their heads together but weren't talking.

'Did your girlfriend arrive?' Muriel asked me.

'Yes, she's talking with Miriam.'

'Is she her type,' Carol asked.

'*Carol!*' said Muriel.

'I don't know. What's Miriam's type? She's French,' I said.

'Oo-la-la,' said Carol, giggling.

'Is your ankle up to a dance?' I asked.

'Only a shuffle,' she said.

'My specialty.'

'Back in a mo, Mu,' she said and giggled again, touching the other girl's cheek.

Muriel watched sullenly as I led Carol back into the lounge.

'I thought you were drunk earlier,' I said.

'I was earlier.'

'You shouldn't tease her,' I said, putting an arm around Carol's waist and taking her hand.

The song on the gramophone was now a two-step that didn't match any dance rhythm I knew, so I ignored the music and shuffled in circles. Carol adjusted to my pace. She was a professional dancer after all, even if this time she'd be the one paying the price.

'Mu?' she asked, pushing closer against me. 'I'm not the one teasing. She's sweet but she's very possessive.'

'I'm not possessive,' I told her. 'I'm always losing things.'

'I'm not French, either.'

'I'm an internationalist,' I said. 'I don't believe in borders.'

'Does that mean you don't know when you're crossing them? Better not tell Mu.'

I didn't think I had to as Muriel was watching us from the kitchen door. Then I saw Lizzie watching us too, *sans* coat and very French in a small black cocktail dress.

'Come and meet Lizzie,' I said. 'She wanted to meet Solly.'

'He's gone home.'

'Will you put in a word with Miriam?'

'I'm not in Miriam's good books at the moment.'

'Lizzie's looking for representation.'

'Who isn't?'

'As a favour?'

Carol leaned back and gave me a provocative look.

'You'll owe me one,' she said.

15

Sunday, January 26th 1947

When I woke up Sunday morning I was alone, which hadn't been the plan.

Although I couldn't remember much, one thing I did remember was having a tussle with Lizzie in the back of a taxi. Since I didn't seem to be bearing any scratch marks and my cheek wasn't bruised, I deduced the tussle had been a good-natured one. I had a headache, though, and my mouth tasted sour from too many cigarettes and too much cheap gin; any strategy I might have had of drinking the stuff neat so as to reduce my input obviously hadn't worked.

Lying in bed with my eyes still closed and taking inventory of other aches and pains – mostly in the legs and back – I assumed I had spent at least part of the evening dancing. Even at my most sober dancing was something I was rotten at, and thinking about it made me cringe. Gin-drunk, I imagined I'd looked quite a spectacle with arms and legs gyrating like an inept gymnast.

The thought was sufficient to preclude any further chance of sleep and so, after a few more minutes of suffering what the Germans call *schadenfreude* – only in my case felt by proxy – I finally got up. It was almost noon anyway so I lit the fire and made some tea. I saw the gas pressure was down again because of the fuel crisis and while I waited for the kettle to boil on a flame that approximated candle-power, I cut a slice of bread and scraped on to it what was left in the dripping bowl.

I spent another hour or so trying to remember enough of the previous evening to assess whether an apology to anyone might be required and, by mid-afternoon, decided it would be easier if I asked the girls in the basement. I put my coat on, took the few slippery steps down to the basement door and rang the bell. I didn't know what sort of reaction I was going to get but at three o'clock on a Sunday afternoon I thought it wasn't likely I'd catch Muriel and Carol still in bed.

But as with many other notions I had about the pair, I was wrong on that score as well.

Muriel answered, wrapped in a heavy dressing gown. To judge from her expression she was less than pleased to see me. She tried to keep me on the doorstep but the draught, blowing with a wind-chill factor somewhere in the minus region, changed her mind. She let me in, shutting the door smartly behind me.

'You don't look well,' she said. 'If it's liver salts you want we don't have any.'

'I am feeling a little fragile,' I admitted.

'We don't do tea and sympathy either. When we got up this morning we found the pipes were frozen. We've got no water.'

'I've got it upstairs,' I said.

'Bully for you.'

'You're sure it's not just the gas pressure? It was down earlier. Perhaps it's back up by now.'

'I'm sure,' said Muriel.

'Why don't you try it again?'

'Harry!' she screeched, the sound going straight through my head, 'the *pipes* are frozen.'

I waited until the pounding subsided. 'Let me take a look.'

She sighed heavily but seemed desperate enough to accept even my help. I followed her down the hall

All the flats had been equipped with Ascot multipoints before the war and, although new at the time, as with everything else they were now showing their age. Like mine, the basement's water heater hung over the tub. Unlike mine, when I turned on the taps nothing happened.

'I'll look under the sink,' I offered. 'That's generally where the pipes come in.

I spent the next ten minutes under the kitchen sink tapping the pipes and achieving nothing except aggravating my headache and giving myself a pain in the shoulder.

'No go,' I admitted eventually, crawling out backwards. 'You must be on a spur down here. Have you got a blowtorch?'

Muriel made a show of looking around the kitchen. 'Now,' she speculated sarcastically, 'where *did* I last see my blowtorch?'

Carol, wrapped in a coat, appeared. She leaned against Muriel and yawned.

'You need a plumber,' I said.

'I *know* we need a plumber,' Muriel retorted. 'You try getting one on a Sunday.'

'They're all busy,' Carol put in. 'Half of London has frozen up. The man we spoke to said it could take days before anyone gets here. We've had nothing to drink since we got home last night, and I want a bath. My ankle hurts again.'

'It was probably all that dancing,' I said.

'If that's the case,' said Muriel, 'I'm surprised you're on your feet at all.'

I decided against going down that route. Instead I said: 'You're welcome to come up for tea. What about the lavatory?'

'What about it?' asked Carol.

'That still works, thank God,' Muriel said. 'The drain doesn't seem to be frozen. But we still need water to flush it.'

'What about buckets?'

Muriel looked at the ceiling.

'Jugs will do,' I said. 'You can bring water down from my place for tea and flushing the lavatory. I assume your gas is still working?'

'Yes,' Carol moaned, 'but it'll take forever to heat up enough water for a bath!'

'Use mine if you want,' I offered. 'At least till you get your pipes fixed.'

'Can we?' said Carol.

'We don't want to get in anyone's way,' Muriel said, referring to Lizzie I assumed.

'No problem,' I said. 'Frances, too, if she wants.' The thought of Frances wrapped in a towel was making me start to feel human again. 'It's no trouble.'

'Oh, Fran's all right,' said Carol. 'She stayed over at Bertram's last night.'

'Oh well, never mind,' I said, trying not to sound too disappointed. 'Buckets and jugs then. Why don't you round up what you can and I'll look upstairs.'

Muriel went off in search of containers while I took a key off my ring and gave it to Carol.

'Here's my spare front door key. Come up when you're ready. I'll get some tea on for you. You must be parched.'

'Harry, you're so sweet,' Carol cooed.

Back in my flat I doubled-checked that my water was still flowing, put the kettle on again and then filled a couple of jugs with water. The kettle had just boiled when there was a knock at the door and the key turned in the lock. Carol and Muriel came in hesitantly, towels draped over their arms and carrying more jugs.

'Tea's ready,' I said. 'I'll run the bath while you have it. Who's first? I'm afraid it takes an age to fill.'

'So does ours,' said Carol. 'Mu says we ought to share so we don't use too much. We do it all the time downstairs to save money on gas. We're quite used to it.'

'Sounds like fun,' I said to Muriel.

She stared at me blatantly. 'Well, it's the sensible thing to do if it takes *that* long to fill,' she said. 'You're not going to want us underfoot all evening, are you?'

Not under*foot* perhaps. But Muriel's expression suggested any riposte of that nature would be a jocularity too far. So I left them to make their own tea and went to run the bath. I gave the tub a quick wipe round while at it, trying to dislodge the grey rim discolouring the enamel, and speculated on how they would have to squeeze up if they were to fit into the thing. With the best will in the world, though, there wasn't room for three.

I had tea with them while we waited for the bath to fill, I asked Carol if she'd twisted her ankle again.

'It's not that bad. Mu put some liniment on it for me,' and she reached across the table and patted Muriel's hand.

'I'd better put some more on after we've had our bath,' Muriel smiled back.

Beginning to feel like a guest in my own flat, I said I'd run the water jugs downstairs and fill their bath for them while they bathed. Muriel gave me their key and I spent the next twenty minutes up and down the stairs like a cold-climate Gunga Din.

I had just let myself in for the last time when I came face to face with Frances.

'What are you doing here?' she said. 'Where are Mu and Carol?'

I wondered if she thought I'd turned Bluebeard overnight but I was too tired to explain.

'Upstairs. Your pipes are frozen.'

Frances used an unladylike expression.

'And I was going to have a bath,' she added.

'That's what they're doing in my flat. You'd better grab your towel and join the party,' I told her, thinking I might get a second chance at Frances in a towel after all.

'You're a dark horse, Harry,' she said. 'I bet you've got that French girl of yours up there too. Who'd have thought it to look at you? Give me a minute and I'll go up with you.'

I waited until she was ready, smarting a little under her thoughtless remark, then went back up.

The other two were in the bath so while I sat with Frances at the kitchen table, I showed her the publicity still of Samuel Wolff I'd taken from his brother's rooms in Oxford. I asked if she'd ever come across him.

'He's rather dishy,' said Frances. 'What did you say his name was?'

'Samuel Wolff. He was an actor before the war. I knew his brother and I'm trying to get back in touch.'

'I think I'd remember if I'd met *him*,' Frances said.

'I asked Solly Epstein last night but he didn't know him. A man at the party thought he might have done rep with him in Manchester but he wasn't a lot of help. Solly told me to ask Miriam but I never got the chance.'

Having been overtaken by gin, I might have added.

'She might know him,' Frances said. 'She's been in the business as long as Solly has and knows more about provincial theatre. Pick your time to ask though.'

'Why?'

'Things have been a bit fraught of late.'

'Why's that?'

'*Muriel*,' said Frances, giving me a knowing look. 'Since Carol turned up ... Well, you know how it is.'

I was beginning to.

'Why don't you get that French girl of yours to ask her?' Frances suggested. 'They seemed to be getting on rather well last night, I thought.'

'Were they?'

'You were drunk I think.'

'A little, perhaps.'

Frances laughed. 'If you don't mind playing the pimp, get her to ask Miriam. She's always had a soft spot for a pretty face.'

'I'm surprised it's not you rather than Muriel she wants.'

Frances patted my hand. 'Keep it up, Harry. I can take any amount of that.'

Carol and Muriel emerged from the bathroom and Frances went in to run another. Carol took my door key out of the pocket of her dressing gown.

'You're a life-saver,' she said.

I told them to keep it until they found a plumber.

'Help yourself if I'm not here.'

'You are sweet,' said Carol, and for a second I thought even Muriel was on the verge of thawing. But then I supposed the chances were their pipes would unfreeze before she would.

They went back downstairs and I sat at the table listening to Frances singing in the bath. She had a good voice and I wondered if she knew any romantic duets we could share while I washed her back. But it seemed things were already complicated enough for the three of them. And there was always Bertram to consider.

What had mostly cooled my ardour though was Frances's remark about my playing the pimp.

16

On Monday Bryce turned up. He said hello to Magdalena, crossed his arms and leaned against a filing cabinet, looking down at me sitting behind my desk.

'I thought I'd let you know we've put a couple of Henry Gifford's men on to Bella. Whatever this "material" of his is, we think it's unlikely he's talking about Begin. It could be someone else, of course. Or maybe a shipment of arms. You've had nothing further from him, I suppose?'

'Only routine stuff,' I said. 'Nothing even a suspicious paranoid could construe as fishy.'

'That's why we've got you on the case, Harry.' He grinned at Magdalena as if it was a joke they shared. 'We don't want to miss anything.'

'No sightings of Begin, then?'

'None. He's gone to ground somewhere. And we're not getting so much as a whisper in Palestine.' He raised a hopeful eyebrow. 'And nothing on the ISPAL traffic even a suspicious paranoid might think twice about either?'

'Nothing gets past Miss Marshall,' I said.

She darted a look at me I couldn't read and squared up a sheaf of paper noisily on her desktop.

'Would you like to take the latest transcripts back with you, Mr Bryce? Or shall I have them couriered over as usual?'

'No, I'll take them please, Magdalena. If they're ready.'

She gathered up her papers. 'Ten minutes? I'll ask Geraldine to get them all together.' She went into the next office.

Bryce paced up and down for a moment after the door closed behind her.

'Do much at the weekend, Harry?'

I wondered if he was working his way round to an enquiry after my family again.

'Oh, much as I ever do.'

'Do you get out much?'

'Now and then.'

'It does us good to socialise.'

'Yes, I suppose so,' I agreed, wondering what he was getting at. 'Actually I was invited to a party Saturday night,' I told him, in case he thought I was a complete wallflower.

'A party? Meet anyone interesting?'

'I went with the girls who live in my basement. Theatrical crowd.'

'West End?'

'Hampstead.'

'Do you have friends there?'

'I didn't know a soul except the girls who live downstairs,' I said.

He nodded as if that made sense, looked as if he was about to say more, then didn't. The atmosphere suggested there was something in the air and it occurred to me he'd heard I'd requested Wolff's file.

'What happened at Wolff's inquest?' I asked casually to test the water. 'Was it a suicide verdict?'

'Wolff?' he repeated absently, as if he'd forgotten the name. 'No. Actually the verdict was accidental death.'

'Accidental? How so?'

Bryce gave me his wintry smile. 'There was no evidence brought to suggest it was a deliberate act.'

'Except I saw him go in. It looked deliberate to me.'

'We could hardly have you called, Harry. Not under the circumstances. It wouldn't do to have it known we had an interest.'

'No? Well you know more about that than me. But what sort of accident is it when a man first takes his clothes off?'

'A swimming accident,' Bryce replied blithely. 'They assumed he got into trouble while bathing.'

'In January?'

Bryce shrugged and turned towards the window. Frost patterned the glass and obscured the view. Not that there was much to see. We overlooked a narrow street and the building opposite. We'd had another snowfall but all that could be seen of it from the window were piles of black slush.

'It's not getting any warmer, is it?' he said. 'I don't believe they've forecast much of an improvement either.'

'In that case,' I observed, 'it's a toss-up what'll last longer, the cold weather or the coal.'

He remained at the window and the silence grew oddly ominous. I thought of Wolff and his file; of his brother and of Hooper; of Miss

Patterson and Katja Tereshchenko and the refugee home – all subjects of outstanding questions that might have filled the silence. But if Bryce knew any of the answers he wasn't saying.

Magdalena returned with a bundle of papers and a large envelope. Bryce looked through them quickly before she put them in the envelope and sealed it.

'Right,' Bryce said. 'I'll be getting back."

Once he left Magdalena sat back behind her desk and started rearranging her files again.

Forgetting I was trying to avoid smoking in the office since neither Magdalena nor the girls smoked, I lit a cigarette.

Magdalena glared at me over the top of her glasses and I put the thing out again.

Bryce's comments about Bella and his "material" had hardly seemed to warrant the journey over from St James's Street, and the papers he took back with him would have been couriered there that afternoon anyway. After a moment Magdalena glanced up at me, seemed to wait for me to say something, then looked down again when I didn't. I was aware she always knew more than I did about what was going on, but, if she knew why Bryce had come, as usual she wasn't saying anything either.

****

I hadn't been home long when Lizzie Lazarus telephoned.

'I have been thinking about you, Harry,' she purred down the line.

'That's odd,' I said, 'I was only thinking about you earlier, too.'

'I have been promised an audition next week,' she said. 'Miriam will arrange it and it is because of you.'

'That's wonderful,' I told her. 'You got on well with her then?'

I remembered what Frances had said and was grateful Lizzie had made the connection off her own back. Or perhaps *on* it. But that was hardly fair and I regretted the thought as soon as it popped into my head. Lizzie was old enough to know what she was doing. Not by much, perhaps, but old enough just the same.

'I want to thank you, Harry,' she said breathlessly down the line.

'You just have,' I said.

'No, properly.'

'Sounds good to me.'

I heard a key turn in the lock and froze. But it was only Carol, jug in hand after water.

'Sorry,' she said when she saw me on the telephone. 'I didn't think you were home. I came up for some water.'

'Who is that?' Lizzie asked down the line.

I put my hand over the receiver.

'Of course,' I told Carol. 'Go ahead.' Then to Lizzie. 'It's Carol from the basement. I introduced you, remember?'

'The plain one with the mousy hair,' said Lizzie.

'Not at all,' I told her. 'Their pipes have frozen and they need water.'

'Sorry,' Carol said again as she edged by me with the jug.

'This is a story, Harry,' Lizzie said, pouting verbally. 'You are not telling the truth.'

'Can we meet?' I asked her.

'You have time for me?'

'Don't be silly. Tomorrow?'

'Where?'

'The ABC tearooms again?'

We agreed on a time and I put the telephone down as Carol turned off the tap.

'You lead a busy social life,' she observed.

'Not really,' I said. 'It just looks that way. Would you like me to carry that down for you?'

'Thanks but I can manage.'

'I know how much Muriel likes me dropping by.'

Carol laughed. 'Mu's a very nice girl when you get to know her. Really.'

'I'll just have to wait for bath night then,' I said.

17

Wednesday, January 29th 1947

'Oh,' said Magdalena, breaking into the reverie I was enjoying about my evening out with Lizzie. We'd had a meal at a decent restaurant and tonight I was taking her to the pictures.

'I almost forgot. Brian Ogilvy rang. Can you meet him for a drink after work?'

'Tonight?'

She picked a note off her desk and brought it round to me.

'Do you have plans? Seven o'clock at this address. He'd appreciate it if you called him back to confirm. That's his office number.'

'As a matter of fact I have arranged something,' I said.

'Then tell him you can't make it.'

I looked at the address and telephone number Magdalena said she had almost forgotten. That in itself was uncharacteristic, and it was more than a little cavalier of her to suggest I put off one of the officers from the St James's Street headquarters.

The address was the drinking club I'd been to with him a couple of weeks earlier and it occurred to me that if the evening was going to be anything like that meeting it would be at least an hour before I'd be able to get away. I was due to meet Lizzie at seven-thirty.

'I don't suppose he mentioned why he wanted to see me?'

'No.'

Her answer, short as it was, implied a volume of meaning. I still wasn't able to read Magdalena, though, and she didn't elaborate. I asked our exchange for his number and when they put me through I spoke to his secretary. Reluctantly, I confirmed I'd meet him and she confirmed seven o'clock. I asked if she might know why he wanted to see me but Ogilvy's secretary was no more forthcoming than Magdalena had been.

At lunchtime I tried ringing Lizzie from a call-box but no one was answering her telephone. I spent the afternoon working through the ISPAL traffic from Palestine and at five-thirty suggested that if Magdalena was walking home through the park I'd go with her. She lived a street or two north of it. Since the bad weather the bus service had become unreliable and rather than wait for a bus that wasn't coming, she often found it quicker to walk. Fine in daylight, I thought, but the crime wave London had experienced during the blackout hadn't shown much sign of abating and Hyde Park in the dark seemed a risk for a woman on her own. Magdalena, though, didn't appear to worry about it.

'Thank you, Mr Tennant,' she said. 'There's really no need.'

'I've time,' I said. 'I'm not meeting Ogilvy for an hour and a half and I can just as well get the Tube at Lancaster Gate.'

Which wasn't exactly true as it would mean changing at Oxford Circus and again at Piccadilly Circus to get back to Green Park. Magdalena would have been perfectly aware of this but she didn't argue. And, since I wasn't meeting Ogilvy until seven, I found it preferable to spend the time walking Magdalena through the park than kicking my heels waiting for him.

Snow had been cleared from the paths through the park but the covering on the grass, without a fresh fall, had become black and pitted by the soot from the capital's chimneys. Beyond the path, trees stood hunched under the weight of the last fall, faintly phosphorescent in the moonlight and possessing an air of unreality. We exchanged a few words about the day's work then walked mostly in silence until I said goodnight by Westbourne Gate. I watched her cross the road then turned towards the Lancaster Gate Tube station.

I couldn't see that I was ever going to get away from Ogilvy to meet Lizzie at seven-thirty and would probably be too late to expect that she might wait for me. I didn't want to leave her thinking I'd stood her up so I stopped at a call-box outside the station and tried her number again. This time she picked up.

'Harry?' she queried. As if I was the last person she was expecting to call.

'Something's come up and I'm going to be late,' I said.

'But we will miss the picture. You know how much I want to see it.' I imagined the pout on those full red lips of hers.

They were showing *The Postman Always Rings Twice* with Lana Turner and John Garfield. I'd not seen it but had read the book and if the film was as steamy as the novel, I'd been entertaining a vague hope that a charged scene or two between Turner and Garfield might arouse Lizzie.

'We can go another evening,' I said. 'What about a drink instead?'

'What time will you meet me?'

'I'm not sure how long I'll be. Can we say nine?'

'This is too late, Harry. What do you want? That I wait for you in some bar?'

'I'm sorry,' I said, 'but it can't be helped. It's work. Would you rather leave it until tomorrow?'

'Perhaps. But you must make it up to me.'

'Anything you want,' I agreed.

'You will have to be nice to me.'

'And will you be nice to me, too?'

'Tomorrow,' she said. 'You will see how nice I can be.'

'I can't wait,' I told her.

But I was going to have to; and worse, spend the time listening to Brian Ogilvy. I edged out of the call-box and walked to Lancaster Gate Tube, cooling my ardour by waiting on the draughty platform for an east-bound train.

****

Ogilvy was sitting by himself at a table in the corner. Smoke hung in the air from a cigarette burning in an ashtray. A glass stood on the table beside a copy of *The Times* open at page two.

'Harry,' he said, his face assuming his customary genial expression as we shook hands. He signalled a waiter. 'What'll it be?'

I asked for my usual gin and French, aware what it would do on an empty stomach. Ogilvy ordered another double scotch.

'How are you finding the new job?' he asked as I sat down.

As far as I could tell it wasn't much different from the old one except I didn't go home smelling like a bonfire.

'Fine,' I said.

'And how are you getting along with Magdalena?'

I half-expected the question to be accompanied by a lewd wink. But Brian Ogilvy was far too well-bred to stoop to that sort of vulgarity.

'Pretty well,' I said. 'She's very good at her job.'

He nodded knowingly as our drinks arrived.

'I looked through your report last week,' he said. 'I think we're beginning to get a picture of what we're up against at last.'

I tasted my drink. 'I didn't think you were involved in this Jewish terrorist business.'

'Indirectly, Harry. Only as it relates to other matters.'

'Anything I should know about?'

He gave the merest of shrugs then pushed the copy of the *Times* towards me without answering my question.

The piece he indicated was about the unemployment caused by the fuel shortages. There were currently one-hundred thousand men out of work because of power cuts and the lack of fuel for industry. *The Times* report suggested that the number was forecast to grow when new electricity cuts came into force next week.

'Bloody country's going to the dogs,' Ogilvy remarked.

'Unfortunately there's not much anyone can do about the weather,' I said.

'We could have been prepared for it.'

'Up to a point,' I agreed. 'But the railways are snowed in. We're having to bring coal in from Hull by boat. Actually there are pictures of them arriving ...' I picked up the paper to show him but Ogilvy wasn't interested in pictures.

'Bloody government's a shambles,' he said. 'Wouldn't you agree?'

I agreed that it was true they didn't seem to be handling matters particularly well. Emmanuel Shinwell, the Minister for Fuel and Power, was the one who was mostly getting it in the neck for not addressing the shortages earlier. The fact he had run down coal supplies in the autumn, and then nationalised the industry in the middle of winter hadn't helped. It hadn't gone down too well in the press. Nor on the streets for that matter.

'But then,' Ogilvy said smiling at me. 'what can you expect from socialists?'

I might have suggested that even the Conservative Party couldn't control the weather, but Ogilvy hadn't finished.

'What concerns us in particular,' he said, 'is that we have a leak.'

'Who? Us?'

'No, not *us*,' he replied irritably. 'I mean the bloody government. Guy isn't convinced, of course. But I'm not as relaxed about this sort of thing as he seems to be.'

'Guy Liddell, you mean?'

On the few occasions I'd seen Liddell he hadn't seemed particularly relaxed to me. On the contrary, I thought he looked more like a man weighed down by his responsibilities.

'Well, perhaps relaxed isn't the best way to describe it,' Ogilvy decided, pulling absently on an earlobe then taking a longer pull at his scotch. 'In my opinion he's let things slip since Petrie left. He was expecting to get the

DG's job himself and between you and me, Harry, being passed over has affected his judgement.'

Sir David Petrie had retired as Director General before I had joined. The new DG was a policeman, an ex-chief constable who had been brought in over the heads of the senior men. A fact that had not gone down well from what I gathered.

'Guy was pretty bitter when Attlee chose Sillitoe over him,' Ogilvy went on. 'He's a decent enough chap, don't get me wrong; a bit of a plodder, but what can one expect of a policeman? The point is it was sheer spite on Attlee's part. Labour have never forgiven the Service for that Zinoviev letter business back in the '20s. And there's nothing like a socialist for holding a grudge. The Party hasn't trusted us since, so when the opportunity came he chose an outsider.'

'Surely he wouldn't—'

'Oh, it wasn't just that,' Ogilvy said quickly. 'Not as far as Guy is concerned. Anyway, the thing is he's none too careful about the company he keeps.'

'What sort of company?'

'You know,' said Ogilvy, 'those with certain *inclinations*, if you get my meaning?'

And this time the wink was certainly implied.

'There was Guy's former secretary, for instance,' Ogilvy said. 'Anthony Blunt. Don't get me wrong. A first-rate mind and a good fellow. No one nicer. But Blunt has an odd circle of friends. Far too close to that Foreign Office chappie, Guy Burgess, for one. Outrageous fellow. Once he's had a few drinks – and he's *always* had a few drinks – his behaviour is quite beyond the pale. How he and some of the others get away with it is beyond me.' Ogilvy shook his head. 'But then, when you have the sort of friends that Burgess and his ilk have it seems you're more or less immune to censure. The wonder is that Guy doesn't see it. Keeping that sort of company has done him no good at all. I mean, people are bound to speculate, aren't they? You heard his wife ran off with her brother, I suppose?'

'Yes,' I said. I had heard it from Ogilvy himself.

'Then there was that business last year. That atom scientist fellow. May, wasn't it?'

I assumed he was talking about Allan Nunn May, not the calendar month. The case had been in the papers: a Russian had implicated May for passing information about the atomic bomb.

'We caught him,' said Ogilvy, 'but apparently that's not enough to satisfy Attlee. That's a socialist for you,' he went on, downing the rest of his scotch.

'What is?'

'Spite, of course. Vindictiveness. They seem to take the view that it was *our* fault the fellow did what he did in the first place. Never mind that half the government would like to jump in bed with the reds anyway.'

'Would they?'

'Bloody Shinwell for one. You know the man once went to prison for inciting a riot? And that's just the half of it.'

'So, what are you saying, Brian? That someone in the government is leaking information to the Russians?'

'The Russians? No, not necessarily the Russians. But something is leaking. I'm just putting feelers out. You understand, Harry. You're in on this Jewish business. All I'm asking is that you keep an eye open.'

'Open for what in particular?'

'Any suggestion that there might be a link between any of the people we're interested in and a government minister. I don't have to tell you that Shinwell is a Jew, do I? And they've all kept some pretty questionable company over the years. Now they're in government that has to change. Perhaps Attlee does have the best intentions, but I'm not sure that goes for the rest of them. It only takes one weak link in the chain, Harry. So, even if it's no more than a whisper, you'll let me know, won't you?'

'Of course,' I said. 'But there's been no suggestion that any of the people we're looking at have those kind of contacts.'

Then I thought of Sydney Stanley. According to Jack, Stanley had government contacts. Perhaps I gave off some sort of subliminal signal because Ogilvy picked it up straight away.

'What is it?' he said.

'Nothing really,' I said. 'It has no connection to what I'm working on ...'

'Go on.'

'It's just that I met someone the other day who claims to know a government minister. Maintains he can get things done. You know, if the price is right. You've met the type. He was just talking himself up.'

'Who is he?'

'I met him through a contact of mine. An old army colleague. He does a bit of business in army surplus. This man's able to facilitate the contracts, apparently.'

'Who is he?' Ogilvy asked again.

'His name is Sydney Stanley. He hasn't turned up in anything I've been working on and I'm far from convinced he has the contacts he claims he does. All the same ... he did manage to run down a little information I was after that was proving difficult.'

'Classified information?' Ogilvy asked.

'No. Something private,' I said.

'You think he might be useful?' Ogilvy said.

'Look, Brian. I wouldn't want to compromise *my* contact because of some other matter.'

Queer Jack's pitch, was what I really meant. Nor did I want it traced back to me that I had been making enquiries about Joseph Wolff and his brother.

'Of course,' Ogilvy agreed. 'A matter of discretion. But this Stanley might be a man who hears things we might not necessarily.'

'It's possible,' I said.

'Jewish, is he?'

'Yes, I should think so ...'

I could see Ogilvy thinking it over.

'Look,' I said again, beginning to wish I hadn't brought Stanley's name up in the first place. 'It might be best if I didn't introduce you to him myself.'

'We can arrange something else,' Ogilvy said. 'Keep your name out of it.'

I took the card Stanley had given me out of my wallet and gave it to him.

'Park Lane,' said Ogilvy, looking at the address before pocketing the card. 'Interesting ... No need to worry, Harry. Mum's the word. And it might be as well if we didn't let Bryce in on this either. Between you and me, old chap. After all, we don't want to go off half-cocked, do we? The way things are these days a man has to tread a fine line. If you know what I mean ...'

And this time there was no mistaking the wink Ogilvy gave me.

18

Thursday, January 30th 1947

'*What* did he ask you to do?' Magdalena demanded the next morning, on the point of sorting the latest transcripts into the appropriate piles.

It was my own fault. I'd brought the subject up, naively supposing that two pairs of eyes might be better than one at spotting if any of our targets could be in contact with a government minister.

'He *said*,' I repeated, 'that if we came across any evidence of someone with links to anyone in government, to let him know.'

She glanced up sharply. 'Let *him* know? And what did he think we would do with that sort of information? Keep it to ourselves?'

I was surprised by her reaction. 'No, of course not. He merely said he wanted us – *me*, that is – to keep it between ourselves. His exact words were that these days we had "to tread a fine line".'

Magdalena dropped a telephone directory she had picked up for no good reason back on to the desk. It landed with disturbing finality.

'If you ask me, it's Brian Ogilvy who's treading the fine line.'

'What do you mean?'

'I *mean*,' she said forcibly, 'it sounds as though he knows what he's looking for.'

'He said he's already found—'

'He's found nothing,' she interrupted. 'But he knows what he wants to find.'

'I don't follow.'

'Brian Ogilvy is running a vendetta.'

'The last time I heard that word,' I said, 'was when I was in Naples.'

'Well, it won't be a knife that Brian Ogilvy uses,' she said. 'Assuming that's what Italians use.'

I was about to say that in my experience Italians used whatever was to hand, but she hadn't finished.

'What Ogilvy uses is disinformation and innuendo.'

'You seem to know a lot about him,' I said.

She didn't reply. Then it occurred to me that perhaps – like the Italians – Ogilvy was using what was to hand – me.

'I got the impression he was rather well thought-of over at HQ,' I said. 'And he has high regard for you.'

She glared at me. 'What did he say?'

'He asked how we were getting on.'

'Getting on?'

'Working together.'

She gave a short contemptuous laugh.

'What's *that* supposed to mean?'

'It means I don't trust him,' she said. 'And I don't think you should trust him either. He's underhand.'

'I thought we all were here,' I said. 'After all, that's what we do, isn't it?'

'You know very well what I mean,' Magdalena replied, dropping a pile of transcripts on my desk then folding her arms. 'And what about Mr Bryce? Are you supposed to tell him if you find anything?'

'Well ...' I said. 'No. That's what he meant by keeping it between ourselves, I suppose.'

'There you are,' she said.

Exactly where that was, I wasn't sure.

'May I ask if this dislike of Ogilvy is anything more than professional?'

'Of course it's professional,' Magdalena said. 'But if you must know, it is also personal.'

'Has he ...? You know ...'

'Has he what?'

'*Approached* you,' I suggested awkwardly.

'Propositioned me, you mean?'

'Well, that's not how I wanted to put it, but yes.'

Then I made things worse by trying to turn the fact into a compliment.

'After all,' I said clumsily, 'you're the sort of girl a lot of men would like to ... to ... well, proposition.'

'Thank you *very* much,' she snapped.

'That wasn't quite how I meant it,' I said.

'And how *did* you mean it?'

'I meant to say that you're an attractive woman. Even if you do have a tendency to intimidate men.'

'Intimidate?'

'Yes. You certainly intimidated me when I first met you.'

131

'Don't be ridiculous.'

'You scared me to death to be honest,' I said.

'Oh, stop it,' she said. 'I was just beginning to take you seriously.'

'Now tell me exactly what *you* mean by seriously.'

She went back to her desk and squared up some files that were in no need of squaring.

'We were talking about Brian Ogilvy, if you recall,' she replied tartly.

'The man with the vendetta.'

'I'm serious.'

'I believe you. Who's he got a vendetta against?'

'When you were talking to him,' she said, 'did he happen to mention Emmanuel Shinwell?'

'What's this, your party trick?'

'Did he?'

'Yes. How did you know?'

'His cousin has an estate in Yorkshire.'

'I'm assuming you don't mean Manny Shinwell.'

'Brian Ogilvy!'

'Well, I know he's a Right Honourable or something. Does that mean he'll inherit a title?'

'Only if two or three others die before him. That's not likely and isn't the point. The estate is no longer worth anything so there won't be much to inherit.'

'What are they, a family of gamblers?'

'No. Coal owners.'

'And they've been nationalised?'

'Not just nationalised,' said Magdalena. 'The estate has been destroyed.'

'How?'

'Opencast mining.'

And as soon as she said it I remembered the furore there'd been the year before about a huge Yorkshire estate where the government had mined a shallow seam right up to the back door of the great house.

'You don't mean that place with the famous gardens?' I said.

'That's the one. There were formal gardens and a park laid out by Humphrey Repton.'

'There was a big fuss about it last year,' I said. 'Didn't Shinwell maintain the coal seam was high grade—'

'And an independent survey said it was so poor it wasn't worth mining,' Magdalena said. 'Even the local miners were against extracting it. Really it was no more than an excuse to destroy the estate. Some people called it an act of class warfare.'

'No wonder Ogilvy's got it in for the socialists,' I said.

'Between nationalisation, the destruction of the estate and death duties, the family has been ruined.'

'I can see his point of view,' I said. 'The world turned upside down.'

'Perhaps it needed turning,' Magdalena replied. 'Although equality is one thing and vindictiveness quite another.'

'Actually that's precisely what Ogilvy accused the government of,' I said. 'Only he was talking about Guy Liddell not getting the DG's job.'

'And there's some truth in that,' said Magdalena.

'He told me there have been leaks from the government.'

'To whom?'

'He didn't give me the details.'

'He's fishing.'

'So you think he wants to smear Shinwell?'

'He'd love to if he could. But I'm sure any Labour minister would suit his purpose.'

I was beginning to wish again that I hadn't given him Stanley's business card. As sharp-eyed as ever, Magdalena noticed.

'Was there something else?' she asked.

I hummed and hawed for a bit but there was no way around it.

'The thing is,' I said, 'I gave him a name.'

'Whose name?'

'Someone who did a favour for me. Well, for an friend of mine.'

'What kind of favour?'

'You're in the wrong branch of the Service,' I said. 'Ever thought of switching to interrogation?'

Magdalena merely waited for an answer.

'It was a man named Sydney Stanley,' I finally said. 'I met him through my old corporal at the war crimes unit. Stanley's been putting a bit of business his way.'

'What kind of business?'

'Army surplus.'

'Is it legal?'

'Of course it is,' I said. 'As far as I'm aware, anyway. Stanley's what they call a "contact man". The sort who claims to know people in the know. If you see what I mean.'

'Is this man Stanley on our books?'

'In what way?'

'In *any* way, Harry.'

'I don't think so,' I said. 'His name's not turned up since we've been looking into this Jewish thing, but then I don't have access to everything, do I?'

'If I were you,' she said, her brows furrowing above her glasses, 'I'd be very careful. You don't want to be caught in the middle of anything.'

'Tread carefully, you mean? Isn't that what I told you Ogilvy said?'

She gave a sigh of exasperation and picked up another file.

'Ah well,' I said to her, 'if nothing else this has at least achieved one thing.'

She glanced up. 'And what might that be?'

'You called me Harry. Does that mean we can now dispense with this *Mr* Tennant and *Miss* Marshall nonsense?'

She sighed again. 'Protocol insists we address our superiors formally.'

'Well no one believes *that* fiction here, do they? That I'm in charge, I mean.'

Magdalena smiled.

'At least, you've learned that much since you've joined us.'

19

Friday, January 31st 1947

'Take me with you, Harry.'

Lizzie was pouting again, stretched languorously across the bed with her hair a dark tangle on my pillow. She was watching me through half-closed eyes.

I don't know when I first thought about going back to Riseborough. While sitting in the dark of the cinema perhaps, as Turner and Garfield plotted to kill the Greek. It was only an idea and I soon forgot it as over a drink afterwards Lizzie said she wanted to see where I lived. With only room for one thought in my head, I skipped the second round I was about to buy and hurried her to the Tube station at Piccadilly Circus before she changed her mind.

I needn't have hurried as it turned out. She had the same thing on her mind. We didn't waste much time once I'd shut the door behind us, leaving our clothes strewn down the hall and into the bedroom like clues in an adult paper chase. I didn't know if Lizzie thought much about John Garfield but, as far as I was concerned, I wouldn't have traded her for Lana Turner even if Barbara Stanwyck came as part of the deal.

It was afterwards, relaxed and contented with Lizzie planning what we'd do on the weekend that I thought about Riseborough again.

'I have to go away tomorrow,' I told her. 'Overnight, perhaps. I'm not sure.'

'Where?'

'East Anglia.'

'Where is East Anglia?'

'East. On the coast.'

'Is this work?'

'No. This is something else.'

'You are going to meet someone? Another woman?'

'Of course not.'

I was planning to see the woman who ran the refugee home again but didn't think Miss Patterson would count as another woman as far as Lizzie was concerned.

'Then you can take me with you?'

'There won't be anything for you to do there,' I said.

'It is on the sea, this *East Anglia*?'

'I'm going to somewhere called Riseborough. It's a small seaside town and it's out of season and bloody cold.'

'Is bloody cold everywhere,' said Lizzie.

'Well Riseborough is colder than most, believe me.'

The pout became more pronounced. 'I do not believe you. I think you are meeting another woman. We make love once and you lose interest in me.'

'That's not true,' I said.

'Then why do you go to this Risselby?'

'Riseborough.'

'I think this is perhaps your secret work. That is why you will not tell me.'

I sighed. She was exasperating. She wanted to know everything. Like a child who demanded a reason for every action, "why" was forever on her lips. I kissed them.

'Riseborough is where Samuel Wolff's brother, Joseph, killed himself.'

'Why there?'

'I don't know why there,' I said. 'Well I might. But I don't understand it. He went there to see someone – a girl. But she wasn't there.'

'Who was this girl?'

I could tell I wasn't going to get any peace until she had got every twist and turn of the story out of me. I didn't tell her why I had been following Wolff – I hardly knew myself – and certainly not who had told me to follow him. But since the reason I'd met her in the first place was because she had known Wolff's brother, I couldn't see that it mattered. So I explained about Katja Tereshchenko and the refugee home.

'I want to talk to the woman who runs it again. Now I know a bit more about Wolff and his brother it might jog her memory.'

'She is young, this woman?'

'No, she is not young. And she is very big.'

'But why do you have to go tomorrow? Why not in the week?'

'Because I work during the week and the weekend is the only time I have free.'

'So you say this is not work? Your people do not tell you to go to this Riseborough?'

'*No*. This has nothing to do with my work.'

Which was hardly true but I wasn't going to explain every detail to her.

She ran a teasing finger across my chest. 'Then there is no reason you cannot take me with you.'

'You won't enjoy it,' I said.

She curled her lips coquettishly and lifted her chin. 'No? How are you so sure?'

She was asking for it so I kissed her again. In a little while she said: 'Is your work really secret, Harry?'

I was running my fingers up the inside of her thigh and her breath was laboured, the words coming from somewhere deep in her throat.

'Do you always talk so much when you're in bed with a man?'

She took my hand and pulled it to her. 'Do you think I sleep with many men?' She shifted a little towards me.

'You're in bed with me,' I said.

'But you are different, Harry.'

'Oh? How?'

'You have secrets.'

'You just think I do.'

'No, it is true. Secrets are an aphrodisiac. Did you not know?'

'That's a big word for a small French girl,' I said, stirring once more as I rolled over and straddled her.

After a while I lay on my back beside her, breathing deeply.

'Do you not find secrets exciting?' she asked again.

'What kind of secrets?'

She ran a hand down my chest. 'That does not matter. Anything that other people do not know. This is an erotic thing. People who know secrets have the power. You do not find this so, Harry?'

I thought of the people I knew who knew secrets, like Bryce and Ogilvy, and couldn't help thinking they were among the least erotic people I'd ever encountered. Then I thought of Magdalena who had a secret or two and suddenly wished I hadn't. For some reason thinking of Magdalena Marshall made me feel guilty.

'Tell me a secret, Harry,' Lizzie was persisting in my ear.

'What makes you think I know anything secret?'

137

'Pah!' she exclaimed. 'It is your work. I know. This is how we met, is it not?'

'I was looking for secrets, not trying to keep them,' I said.

'You are teasing me.'

She rolled over and sat astride me, loose hair straggling down over her small breasts. She leaned forward, swaying left and then right so her nipples brushed against my lips.

'We had secrets in the war,' she said. 'My mother always had secrets.'

'Let's not talk about your mother,' I said.

'You would think my mother was very beautiful. I showed you her photograph.'

Lizzie's mother seemed an odd topic to discuss while I was in bed with her daughter, but I wasn't exactly in a position to walk out on her. Besides, I liked listening to her French accent. I let her talk.

'I remember the photograph,' I said, 'and yes, your mother was very beautiful. Like her daughter.'

'Did I tell you she was Russian?'

I stiffened, although not in any way that would have been useful to Lizzie. She stared down on me.

'This surprises you?'

'Not at all,' I said.

'Is it that you should not be seeing the daughter of a Russian? What would they say about this at your work?'

'I think I'd better not tell them,' I said.

'So,' she replied teasingly, 'now you have more secrets.'

'No. I don't have anything to do with the Russians.'

'Only this Russian,' she said, sitting back hard against me and beginning to move rhythmically. 'So what is it you do have to do with if it is not Russians?'

It was like an exquisite torture, Lizzie upright above me, breasts rising and falling as she breathed.

'Other things,' I managed to say. 'Anyway, you're only half-Russian, aren't you? The rest is French and the French are our allies.'

'French, yes,' she said. 'But I was brought up Jewish. My step-father was a Jew.'

This was too much.

Lizzie stopped moving.

'Ah,' she said. 'You do not like Jews?'

'Of course I like Jews,' I said. 'I'm with you, aren't I?'

'You did not know I was Jew.'

'Not by birth.'

'When I was a girl I wanted to join the Catholic Church,' Lizzie went on, resuming her work with religious fervour despite the fact I'd lost my stride. 'But my mother was very angry. Now I am nothing. I am myself, that is all.'

'Making love to you while listening to your life story is very disconcerting,' I said.

'There are Jews who still fight in Palestine,' said Lizzie. 'I have read about this. But of course you will know, Harry.'

'Why should I know about it?' I said.

She bent forward, her face to mine. 'You are teasing me again. You want to know all about Samuel Wolff. Was he not Jewish like my stepfather? And his brother, Joseph, too? Is it because they were Jewish that you are interested in them?'

She straightened up again, threatening to break me in two.

'Did Stanley tell you this?' I managed to ask.

'Stanley?'

'Sydney Stanley, the man who sent you to meet me,'

'No, no Harry. I told you I do not know this Stanley. It was you who told me that Samuel Wolff had a brother, remember?'

I was finding it difficult to remember much at all. She was arching her back and urging me on like a jockey who has found her mount flagging in the last furlong. I stepped up, trying not to disappoint, galloping on and hoping I might last until we reached the finishing post. Finally crossing it together, I collapsed in a heap, feeling fit for little but the knackers' yard.

'So,' said Lizzie, snuggling beside me, 'you think you will find out more about this man Wolff in Riseborough?'

****

It wasn't yet light when I felt her slide out of bed. I heard water running and a minute or two later she came back to the bedroom and began to dress.

'Where are you going? It's only seven o'clock.'

She bent down and kissed me. 'I must go home and pack a suitcase. I will need clothes in Riseborough.'

'Are you sure you want to come?' I asked again, pushing myself upright. 'I told you there's nothing to do there.'

'But of course I want to come. I will do what you do in the day. At night we will think of something else.' She smiled wickedly.

'We could stop at your flat and pick up what you need on the way to the station,' I suggested. 'You won't need much.'

'No, Harry. I must have proper things for a weekend. It is how I am.'

'If you must,' I said. 'But you won't need evening clothes and you'd better bring a book. So you won't be bored.'

I yawned and got out bed and started pulling on my clothes.

'I'll walk you to the station.'

'No,' said Lizzie. 'You stay inside and be warm.'

Warm wasn't how I would have characterised my flat but I didn't argue.

'At least have a cup of tea before you go,' I said.

'No, I have no time.'

I got dressed anyway and told Lizzie to meet me at Liverpool Street Station at eleven sharp for our train. I had to pack a change of clothes myself, as well as telephone the hotel in Riseborough to make a reservation. There was probably no need as I couldn't imagine they wouldn't have a vacancy given the weather, but I would anyway.

I kissed Lizzie goodbye and opened the door for her only to find Carol and Muriel on the step, jugs and towels in hand.

The three girls exchanged glances. Lizzie lifted her chin.

'We didn't think you'd be up,' Carol said.

'You remember Lizzie,' I said to them. 'She came to Miriam's party.'

'Of course we do,' Muriel said. 'How could we forget? Miriam told me all about you, Lizzie. Working yet?'

'I will see you at the station, Harry,' Lizzie said to me, ignoring the girls and hurrying down the stairs.

'Someone going away?' Muriel asked.

I stepped aside to let them in.

'Only tonight,' I explained. 'Your pipes are still frozen, I take it.'

'This must be awfully inconvenient for you,' Carol said. 'We thought we'd get out of your way early.'

'I'll be back tomorrow afternoon at the latest,' I told them. 'Make yourselves at home.'

'I hope we didn't embarrass your friend,' said Muriel, looking as if she didn't hope so in the least. 'She must think you have a string of girls coming up to visit you.'

I took their jugs to the kitchen and filled them, then I filled the kettle.

'Don't worry about it Muriel,' I said. 'Anyone can see I'm not your type. Would you like a cup of tea while you're waiting for the bath to fill?'

20

Saturday, February 1st 1947

Wrestling Lizzie's case on to the platform, I was struck by how Riseborough looked even bleaker than it had on my first visit. The case was as big as a steamer trunk and I wondered as I pushed it aside and helped her down why she thought it appropriate to bring so much for a single night away.

Lizzie caught her breath, what little colour was in her cheeks draining as she stepped out of the train.

'It is freezing,' she complained.

'I warned you. Mind the ice.'

'How far is our hotel. Do we take a taxi?'

'No, we walk. It's not far.'

Snow had piled in frozen heaps against the railings outside the station and I thought this was probably how a Siberian town looked. The Russian wind may have blown itself out but it had left behind it sheets of ice that glazed the road and pavements.

Lugging her case behind me, I walked through the empty town, conscious of an icy stillness that was almost tangibly solid.

It was a short walk to the hotel but nearly too much for Lizzie. She had taken on the pallor of an ice sculpture and her teeth were chattering as we pushed through the front door and up to the desk.

The girl I remembered from my previous visit was still on reception. She smiled brightly at us.

'Mr and Mr Tennant, nice to see you again.'

She had never seen Lizzie before but I supposed it was possible she remembered me. Then we were probably the only guests due that day. I signed the register, suppressing the temptation to flick back through the pages to see whether Joseph Wolff's name had disappeared from their register in the same way his file had vanished from ours.

'Any chance we could we get a drink to warm us up?' I asked.

'Of course,' said the receptionist. 'The bar is closed, I'm afraid, but I can have something sent up?'

****

After we'd had our drinks and settled into our room, I decided that as it still wasn't quite five o'clock I'd try the refugee home straight away. I had been counting on the fact that Miss Patterson was there on Saturdays but was worried I might not catch her on a Sunday. Lizzie, already in bed and wrapped in blankets made a face at me. I promised I would not be long.

'You do not want me to come with you?'

'I'd have a hard time explaining you,' I said.

I had told Miss Patterson on my previous visit that I represented a refugee organisation. I didn't want to confuse her by turning up now with a wife in tow. The bar would open at six, time enough to get a drink or two into Lizzie to placate her before dinner.

Out on the street the afternoon light had been replaced by pale moonlight reflecting off the snow-covered cliff top with luminous florescence.

In the dark, the refugee home loomed larger than I remembered. Oppressively gothic and almost menacing, I wondered how the inmates felt about having exchanged their homelands for this forbidding institution. I recalled what Miss Patterson had said about Joseph Wolff when he arrived: disturbed, she had said, almost incoherent. But while I imagined the look of the place might possibly affect someone of a nervous disposition, I didn't think it likely that Wolff's first sight of the home could have disturbed him to such a degree.

Michael Wright, Wolff's student at Oxford, had told me Wolff had been looking forward to his trip to Riseborough; that he had been in a better frame of mind than for some while. That suggested to me it had been something else that had disturbed Wolff, something more than the curiously introspective depression Wright had told me Wolff had been suffering.

Something, perhaps, that had happened to him between leaving Oxford and arriving in Riseborough.

Miss Patterson was still in her office; her paraffin heater was still throwing out more fumes than a DDT de-louser; and the air was still thicker than a pot of pre-war clotted cream.

'Why, it's Mr … ' she began before her memory failed her.

'Tennant,' I reminded her, trying not to breath too deeply. 'Harold Tennant?'

'Of course,' she said, coming round her desk to shake my hand.

143

My earlier impression of her resembling a dreadnought returned as she cut a swathe through the paraffin fumes.

'Department for Displaced Persons, isn't it? You were enquiring about Katja Tereshchenko. Have you made any progress?'

'I've just a few more loose ends, I'm afraid,' I said. 'You told me Katja had a sister. Her name was Oksana?'

'That's right, Oksana. Katja came to England to find her. She had heard that Oksana was in Yorkshire. That is where Katja went first, anyway. She told me she had received a letter with an address for Oksana. By the time Katja got there, though, her sister had already left.'

'You don't know where Oksana went.'

'I'm sorry, Mr Tennant, but Katja was never able to find out. By then her health had started to give way. She was quite ill, poor thing. Not well at all by the time they came for her.'

'It's just that we have traced a displaced person by the name of Oksana Tereshchenko. We are wondering, of course, if she might be your Katja's sister.'

'Do you think she might?,' said Miss Patterson eagerly. 'I believe Oksana used her married name, though. Katja did tell me her sister's husband had died, so it's possible she reverted to her maiden name.'

'And you told me a visitor had come looking for her just a day or so before I did. Joseph Wolff, I think you said his name was. Do you remember?'

'Certainly.'

'You said he seemed very disturbed.'

'Indeed he was, Mr Tennant. Particularly after I told him that Katja had already been resettled.' She lowered her voice a little. 'I don't know if you heard, Mr Tennant, but the poor man drowned. His body was washed up a few miles along the coast.'

'Yes, I heard that.'

'Well,' she said, resuming normal volume, 'word gets around as you can imagine. Naturally I went to the police. I told them how Mr Wolff came here asking after Katja. How agitated he was when he arrived and how distraught he became when I told him she'd already gone. They told me I would most likely be called to give evidence on his state of mind at the inquest. I attended, of course, although in the end I wasn't called. And do you know, the coroner brought down a verdict of accidental death? A swimming accident. Well! I must say I found that *very* difficult to understand.' Miss Patterson shook her head. 'It was quite obvious to *me* that news of Katja's death had unbalanced the poor man's mind and that he had very possibly killed himself. But I'm afraid no one was prepared to listen to me.'

'It does seem a curious verdict,' I said. 'But I suppose they must have had some evidence to support it.'

'Well I can't think what that might have been, Mr Tennant. The local police no longer seemed interested and the plain clothes man who came down after the poor man's body was found seemed more interested in what Mr Wolff had asked me about Katja than in his death.'

'A plain clothes detective, you mean?'

'That's what he told me he was. I tried to remember what Mr Wolff had said, of course, but I couldn't tell him any more than I told you.'

'And did you mention that I'd been to see you?'

'Oh yes. I thought it best to tell him everything that happened that day because apparently that was the day Mr Wolff drowned. A Sunday, I believe it was.'

'Yes, you're right,' I said. 'Sunday January the 5th, if I recall. I remember because it's not often I find myself working on a Sunday.'

Miss Patterson nodded. 'I live in, of course, so I can always be found in the office.'

'And I'm sure it's much appreciated,' I assured her. 'One thing I do remember you telling me is that you thought Mr Wolff said something about a brother? I believe at the time you thought he was talking about Katja's brother. The Oksana Tereshchenko we have details for, though, has no brother.'

Miss Patterson brightened. 'Well, it now seems it was his *own* brother he was referring to. They said at the inquest that he had a brother who was killed in the war. Samuel, they said his name was.'

'So it was Wolff's own brother he was talking about?'

'I'm afraid so,' she sighed. 'So much tragedy.'

'Indeed,' I muttered. 'And you don't recall exactly what it was he said.'

'I'm sorry, Mr Tennant. The plain clothes policeman asked me as well. But as I told you, the poor man was so distressed he wasn't making any sense.'

Although I had glimpsed Wolff as he checked into the hotel, I never saw anything more of him until the following day when he came down to lunch. It was true he hadn't eaten much and had looked preoccupied, but it didn't strike me at the time that he was showing signs of distress. Yet, according to Miss Patterson he had certainly been distressed on the evening of his arrival.

It was obvious she couldn't tell me anything more. No more than she had been able to tell the plain clothes man. He had been sent down by Bryce, I assumed, after I told him about Wolff and Katja Tereshchenko.

I smiled at Miss Patterson and told her we'd do what we could to confirm that the Oksana Tereshchenko on our books was Katja's sister, even if we couldn't yet tell her where her sister had gone.

'I've tried to find out,' Miss Patterson assured me. 'I was in London attending a meeting of the charity trustees when they came for her, otherwise I might have been able to persuade them to wait until she was stronger. I've written letters and made phone calls, all to no avail I'm afraid.'

'Well,' I said, 'we'll do what we can our end.'

'I must say,' she went on, 'I do admire the length organisations like yours go to in order to reunite families. If this Oksana does turn out to be Katja's sister at least she will know she is still alive. So many of our poor refugees never learn of the fate that befalls their loved ones.'

'Indeed,' I said again, at a loss to add anything more.

'Would you wait a minute?' she said suddenly, turning and steering a passage around her desk and through a door into a room beyond. A moment later she was back carrying a small battered box. 'This was Katja's. It was all such a rush that morning the men came for her that apparently she left it behind. She didn't have much but she treasured what few things she did have, so I was very surprised when we were cleaning her room to find the box still here.'

She placed it on the desk and opened it.

There was nothing of value inside that I could see: a rustically carved wooden crucifix and a cheap string of rosary beads; some buttons that probably weren't silver; a fountain pen; a cheap brooch; and a couple of letters in envelopes. Beneath that Miss Patterson found a photograph.

'She showed me this once. Her family. It's an old photograph, of course.'

A group of people stood in front of a farmhouse. Father and mother with two sons and two daughters. Miss Patterson laid a podgy finger on the figure of a girl standing by her mother.

'That is Katja,' she said. 'And this would be her sister. Oksana was a year or two older than Katja, I believe.'

146

Katja was just a kid, pretty in a rural sort of way, farm fresh with wavy hair and a nice smile. Oksana looked far more attractive. Still young in the photo, she looked as if she might grow up a beauty.

Miss Patterson put the photo back in the box.

'I've been at a loss as to what to do with it. I've been hoping Katja would get in touch but we've heard nothing as yet. When a resident dies we usually keep any possessions for a year if they haven't indicated what should be done with them. Then, if no one claims them, I pass them to a local man who deals in second-hand items and bric-a-brac. He sells anything of value for what he can get and we halve the profits. For the charity, you understand,' she added quickly. 'Any personal papers I burn, of course.'

'Of course,' I concurred, looking at the two envelopes and about to suggest I examine them.

'Naturally I'd hold on to the box. But it might help you establish whether your Oksana Tereshchenko *is* Katja's sister. If she is, it might be better if she has it. If not perhaps you could arrange to return it? There's little of value here but Katja might still want it sent on.'

Miss Patterson put the lid on the box and thrust it into my hands.

'I'll make sure Oksana gets it,' I said. Then, feeling a pang of conscience about the lies I'd been feeding her, I took a ten-shilling note out of my wallet and gave it to her.

'For the charity,' I explained. 'I know you were going to keep the box rather than sell Katja's belongings ... but just so the charity doesn't lose a donation ...'

'Oh that's far too much,' Miss Patterson objected, folding the note through a slot in a tin moneybox on her desk nevertheless.

I thanked her again for her help and assured her my organisation would be in touch. Then I left, Katja Tereshchenko's few possessions clutched tightly under my arm.

****

Lizzie was waiting impatiently in our room. On my way up I'd noticed the hotel bar was open so I told her to get dressed and that we'd go down for a drink before dinner.

She jumped out of bed, kissed me and began the process of choosing a dress from the unfeasibly large number she had in her case.

'What happened?' she demanded, holding a dress to herself in front of the mirror. 'What did your woman tell you?'

I put Katja Tereshchenko's box on the table beside the bed and took out the letters. Lizzie, now in bra and panties, stood over me watching, her curiosity overcoming the temperature in the room.

'What are those?'

I told her they had belonged to the girl Samuel Wolff's brother had come to Riseborough to see.

She peered at the first as I took it out of its envelope. 'They are secret?'

'No, they're not secret, Lizzie. This one seems to have been from Wolff, though.'

'Samuel?'

'Joseph.'

It had been addressed to Katja at the refugee home and was handwritten. The date at the head of the letter was the same as the date on the postmark: December 19th 1946.

"Dear Miss Tereshchenko,
I received your letter only yesterday (December 18th) as I am afraid it appears to have been much delayed in the post. My full address, should you wish to correspond further, is as above. However, I would very much like to visit you in Riseborough if I may. My brother, Sam, told me of having met your sister, Oksana, and that they had formed an attachment. I am afraid I have to tell you that I fear they are now both beyond our help. I had been informed in November 1944 of Sam's death while on active service. I made some effort to contact your sister at the time only to be told that she was no longer at the camp. It was only two weeks ago that I learned further details concerning both my brother and your sister which I find deeply disturbing. There is too much I wish to tell you to commit to paper so, if you will allow me, I will visit you in the New Year. Saturday January 4th, if that is convenient. I would have liked to be able to meet you sooner but I am afraid commitments prevent this. Should this date not be

convenient, please write to me at the above
address as soon as you are able.
Yours most sincerely,
Joseph Wolff."

LIZZIE READ THE LETTER OVER MY SHOULDER. 'WHAT DOES IT MEAN?' SHE DEMANDED.

'THIS GIRL, Katja Tereshchenko, HAD WRITTEN TO WOLFF LAST YEAR. SHE'D ADDRESSED THE LETTER SIMPLY TO PROFESSOR WOLFF, OXFORD, AND IT MUST HAVE TAKEN WEEKS TO FIND HIM. BY THE TIME HE GOT IT AND ARRANGED TO COME HERE SHE HAD ALREADY LEFT.'

'NO, HARRY,' SAID LIZZIE, APPARENTLY UNTOUCHED BY THE PATHOS OF FATE'S MACHINATIONS. 'I MEAN WHAT IS IT ABOUT? WHAT DID HE HAVE TO TELL THIS KATJA GIRL? WHY DID HE SAY IT WAS DISTURBING?'

'THAT'S WHAT I DON'T KNOW,' I SAID.

SHE POUTED AT ME. 'NO,' SHE SAID. 'I THINK YOU DO KNOW BUT WILL NOT TELL ME.'

SHE REACHED PAST ME FOR THE SECOND LETTER IN THE BOX. I PULLED IT OUT OF HER HAND. THERE WAS NOTHING WRITTEN ON THE ENVELOPE AND WHEN I TOOK OUT THE LETTER I WAS DISAPPOINTED TO FIND IT WAS WRITTEN IN CYRILLIC.

'YOU CAN UNDERSTAND THIS?' LIZZIE ASKED.

'NO.'

'LET ME,' SHE SAID, TAKING THE LETTER FROM ME AGAIN AND SCANNING THROUGH IT.

'IT'S RUSSIAN, ISN'T IT?' I ASKED.

LIZZIE DIDN'T REPLY.

'CAN'T YOU READ IT? I THOUGHT YOU SAID YOUR MOTHER WAS RUSSIAN.'

'YES, BUT I DO NOT THINK THIS IS RUSSIAN.'

'WHAT IS IT IF IT'S NOT RUSSIAN?'

'UKRAINIAN?' LIZZIE SUGGESTED DOUBTFULLY. 'YOU SAY THIS GIRL Katja was Ukrainian? Tereshchenko is a Ukrainian name, no?'

I wondered if this might be the letter Miss Patterson said Katja had received from her sister, Oksana.

'Yes,' I said to Lizzie, 'but aren't the languages similar? Can't you make out any of it?'

'Anyway,' she said, dropping the letter on the bed and going back to her dressing, 'writing by hand is different from printed words. This is true in Russian so perhaps in Ukrainian also.'

She pulled her dress over her head.

'We have dinner now?'

'Yes, when you're ready,' I replied distractedly, picking up the letter and gazing at the incomprehensible characters that filled every page.

Then, as unexpected as a finger in the eye, I was brought up sharply by an English word. *"Butterwick"*. I didn't know what it meant and could make neither head nor tail of the context in which it had been used. I stared at the word for a while longer then slipped both letters into their envelopes and put them back in Katja Tereshchenko's box.

Lizzie was dressed and waiting, standing over me with her little handbag gripped in her fist. I grinned at her, reached over and pulled her on to the bed.

'No, Harry!' she complained. 'You crease my dress … you mess my make-up.' She struggled upright, smoothing her hands down the fabric and then over the tangle that was her hair. 'Maybe later,' she said. 'But only if you are good to me. You say this girl, Katja, is not a secret because you think I cannot keep a secret. I was in the French Resistance. To talk too much then is dangerous. With Germans it means death. I know how to keep a secret. How you say, to keep my mouth shut?'

'Do you? I don't think now is the time.'

'Time for what?'

I stood over her. 'To keep your mouth shut.'

She opened it again. 'What do you—'

I covered her mouth with mine, smothering her words. We tumbled back on to the bed again.

****

Half an hour later wE WERE IN THE BAR, HAVING A DRINK BEFORE DINNER. THE DINING ROOM WAS EMPTY. LIZZIE, FULL OF QUESTIONS AS EVER, BEGAN DEMANDING TO BE TOLD EVERYTHING I HAD LEARNED ABOUT KATJA. I WENT THROUGH IT AS WE ATE, THEN ASKED HER ONCE MORE WHAT SHE REMEMBERED ABOUT SAM WOLFF. SHE SAID AGAIN THAT HE HAD BEEN A FRIEND OF HER MOTHER'S AND THEN TOLD

ME A STORY ABOUT HIM I HADN'T HEARD BEFORE. BUT I WAS BEGINNING TO SUSPECT SHE WAS MAKING IT UP. EITHER TO COVER FOR THE FACT THAT SHE COULDN'T ACTUALLY REMEMBER MUCH ABOUT HIM, OR SIMPLY TO PLEASE ME. IT HARDLY MATTERED ONE WAY OR THE OTHER. IF JOSEPH WOLFF'S LETTER WAS ANY INDICATION, HE HAD LEARNED, TWO YEARS AFTER HE HAD BEEN NOTIFIED OF SAM'S DEATH, THAT THERE HAD BEEN MORE TO THE DEATH THAN HE HAD BEEN LEAD TO BELIEVE. LEARNED SOMETHING THAT HAD DEEPLY DISTURBED HIM. IF THIS WAS THE CASE, IT MIGHT ACCOUNT FOR THE STATE OF MIND MICHAEL WRIGHT HAD DESCRIBED, ALTHOUGH NOT NECESSARILY FOR THE DISTRESS HE HAD SHOWN IN FRONT OF MISS PATTERSON. WOLFF HAD WANTED TO MEET KATJA AND APPARENTLY BECAME DISTURBED ON LEARNING SHE WAS NO LONGER AT THE HOME. BUT SHE HAD ALSO SAID WOLFF WAS AGITATED WHEN HE ARRIVED. I SUSPECTED SOMETHING ELSE HAD HAPPENED, SOMEWHERE BETWEEN OXFORD AND RISEBOROUGH, AND IF I WAS RIGHT THERE MIGHT VERY WELL BE SOMEONE WHO KNEW WHAT IT HAD BEEN.

I NEEDED TO SEE HOOPER AGAIN.

'HARRY! YOU DO NOT LISTEN,' LIZZIE COMPLAINED.

'I WAS LISTENING,' I INSISTED. 'WHAT WAS IT YOU SAID?'

****

AFTER DINNER WE WENT BACK TO OUR ROOM. THE DRINK AND THE MEAL HAD ANIMATED HER AGAIN AND, ONCE IN BED, SHE WANTED TO KNOW ALL ABOUT MY LIFE – MY ARMY CAREER, MY MARRIAGE … WHAT I DID WHEN I GOT BACK TO ENGLAND … SHE WAS AS PERSISTENT AS A SPANISH INQUISITOR WITH A TRICK OR TWO I DOUBTED WOULD HAVE OCCURRED TO A RELIGIOUS INTERROGATOR.

IT WAS THE WELL INTO SMALL HOURS BEFORE SHE FINALLY EXHAUSTED HERSELF – AND LONG AFTER SHE HAD EXHAUSTED ME.

WE FELL INTO A DEEP SLEEP. MINE WAS DISTURBED BY VISIONS OF JOSEPH WOLFF WADING INTO A GREY NORTH SEA TOWARDS TWO FIGURES WHO WERE WAITING FOR HIM. HAZY AND INDISTINCT FROM WHERE I STOOD ON THE CLIFF, I

SOMEHOW KNEW – THE WAY ONE DOES IN DREAMS – THAT THE TWO FIGURES WAITING FOR WOLFF WERE SAMUEL AND OKSANA. WHEN HE REACHED THEM, THE THREE EMBRACED BEFORE SINKING FROM SIGHT BENEATH THE WAVES.

THE DREAM WOKE ME. I LAY ON THE BED AS RIGID AS A CORPSE, BATHED IN RAPIDLY FREEZING SWEAT. I COULD HEAR LIZZIE BREATHING BESIDE ME. HER BREATH WAS SLOW AND REGULAR. IF SHE WAS DREAMING, I SUPPOSED HER SLEEPING IMAGINATION TO BE SERENELY UNDISTURBED BY MY GHOSTS.

AND SO, LYING NEXT HER, I DIDN'T GIVE LIZZIE LAZARUS'S DREAMS A SECOND THOUGHT.

21

Monday, February 3rd 1947

I was late getting into the office. As with my previous visit to Riseborough, the train on Sunday was delayed by the weather and our connection missed. It was almost midnight by the time we reached London. Lizzie stayed the night and we both overslept.

Magdalena was already at her desk, sorting the weekend's intercept traffic as I walked in. She examined each sheet before placing it in the appropriate pile or discarding it altogether. I took off my coat and hung it on the stand, trying to suppress a yawn.

'Good morning,' she said. 'Did you have a nice weekend?'

'Pleasant enough,' I told her, giving into the yawn while trying to detect any note of sarcasm.

'Late night?'

'I didn't sleep well,' I admitted.

'Something on your mind?'

There had been, but it wasn't anything I could talk about.

'I'm just a light sleeper,' I said.

It was the truth and so I trusted it wouldn't disturb the polygraph that I had come to appreciate was Magdalena's intuition.

I saw her eyebrow rise a fraction, but there was little enough in my reply for her to go on and she soon went back to the papers in her hand. I settled behind my desk and began flipping through the pile she'd already placed there, my mind still on other things.

****

On Sunday after breakfast at the hotel in Riseborough, I'd wanted to walk back along the cliff to where I'd watched Wolff wade into the sea. Lizzie hadn't been keen – apart from her aversion to cold weather, anywhere beyond touching distance of brick or concrete appeared to invoke some sort of physical antipathy in her. Even so, she seemed unwilling to let me out of her sight and hobbled along behind me in totally unsuitable shoes, complaining interminably about the cold.

The cliff and the shoreline looked as desolate as I remembered. Not a human soul was in sight. A few seagulls wheeled listlessly over the shingle on the strand, but even they didn't have their hearts in it. A mile or two out to sea I saw a trail of smoke from a ship. One of Manny Shinwell's colliers from the north, I supposed, with coal bound for London.

All part of the great effort to keep the capital from freezing to a standstill.

Beside me Lizzie had already frozen to a standstill. Since there was nothing to see of Wolff's last point of conscious earthly contact, we walked back to the hotel and packed our bags. The train we had planned to take from Riseborough was delayed and we missed our connection at Norwich. The next, to Liverpool Street Station, was cancelled and the last late getting in. By the time we arrived, we were both exhausted, cold and hungry and getting tired of each other's company.

I sensed rather than felt some small residual warmth hanging in the air at the flat, an indication that one of the girls had been up to have a bath. As they still hadn't been unable to find a plumber, on returning home some days I often found that one or another had been up to use the hot water. Unlike Saturday morning, I rarely saw them. Carol and Frances, I believed, were a little embarrassed at the perceived imposition. And no doubt Muriel felt humiliated by being beholden to me. So often the only evidence of their passing would be a lingering trace of steam in the air and, more rarely, a shilling for the gas meter on my kitchen table.

Lizzie had turned her nose up at the meal I was able to put together from what I could find in the kitchen and went straight to bed. I made myself some tea and then, like an unexpected beneficiary who couldn't quite remember the deceased, I sorted through the few pathetic possessions Katja Tereshchenko had left at the refugee home. The rosary and the photograph no longer meant anything to anyone, and the few other bits and pieces I assumed she had treasured were of no more value. All the same, I couldn't throw them away. I would have to hang on to them for a week or two then send them back to Miss Patterson with a note explaining that my – fictitious – Oksana had turned out to be no relation of her – all too real – Katja.

I scooped the bits back into Katja's box and put them in a cupboard.

That left the two letters; the one from Wolff and the one in Ukrainian. I could have given them to Bryce – as he would have expected me to do – although if I did I would have to explain why I'd gone back to Riseborough again. And, as with everything else concerning Joseph Wolff,

I doubted that Bryce would tell me what was in the Ukrainian letter once it had been translated. The alternative was to find someone to translate the letter into English myself.

The fact I didn't know any Ukrainians wasn't really a problem. I worked for an organisation that did.

****

It was almost lunchtime when Magdalena dropped another armful of transcriptions on my desk. They landed with a bang, raising a cloud of dust. Mondays were always a busy day. Not only had the SIME and ISPAL traffic increased, we also had to catch up on the weekend's intercepts.

'We're getting behind,' she said, taking half the pile for herself. 'Do these people do anything else except talk to each other over the telephone?'

The transcripts arrived by courier every morning, all attached to specially prepared forms and clearly marked as to whose telephone the tap had been made on, and – where possible – who was talking to whom. Although this helped us to place the transcribed conversations in the appropriate files, we still had to read them for anything of substance that might need to go straight to Abel Bryce.

All tedious work, I found – a window on to other people's lives which, out of choice, I'd never have looked through.

One positive result of our mutual boredom, though, was that since our conversation following my meeting with Ogilvy, some of Magdalena's formality had begun to erode. She didn't rear up when I occasionally used her Christian name, and had even been known to respond by sometimes calling me Harry.

'Where do they do the listening?' I asked casually after we'd been quiet for a while.

I had never bothered to ask before and, not wanting to arouse her suspicion, now made it sound no more than a matter of curiosity.

'What do you mean, where?'

'Well, I don't imagine they're squeezed into cupboards somewhere in the buildings we've got tapped, earphones strapped to their heads and notebooks at the ready.'

'Of course not,' Magdalena replied impatiently. 'The lines go through Dollis Hill.' She put one sheet of paper aside and picked up another.

'Dollis Hill?'

'The Post Office Special Investigations Unit at the Paddock. Post Office engineers do the actual tapping. They run the lines through Dollis Hill.

Most of the mail is intercepted at an outstation in St Martin Le Grand, near St Paul's. They steam open the envelopes and make Photostats with peddle-operated cameras. The telephone taps are recorded on cylinders there then passed to our interpreters to transcribe.'

'Quite an operation,' I said.

She raised a mordant eyebrow. 'We've been doing it for quite some time.'

****

As there was no canteen in our building, or any tearoom within walking distance, we usually had to bring our own lunch into the office. The nearest pub was down in Brompton, too far a trek on icy pavements and in a usually freezing wind. If I happened to have nothing in the flat and neglected to stop and buy anything to eat on the way in, I generally had to go hungry. Once or twice when this happened, Magdalena had been known to offer me a sandwich from her packed lunch. When in a position to reciprocate I always tried. One look at my effort at making myself a sandwich, though, was usually enough to persuade Magdalena to decline.

That morning, as I was late anyway, I had taken the time to stop of at a Lyons teashop and buy a sandwich and a couple of tea cakes. I unwrapped them at one o'clock when Lily brought in our tea and put one in front of Magdalena. It was small and not very prepossessing – as was the way of most available food just then – and so I doubted she would recognize it as being an inducement.

'So,' I said, back at my desk, 'a lot of these conversations must presumably be in foreign languages.'

'Many are,' Magdalena said. 'And so is most of the SIME and ISPAL traffic.'

'We employ a team of interpreters who speak Hebrew and Yiddish and the like, I suppose.'

'And all the east European languages,' she confirmed. 'We're only seeing the Zionist material, of course. B Branch deal with the Russians and their allies.'

'Like Poles and Ukrainians?'

'All the Slavic and the Germanic languages.'

'And all these interpreters work for us full-time?'

Behind her glasses she batted her eyelids innocently at me in that way she had.

'Naturally.'

I dropped the subject. It was all I wanted to know. By mid-afternoon we had gone through all the transcripts, compared our notes and sent through to Lily and Geraldine those we needed typed up. We spent an hour assimilating the new material into our existing files, then Magdalena disappeared down the corridor as she usually did at that time to look through the regular office work and check on her other girls. I gave her ten minutes before going upstairs to the office in which our personnel files were stored.

The girl there asked if I needed any help. I smiled and thanked her and said that I only needed to consult a couple of files before the morning. She went back to her work and I began looking through the cabinets.

I had no individual names but since most of our personnel were cross-referenced by Branch and occupation – excluding those whose work was deemed too sensitive for the eyes of the girls who did the filing – I soon found a list of our interpreters and, helpfully, those languages in which they were proficient.

I read through a couple of résumés and decided on a man named Konstantin Berezin. He wasn't a Ukrainian but a Russian who spoke it, along with German and Polish. He was aged fifty-five according to his file, and had arrived in London via Paris, having left Russia in 1921. He had been employed by the Service since the mid-1930s.

I noted his address then went back downstairs. Magdalena was putting on her coat.

'That was a productive day,' I said as I pulled on my own.

'Yes,' Magdalena agreed. 'We've almost managed to catch up. Although it has to be said we've not found much of interest yet.' She smiled as I held the door for her. 'It can't be as exciting as the work you used to do.'

'Oh, I don't know,' I said. 'It has its moments.'

22

Tuesday, February 4th 1947

I had arranged to see Lizzie that evening at the ABC tearooms where we first met and so decided to leave contacting Konstantin Berezin until the following day. I was supposed to see her at seven-thirty, but by eight-thirty she hadn't arrived.

I called her number from the nearest telephone kiosk. There was no reply. Even the man who sometimes answered wasn't picking up the telephone.

I still didn't have an address for her – she had told me her landlady didn't appreciate gentlemen callers – so I went back to the ABC, deciding to give her another half-hour. By nine she still hadn't turned up. It was too late to see Berezin – the address I had for him was out by Gladstone Park and I thought by the time I found the place it would be gone ten. So in the end I gave the evening up and went home.

Even though Lizzie and I had not parted on the best of terms on Monday morning, I hadn't thought the matter serious enough to warrant her standing me up. There was a chance she had tried to telephone my flat to say she couldn't make it, although unless one of the girls from the basement happened to be using the bathroom at the time and left a message, I wasn't going to know. And since there was no note waiting for me when I got home, I was left none the wiser.

I listened to the wireless until eleven, giving her plenty of time to call if she had a mind to, then went to bed. I even forewent my usual last cup of tea, having already drunk my fill at the ABC.

****

In the office the next morning Magdalena looked brighter than the cold and dreary weather warranted and by the time I arrived had already sorted the previous day's transcripts couriered in earlier from Dollis Hill.

She smiled and chirped, 'Good morning,' as I walked in and told me there had been more than usual ISPAL traffic overnight as I dropped behind my desk.

We were always at least a day behind with the SIME and ISPAL material and generally longer after a weekend. The cipher intercepts were gathered by the Government Code and Cipher School at a station in Sarafand in Palestine, under the Signal and Intelligence umbrella known as SIGINT. Since these had to be decoded and translated – if written in anything other than English – before being transmitted to the GC&CS establishment in England, decoded again and then sent on to us, it always surprised me we got them as quickly as we did. Even so, it seemed an extremely tedious and long-winded business for what, in the main, turned out to be little more than tiresome chit-chat. But as it all came under the catchall of Defence of the Realm I supposed they knew what they were doing.

'In that climate,' I said to Magdalena as she brought me some of the Palestine intercepts, 'you'd think they might take the weekend off now and again and go to the beach.'

'Oh don't,' she said. 'It's too much to bear thinking about, beaches this winter.'

'Hot sand and blue skies?'

'And swimming in the sea?'

I thought of Riseborough and Wolff. There hadn't been much sand there, hot or otherwise, and the sky had been an unrelieved grey as I remembered.

'I bet you used to spend your holidays by the seaside when you were a girl,' I said.

'Eastbourne. Why, didn't you?'

'No. My mother never liked the seaside. She used to make me and my brother spend our holidays doing the gardening.'

'Poor you,' she said.

'Poor George. He never knew any better. Now he wants to be a farmer.'

'But you knew better?'

'Of course I did. I grew up to be a civil servant.'

Magdalena laughed. I pulled the first telephone tap of the day towards me.

****

It was a little before lunch when one of the girls from down the hall put her head round the door and said Abel Bryce was upstairs in the interview room and would like to see me.

I glanced at Magdalena. She usually knew in advance what a surprise visit from HQ was about, but this time gave no indication. Apprehensively, I heaved myself out of my chair and made my way up to the floor above.

If Bryce had got wind of the fact I'd gone back to Riseborough, I supposed I was going to have to tell him everything, hand over Katja's letters and try to think of a good excuse for not already having done so. By the time I reached the door of the interview room, though, I hadn't even come up with a bad excuse.

The room was usually kept empty in case of special meetings – interviews, or for the use of visiting officers, or any other business where one wanted some privacy. About the only thing it wasn't used for was canoodling with the secretaries, but that was only because someone had stolen the key.

I knocked and walked straight in. Abel Bryce was sitting behind the long table. Another man was standing by the window looking down on the street. He didn't have to turn round for me to know it was Henry Gifford. I hadn't seen him since the previous autumn, having had no dealings at all with Special Branch.

I looked from one to the other and wished I'd stopped in at the lavatory on my way up.

'Harry,' said Abel Bryce, getting to his feet and extending his hand across the table. 'Good of you to pop up. I know how busy you are at the moment. You remember Henry, of course.'

Gifford turned around.

He hadn't changed much. His bristle moustache might have been a little greyer, his lank hair a little thinner; his face, still as lugubrious as a bloodhound's, was perhaps stretched a little longer. But gravity will do that to us all.

'Sit down,' said Bryce.

'Isokon Flats, Lawn Road,' Gifford said without preamble. 'Ring any bells?'

'From what I hear you don't have to,' I quipped. 'Door's always open.'

That brought the shadow of Bryce's wintry smile to his lips although Gifford seemed immune to that sort of seasonal cheer.

'You were there, 25th of January,' he said. 'A Saturday night.'

'Are you following me, Henry?'

This time he did smile. 'Not me. We have others to do the leg-work.'

'I went to a party there,' I said to Bryce. 'You remember, I told you about it. A theatrical crowd. Is that why you asked me what I'd been up to that weekend? What is it you think I've done this time?'

'We don't think you've done anything, Harry,' Bryce said.

'So why the questions?'

'You remember how we first met?' Gifford asked.

'Of course,' I said. 'I was a beat copper and – if I remember your words correctly – you said I'd put my big boots into one of your operations. Don't tell me I've done it again?'

'Not an operation,' Gifford said. 'Let's say you just popped up somewhere we're interested in.'

'Isokon Flats? What on earth for? I know the music was a bit loud but you don't call out Special Branch for that. And don't tell me you're doing the Vice Squad's work now. Anyway, you know what actors are like … I thought it was live and let live these days unless they're caught soliciting.'

A shadow of distaste passed across Gifford's face.

'You should have let me know you were interested in the place,' I went on. 'I could have kept an eye out and saved you paying the overtime. How *did* you know I was there, anyway? I saw some people hanging around outside. As I remember it, it wasn't exactly a night for photographs.'

'You were recognised,' Gifford said.

'Who by? Or have you been handing out *my* photograph?'

His face remained blank. 'Never mind who. You were a copper. You know how enquiries work.'

'I've forgotten,' I said.

'You told Bryce here the girls you went to Isokon Flats with live in your building.'

'That's right. The basement flat. So what's special about the Isokon Flats?'

'It's been a place of interest since before the war,' Gifford said. 'We just keep tabs on it now and then. To see if anyone new turns up.'

'I imagine people are turning up there all the time.'

'Yes,' Bryce put in, 'but they don't all work for the Service, Harry.'

I laughed. 'What? Am I suspected of passing on what I know? What do I know, Abel? Beyond the tedious material you send me to read every day, that is?'

Bryce started shaking his head but I was getting irritated now.

'There were some Jews there,' I told him, 'but that's the theatre for you. They're a creative people even if you wouldn't know it from the ones I have to listen in on. And I didn't twig any of the guests there as terrorists. Or is it the Russians you're interested in? I suppose some of the crowd might have had left-wing leanings ... But then, with a socialist government in power, you could say the same about a majority of the British electorate.'

He sighed. 'There's no need to—'

But I was getting up a head of steam.

'Oh,' I said to Gifford as if I'd just remembered, 'I was told George Orwell used to live there. He was left-wing as I remember. Now who was it who told me? Solly Epstein, I think. He's a fat little theatrical agent though I can't vouch for what he gets up to on the side. He did say the place used to be quite Bohemian before the war. All sorts of people used to drop by apparently. One of those modernist painters too, I recall. But Orwell is the only name I can remember at the moment.'

Gifford grunted, unperturbed. 'Orwell's living up on one of those god-forsaken Scottish islands now,' he said.

'Is he? Well that lets him out, I suppose. A bit too far to travel even for a decent party. And from what I remember of it I'm not sure it was that good an evening.'

'From what I'm told,' Gifford remarked, 'you looked to be having a good time.'

'That'll be the gin,' I told him. 'And it wasn't the bathtub variety so no call to alert customs and excise.'

'No one's accusing you of anything, Harry,' Bryce said again.

'No? So if it's not me who *are* you interested in?'

Gifford finally pulled out a chair and sat down. 'No one in particular,' he said. 'But perhaps everyone in general.' He took out his pipe and began thumbing tobacco into the bowl. 'Let's start with who you know who was there. Then we'll cast the net a little wider.'

I glanced from him to Bryce. Two contrasting styles: Gifford calm and unemotional; Bryce conciliatory and helpful. I wasn't sure I was convinced by either of them.

'I hardly knew anyone there,' I said. 'Two of the girls I went with work for Solly Epstein. The third is an actress. Her boyfriend drove us there. Bertram something. I can't remember his surname.'

'Wilkinson,' said Gifford.

'Then you probably know if he works for the Comintern or not.'

'Be serious, Harry,' said Bryce.

'I'm trying,' I said. 'Believe me. I spoke to quite a few people as I recall but I don't know their names. There was Miriam … she's Solly's partner at the agency. Not that I spoke to her much. She's the type who doesn't waste time with men, if you know what I mean.'

'And the brunette in the fur you were waiting for outside?'

'Just a girl I know,' I said. 'A friend. I only met her a week or so ago. She's an actress, too. I said I'd introduce her to Solly Epstein. That's why I was at the party.'

'Has she got a name?'

'Lizzie Lazarus.'

'Lazarus?' Gifford repeated. 'Odd name.'

'She's French,' I said, omitting the Russian half. And also electing not to tell him about Jack Hibbert and Sydney Stanley, and how I met Stanley and Lizzie because I'd been making inquiries about the Wolff brothers.

'The thing is, Harry,' Bryce said, 'we're pretty sure a Soviet spy ring operated out of the Isokon Flats before the war. Only we could never prove it.'

As far as I knew, Bryce had still been at school before the war but I let that pass.

'And you think I'm going to queer the pitch for you if they're still there?' I said.

'We're pretty sure they've cleared out,' said Gifford 'but we keep an eye on the comings and goings just in case.'

'So what next? Should I go home and pack my bags and expect a transfer to the Outer Hebrides?'

Gifford chuckled between puttering on his pipe. Bryce looked blank. I told him how the last time I'd put my "big boots" into one of Gifford's operations he'd had my shift changed at my station to get me out of the way.

'Nothing like that,' said Bryce. 'We just wanted to put you in the picture. In case you're invited to another party there.'

'That's not likely,' I said. 'But it might help if you tell me who your informant is.'

Gifford knocked his pipe out in an ashtray and pushed his chair back. 'Hooper,' he said.

I might have guessed that. Hooper was the only Watcher I'd met face to face. But he'd hadn't been in the flat.

'You must have someone inside, too,' I said.

Gifford stood up. 'I don't think you need to bother about that,' he said. 'You probably won't run into each other again.'

'Need to know, you mean.' I said, glancing from one to the other again. 'Well, I'm getting used to that.'

'It can be frustrating,' Bryce agreed. 'But there is sound reasoning behind it.'

'Mondrian,' said Gifford, walking me to the door. 'The painter you couldn't remember?'

'That's right. Mondrian. Never did reckon his stuff,' I said.

Gifford grunted again. 'Me neither. Though there was another writer apart from Orwell who lived there for a while. Much more up my street.'

'Oh? Who was that?'

Gifford gave me his tobacco-stained smile. 'Agatha Christie,' he said.

****

This time I did stop at the lavatory on my way back to my floor. I shut myself in a cubicle and sat down. I had no urge to use it but felt uncomfortable all the same. I'd never been comfortable with coincidence but was willing to accept that on occasion it does happen. What I wasn't so willing to accept was that Special Branch still regularly checked on all new characters who turned up at the Isokon, even if it was true that the Russians had operated out of the flats before the war. Hooper was supposed to have seen me, but I never saw Hooper. So if they were lying about that, the only way they could have known about me was that they *did* have someone on the inside and I had drawn attention to myself by asking questions about Samuel Wolff.

Yet Bryce hadn't brought the subject up. It might have been that they were playing cat and mouse. If that was the case, then I'd been cast as the mouse.

Back in the office Magdalena asked: 'Is everything all right?'

'Yes, fine,' I said.

I sat down at my desk and picked up the transcript I had been reading when I'd been called away. I read it twice more, although the content didn't register with me either time. If Bryce knew what I was doing I was either going to have to come up with an excuse and come clean – which was going to make me look bad – or brass it out and be more careful, which would make me look even worse if I was eventually caught. I could have dropped the whole business, except I felt I'd come too far for that. And, if I did, I knew I'd always be troubled by what it was I'd never found out.

So it was a case of being more careful. I had planned on visiting Konstantin Berezin that evening but decided it might be better to act as if nothing had happened and do nothing out of the ordinary for a few days.

I glanced at Magdalena and saw she was still looking at me.

'What?' I said.

'It was nothing to do with our work, then,' she asked. 'Your meeting, I mean.'

'No. Nothing.'

'Oh.' She waited a moment longer, as if she hoped I might explain, then went back to her work, plainly dissatisfied.

After a while, I said casually: 'I was under the impression you knew everything that went on around here.'

'No,' she said, looking up again. 'I know what I'm told, that's all.'

'That, and what you can find out,' I said.

'I don't think I'm alone in that, do you?'

She held my gaze, her tone full of meaning.

And pertinence, too, I couldn't help thinking.

23

Friday, February 7th 1947

Despite my best intentions, by Friday Katja Tereshchenko's letter was burning the metaphorical hole in my pocket. I'd heard nothing from Lizzie since she'd stood me up on Monday and by the end of the week I'd given up trying to ring her. No one was answering her phone. The pipes in the basement flat were still frozen so I'd seen the girls now and then as they'd come up for water or to use the bath but, with nothing much else to do in the evenings, I had stayed at home listening to the wireless while trying to decode the frustrating enigma that was Katja's letter.

By Friday, though, I had had enough. Copies of Berezin's pay slips in his file at the office suggested he wasn't on shift-work and I thought if I turned up one evening I would have a decent chance of catching him in. At any other time I would have contacted him beforehand. Since the interview on Tuesday, I didn't want any hint of my interest getting back to Bryce.

The address in Berezin's file was given as Randall Avenue. The street map showed it to be north of Gladstone Park near Dollis Hill, which suggested that was probably where Berezin worked. Although the Hendon Police Cadet College was located a little north of there, I didn't know the area. I had been due to attend Hendon before the war until it had been decided to reserve that college for future Metropolitan Police of officer class. That meant I had to learn my trade at the Peel College in Westminster alongside the rest of the plebeian beat coppers.

Dollis Hill on the Bakerloo Line was the nearest Tube station to Randall Avenue. It would still leave me a mile or more to walk, up Hamilton Road and through the park, then across Dollis Hill Lane to Randall Avenue, but I judged it a better bet than to put my trust in the presently unreliable bus service.

Coming up to street level I found the lighting in the area was as intermittent as everywhere else. Whether this was through a shortage of light bulbs or because Manny Shinwell was trying to save on electricity was anyone's guess. In the park where the snow lay thicker, it gave the evening a ghostly sheen, as if a shroud had been spread over a dying city.

Crossing Dollis Hill Lane I was confronted by the now familiar tangle of brick and masonry of a bombsite, what was left of a former terrace rising out of frozen pools of stagnant water.

There was more damage where Randall Avenue met Tanfield Avenue but the address I had for Konstantin Berezin was still intact: an old Victorian house climbing tall and dark out of the night like something out of a Boris Karloff picture.

The front door wasn't locked and a single dim light on the stairs and the pervading silence served only to make the shadows deeper. Berezin, I discovered, lived at the top of the stairs in the attic flat.

There was something almost priestly about the bearded figure who answered my knock. The door opened a crack and a pair of watery eyes peered at me out of a face that would not have looked out of place under a *kalimavkion*, one of those long cylindrical hats that the orthodox clergy wear.

'A Branch,' I said. 'Administration.'

I held up my Service ID card while he examined it closely.

He ran a hand down his beard. 'There is some problem?'

'No,' I assured him. 'But I would like your help with a translation.'

He pulled the door open and I stepped into a cramped corridor under a sloping ceiling, almost disappointed that I could not smell incense.

He regarded me sadly. 'You could not send it to the office?'

'This is a private matter.'

I took the letter out of my coat pocket, along with the half bottle of Russian vodka I had scoured several pubs to find. Berezin's moist eyes lit brighter than the light on his stairs.

'Not work?' he asked, eyes on the vodka.

'Not exactly,' I said. 'It's written in Ukrainian, I believe. You know Ukrainian?'

He took the bottle off me then the letter. He led me the few paces along the narrow passage to his sitting room. A dim bulb struggled to light the room. Two worn armchairs sat in front of a gas fire. In a corner, almost lost in shadow, I saw an icon fixed to the wall.

'Sit,' he said, beginning to examine the letter under the lamp.

After a moment he glanced at me, put the letter on the table and went into a small kitchen. He returned with two glasses, poured a modest measure of the vodka into each and passed me one. He sniffed at his own before sipping at it, picking up the letter again.

'You want me to transcribe into English?'

'There's no need,' I said. 'Just give me the gist.'

'The *gist*?'

'I just want to know what it's about.'

He sat at the table near the lamp and peered at the letter.

'Who is Katja?'

'A woman who lived in a refugee home until Christmas. I know very little about her. I think the letter might be from her sister. It was found among her belongings.'

'And this is not work?'

'Indirectly,' I said.

Berezin observed me dolefully and I felt a sudden need to confess.

'A man went to visit her. He didn't know she was no longer at the home. He drowned himself a couple of days later.'

Berezin tossed back the rest of his vodka and smoothed out the letter.

'I will read it first to myself.'

I readied a notebook and pencil, like a junior reporter hoping for a scoop. Berezin angled the pages to the light.

'It is from her sister and her name is Oksana Janowski. The letter begins, "My dearest sister". She writes her address as Butterwick Camp, Malton, Yorkshire.'

'Butterwick?' It was the one word I had been able to read. I scribbled down the address. 'Does she say what sort of camp it is?'

'It is an internment camp. I have heard of it.'

'POWs?'

'No, these were workers captured in France after the invasion.'

'Workers?'

'Todt workers. You know?'

'You mean the Todt Labour Organisation? Labour recruited by the Nazis?'

He shrugged. 'Recruited … forced …'

'Are they Ukrainians? Is that why she is in the camp?'

He went back to the letter, read a few lines then looked at another page.

'Mostly they are Russians. Soldiers the German army captured when they overran Poland. Some civilians also.'

'What is she doing there?'

'She says she is translator.'

'For the men in the camp?'

'For authorities and men in camp.'

'What else does she say?'

Berezin glanced back at the letter.

'That her husband is dead. Typhoid, perhaps … I am not sure of word she uses.'

'Her husband was a Todt worker?'

He turned back the page. 'Doctor. But he is not at camp. She tells her sister he died in France. He was a doctor for workers.'

'The Todt workers.'

'She was nurse. When the British captured them she is taken too. First to camp Kempton Park – this is in Surrey, I think. Then she is taken to Butterwick.'

'Does she mention a man named Samuel Wolff? Is there a Ukrainian equivalent? He was one of the officers in charge of the camp, I think.'

'Samuel is name from Bible. She writes it in Ukrainian.'

'And Wolff?'

'*Vovk*,' he said. 'She uses animal name.'

'She tells her sister she and Samuel Wolf have become good friends. I think she means more than this and that her sister will know.'

'Anything else about him? Or his brother? He had a brother named Joseph.'

Berezin sighed as if my requests were in some way unreasonable. He returned to reading the letter and said nothing for a minute or two.

'Brother of Samuel,' he finally said, 'is academic at Oxford. She tells sister she hopes to meet him. Maybe next time Samuel gets army leave. She would like sister to come to England if ever possible. She says it is good here and no one is afraid of soldiers and policemen.'

Berezin paused and settled his rheumy gaze on me, as if I'd turned up in jackboots and a Gestapo leather coat.

'Is the letter dated?' I asked.

He went back to the first page. 'September 15th, 1944.'

'Before the end of the war? Almost two and a half years ago. Does she say how she is sending the letter? To where?'

Berezin waited until I had finished.

'No address,' he said. 'No envelope. How will I know?'

'Sorry,' I said. 'Katja came to England to find her sister. She went to Yorkshire but Oksana had already gone.'

'Butterwick Camp closed,' he said.

'You said you knew it.'

'This camp and others.'

'For Todt workers?'

'And POWs.'

'Where did they go? To another camp? The German POWs are still here.'

Behind his beard Berezin's lips curled into a humourless smile. 'Germans were enemy. Russians were allies.'

'So they went home?'

'You know this.'

I'd not given it any thought. I hadn't known there'd been any Russians in the country apart from the kind in Miss Patterson's refugee home. And like Berezin himself – refugees from Lenin's revolution.

'But Oksana wouldn't go with them, would she? Unless she went as an interpreter. She says nothing in the letter about leaving the camp?'

Berezin gazed at me as if still not sure what it was I wanted. He looked at the end of the letter.

'No. But she says men in camp are not happy. She says there are many rumours.'

'Rumours about what?'

He folded the letter quickly and passed it back to me. 'She does not say. She says Russian general is coming to talk to men. That is all.'

'All?'

I took the letter from him, glanced down at the notebook on my lap. I had written nothing but the address of Butterwick Camp. I pushed Oksana's letter back towards him.

'Make a transcription for me, will you? I'll pay you for it, of course.'

He eyed me warily. 'I am good worker,' he said. 'I work for British government for long time. I am no trouble.'

I didn't suppose he was, or what that had to do with anything.

'And you say this is not work?' he went on. 'What is it then if not work?'

I explained how Katja had written to Joseph Wolff and he had replied. 'Now both Joseph Wolff and his brother Samuel are dead,' I said. 'I want to know why.'

'Why?' he repeated, looking almost bemused. 'You tell me brothers are dead. Maybe Oksana dead too.' He shrugged. 'Everybody is dead.'

'I don't know that Katja's dead,' I said. 'She was taken for resettlement.'

'Resettlement?' Berezin repeated. 'Where?'

'I don't know.'

'You do not know?'

'No.'

'And the others from the camp. The Todt workers. You do not know. Truly?'

'No,' I insisted. 'Why should I?'

He said, 'You do not know,' again, but this time almost to himself.

'Know what?' I said. 'What should I know?'

'That Russian Todt workers were sent back.'

'Repatriated? Yes. So what?'

This appeared to offer him some grim amusement. He grunted softly, poured himself another glass of vodka and stared at me.

'*Repatriated*,' he said. 'Such a gentle word. What does it mean, to be repatriated? To go home to your fatherland? Or for us, home to Mother Russia? Not these men, I think.'

'Why not?'

Berezin drank his vodka and looked at the date on the letter again. 'September 1944 Some may still be alive but I think not. After Todt they would not be in good shape. The British they feed them well for three, maybe four months, but it is harsh in the camps. Worse than the Nazis.'

'What camps? Like Butterwick?'

'No, not like Butterwick. Russian labour camps.'

'But they were returning POWs. Why would they be sent to labour camps?'

Berezin grunted but did not reply. He picked up the letter. 'You are sure you want me to transcribe this?'

'Yes,' I said. 'If you would.'

'I should give it to someone at office to pass to you?'

'No,' I said. 'Do you have an envelope?'

Berezin leaned across his table to a pile of papers. Sorted through them and found an envelope. I wrote my address on it and took out my wallet. I gave him two pounds. Berezin's eyes widened.

'Is that enough? Perhaps you could put Oksana's letter in with the transcription. And if we can keep this between ourselves …?'

'Between ourselves …?'

'It might be as well,' I said, 'if you don't tell anyone at work about it.'

He took the money but I saw I had touched some sort of nerve. The look on his face was one of contempt.

'The big secret,' he said.

24

Monday, February 10th 1947

On Saturday blizzards hit the country paralysing everything.

Already paralysed, I spent the better part of the weekend trying to fit what Konstantin Berezin had told me into the jigsaw I had begun to assemble around Joseph Wolff. Since his brother Samuel was part of the Field Security Service charged with guarding Butterwick Camp, and had died – according to Sydney Stanley's source – somewhere near Murmansk, it seemed reasonable to conclude he must have been on the boat repatriating the camp inmates back to Russia. Although whether Katja's sister, Oksana, was also on the boat I couldn't be sure. Neither could I be sure of how much of what else Berezin had said had been true.

As a refugee from Bolshevik Russia in the 1920s, Berezin was hardly going to be sympathetic to Stalin and his regime. I was inclined to take with a pinch of salt his assertion that returning POWs were routinely shipped off to Russian labour camps; what was there to gain by doing that? Besides, I couldn't believe the British government would collude in such an initiative. POWs were protected under the former Hague – and now the present Geneva – Convention and Todt workers, whatever they'd been forced to do, were, after all, the helpless flotsam caught up in the tides of war.

I might have asked someone at the office if they knew anything about it all if I could have been sure that I wouldn't be asked in return exactly what my interest in the business was.

****

I got into the office before Magdalena on Monday and when she arrived and took off her coat, I saw she was dressed more smartly than usual. Never less than presentable, Magdalena this particular morning seemed to have made an extra effort and beneath her cardigan was wearing a frilly blouse on top of an elegantly tailored skirt.

I told her how nice she looked, managing not to make a mouthful of it as I generally did, and was rather surprised when I saw her cheeks colour. Encouraged, I might have gone further had Geraldine not come in just then

173

with the previous days' intercepts and a note for Magdalena. She stood at her desk, stacked the intercepts in a pile and read the note. Her face fell.

'Bad news?' I asked.

'Oh no, nothing really.' She tucked the note into her handbag and sat down.

'You look disappointed.'

'I was going out to dinner after work,' she said, 'but my friend can't get away.'

'I hope you still brought sandwiches,' I teased. 'You know I've come to rely on them.'

It wasn't much of a joke as it wasn't often she shared her lunch, but my apparent dependency seemed to be one of the few things that could make her smile.

'Then you'll have to look after yourself for once,' she retorted.

'Was it a special occasion?'

'If you must know, it's my birthday today.'

'I had no idea,' I said. 'Many happy returns, Magdalena.'

'Thank you … Harry.'

'I'd offer to sing *Happy Birthday*,' I suggested. 'But you've already had one disappointment.'

'I doubt you would have exceeded expectations,' she replied dryly, beginning to sort through the heap of intercepts.

'Were you going anywhere special?'

'Only the Mountview at the Oxford Corner House.'

'I'd ask if I knew the lucky man,' I said. 'Although I'd be tempted to use another adjective if he's stood you up.'

She glanced over at me. 'You're trying too hard, Harry. And for your information, *she* is a woman friend.'

'Sorry,' I said.

'We had a table booked. Now I'll have to telephone and cancel.'

She reached for the directory and began thumbing through the pages.

Without thinking, I said: 'If the table's already booked, why don't I take you?'

She looked up in surprise. '*You?*'

'The suggestion isn't *that* outrageous, is it?' I said, a little stung. 'And if you haven't brought any sandwiches I'm going to need a decent dinner this evening.'

'Be serious,' she said, which was her usual reply to anything I said that didn't quite accord with office protocol. Then relenting, added, 'I didn't mean to sound brusque. You surprised me, that's all.'

'Isn't that what you have to expect on birthdays? And I think even I could stretch to the Mountview. Birthday treat,' I said.

'Certainly not. I always pay for myself.'

'Can I take that as a yes, then?'

She made a show of huffing and sighing but I didn't think she was displeased.

'Very well,' she finally said, 'but only on the understanding we each pay for our own meal.'

'You don't like being under an obligation, do you?'

'Not to a man,' she said.

'You realise that does put me at something of a disadvantage.'

'Then you'll just have to try extra hard, won't you?'

****

The rest of the day seemed to drag after that. We were busy as usual and Magdalena said no more about us having dinner together. Several times I felt like bringing the subject up but was worried I'd spoil it. Fortunately, after lunch she spent much of the afternoon out of the office supervising the other girls. It was almost six o'clock by the time she came back.

'The table's booked for seven,' she said.

'Had I known I was going out I would have put something smarter on,' I said, embarrassed by my old suit.

She looked me up and down. 'You'll do. It's only the Mountview. Not the Ritz.'

'It may be only the Mountview to you,' I said, 'but I lead a sheltered social life.'

'Nobody will look at you as long as you don't eat with your hands,' Magdalena said.

The weather hadn't improved and there had been a few fresh flurries of snow during the day. As cold as ever, the pavements had had no chance to thaw out and hard-packed areas of black ice threatened the unwary. Magdalena made no objection to taking my arm as we walked to the bus stop. We rode down the Bayswater Road and along Oxford Street to the Corner House at the junction with Tottenham Court Road. The imposing façade looked much the same as it had in pre-war days. Inside, the Art-Deco interior had faded a little but few of us looked as good as we had before the war. Upstairs, though, the Mountview restaurant seemed as grand as ever. The capitals of the room's great pillars opened above us like flowering buds, blooming into the up-lighting that illuminated the almost fluid ceiling.

Magdalena slipped out of her coat as a waiter showed us to our table and I couldn't help thinking she was the smartest woman there. We sat down and Magdalena put her glasses on to examine the menu. My eyes ran down fare I'd hardly thought of since the beginning of the war. The prices, too, seemed to have hardly changed since 1939. I wondered how the Lyons restaurants managed it and why I didn't eat out more often, hard-up as I was. The Corner Houses were thriving. Most of the tables ranked between the wide pillars had already been taken. A buzz of conversation filled the room.

'I'd forgotten how nice these places are,' I said.

Magdalena placed her small handbag by her side. 'Don't you ever come here?'

'I haven't been here since before the war. It seems an extravagance to take a table for one in a place like this.'

'I hadn't taken you for the thrifty type.'

I gave her a mock scowl. 'I didn't mean I was a penny-pincher. I did offer to treat you, remember.'

She started to tell me again how she always paid her own way and I *was* listening. But having just spoken about a table for one my eye had been caught by a man sitting by himself two or three tables away, and then only because he was leaning around a pillar and looking in our direction. For a brief second, our eyes had met.

Although half-hidden by a pillar, I could tell by his demeanour he was on his own. Even then I might not have thought anything of it had I not been almost certain that he was the same man I had noticed as we had boarded our bus on the Bayswater Road. And now I saw him again I realised he had only caught my attention on the bus because he had seemed to me to epitomise Harry Hunter's ideally dressed Watcher. In the Mountview, though, he didn't blend in at all despite having removed his trilby and taken off his raincoat. There seemed something so *ordinary* about him that, paradoxically, he looked out of place. Most people dining out at a Lyon's Corner House restaurant generally made an effort to dress accordingly. And even though I'd come straight from work in the suit I wore to the office, I had taken the trouble to brush myself down so that I looked reasonably presentable. The man behind the pillar gave every appearance of not having expected to be there.

'Harry …?'

'I'm sorry,' I said. 'What were you saying?'

Magdalena pierced me with one of her mordant looks. 'I might just as well have dined by myself.'

'Sorry,' I said again, 'but I've just noticed someone at another table—'

'If you'd rather sit—'

'No, I mean someone I saw on our way here.'

Magdalena huffed and scowled at me.

'Look to your right,' I said, 'but be casual about it. The man by the pillar three tables over. Have you seen him before?'

She didn't turn her head. Instead she reached into her bag, took out her powder compact and pretended to check her make-up, angling the mirror towards the man's table.

'You've done this before,' I said.

She snapped the compact shut. 'I don't recognise him. Who is he?'

'I saw him getting on our bus. He was certainly looking our way just now.'

'That hardly signifies anything,' she said wryly. 'Perhaps he recognised *you* from the bus.'

'Possible,' I said to her. 'Although it crossed my mind that he might be B6.'

This time she laughed. 'A Watcher?'

The waiter came to take our order, saving me from having to make a reply. As soon as he left Magdalena leaned a little closer towards me.

'What possible reason would a Watcher have to follow us here?'

'They've got to eat,' I suggested.

'Be serious. Have you been up to something, Harry?'

'No. Nothing at all.'

She flicked out her napkin and arranged her cutlery.

'I don't believe you think he's a Watcher for a minute,' she said.

'I'm serious,' I insisted.

'In that case you're showing all the symptoms of a guilty conscience.'

'Now they're giving the staff training in psychoanalysis?' I asked.

'I mean it.' She regarded me coolly for a moment, then her expression became severe. 'What *have* you been up to?'

The waiter returned. I'd pushed the boat out and ordered a half-bottle of wine over Magdalena's objections. He uncorked it and poured a little into my glass. I raised it to her.

'Many happy returns of the day,' I said again.

The waiter beamed at her, filled our glasses and retreated. I looked down into my wine considering how much I should tell her.

But she was there before me.

'Is this still about Joseph Wolff?'

I was surprised she remembered the name.

'What makes you think it has anything to do with Wolff?'

'You requested his file.'

'I've asked to see several files.'

Magdalena shook her head. 'Don't play games with me, Harry. Wolff is the man you followed to East Anglia last month, isn't he? The one who drowned?'

I was beginning to wish I'd never mentioned the man at the other table. I glanced in his direction but a foursome was now sitting at a table between us.

'It's a weakness of mine,' I admitted in an attempt to make light of it. 'I get a hunch about something and feel the need to follow it up. The ex-policeman in me, probably.'

'Even when you've been told the case is closed?'

I grinned at her. 'Perhaps it's *because* I was told the case is closed.'

She didn't appreciate the joke.

'Actually,' I went on pedantically, in the vain hope she'd drop the subject, 'I didn't follow Wolff. I was waiting for him at the hotel there.'

'Don't split hairs,' she said. 'Did Wolff go there to meet someone?'

Our dinner arrived and the waiter fussed over us for a moment.

'Well? Did he?' she asked again once he'd gone.

'A Ukrainian girl. Katja Tereshchenko. Only by the time Wolff got there she'd already gone.'

'Do you know why he wanted to see her?'

'Not exactly,' I admitted. 'Something to do with his brother and her sister.'

'Just a family affair?'

'No. There was more to it than that. Wolff's brother was killed in the war. I'm not sure what happened to Katja Tereshchenko's sister.' I paused, put my knife and fork down deliberately and said, 'Look Magdalena, it's probably better if you don't get involved. All I've done so far is ask a couple of people a few questions. I've not done anything wrong, but I doubt that Bryce and the rest of them over in B Branch will see it that way. They won't care for me sticking my nose into something that is none of A Branch's business. You've got your career and a reputation to think of. I'm new to this and they can write me off as a mistake if I put a foot wrong. You're supposed to know what you're doing.'

'I appreciate your concern for my reputation,' she replied curtly. 'Who have you seen, exactly?'

I realised then that she hadn't wanted to get involved, but might very well now report what I told her to Bryce. Or to whoever it was had been interested in Wolff in the first place. I sighed, more in disappointment than anything. I had thought, perhaps naïvely, that she had been beginning to unbend.

'Hooper, for one,' I said. 'He was the Watcher who followed Wolff down to Riseborough on the train. I went back there again last weekend and spoke to the woman who runs the refugee home where the Ukrainian girl was living. Then last night I went to see one of our interpreters—'

'What for?'

'The woman at the home – a Miss Patterson – gave me a letter Katja received from her sister. It was in Ukrainian and I wanted to get it translated.'

'You didn't give it to Abel Bryce?'

'No.'

'Why not?'

'Because Bryce said the case was closed.'

She stared at me accusingly. 'You told me you hadn't done anything wrong! You've been withholding information. Do we have anything on this Katja Tereshchenko?'

'Bryce said we didn't.'

'But you don't you believe him?'

'Yes,' I said, 'about that. I'm pretty sure he didn't know anything about Katja Tereshchenko. What I do find difficult to believe is that we don't have a file on Joseph Wolff any more. Not when he was being specifically watched.'

'And you still don't know *why* he was being watched?'

'No,' I said. 'Do you?'

179

Magdalena reached for her wine. 'Not my department,' she said. 'I'm just an office girl.'

'Well,' I replied, 'maybe they'll give you a promotion when you tell them.'

'Tell them what?'

'About me withholding information.'

'Is that what you think I'm going to do?'

'Isn't it?'

The waiter took our plates and brought the dessert. I glanced across at the foursome and saw that the table beyond was now empty. If he really was watching me I hoped he was getting cold waiting out on Oxford Street. If he wasn't, I'd tipped my hand to Magdalena for no reason.

'I'm certainly not going to tell anyone,' she said, slicing her pie with her spoon. 'But you should tell Bryce about the letter. Say you forgot about it. Do you know what'll happen if they find you've deliberately withheld information?'

'Not compliment me on my initiative I suppose?'

'Sack you more like.'

'Well,' I said, 'that's why I was wondering if that chap wasn't a Watcher. Keeping an eye on me to see what I was up to.'

'I doubt they'd bother,' Magdalena said. 'They'll just get rid of you. It's not too late. You should see him first thing in the morning.'

I thought even first thing in the morning was by now already too late. And given that, there didn't seem a lot of point in not telling her the rest. So I explained how I'd taken a look at Wolff's rooms in Oxford and talked to one of his students, then asked a contact of mine to make enquiries about his brother. I didn't mention Lizzie Lazarus or Sydney Stanley. I just said I'd found out that Samuel Wolff had been in the Field Security Service and had apparently gone overboard from a ship somewhere near Murmansk.

'Murmansk in Russia?'

'Is there another?'

'Don't be flippant,' she said.

'I don't know whether Samuel Wolff's death was an accident, suicide, or something else. I thought it might be the reason Joseph Wolff killed himself.'

'I thought *that* was an accident.'

'I saw him go in. It was no accident.'

'So you think he chose drowning because it was symbolic? Isn't that rather Greek?'

'You mean Greek theatre, I assume. Well,' I said, at the risk of being flippant again, 'his brother was an actor before the war.'

'And what about Joseph Wolff?'

'He was a mathematician.'

'That's not what I meant.'

'What did you mean?'

'Oh Harry,' she said. 'If there's a Russian connection you're in deeper trouble than I thought.'

'At first I wondered if it was something to do with Jewish terrorism.'

'Because they were Jews? Is there any other reason to think it might?'

'None. But if there was it would be another reason for you not to get involved. Particularly if you're not going to tell them what I've been up to.'

'I'm not,' she said again. She finished her wine. 'As I said, it's not my department. So, what are you going to do next? Take it to Bryce?'

'Not if I want to get paid this month.'

'What else was in the letter?'

'I can't be sure until I get the transcription. It's possible there might be a Russian connection. The translator told me the camp where Wolff's brother and Katja's sister met was holding Russian Todt workers captured in Normandy. But if it has got something to do with the Russians, I would have thought there'd be something in the Registry on the Wolffs. And you couldn't find anything.'

'What about SIS?' Magdalena asked. 'Have you thought of them?'

'Are they likely to have a file on Joseph if we haven't?'

'Possibly,' she said. 'We may be sister organisations but there has always been a rivalry. We don't necessarily tell each other what we're doing.'

'Perhaps not,' I said, 'but I can hardly waltz up to their door and ask to see their files.'

Magdalena smiled. 'I might be able to. I'll have a word with Jane.'

'Who's Jane?'

'You're sitting in her chair,' she said. 'It was Jane Archer I was meeting tonight.'

I'd never met Jane Archer although her name was familiar enough if you worked in the Service. She had been the first woman who worked there to be made an officer. I'd heard she had joined during the Great War, risen through the ranks and had at one time run the Registry. At the beginning of the war she had married someone in the RAF with links to Intelligence. Critical of Jasper Harker, Kell's successor as Director General of the Service, she had been sacked after some particularly intemperate remarks. SIS had had no compunction about offering her a job, though.

'She's a friend of the family,' Magdalena explained. 'In fact, Jane is the reason I joined the Service. I was going to resign after they sacked her but she persuaded me to stay. She said I was doing useful work and not to throw my career away because of the petty jealousies of others.'

'I hope you're not going to throw it away over the petty obsession of a colleague,' I said.

'I'll be careful. She'll know if SIS have anything on your Joseph Wolff.'

I was none too sure about involving Jane Archer.

'Won't she feel obliged to tell someone? I'm already in trouble. I don't want either of you getting caught in the crossfire.'

For some reason the thought amused Magdalena.

'Jane can keep a secret. She knows all about the politics of the Service. She's been a woman in a man's world most of her life.'

'And suffered for it from what I've heard,' I said.

'Which is precisely why she might help.'

****

We had a brief and inevitable argument over settling the bill then walked across the street to the Tottenham Court Road Tube station. I looked for the man I'd seen in the Mountview; there were still people out despite the weather but I didn't see him.

Magdalena lived north of Hyde Park, handy enough for the office and a just a short walk from the Tube stations at both Lancaster Gate and Marble Arch. I offered to see her home but she wouldn't hear of it. I waited with her at the Tottenham Court Road station from where I could take the Central Line with her as far as Oxford Circus. There I'd have to change to the Bakerloo Line for Marylebone.

We waited standing close together on the platform while the wind howled through the tunnels around us. I was tempted to put my arm around her until, as if she had sensed my impulse, she gave me a look severe enough to remind me it was her birthday not mine. In the carriage we sat beside each other in silence until the train pulled into Oxford Circus.

I stood up and she offered me her hand.

'Thank you for a very pleasant evening, Harry. It was so much nicer than spending my birthday on my own.'

I took her hand in mine without actually shaking it and muttered something in reply. Then I stepped on to the platform and watched as her train pulled out.

25

Tuesday, February 11th 1947

The next morning I thought Magdalena might say something about our evening together although she merely contented herself with a smile which left me less than contented.

I smiled back then started ploughing through the intercepts already on my desk. As usual nothing out of the ordinary came to my attention, not until I began reading a transcript of a telephone conversation between Harry Isaac Presman and an unidentified caller. Their exchange seemed innocuous enough until a cryptic phrase caught my attention:

PRESMAN: DID YOU MANAGE IT?

UNIDENTIFIED CALLER: I USED THE LITTLE SCRIABINA. IF THERE'D BEEN ANYTHING WORTH FINDING, THE SCRIABINA WOULD HAVE FOUND IT.

PRESMAN: NOTHING THEN?

UNIDENTIFIED CALLER: NO. WE DECIDED IT ISN'T WORTH RUNNING ANY LONGER.

SINCE THE CONVERSATION HAD BEEN IN ENGLISH THE WORD IN QUESTION HAD OBVIOUSLY NOT BEEN A PROBLEM POSED BY TRANSLATION.

'Have you any idea what a "scriabina" is?' I asked Magdalena.

She blinked her doleful eyes at me. 'A "scriabina"? How do you spell it?'

I spelled it.

'No, none,' she said. 'What's the context?'

'Harry Isaac Presman and an uNIDENTIFIED CALLER.' I read out the passage.

She came over to my desk. I could smell her scent as she leaned over me, her hair brushing my cheek. I cleared my throat and pointed to the relevant passage.

'It sounds Russian,' she said.

'Do you think so?'

She straightened up and I began breathing more easily.

184

'Suppose it's not a *what* but a *who*?'

'How do you mean?'

She touched a speculative finger to her lips.

'Suppose they're talking about a person. The person transcribing wouldn't have known to capitalise the word. "Scriabina" sounds like the feminine form of Scriabin. There was a Russian composer named Scriabin.'

'Was there?'

She went to the door of the adjoining room and asked Geraldine to come in.

'Geraldine, could you please consult the Registry and see if we have anything on a Scriabina? Any reference at all.'

Geraldine was a meticulous, coolly efficient girl in her early twenties. Always well turned out she remained unfazed if, on occasion, she was ever asked to work late. In marked contrast to Lily, I had noticed. Lily had a whiff of Bohemia about her, usually giving me the impression of having come straight to the office from some all-night party in Chelsea or Soho. While Lily's office work was eminently satisfactory, Geraldine was the girl Magdalena usually favoured whenever anything beyond our usual routine was required. Consequently Geraldine was always in and out of the office, generally commuting between us, the St James Street headquarters and the new Leconfield House offices where Potter, the business systems expert, was trying to untangle the mess that the Registry had become.

'Scriabina,' Geraldine repeated, writing the word in her notebook and making sure she had spelled it correctly. 'Shall I try alternative spellings in case it was incorrectly transcribed?'

Magdalena smiled at her. 'If you can find any, dear.'

Geraldine hurried off.

It was over two hours before she returned, making straight for Magdalena's desk as she always did rather than mine.

'No file I'm afraid, Miss Marshall,' she announced, tapping her pencil against her notebook. 'under any variant spelling. I did find one reference to an Ariadna Scriabina, though. In a memo to B Branch from SIS concerning an SOE arms drop in France in 1943. They allowed me to photocopy it.'

Geraldine handed Magdalena the copy.

Magdalena read it, said 'Bloody cheek,' and passed it to me.

I stared at her.

'Sorry,' she said, 'but that is so *typical* of SIS as far as SOE was concerned. Always trying to undermine them. And then to suggest a leak might have come from *us*!'

I read the memo.

It was a brief complaint to SIS from SOE about the fact that an arms drop of theirs made to a local Toulouse resistance group had been pilfered by another group led by Ariadna Scriabina. SOE implied SIS interference in their operation. SIS passed the memo on to the Security Service in case we were interested in a possible SOE leak.

Magdalena took the memo back. 'You know who SOE were, I suppose?'

'Special Operations Executive, wasn't it?'

I had briefly come across the organisation while with my war crimes unit. The case had involved an accusation of betrayal of one of their agents. We never handled the matter, though, and I never learned much about them. Nor what had become of any subsequent investigation.

'It's still all a bit secret, isn't it?' I said.

Magdalena huffed. 'Only because SIS want to keep it that way. When SOE were wound up at the end of the war, SIS made sure they took anything of value from the information that had been gathered. *And* the pick of SOE personnel. Then they more or less threw the rest of them out on the street.'

Geraldine, still standing between us, looked a little embarrassed. Magdalena passed the memo back to her.

'Thank you, Geraldine. That'll do. You're sure there was nothing else on Ariadna Scriabina?'

'Nothing Miss Marshall.'

'Very good. Make sure you shred the memo and any notes you've made, please.'

'Of course, Miss Marshall.'

Geraldine went back to the room she shared with Lily.

Magdalena fell into a reverie.

'So,' I said after a moment. 'What do you think?'

She shook herself free of her trance.

'I'm sorry. Did you say something?'

I made a comment about "dining by myself", repeating the phrase she had used in the Mountview when I was caught not listening to her. She deliberately ignored me so I said again: 'Do you think it has any relevance for us? An arms drop near Toulouse in 1943?'

'That's hardly likely, is it?'

'The remark must have meant something,' I pointed out. 'After all, Presman didn't ask his caller what the hell he was talking about.'

'Sorry. You're right. If he was talking about a person it must have been another Scriabina. We'd better make a note and open a miscellaneous file for it. We might get more later.'

'Will do,' I said, going back to the intercept. I made some notes for the girls to type up later and opened a new file.

'By the way,' Magdalena said. 'I'm seeing my friend this evening. The one I mentioned to you yesterday? I'll speak to her about the matter we discussed.'

It was a moment before I realised she was talking about Jane Archer from SIS.

'The last thing I want is for you to compromise your principles, Magdalena.'

'I beg your pardon?' she said.

'The memo,' I said. 'You obviously feel strongly about the Sisters.'

She glared back at me. 'Don't be ridiculous,' she said.

26

Wednesday, February 12th 1947

When I got home on Wednesday evening I found the letter from Konstantin Berezin waiting for me on the table in the foyer. I had just picked it up when Frances breezed in.

'Hello, Harry,' she said running a hand over the envelopes on the table. 'You'll be pleased to hear we finally found a plumber to unfreeze our pipes. We've got running water again. Sometimes it's even hot!'

'You must be relieved,' I said.

'Oh, I don't know.' She picked out a couple of letters. 'It's kept us in shape, carrying those buckets up and down your stairs. 'Bye sweetie …'

I spent a moment admiring that shape then took Berezin's letter upstairs. I would be glad to have my bathroom back to myself but was going to miss seeing the girls come and go – be it flushed from the bath or smeared with face cream and usually in various stages of undress.

In the flat I put the kettle on and opened Berezin's letter. He'd not enclosed any note, just Oksana's original letter and his translation, written out on two sides of a single sheet of foolscap. I sat at the table and read it.

Oksana began by saying she had received a letter from Katja while still in France in May 1944. As it was at least two months old when it arrived she assumed there must have been others that hadn't reached her. She had replied at once, she said, but given what had subsequently happened wasn't sure if Katja would get the letter. She was sending this one through the Red Cross and, in case Katja had not received the earlier ones, was giving an account of what had happened to her again and hoped her sister would forgive her if she had already heard this news.

She went on to say how she had learned about the fate of the rest of their family and was praying that Katja was safe. Frederick, her own dear husband, had died of typhoid soon after they reached France. The Germans had not allowed her to return home as her nursing skills were valuable and she was put into a medical unit at the Todt workers camp near the coast where they were engaged in building fortifications. She was treated better than the workers, she said, but life was hard.

Picturing Oksana's life in the camp dulled my appetite and although I made myself some tea I left supper until later. I lit a cigarette and picked up the letter again.

Oksana recounted how, after the invasion of Normandy, the Germans had retreated and how the abandoned Todt workers had merely sat and waited for the Allies to arrive. She wrote Katja that she had waited with them. She hadn't known what to expect but believed whatever happened could not be worse than what they had already been through.

When the Allies found them they were all taken prisoner and shipped across the Channel to a camp in southern England called Kempton Park. She already spoke Russian and had learned some English from her husband and so, when they were later transferred north to Butterwick Camp, she was asked by the authorities to act as a translator. It was in Butterwick she met Samuel Wolff. Oksana described him as a very handsome man, kind and considerate, and not a bully like some of the guards. The security officer in command at the camp was a Major Fairfax and all communication from him went through Samuel Wolff and her. She told Katja how she worked with him every day and, she said, became very fond of him. She was overjoyed when she found Wolff felt the same way about her. She spent some lines telling her sister that she was no longer the pretty girl Katja would remember, that life had been hard and had taken a toll of her looks and that she couldn't quite believe someone like Samuel Wolff could care for her.

I tried to picture them together – Sam Wolff, nearly ten years on from playing Shylock and probably still dreaming of a career in the theatre, and Oksana, a once beautiful girl worked to the edge of exhaustion – finding some happiness together in the last place that either of them could have imagined. They were making plans about what they would do when the war ended, and Wolff had said he would take Oksana to visit his brother who was an academic at Oxford University.

Then, at the end of the letter she wrote about some trouble brewing at the camp. Conflicting rumours about repatriation were circulating. Some said the men held there were to be repatriated before the end of the war, those who had been soldiers returning to their Red Army units to fight again on the eastern front. The civilians, it was said, would be recruited into labour battalions. But others, she wrote, maintained they wouldn't be put back into the army at all but sent to the labour camps in Siberia and the north. Some were even hinting they might face a worse fate.

Major Fairfax, Oksana said, was attempting to reassure them. He told them a Russian general was visiting all the camps where Russians were being held to ascertain who wished to return to Russia and who did not. This general was due at Butterwick the next day, Oksana said, and she was expected to act as the interpreter between the general and Major Fairfax.

Oksana ended the letter promising to write again soon, and in the meantime would be praying for Katja and for the souls of their dead family. She hoped most fervently that this letter would reach her dearest sister …

27

Friday, February 14th 1947

Since Tuesday, I had asked Magdalena several times if she had seen Jane Archer; if her friend was prepared to check SIS files to see if they had anything on Joseph Wolff. All I ever got in response, though, was a silent shake of the head, as if it were a subject not to be discussed. It wasn't until late on Friday afternoon, once Lily had come in for the files to lock them away for the night, that Magdalena broached the matter.

She had been out of the office for longer than usual at lunch. She worked on for another hour or two after she returned then, at five o'clock, put on her coat and said out of the blue: 'Take me for a drink, will you Harry?'

'You're very forward,' I joked back. 'When I didn't get a Valentine card this morning I assumed you must have tired of me.'

She compressed her lips the way she did when biting back a reply and glowered instead, fussing with her handbag.

I reached for my coat and hat. 'Anywhere in particular?'

'The Great Western Royal at Paddington Station.'

I held the door for her. 'Is this a date? What are we celebrating this time? It's not *my* birthday.'

'A date?' she repeated. 'You watch too many American films.'

'An assignation, then,' I suggested, wiggling my eyebrows at her.

'Be serious.'

****

After work I generally took the Tube from South Kensington Station, riding the Metropolitan and District line to Edgware. Magdalena took the number 73 bus to Hyde Park Corner and Marble Arch and walked the rest of the way home. Of late, though, with the weather and an unreliable bus service, she had found it was just as quick to walk across Hyde Park to Lancaster Gate, which wasn't any great distance from where she lived. She maintained that walking through the park after dark didn't bother her. Since the day I'd gone to meet Brian Ogilvy and walked with her across the park, I would often accompany her, then take the Tube at Lancaster Gate and ride the Central Line to Oxford Circus, changing on to the

Bakerloo Line for Marylebone. It was a longer way round for me but I didn't mind. Magdalena no longer objected either.

It was about a mile on foot to Lancaster Gate, along South Carriage Drive and over the Serpentine, and on this particular evening we automatically crossed the road towards Prince's Gate.

After the blizzard the previous Saturday we'd been promised a thaw that hadn't materialised. I'd read in *The Times* that morning that the temperature at Greenwich had been the lowest for February for more than a hundred years. Most of the vehicles snowed in over the weekend had been pulled out by then but no one was driving much if they could help it. Those that were moved at a crawl. Even milk deliveries were being made by sledge.

Out of the park we walked up Gloucester Terrace and on to Craven Road towards the station. Behind the façade formed by the hotel the station was busy and, although it wasn't much past six-thirty, the hotel bar was crowded. Food and petrol might be short, electricity subject to cuts and water pipes frozen, but the beer was still flowing.

Despite the expectation that railway termini would become targets for German bombers, the hotel had survived the war and having once been the Great Western Railway's showpiece the place still looked classier than most of the other railway hotels. Inside I found a table and a couple of comfortable chairs in the corner of the bar. A waiter came for our order and I asked for a pint of beer and a tot of rum for Magdalena. It was an odd drink for a bishop's daughter, but by then – and casting no aspersions on her father – I had come to realise that Magdalena was an odd bishop's daughter.

'Cheers,' I said when the drinks arrived, raising my glass to her. 'Although what there is to be cheerful about I don't know.'

Magdalena sipped her rum, looking at me across the table. 'In the Middle Ages,' she said, 'a doctor would have diagnosed you as having a melancholic humour.'

'In the Middle Ages,' I told her, 'I'd have avoided doctors like the plague. If that's not an oxymoron or whatever they call it. Anyway, in the Middle Ages I'm pretty sure the sun used to shine now and then. I would have been more cheerful.'

'If it's sun you need perhaps you should consider going abroad. Ever thought about Africa or Australia? The sun shines there all day if you believe the posters. There are schemes to help servicemen who want to emigrate.'

'Are you trying to get rid of me? You're a very capricious girl, Magdalena Marshall. First you ask me to buy you a drink and then suggest I ship out to Africa.'

'I thought it might suit you,' she said.

'I doubt it. I don't much fancy Africa, thank you very much. All that big-game … I've had enough of guns and shooting for one lifetime. And I don't want to emigrate to Australia, either. It might suit my brother – I can see him as a sheep farmer. But it doesn't hold any attraction for me. I doubt it would suit my wife much either.'

Her eyes widened. 'Your wife? I thought you were separated.'

'So we are,' I said. 'Didn't you know my brother wants to marry her? If he went, I suppose she'd have to go sheep farming with him.'

'Why should I be privy to your marital arrangements?' she replied curtly. 'Office gossip?'

'I don't listen to office gossip. Anyway, what makes you believe people in the office are talking about you? Male arrogance, I assume. It's typical of men to think they're the centre of other people's concerns.'

I laughed. 'I can't help my gender I'm afraid. And had I known you only asked me here so you could abuse me out of Geraldine and Lily's earshot, I would have gone home to my empty flat and snuggled up to my wireless.'

'Oh, *please*,' Magdalena said. 'I'd hardly ask you here to abuse you. I could do that perfectly well in the office.'

'As you wish,' I said. 'Although, like it or not, if Geraldine or Lily saw us having a drink together we really would be the subject of their gossip.'

'That's why I suggested we come here. We're unlikely to run into anyone we know.'

'So it is an assignation,' I said. 'Does that mean I've finally worked my magic on you?'

She threw me a pityingly look. 'I'm very much afraid, Harry, that sooner or later you're going to have to come to terms with the fact you haven't got any magic. At least none that's readily discernible.'

'Then why are we here?'

'Because I met Jane Archer for lunch today and I didn't want to discuss the matter in the office.'

'I wondered where you got to. It's a good job I brought sandwiches this morning. The way you've been acting all week I was beginning to think the subject of Mrs Archer was verboten. So, has she managed to turn up anything in the SIS files on the Wolffs? Or do I mean Wolves?'

Magdalena glanced over her shoulder. 'For heaven's sake keep your voice down, Harry.'

'Sorry,' I said. 'I'm new at this game, remember?'

'That must be why you haven't learned the rules yet.'

'Touché. Well, has she found anything?'

'Not on Samuel, no. But there is a file on Joseph.'

'So he was under suspicion?'

'No. At least, Jane doesn't think so. The file on him exists because of the nature of the work he did during the war. Jane couldn't tell me any details, nothing beyond the fact it was very sensitive. And apparently still is.'

'And that's why we were watching him?'

'Jane didn't know.'

'Well, if his work was so sensitive why don't *we* have a file on him?'

'That's something else neither of us can understand. We should have a file, of course. Jane gave me the name of two colleagues he worked with during the war and suggested I check to see if we have files on them.'

'And do we?'

'Yes.'

'Perhaps I should talk to them.'

'I doubt they'd talk to you,' she said. 'Not about the war.'

'Then is it because he's dead there's no file?'

'We don't destroy files simply because the subject has died. Besides, there is usually other pertinent material in their files, so when someone dies their file gets marked "Deceased" but remains active.'

'Not in Wolff's case. Does your friend have any theories?'

'Not at the moment. She's going to look into it. She also wants to know what else you've found on Joseph and his brother.'

A ripple of trepidation began to work its way up from my stomach. When I first began looking into Joseph Wolff and his brother, it seemed prudent to ensure that the fewer people who knew about it the better. And where that proved unavoidable, I tried to keep them in separate boxes. Hooper knew I was asking questions about Joseph Wolff, but Jack was only aware of my interest in his brother, Samuel. He had told Sydney Stanley and then Lizzie. She certainly had a way of winkling information out of people although I didn't suppose she knew anyone who'd be interested in the Wolff brothers.

It was true I'd also mentioned Wolff to Brian Ogilvy as well as given him Sydney Stanley's name – which I now thought might have been a mistake – and I'd consulted Konstantin Berezin about translating Katja's letter. The point was, though, no one really knew much about any of the others. Except Magdalena. I had told her everything. Well, almost everything. But now she had told Jane Archer.

The circle seemed to be widening and threatened to get beyond my control.

'Do you trust her?' I asked.

Magdalena stiffened. Anyone watching us might have thought I'd slapped her across the face.

'Of course I trust her!' she whispered back fiercely. 'Jane has spent over thirty years working in the security services. How can you—'

'Keep your voice down,' I said, grinning at her.

She scowled.

'I meant no offence,' I said. 'All I meant was, is it likely she'll talk to anyone else? Will it get back to our office?'

Magdalena raised her eyes to the ceiling. 'Of course not. I told her you're out on a limb. She does want to meet you, though. She'll be at our office tomorrow afternoon at three. She'll be bringing some files with her.'

'Is that wise?'

'The security staff at the office know her. She has clearance and can make a plausible excuse for being there. There won't be anyone else around and she'll come to our office. She can't leave the files, of course, but thought it safer to come to us rather than have us go to her.'

'I hope she knows what she's doing,' I said.

'Jane has better reasons than most to be guarded,' Magdalena replied tartly. 'She made enemies while she was with us and believes there is a faction in SIS who would like to see her removed from there too.'

I was beginning to see what it was they might have against her. In fact, I was none too sure that Jane Archer was the sort of person I should be trusting my career to – and perhaps more than just my career. Having signed the Official Secrets Act I was over a barrel. But it seemed too late to backtrack now. Magdalena appeared devoted to the woman and the last thing I wanted to do was upset Magdalena. It would have been wiser not to have involved her in the first place.

'I should never have said anything about all this to you,' I said.

'Why?'

'Because I don't know what I'm getting you into. Do you know?'

'I haven't a clue,' she said blithely.

'Then why on earth are you helping me? My barely discernible magic aside, of course.'

'I didn't say *barely*. I said *none* I could discern.'

'Let's not quibble,' I said. 'You told me yourself they'd take a dim view of my investigating a man whose file they've closed. Closed then *lost*, apparently. They can always regard me as an idiot they shouldn't have trusted in the first place. Someone who didn't know any better. Not you, Magdalena. You know their business inside out. What excuse do you have?'

I expected some sharp retort. Instead she looked down at her glass, turning it between fingers and thumb.

'Early in the war,' she said, 'I applied to join SOE.'

Surprised, all I could think to say was: 'You joined SOE? Is that why you said "undermine *us*" in the office Tuesday?'

'Did I?' she asked.

'How did you know about them? I thought they were a big secret during the war.'

'Actually,' Magdalena said, 'I had no idea who they were. At the time I wanted to do something more than I was doing and answered an ad in the paper. They were looking for people with good French. I was asked for an interview in a rather grubby office in Holborn. They tested me on my French and gave me some aptitude tests. There was another interview and a few days later a group of us was sent away for training. It wasn't until then that I found out what sort of organisations they were. I was still keen and spent some time in a rather grand house in Scotland doing night marches and being left in the middle of nowhere and told to find my way back.'

I found it difficult to picture Magdalena marching through Scotland and told her so.

'Can't you?' she said. 'Well, I admit it wasn't the sort of thing I usually did. It was uncomfortable, usually cold and often wet. But I enjoyed it. Not that it made any difference. When the time came, I was rejected. They told me I was too tall and that I might stand out, then that my French wasn't good enough. I think my being tall was just an excuse. And as for my French, some of the others in my group weren't as fluent as I was. They took them.'

'What do you think it was then?'

Magdalena lifted her chin. 'I think they thought I didn't have the nerve. For the work, I mean.'

'Going behind the German lines.'

'Yes.'

'Would it have scared you?'

'Of course it would. But I still could have done it.'

The pain of the rejection was still evident in her voice. She looked at me steadily, but the defiance was a veneer. Beneath she seemed more vulnerable than I had ever seen her.

'It was their call,' I said, trying not to sound patronising. 'From their point of view every agent was a link in a chain. If one breaks the whole chain is broken.'

'I know that,' she said.

'Did you lose a friend in SOE?'

Her eyes narrowed. 'Office gossip?'

'Personal observation,' I said.

She finished her rum and toyed with her empty glass before putting it on the table.

'Not in SOE. In the navy. He was on the Atlantic convoys. His ship was torpedoed in '41. There were no survivors.'

'I'm sorry.'

'I was hardly the only one,' she said.

'That doesn't make it any easier.'

'No.'

'Was that why you wanted to join SOE?'

'I suppose it was one of the reasons,' she said.

'And did they know that?'

'By the time they finished with you they knew everything there was to know. That, though, wasn't a bar. Revenge is a very strong motive.'

'Sometimes that sort of emotion can become a bar in itself,' I suggested.

'I'm not an emotional person,' she insisted.

'Then or now?'

She didn't reply. I had made her uncomfortable. She straightened in her chair, cleared her throat and spent a moment looking around the hotel bar.

'Anyway,' she said finally, 'now you know. After I was rejected they offered me a clerical post with them. I told them I wasn't interested in typing reports about people doing things I should have been doing. It was stupid of me, but that's how I felt at the time. Then Jane Archer found me a position in her office and I've been living a mundane, clerical life ever since.'

'I thought you enjoyed your work,' I said. 'You're good at it.'

'Oh, it's interesting enough,' she said, making it sound as if for her it held no interest at all. 'God knows there are worse jobs. And I tell myself that I know things that very few other people know.'

'But that's not enough?'

'It's not that. It's just that I never got the chance. I never found out if they were right. If I could have done it. Had the nerve, I mean.'

'And that's why you want to help me? To see if you have the nerve for it?'

'Perhaps it is. In a way.'

'It's hardly the same thing,' I told her. 'I doubt they'll put you up against a wall and shoot you if they find out you knew what I was doing. It's not exactly a matter of life and death.'

'Perhaps not for you,' she replied. 'But both the Wolff brothers are dead and no one seems to know why.'

'Someone knows. I think the point is, they don't want anyone else finding out.'

'Then why don't we see if we can,' she said.

I smiled at her. 'No magic, eh?'

She rolled her eyes but didn't argue when I said I'd walk her home.

She lived in Archery Close, off Connaught Road. It was the kind of quiet mews one could have found tucked away all over London twenty-five years ago, barely changed in the last hundred years if one discounted the fact it now housed people rather than horses. This one, though, had had a rude introduction to the 20th century. An air raid had taken out some houses in Connaught Square and one whole side of Archery Close had been damaged. Magdalena hadn't lived there then but for those who had there was an ever-present reminder in the empty houses and the rubble that lined one side of the close.

The terrace was bathed in darkness as we walked up the mews. A few weak streetlights struggled to illuminate the cobblestone path cleared through the snow, leaving them shining with frost like glazed buns.

I said goodnight at her door, lingering for a moment in the hope of an invitation inside. When it didn't come, I said I'd see her at the office at two o'clock the next day then walked back down the close. As I turned into

Connaught Square, I glanced back down the road and noticed a man in a trilby pass under a streetlight fifty yards behind me. Cast in shadow, I couldn't see his face but he paused as I turned, then crossed the road and walked off in the other direction.

Quickening my step I hurried along the road back towards Lancaster Gate Station, repeating to myself what I had told Magdalena: '*I doubt they'll put you up against a wall and shoot you ...*'

At that moment I was no longer as sure.

28

Saturday, February 15th 1947

I was already in the office when Magdalena arrived. With all our files locked away for the weekend there was nothing for me to do so I sat at my desk with my feet up, smoking. I always did my best to remember not to light up in the office, but it was Saturday so when Magdalena walked in I was puffing away like a locomotive. She waved her hand in front of her face as if the wind had changed on bonfire night and I crushed the offending thing out in my ashtray.

'Sorry,' I said. 'Is she here?'

'Upstairs. Are you ready?'

I followed her along the corridor and up the stairs to one of the offices used by the clerical staff. Jane Archer was sitting at a desk. She stood up and Magdalena introduced us.

She must have been almost fifty but age hadn't yet robbed her of what was usually described as classical beauty. Hers was the kind of face one encounters on Grecian statuary – serene yet enigmatic.

According to Magdalena, Jane Archer had qualified as a barrister after her first stint in the Service following the Great War. I had appeared in court a few times myself in my capacity as a police constable but I'd never encountered her like before. She had the kind of presence that didn't countenance contradiction.

'Harry Tennant,' she said as we shook hands, as if to speak my name aloud would fix me forever in the Jane Archer catalogue of characters. 'Magdalena tells me you're a bit of a loose cannon.'

I gave her my most endearing grin, avoiding Magdalena's eyes while doing it.

'Only when there's something to aim at,' I said.

But Magdalena was right. The charm was no longer working. All Jane Archer did was raise an eyebrow in a manner that must have given unreliable witnesses sleepless nights.

She sat down again, smoothing her skirt under her. Magdalena and I took chairs on the opposite side of the desk like a pair of interviewees.

'Joseph Wolff,' Jane Archer began without further to-do. 'I can't tell you the nature of the work he was involved in during the war beyond the fact that it was highly sensitive and remains so. I would hardly be revealing any secrets if I said it stemmed from his academic career.'

'He was a mathematician,' I said. 'That leaves a lot of scope.'

Mrs Archer smiled slightly. 'Which is why I am able to mention the fact without revealing any secrets.'

'And when he went back to Oxford?'

'He did just that,' she said. 'He resumed college life. He retained no ties to the government nor to his wartime work.'

'I assume Magdalena told you of his interest in Katja Tereshchenko?' I said. 'Am I to take it then that this interest had nothing to do with his former work?'

'That isn't what I said,' Jane Archer replied equably. 'According to Magdalena, however, the matter appears to have been more to do with his brother. Or, to be more precise, the death of his brother.'

'He died near Murmansk. Any Russian connection, then, would be coincidental?'

'I doubt it,' said Jane Archer. 'But I think we can dismiss the possibility that Wolff was attempting to pass information to the Russians through his brother.'

'Which leaves us where?' I asked.

Jane Archer smiled again and shrugged. 'Isn't that what you're trying to find out?'

I glanced at Magdalena. She was watching her friend in a way that suggested she would have liked to be taking notes.

'But we *were* watching him,' I said. 'There must have been a reason.'

'Indeed.'

'And he killed himself. That was hardly on a whim.'

'I agree. And if you find an answer to either question I will be very pleased to know what it is.'

'Well,' I suggested, 'you might get an answer to the first by simply asking someone at St James's Street why we were watching him.'

'I could,' she agreed, 'but am I any more likely to receive an answer than you, if you posed the same question?'

'You've got a reputation,' I said, trying to suppress the endearing grin again. 'I would have thought—'

'I'm sure,' Jane Archer cut in, 'that Magdalena has outlined for you precisely what sort of reputation I have, Mr Tennant. As you pointed out yourself, Joseph Wolff's Service file is absent. Destroyed, perhaps ... At least, it has been put beyond view. There is nothing in his SIS file to indicate why he was of interest to us now, or why he might have been inclined to commit suicide. It seems reasonable to surmise from this that whatever the interest in Wolff was, it is not one that whoever held it cares to share with anyone else. And I can assure you that would include me.'

The defence rests, I thought. Which led inexorably to the next question which was: why was she here? Why did she want to meet me?

It occurred to me that it might be because I was involving Magdalena in something she'd be better out of. But if that were the case and all she wanted to do was warn me off, she could easily have sent me a message, or arrange to meet under other circumstances.

Or was it something else? Something which not only required that she see me but that Magdalena should be there as well.

A novel idea sprang to mind and I glanced sideways at Magdalena, only to find she was looking at me.

'The other matter,' Jane Archer said briskly, while I was still weighing up the possibilities, 'is your having encountered the name Scriabina.'

She leaned forward and touched a file that lay on the desk in front of her. I had seen it as we walked in and had assumed it to be connected to Wolff. But I was wrong. She opened it and I saw that within its buff covers lay another, its own cover old and torn.

'This is Ariadna Scriabina's SOE file,' Jane Archer said. 'Given the nature of the work on which you and Magdalena are currently engaged, I thought it had some relevance.'

'In what way?' Magdalena asked.

Jane Archer pulled the old file a little closer.

'To summarise,' she said, 'Ariadna Scriabina was the daughter of the Russian composer Alexander Scriabin. She was born in Italy, although she lived in Russia from 1910 until 1922 ...' she scanned through the pages, '... moved to Paris and seems to have been married three times. It is her last husband who is the important one from our point of view.' She looked up. 'His name was Dovid Knut and he was a Bessarabian Jew. It is after she married Knut that she became interested in Zionism—'

'Zionism?' I said. 'I thought she was in the French Resistance?'

Jane Archer nodded. 'And so she was. She apparently converted to Judaism after her marriage to Knut. When he was mobilised at the start of the war and sent to Toulouse, Ariadna joined him there with her two daughters. These were issue from her first marriage. It was in Toulouse that she became involved in Resistance work and came to the attention of SOE. More importantly, as far as we are concerned, is that along with her husband and two friends she formed the Armée Juive.'

'And what was that?' I asked.

'The Jewish army. It was a resistance cell. They began by helping Jewish refugees from Germany who were being held in Camp du Récébédou, one of the internment camps near Toulouse. The Armée Juive committed acts of sabotage and smuggled Jewish children to Switzerland and Spain. They also used arms we dropped for the use of resistance groups to assassinate local Milice agents. This is how they came into conflict with SOE.'

Jane Archer turned the file around so Magdalena and I might read it.

'She was killed by a Milice agent in 1944 while on her way to a meeting. The French government posthumously awarded her the Croix de Guerre and Médaille de la Résistance after the war.'

'There's no doubt she *is* dead, I suppose?' Magdalena asked. 'Could the reference to Scriabina in our intercept refer to her?'

'No,' said Jane Archer. 'There's no doubt she's dead.'

I read the account of her death SOE had received. She had been ambushed along with an associate by two Milice agents. He had escaped but Ariadna had been shot.

'Then who might "the little Scriabina" that was being talked about on our intercept be if it wasn't Ariadna?' Magdalena asked.

I went back to looking at the biographical detail SOE had collected on her.

'Ariadna Scriabina was highly thought of,' Jane Archer told Magdalena. 'It is always possible that someone has taken her name as a nom de guerre …'

I saw it noted in the file that Ariadna had had two daughters by her first marriage, Tatiana-Miriam and Gilbert-Elizabeth. The younger of the two was known as Betty.

'… or perhaps,' Jane Archer was suggesting, 'someone who had been close to her …? You should try contacting the French and our office in Palestine. See if they have any record of what became of her daughters.'

But I didn't need to go that far afield.

Betty's father – Ariadna Scriabina's first husband – was a French composer. His name had been Daniel Lazarus.

29

Saturday, February 15th 1947

Outside the sky had cleared. The sun was setting behind the Royal Albert Hall and throwing long shadows down the Kensington Road. In the park, the snow sparkled in the late afternoon light. For once the city smelled fresh, the air crisp with frost.

I suggested we walk across the park.

I had not said anything about Ariadna Scriabina's daughter to Jane Archer in front of Magdalena. I told her I appreciated her help then had left Magdalena to say goodbye to her while I went downstairs to our office to retrieve our coats. I gave the two of them a few minutes alone before going back up.

Minutes I needed to myself.

There could be no question of coincidence. Lizzie Lazarus had come to me through Sydney Stanley's suggestion of putting an advert about Samuel Wolff in the theatrical trade pages. The ad had appeared – I'd seen it – but it was clear to me now that Stanley had had his reply ready even before the paper had come out.

Jack and I had been set up. I had been played like a fish on a line.

Lizzie had always been inquisitive about my work – it excited her, she said – a claim that had always held a hint of libidinous promise. She had told me her mother had worked for the French Resistance and that she had helped – a risky strategy, it seemed to me now but one meant, I presumed, to suggest that she could keep secrets too. If I was prepared to share them with her. I had swallowed that, too.

I was going to have to tell Magdalena. I could see no way around it. It was obvious Lizzie had been planted on me to get as much detail as possible about the work I was doing and I sat on the edge of my desk and smoked a cigarette while I tried to remember how much I had told her. The desk was uncomfortable and so was I. But I didn't deserve to feel comfortable. I had been a fool and, finally, when I could string it out no longer, I put the butt of the cigarette in the ashtray and went back upstairs.

Jane Archer had gone.

'She thought it best is she left first,' Magdalena said. 'You were a long time.'

'Sorry. I thought you might want a few words alone together.'

Magdalena raised an eyebrow. 'To talk about you, you mean?'

'No, I didn't mean that at all.'

'She's coming back, you know.'

'Back? What, back to the Service?'

'Yes. Politics again. She's joining C Branch.'

'Credentials Investigation? Are you serious?'

'Yes. And what an utter waste of her talents,' said Magdalena. 'But it's all they're offering.'

'I know what I'd tell them to do with C Branch,' I said.

'Fortunately Jane is more refined than you.'

'Even so. Why would she agree?'

'It's addictive,' Magdalena replied. 'The secret world. You've got the habit, Harry, only you don't know it yet.'

****

We passed through Prince's Gate, different phrases running through my head as I tried to frame what I had to say to her. I would tell her as we walked, I decided. It would give her time to burn off any anger at me for jeopardising our work. What I was afraid of mainly, though, was that her response would be contempt – contempt for me and for how easily I had been duped.

Given my preoccupation as we entered the park, I barely noticed the man behind us. Not until I happened to glance back as we started up South Carriage Drive.

He was some yards away and incongruously dressed, I couldn't help noticing, in a leather coat and a hat that looked like a beret. The Milice sprang irrationally to mind as I took another look to see if he might be the man I had spotted in the Mountview. But he didn't seem to me like one of Harry Hunter's men from B6, or even one of Henry Gifford's men with a penchant for outrageous disguise.

I hadn't got a good look at the man in the Mountview, it was true, but this one appeared oddly conspicuous. Then I decided that Magdalena might be right; I had acquired an addiction to secrecy and it had warped my thinking. Like the man I'd glimpsed on leaving Magdalena's house the previous evening; I was seeing people following me everywhere.

Even so, reluctant to dismiss the idea altogether, I took Magdalena's arm and quickened my pace.

'Let's go through Kensington Gardens.'

'They'll be locking the gates soon,' she said, frowning as she matched my stride.

'We'll still be able to get out through the turnstiles the other side,' I assured her.

The Coalbrookdale Gates leading into Kensington Gardens weren't yet shut, the damage they had sustained when a nearby bomb had exploded not obvious until we were close to them. I could see the chipped paint and the twisted metal as we passed through but, like most of London, the gates were still upright. Still standing.

'Why do you want to go this way?' Magdalena asked.

'There's a man behind us,' I said. 'I want to see if he's following us.'

'We're being followed?' Magdalena demanded. 'By whom?'

I smiled. Her grammar remained precise even under duress. I pictured her being interrogated by the Gestapo, replying to their brutal questions in impeccable English.

'What's amusing you?' she demanded.

'And they turned you down.'

'Who turned me down? What are you talking about?'

Once beyond the gates, I looked back again. The man was still behind us and, I was now sure, following us. I wondered how they had got wind of our meeting with Jane Archer.

'He's still there,' I said to Magdalena. 'When we get a little closer to the trees I'm going to stop. I want you to keep walking.'

'Is it the man from the Mountview?'

'I can't be sure. Another one I think.'

'What are you going to do? Not challenge him?'

'Why not?' I said. 'I'm curious to know how long I'm going to have to drag a tail behind me.'

'All right, but this isn't a joke, Harry. Be careful.'

'If he's a Watcher,' I pointed out, 'he'll have just been told to follow me. We don't pay them enough to do anything else.'

I looked back over my shoulder again. He was the only person in sight and it seemed to me, that if they no longer cared how obvious they made the fact I was being followed, there was no reason why I should be worried about letting them know I knew.

'What if he's not a Watcher?' Magdalena asked.

Oddly, I hadn't given that possibility much thought.

The park around us was deserted. The few people by the gates in Hyde Park were now out of sight beyond the fence dividing it from Kensington Gardens. The sun had gone down and dusk was falling quickly. It was already dark under the trees, the snow hanging in the branches like icing sugar catching the last of the light.

A few yards further on I told Magdalena to keep walking. I said I'd light a cigarette and catch her up. I stopped and turned and reached into my pockets for my cigarettes. The man in the leather coat was now sixty or seventy yards behind me and, instead of his being surprised by my stopping as I had expected, he quickened his pace towards me.

He was no more than forty yards from me when he drew the gun out of his pocket.

Screaming soundlessly to myself for being so stupid, I turned and began to run. Ahead of me Magdalena had stopped and was watching.

'Go!' I shouted. 'Get into the trees—'

I heard the whine of a bullet close to my ear even as I heard the shot. In a dozen yards I had caught up with Magdalena, grabbed her arm and pulled her off the path towards a thick clump of trees. A second shot kicked up a spray of snow in front of us.

'He's shooting at us!' Magdalena gasped as I dragged her under the cover of the trees. 'Why is he shooting at us?'

It was dark beneath the thick canopy. I dodged between the trunks, hauling Magdalena behind me. I looked back but couldn't see him. I stopped and listened but could hear nothing except our own ragged breath.

'Have you got a gun?' Magdalena whispered hoarsely.

'A gun?' I gasped back. 'Of course I haven't got a gun. Why would I have a gun?' I pulled her behind the trunk of a big oak. 'Have you got one?'

'Certainly not,' she replied indignantly, as if the very idea was preposterous. 'Why would I carry a gun?'

I strained my ears but could hear nothing except the faint sound of traffic beyond the park.

'We need to get deeper into the trees,' I whispered, peering around the trunk.

The light had gone and the trees were beginning to loom menacingly above us. My imagination placed an assassin behind each one.

'Ready?' I whispered.

Magdalena nodded. I took her hand, squeezing it to encourage her. We ran a dozen yards through the snow then stopped. I pulled her behind the bole of a broad beech, pinning her to the smooth bark to flatten our profile. Her face was level with my face. Her eyes stared into my eyes.

I turned my head to whisper in her ear.

'We'll go another fifty yards then get down in the snow. It's so dark he'll be on top of us before he sees us.'

'All right,' she whispered, breathing heavily.

My lips brushed her hair. 'It's not SOE,' I said, 'but you're doing just fine.'

It was so dark all I could see of her face was a faint gleam in her eyes. On impulse I touched my lips briefly against hers. Then, before she could react, pulled her out from the cover of the beech and darted into the thicker copse.

I had lost my bearings in the trees. For all I knew the man might be in front of us. Still running, I looked around again but it was too dark to see anything. Suddenly Magdalena jerked me to one side. But it was too late. I tripped on a branch in the snow, pitched forward and hit my head against a tree. I grunted and went down. Magdalena dropped beside me.

We lay still, chests heaving in unison like a pair of spent lovers who had somehow circumvented all the pleasure.

Dazed and winded, I put a hand against Magdalena's mouth and tuned my ears to the darkness, listening. As if she understood, she stopped breathing.

I heard the sound of cracking of wood and felt her stiffen. Turning my head, I saw the beam of a torch darting between the trees. Something was jabbing into my back and I shifted my weight. I was lying on the end of the branch I had tripped over. I took hold of it. The branch was at least three feet long and felt weighty. I held a finger to Magdalena's lips again.

'Can you stay still?' I whispered.

I felt her nod. Slowly I got to my knees, hefting the broken branch. The torch was closer but angled away from us.

'Make a noise to attract him,' I said softly to her. 'Moan as if you're hurt.'

I stood up, flattening myself against the tree trunk. A second later I heard Magdalena whimper. She did it again and the torch beam swung in our direction. I heard shoes crunching in the snow as he approached.

Magdalena didn't stir and I edged around the tree, holding my breath as he moved closer, the branch ready.

Magdalena whimpered again and the torchlight swung our way. As he breasted the tree I stepped out and brought the branch down on him with all the force I could summon. I heard him grunt and he dropped to his knees. I hit him again, hard across his head. The branch broke and the torch fell from his hand. He pitched forward into the snow and lay still.

Magdalena jumped to her feet. I dropped what was left of the branch and reached for the torch, playing it over the snow until I found the gun. It lay just beyond his outstretched hand.

'Is he dead?' Magdalena asked.

'Not yet,' I said.

I picked up the gun and levelled it at his head.

'No, Harry,' said Magdalena. 'Don't do it.'

I couldn't think of any good reason I shouldn't, except that she asked me not to. I lowered the gun and knelt in the snow beside him, rolling him over and shining the torch in his face.

'Have you seen him before?' I asked her.

'No.'

'Me neither.'

I went through his leather coat. He had some papers in an inside pocket, a bunch of keys and some money. I tossed the money into the snow, as far as I could. Without his torch he was going to have trouble finding it. Then I put his papers and keys into my pocket and slipped the gun in beside them.

'Come on,' I said. 'Let the bastard freeze to death. It's not as quick as a bullet.'

I took Magdalena's hand and, by torchlight, hurried back through the trees until we found a path. Following it, we came to the Speke Monument. We were on the north side of the park. Ahead of us was the frozen Long Water, starlight lying like a ghostly reflection on its icy surface. Away to our north the muffled sound of traffic hardly intruded on the air of unreality.

Five minutes later we pushed through a turnstile and out on to the Bayswater Road. As we passed beneath a streetlight Magdalena looked at me and gasped.

'What's the matter?'

'Your face. You're bleeding. Have you been shot?'

I reached a hand to my forehead. Blood was matted in my hair.

'It was that damned tree I ran into,' I said. I looked down at the blood on my hand and a wave of nausea washed over me. I staggered. Magdalena grabbed me by the arm.

'It's not far to my house,' she said. 'Can you manage or shall I get a taxi?'

'I can walk,' I muttered, leaning on her. 'I'd have been all right if you hadn't told me.'

'I'll let you bleed next time,' she said.

I raised a weak grin. 'You SOE people are all the same,' I told her. 'Hard as nails.'

'Come on,' she said pulling me by the arm. 'You're frightening the pedestrians. We'll get you cleaned up and put a drink inside you.'

'That's almost worth getting shot for.'

People on the street, I noticed, were staring at us. Buses ran past and cars drove by. I looked at my watch and was astonished to see it was only quarter past six. I felt as though I'd been up all night.

We turned up Albion Street on to Connaught, leaving the traffic and people behind. Archery Close was deserted. Lights showed behind curtained windows, still a novelty for some, I supposed, after years of blackout. At her door Magdalena rummaged in her bag for her key. I leaned against the wall. She found the key and slipped it into the lock.

'If it had been me,' I said, 'I'd have dropped the bag in the park.'

'I'd sooner have left you than lose my bag,' she said.

'Next time we'll bury it for safekeeping,' I told her. 'X marks the spot.'

She turned on the hall light and led me into the sitting room.

'You think they'll be a next time?'

'Excitement,' I said. 'You told me it was addictive.'

'I meant secrecy, not getting shot at.'

She turned on a table lamp, pushed me into a chair and took off her coat. She went into the kitchen and I looked around at the comfortable furniture, the paintings on her walls and the rugs on her floor. The polished wooden case of a wireless stood on a side table and some paper and a few sticks of kindling lay in the grate ready for a fire. A coal scuttle stood beside it. I felt in my pocket for my matches and found the gun and the man's papers and keys there. I pulled them all out.

The papers weren't in English. I thought they might be Hebrew, but what did I know? I dropped everything on to the table beneath the lamp and took out my wallet. I pulled a card from it and lay that beside the papers, the keys and the gun. Then I lit the fire.

Magdalena returned with a bowl of water and a cloth.

'Making yourself at home?' she asked, seeing the fire.

'I can do that,' I said, reaching for the bowl. 'You had better ring this number.' I gave her the card. 'Ask for Henry Gifford. Tell him what happened.'

'Chief Superintendent Gifford?'

'You know him?'

'We've met.'

'I think the man who just tried to kill us was a Jewish terrorist.' I pointed at the Hebrew papers. 'So much for my thinking he was a B6 Watcher. You better not mention that to Gifford.'

She put the bowl on the chair beside me. 'First things first,' she said. 'Your head might need stitches. Take your coat off.'

'Do you live here alone?' I asked. I hadn't seen any evidence of any once else living there.

She wiped the blood off my forehead and rinsed the cloth in the bowl. 'Did you think I had a man here?'

'Of course not,' I said, although there was no reason why she shouldn't. 'Have you lived here since you got back from Blenheim?'

She dabbed at my forehead. 'Before. I bought it when my father died. My mother lived with me until she died. I rented the place out while I was at Blenheim. American army. They put an officer in here. He didn't do too much damage.'

I smiled then winced as she put some disinfectant on the cut.

'You did well,' I said as she bathed my head.

'Why, did the Americans always cause damage?'

'I meant in the park.'

'I didn't do anything.'

'You whimpered on demand,' I reminded her.

'That was more involuntary than by design,' she said.

'You were wonderful.'

'I was scared.'

'That makes two of us,' I told her.

She dropped the cloth in the bowl. 'That'll do until I've rung Gifford. Sit by the fire. You look frozen.'

'That's funk,' I said.

'A big man like you?' She put her hand to my cheek. 'You feel cold.'

I'd liked to have proved her wrong but I had to tell her about Lizzie first.

'There's something you need to know before you speak to Gifford.'

'Oh?'

'The file on Ariadna Scriabina that Jane Archer showed us. I know who Presman's friend was referring to when he said "the little Scriabina".'

Magdalena withdrew her hand. 'Who?'

'One of her daughters. Gilbert-Elizabeth. She told me her name was Lizzie Lazarus.'

I thought I saw Magdalena's eyes narrow, but it might have been the firelight.

'How well do you know her?'

'Well enough,' I said. 'I was looking for anyone who had known Samuel Wolff. My former corporal at my old unit put me on to contact of his. He called himself Sydney Stanley.'

'The man whose name you gave to Brian Ogilvy?'

'Yes. He was the one who came up with Lizzie Lazarus.'

'Is he Jewish?'

'Stanley is. Lizzie is French. Well,' I added, reluctantly, 'half French. The rest is Russian.'

Magdalena sat down. 'Harry ...'

'I know,' I said. 'It was stupid. But it just didn't occur to me that she might be a plant.'

'How far did it go?'

I shrugged, embarrassed to put it into words. 'Far enough.'

Magdalena closed her eyes for a moment. 'What did you tell her?'

'I've been trying to remember,' I confessed. 'She was always asking questions ... wanting to know what I did, that sort of thing ...'

'She knew you worked for us?'

'Yes. I'm not sure how. I certainly didn't tell her. Whether Jack had guessed or Stanley had found out through some other source ... But I don't think I told her much at all. About Joseph Wolff and his brother and what happened at Riseborough, certainly. But not about what *we* do.'

'Did you tell her what Wolff did during the war?'

'No. I have no idea what he did. And now, after what's just happened, I don't believe that's what she was interested in. Anyway, a week or so ago we were supposed to meet and she didn't turn up. I haven't seen her since.

I assume they weren't learning anything and called her off. Like Pressman's contact said on the intercept.'

'Did you try to contact her?'

'Yes, but no one is answering the number she gave me. I never knew where she lived.'

Magdalena stood up and went into the hall. I heard her speaking to the operator and ask for Gifford's number. A moment later she was connected.

'Superintendent Gifford? This is Magdalena Marshall. That's right, from the Kensington office. I'm at my house with Harold Tennant. A man has just tried to kill us.'

I winced again. I hated to be called Harold. Whenever I was in trouble as a boy my mother would call me Harold. I'd always found that worse than her displeasure. But even that wasn't going to be as bad as Magdalena's.

'Yes,' she said in the hall, 'Archery Close. Off Connaught – Oh, you know it? Good. About half an hour? We'll be waiting.'

She came back to me. 'Half an hour.'

'He already knew where you lived?'

'Well that doesn't mean anything,' she said. 'I bet he knows where you live, too.'

'I bet he does,' I agreed.

She stared at me, nibbling at her lower lip. 'Why did you tell me?'

'About Lizzie Lazarus? Because after what's happened you've got a right to know. I didn't want there to be any secrets between us.'

She smiled. 'That's an odd attitude given the kind of work we do.'

'Perhaps, although I don't know how much longer I'll be doing it.'

'You'll have to tell him everything, of course.'

'I know. Which means it'll get back to Bryce which means they'll probably sack me. Or worse. But that's still no reason for you to be involved. I'll tell him I happened to be walking you back across the park. You didn't know anything about Lizzie Lazarus …'

She shook her head, whether in disappointment or exasperation, I couldn't guess.

'Come on,' she said. 'Up to the bathroom. Let's get you properly cleaned up before he gets here.'

I took off my jacket and sat on the edge of the tub while she ran warm water into the basin. She bathed my forehead again and began washing the matted blood out of my hair.

'Would you have shot him?' she asked suddenly.

'The man in the park? Certainly. He was going to shoot us.'

'Even so. It still would have been murder.'

'Proactive justice, I call it.'

'*Proactive*? What is that supposed to mean?'

'Doing unto others before they do it to you,' I said.

'That's not quite how my father might have put it.'

'Perhaps not. Then he might have thought differently if someone was shooting at him.'

'That wouldn't have been very likely,' she said.

'No,' I agreed. 'The Anglican Church always takes a more *meta*physical view of things. If you know what I mean.'

'Exactly what do you mean?' she asked. 'Is this some veiled allusion to my being a bishop's daughter? Was she pretty?'

'You mean Lizzie? I suppose you'd call her pretty – in a half-French, half-Russian sort of way.'

Sitting on the edge of the bath, Magdalena standing inches in front of me, I had a sudden urge to put my arms around her waist. So I did. I expected her to pull away, but she didn't. She looked down at me.

'I'm feeling light-headed again,' I explained.

'You're certainly feeling something. You kissed me under the trees in the park, remember?'

'It was a spur of the moment thing,' I said.

'Was it? I suppose that means you'll need to think about it before you do it again.'

'That depends on the situation,' I said.

She hesitated and leaned down towards me.

'What sort of situation would you say we were in now?'

I reached up and pulled her gently towards me. Her lips opened. As they touched mine the doorbell rang.

'He's early,' she said, straightening.

'That's the police for you,' I mumbled. 'Always stopping people enjoying themselves.'

30

Saturday, February 15th 1947

The three of us were sitting around the fire. I finally had the promised drink in my hand and Gifford was nursing a scotch and water. Magdalena was beside me on the sofa, drinking soda water.

'Tell me again,' Gifford said.

So I went through it once more, from when Magdalena and I left the office and when I first became aware that someone was following us. I had told him we had been followed before but not by this particular man.

'And you left this one alive,' he said, alluding, I presumed, to the body he'd moved from my old Cowcross Street flat the previous summer. I felt Magdalena's eyes on me.

'We left him alive,' I said. 'But it's no night for lying around in the open.'

Gifford stood up. 'If I can use your phone I'll get some men in the park.'

'South and west of the Speke Monument,' I told him. 'He was bleeding and the snow was fresh so if he's moved he's likely to leave a track.'

'He's not the only one bleeding,' said Gifford, looking at my bruised face.

He went into the hall and held a brief conversation with someone on the other end of the line. Magdalena and I turned to at each other but said nothing. I was about to reach for her hand when Gifford came back.

'Either of you read Hebrew?' He gestured at the papers on the table. He had already pocketed the gun and the keys.

'No,' I said. 'And neither of us knew him. He obviously knew us, though.'

'And what your work involves?'

'I can't see any other reason for him trying to kill us. Not that it's much of a reason anyway. Someone else would carry on doing what we're doing even if he had killed us.'

Gifford sipped his scotch. 'There doesn't have to be any particular reason,' he said. 'The act itself is sufficient as far as they're concerned. Terror for terror's sake. More to the point is, how did he know you both?'

216

I glanced at Magdalena.

'A few days ago one of our intercepts made reference to someone they called Scriabina.'

'Russian?'

'Yes,' I admitted, 'although I don't think there's a Russian angle to this. It turned out that a woman named Ariadna Scriabina had been in the French Resistance. She was killed by the Milice—'

'Scum of the earth,' Gifford muttered. 'So what's the connection?'

I was on the verge of coming up with some evasive explanation when Magdalena pushed her leg against mine. Gifford saw her do it.

'We had no file on her,' she told him. 'I have an acquaintance who works at SIS—'

'This will be Jane Archer, will it?' Gifford said.

'You know her of course,' said Magdalena, 'from when she worked for the Service.'

Gifford nodded. 'Getting rid of Mrs Archer was one of the former Director General's worse decisions.'

'I'm glad someone agrees with me,' Magdalena said.

Gifford's expression soured. 'We're all supposed to be on the same side yet I could name a dozen I would have let go before her. Not my decision though,' he said. 'So, you asked Jane Archer to look into the SIS files?'

'She found Scriabina in an old SOE file.'

She was about to continue but I thought if there were any further confessions to make I had better be the one making them.

'It turned out,' I said, 'that Ariadna was married to a Jew named Dovid Knut. She converted and became a supporter of Zionism. Together with two friends, Ariadna and her husband formed the Armée Juive – that's the Jewish army. They started by helping the Jews held in the camps in the south of France. Getting their children out.'

'And very admirable too,' said Gifford. 'So what's she got to do with this? You did say she was dead?'

'Yes. But she had a daughter who seems to go under several names. One of them is Elizabeth Lazarus.'

'Ah,' he said, as if the scales had dropped from his eyes. 'The girl you took to Isokon Flats in Hampstead.'

'Yes,' I said.

'And she's inherited her mother's enthusiasm for the Zionist cause?'

'I didn't know that that when I met her,' I said quickly, and making it sound like an evasion of responsibility.

'I don't suppose you've an address or telephone number for her?' Gifford asked.

'No address. I've got a telephone number no one is answering.'

I wrote it down.

'I don't know for certain she was involved in what happened this evening,' I said, passing him the number. 'But she was certainly put on to me to get information.' I glanced at Magdalena again but she was watching Gifford. 'She was always asking questions about my work. I never told her anything, of course. I assume that's why her colleagues decided I wasn't of any further use.'

'It seems the most likely explanation,' Magdalena put in helpfully.

Gifford turned back to me. 'And you never suspected anything?' he asked. 'Even when she wanted to know about your work.'

'No,' I said. 'I know it sounds naïve, if not downright stupid. But she ever asked me anything outright … She had a way …'

I decided to shut up. The hole I was digging was getting deeper.

Gifford was watching me as if he sensed there was more to it.

'You told me when we spoke about the Isokon Flats that this Lazarus was an actress? That you introduced her to an agent.'

'She told me she was looking for work. I introduced her to Solly Epstein, the man the girls who live in my building work for. I suppose she might have given him a contact number although it's more likely the whole thing was a story she concocted just to get close to me.'

'You're probably right,' Gifford remarked mordantly. 'It sounds to me as if she already had a job. Worth a try, though. Epstein has an office, I take it? I assume from the name he's a Jew.'

'Soho.' I gave him the address. 'I can't imagine Solly's any more involved in this than Miss Marshall here.'

I was spreading it on too thick and could see Gifford wasn't swallowing it.

'And what would Epstein's connection to the Isokon Flats be?'

'His business partner lives there. Miriam something. It was her party.'

Then I remembered Ariadna's other daughter's name was Miriam. For a second it all seemed to fall into place. But the pieces didn't quite fit. Solly's Miriam would be too old and the whole thing seemed a coincidence too far. Besides, if what Frances had implied …

'Cohen,' said Gifford, breaking my train of thought. 'Miriam Cohen.'

'You know her?'

He didn't reply immediately. Instead he finished his drink and stood up.

'Right. I'll get over to the park then have a word with this Epstein chap.' He skewered me with his cold eyes. 'You don't look too bright. Want me to run you home?'

I turned to Magdalena again. It was the last thing I wanted. If Gifford hadn't already guessed, though, I didn't want him to think there was anything between Magdalena and myself beyond our work.

'Thanks,' I said. 'I'd appreciate it.'

Magdalena and I stood awkwardly for a moment before moving towards the door. I clumsily offered her my hand and thanked her for cleaning up my cut head. I said I'd see her in the office on Monday morning.

I saw none of it was fooling Gifford but once I'd started playing the idiot I didn't seem able to stop. Magdalena muttered something about it being the least she could do and not letting me go home in the condition I'd been in, then Gifford and I were outside, walking down Archery Close to where he'd parked his Wolseley.

'Smart woman, Miss Marshall,' he said as we climbed into the car.

'Smart?' I repeated as he started the engine. 'Yes, I suppose she is rather attractive.'

'Clever, I meant,' Gifford replied caustically. He turned into Connaught Street. 'Anything between you and this Lazarus girl? Or is that a silly question?'

'Yes,' I said. 'I mean no, it's not a silly question. We had a bit of a fling. It's obvious now she was trying to pump me for information.'

'On how much we knew about the Zionist threat specifically? Or other things? Her mother was Russian, you said.'

'Yes, although I don't think that was her angle. She never asked me anything directly. Not in so many words.'

I tried to remember what she *had* asked me exactly. All I could recall, though, was her general wheedling manner. Reflecting on the brief time we'd spent together, it was now obvious that she was always pumping me for information. Whilst she was doing it, though, it hadn't seemed like that.

'She was just after anything in general I might be able to tell her,' I finally said. 'As far as I remember.'

'And how was it you met her? Through those girls who live in your building? Or was it Epstein?'

'No, neither,' I told him, unwilling to drag any of them into it. But if I didn't, it meant I had to drag the truth in. Eventually I said, 'I was trying to find out what I could about a man named Joseph Wolff and his brother Samuel.'

'Wolff? Who are they? What have they got to do with it?'

He turned the Wolseley left on to the Edgware Road. I couldn't tell from his tone whether he was playing me along or not. There was hardly any light off the dashboard and in the darkness his face was no more than a profile in silhouette. But if he knew about Wolff already there was no point in being evasive; if he didn't, there was no longer a reason for not telling him.

'The beginning of January,' I said. 'Abel Bryce asked me to go to Riseborough on the East Anglian coast. I had to keep an eye on a man named Joseph Wolff. Bryce didn't tell me why or much about him beyond the fact he'd been doing some sort of secret work during the war. So when this Wolff waded into the sea and drowned himself it came as a bit of a surprise.'

'You saw him do it?'

'Yes. There was no doubt that he did it deliberately although the inquest found he drowned accidentally.'

'And what did Bryce have to say about it?'

'That's the thing. Nothing at all. Case closed, he said. No one seemed to be interested once Wolff was dead.'

Gifford turned his head. 'Except you?'

'I was curious.'

'Even though that's what gets cats killed,' he said.

'Men don't generally kill themselves for no reason,' I told him. 'But no one else seemed to want to know why.'

'Perhaps they already knew.'

'Perhaps they did. But it seemed to surprise Bryce when I told him what had happened. Even so, he told me the case was closed.'

'But you weren't prepared to drop it.'

'I wasn't specifically told *not* to make enquiries,' I said. Which was true. But Bryce hadn't told me *not* to jump into the Thames, either, and I hadn't gone ahead and done that.

We were approaching Broadley Street and I pointed to the turning.

'This is my road. On the right, a couple of hundred yards.'

'I know it,' Gifford said. He slowed the car and turned into Broadley Street. 'So you decided to "make enquiries"?'

The way he said it put the phrase in quotes. And there was just a hint of derision in his voice, enough to suggest I had been encroaching on a job for which I was not fitted.

'Wolff's a Jewish name,' I offered in mitigation. 'I thought there might be some connection with the terrorist threat.'

'And Bryce wouldn't have told you if it were true?'

'I wasn't on the Zionist business at the time,' I said, cutting my case for mitigation off at the knees.

'So you started playing Buck Ryan, again,' he said.

'Look,' I said, turning to face him as he drew up outside my flat. 'I played the patsy for you and Bryce last time and wound up in this job. If you didn't want me to continue doing what I'm good at, why am I here? Is this another set-up?'

I was reminding him of how the previous summer they had used me to gather information which they had difficulty in getting any other way. It hadn't ended too well for me and I was beginning to think the job had been a sop thrown my way to keep me on-side. Gifford appeared unconcerned, though. He put the handbrake on and turned off the engine.

He shifted in his seat to face me. 'At the time we thought you could be useful because of who you were and who you knew. What makes you think anyone is pulling your strings now? Did you have any connections to Wolff? Anything at all anyone might think useful?'

'No.'

'All right, then. So what did you do?'

'I started asking around,' I said.

'Anyone in particular?'

'I've still got a few contacts from my war crimes unit.'

He grunted. 'Like your old corporal, Jack Hibbert?'

'Is there anything you don't know?' I asked.

'Too much. I know Hibbert deals in black market goods. What else is he into?'

'Nothing,' I said. 'And he's out of that sort of stuff now. He deals in army surplus these days. Legitimately.'

'Is that a fact? Well, what did he turn up?'

'Lizzie Lazarus, mainly,' I said, which wasn't exactly a ringing endorsement of what I'd told him I was supposedly "good at". 'I hadn't been getting anywhere with Joseph Wolff so I started looking for anyone who knew his brother. Lizzie came to me with a story about how she'd met Samuel in Paris before the war. She would have been just a kid but she said Wolff was a friend of her mother's. It was all a fiction, obviously.'

'Obviously,' Gifford echoed.

'And exactly how *did* she come to you?'

So then I told him about Sydney Stanley.

'Since Sam Wolff had been an actor, Jack advertised in the theatrical papers for anyone who had known him. Although it turned out that this was Stanley's idea and he already had Lizzie primed. Then Stanley said he wanted to meet me so Jack introduced us. He told me Stanley had useful contacts and he was the one who told me Sam Wolff had been in the Field Security Service and that he had gone overboard from a troop transport somewhere around Murmansk in 1944.'

'So there could be a Russian connection after all?' Gifford said, ears pricking up and nose twitching like a dog who's sensed something in the undergrowth.

I shook my head. 'I can't see it. Like I said, Sam Wolff was an actor before the war.'

'You just said he went overboard. Is it possible he could have defected?'

'Well, I suppose so. But what's an actor got to offer the Russians?'

'Maybe Eisenstein's remaking *Hamlet*,' he suggested sarcastically. 'What if he had details of what his brother was doing during the war?'

'That had occurred to me,' I said. 'But since I don't know what it was he was doing it's not got me very far.'

'So what else have you turned up?'

'Not much,' I admitted. 'Only that there's no Jewish connection to Joseph Wolff as far as I can make out. It seems to me his suicide had more to do with his brother's death.'

'And you maintain you told the Lazarus girl nothing about the people we're interested in.'

'Absolutely not,' I said emphatically. 'As far as she was concerned Wolff was the only person I was interested in.'

'And does Bryce know about these extra-curricular activities of yours?'

I wasn't sure if he meant my interest in Wolff or my interest in Lizzie. I said no anyway, whichever he meant.

'I was waiting to see what I turned up first.'

'Which hasn't been much,' said Gifford. 'The man in the park was on to you because of the Lazarus girl and your work on the Zionist terrorists. Wolff's a red herring.'

'If you put it like that,' I said.

He sat still for a minute, hands on the Wolseley's steering wheel. I felt obliged to ask if he wanted to come in for a cup of tea or something stronger. He shook his head.

'No thanks. I need to see how our search in Kensington Park is going. I should imagine our Hebrew friend is long gone by now. If he's not, he won't be in any condition to tell us much anyway.'

I opened the car door. The interior light came on and I saw Gifford raise a speculative eyebrow.

'Getting to be a habit of yours this, leaving bodies for me to clean up.'

'I didn't hit him that hard,' I said. 'Although if it had been up to me I'd have put a bullet in him. I might have done if Magdalena hadn't stopped me.'

Gifford grunted. 'As I said, smart woman.'

I got out the car and Gifford drove away. It was still only early evening and there was a light showing in the basement flat.

But I wasn't in the mood for any more company. I let myself in and climbed the stairs. The flat was cold and empty. A sudden tide of exhaustion washed over me and I lay on my bed in the dark. The events in the park played over in my head and I could see Magdalena in front of me as I pinned her to the trunk of the tree. I tried thinking about the man I'd left unconscious but mostly I thought about Magdalena; wondering if she might be thinking about me.

31

Monday, February 17th 1947

I woke in the small hours, cold as meat in a freezer. I undressed, climbed between the sheets and then lay awake until dawn. The cut on my head had dried but a bruise and swelling around my left eye prompted an unsuspected vanity that left me vacillating for the rest of Sunday whether or not to go and see Magdalena. I would have telephoned only I didn't have her number and, by the time I had made any sort of decision, it was so late in the day it seemed more sensible to wait until I saw her at the office the following morning. So I kicked my heels in the flat, catching up on my cleaning and ironing, thinking I might hear something from Gifford. But I didn't, and in the end I went to bed again, disconsolate and feeling a sense of trepidation about the morning.

When it came, I found it had not been misplaced.

I had only been in the office a minute or two when the phone rang. Magdalena was looking in concern at my bruised face while I was standing awkwardly in front of her, trying to put into words the thoughts that had been ricocheting around my head for the last twenty-four hours. The jangle of the telephone scattered the few phrases I had managed to collect. I scowled and, muttering under my breath, reached for the receiver.

'I thought you'd want to know,' Gifford said down the line. 'We got a name from those papers you took off your friend last night ...'

He paused – either for effect or to stick his pipe in his mouth – and I asked irritably, 'So what is it?'

'... Jacob Elias. We've nothing on him – that's assuming it's his real name – but you'll want to check your own files. And Abel Bryce will be over to see you.' He paused again. 'Just a word to the wise.'

I wasn't feeling very wise. I wasn't sure what I *was* feeling; more like a love-struck adolescent than anything. But the thought of Bryce coming was enough to sober me up.

'That was Gifford,' I said to Magdalena. 'The name of the bloke who tried to shoot us was Jacob Elias according to the papers he was carrying. Special Branch have nothing on him. He said Bryce is on his way, too.'

She looked bewildered. I stepped towards her just as Geraldine came in carrying the weekend's intercepts.

'Jacob Elias?' Magdalena repeated, suddenly discomposed. 'No, I don't know the name.' She turned to the girl. 'Geraldine, see if we have anything on a Jacob Elias, will you?'

Geraldine laid the intercepts on the table, took her notebook from the pocket of her dress and wrote the name down.

'Yes, Miss Marshall. Anything else?' Then she saw my face and went pale.

'Tell Mr Bryce when he arrives,' Magdalena said, 'that we'll see him upstairs please.'

Geraldine closed the door behind her and Magdalena and I stood looking at each other again.

'About last night ...' I said.

'Yes?'

'Before Gifford arrived ... we were ...?'

'About to kiss? Yes, we were.'

I took a step towards her. She glanced towards the girls' office.

'Not here,' she said.

'No, of course not. But somewhere?'

'Yes.'

A wave of relief washed over me and at that moment I didn't care a hoot that Bryce was coming to see us.

'Are you all right?' I asked.

'Yes. I didn't sleep very well.'

'No. Neither did I. I wanted to call you but like an idiot I haven't got your number.'

'Oh, I don't know,' she said, smiling at me slyly.

'That's not what I meant.'

'I know it's not. You'd better take the number now or you'll forget.'

She wrote it down and gave it to me.

'You could have asked the operator,' she said. 'You know my address.'

'I thought it might be restricted ... you know, because of what you do. I can be dense sometimes.'

'Because someone had just tried to kill you?'

'No,' I said, 'they don't shoot you for that. Not yet, anyway.'

She smiled again and I had a sudden urge to take her by the hand and run away from the office, from Geraldine and Bryce, from all the clandestine nonsense we were mired in. But I stood rooted to the spot and a moment later Lily put her head around the door and told us Abel Bryce had arrived.

He was waiting in the office where I'd seen him and Gifford a fortnight earlier. We walked in and, judging from his expression, I didn't think he had been expecting Magdalena as well. We all shook hands and sat down. He looked at my bruised eye and tutted but before he could say anything I said: 'Gifford told you what happened on Saturday night, I assume?'

Bryce nodded soberly. 'He got a name from the papers you found on the man. Jacob Elias.'

'Yes. He phoned. He didn't tell me if he found Elias himself.'

'No. Some blood in the snow, that's all. You hit him, apparently?'

I laughed. 'There was nothing apparent about it. I gave him everything I had.'

'Well,' Bryce said, as if that were neither here nor there, 'he got away. His name hasn't come up in the intercepts, I take it?'

'No,' Magdalena said. 'And nothing at all on Menachem Begin yet, either.'

'There's a rumour he's in Paris,' Bryce said. 'But it's only a rumour.'

'So what next?' I asked, feeling like a man poking a stick at a wasps' nest.

'Henry is making enquiries about the Lazarus girl. Anything you can add about that, Harry?'

'Nothing I didn't tell him,' I said.

'No. Well …' he turned his gaze to Magdalena and his rather boyish looks softened. 'And how are you feeling, Magdalena? It was quite an ordeal, I should imagine.'

'Mr Tennant took the brunt of it,' she said, glancing at me.

I wondered if I ought to put a hand to my forehead and feign faintness. But Bryce didn't seem as concerned about me as he did about Magdalena.

'Why don't you take a day or two off,' he suggested to her. 'We can manage. Just to steady the nerves.'

'They are quite steady enough, thank you Mr Bryce,' she replied primly. 'I'm in no need of time off.'

'Well, if you're sure?' He stood up and so we did as well. 'We'll pick up this Elias fellow before long, I'm sure. Just to be on the safe side, though, Henry Gifford is arranging for a man to keep an eye on your house until we do. And it will be prudent if you were to use public transport to and from work rather than walking through the park. Or we can arrange a car if you prefer?'

'The bus will do,' Magdalena said.

'Very well.'

We turned to leave.

'Harry ...? If you have a minute?'

I managed to give Magdalena's arm a small squeeze as I held the door for her, then turned back to Bryce. He was in his chair again and no longer looking boyish.

'Sit down, Harry,' he said. 'I didn't want to say anything in front of Miss Marshall, but I have to tell you, back at St James's Street they're a bit worried about your involvement with the Lazarus girl.'

I sat down, lit a cigarette and thought they were probably worried about a bit more than Lizzie.

'I didn't tell her anything that could be remotely useful,' I said through the smoke. 'It's embarrassing, I know. And I was pretty naïve, but at the time I wasn't working on this Jewish business, if you recall—'

'In some ways,' said Bryce, 'that makes it even worse. How did she know you worked here in the first place?'

'I was looking into something else at the time,' I persisted, ignoring the implication.

'Joseph Wolff.'

'Yes.'

'I told you the case was closed.'

'But not that I shouldn't ask any questions about him,' I said, still picking nits while there were any left to pick.

He gave me his wintry smile. 'I'm afraid it amounts to the same thing.'

'I'm new around here,' I reminded him. 'I didn't know that.'

I even tried smiling at him although it didn't make much impression on the gloom that had settled on his side of the desk.

'And what have you found out, exactly?'

'About Wolff? Not a lot,' I admitted.

I told him then that I'd been to see Hooper and back to Riseborough again; that Stanley had found out Wolff's brother had apparently been lost at sea near Murmansk and that in my opinion Joseph Wolff was depressed over his death. The fact that the onset of any depression seemed to have been delayed by over two years was an obvious flaw in my reasoning, but neither of us brought that up.

What I didn't tell him was that I'd been given a letter that Katja Tereshchenko had received from her sister, Oksana. And that I'd had it translated. He might have already known, of course, and if he did I thought I'd give him the opportunity to say so.

'Perhaps it was a mistake not telling you more about Wolff at the outset,' Bryce said.

'You make the rules.'

'As a matter of fact I don't, Harry. I just follow them.'

'Point taken.'

'I can see now we should have told you why we were watching him.'

He leaned forward and put his elbows on the desk. His jacket was getting worn, I noticed, and the cuffs frayed.

'Wolff was a mathematician – but you probably know that. He worked on the development of codes during the war. Based on prime number theory, I'm told, although I don't understand these things myself. Developing codes and breaking them. It was important work but of course it couldn't be acknowledged. Not at the time or since. Given the world we live in nowadays, codes are just as important as they were during the war. You understand, I'm sure.'

He waited for my acknowledgment so I nodded.

'Wolff wasn't the kind of man who minded that his work wasn't publicly recognised. He didn't seek honours and that sort of thing. Knowing he had made a contribution was enough for him. His family had come out of Russia after the 1905 revolution. They were Jews, of course – Wolfovich had been the family name. They had suffered in the pogroms by all accounts, although some family members went back after the first war. Apparently they thought things had changed. They soon fell foul of the Bolsheviks, though. It was one of the reasons why Wolff was so contemptuous of dictatorships of any stamp. He was immensely proud of our British democracy. It was enough for him to know that his contribution had helped defeat Nazi Germany and that we now oppose totalitarian Russia. We knew all about his background, of course. We also knew he was a sound man. His death was a tragedy.'

'There's no chance his brother defected, I suppose?' I asked. 'If there was family there? Wolff finding out something like that might have affected him perhaps?'

'No, I don't think there's any chance of that,' Bryce said. 'None of the family in Russia survived as far as we are aware. Samuel Wolff's death seems most likely to have been a shipboard accident. It was November, remember, and the seas in that part of the world can be pretty bad.'

'I appreciate your telling me,' I said.

'This other matter, though. Sydney Stanley and the Lazarus girl. Gifford is making enquiries but it's been decided that it's best if we didn't show our hand. Now we're on to them we're going to give them a little more rope. Jacob Elias is a different matter, of course, and we're actively looking for him. The point is, we know that they know you, and Brian feels it's probably wisest if you keep your head down for a while.'

'Brian Ogilvy?'

'Brian was handling Wolff.'

'Right,' I said. 'I wasn't aware of that.'

Ogilvy, I realised, had been something more than disingenuous when I spoke to him about Wolff. I had even told him I'd ask to see the man's file. He had feigned ignorance of the matter.

'So, what does "keeping my head down" mean, exactly?' I asked Bryce.

'Miss Marshall declined when I suggested she might like a few days off. We don't think you should decline, Harry. In fact we insist. We'd like you to take a week or so off while we await developments. Paid leave, naturally. Nothing more than that at the moment. Unfortunately you've been compromised and the DG wants time to consider our options.'

'It's gone as far as the Director General?'

'Under the circumstances Brian thought we had no choice.'

'If you think it best,' I said. 'Although we've been pretty busy with the intercepts ...'

'We know you've had a lot on your plate recently, Harry,' he said. 'You could probably do with some time off. We'll have someone stand in for you.'

He smiled. A little grimly perhaps but it signalled the end of the interview. We shook hands and he said he'd be in touch. I went back downstairs to our office. Magdalena was working on the weekend's wire and telephone taps.

'Leave of absence,' I said to her as she looked up. 'They're not taking no for an answer in my case. Bryce said they'd find someone to cover for me as far as the work goes.'

'Geraldine,' Magdalena said. 'I won't have anyone else in here.'

I grinned at her. 'I think they believe I'm a corrupting influence.'

She smiled back. 'I think they're probably right.'

I gave her hand a squeeze then took my hat and coat off the peg. 'I'll call you,' I said. 'Will that be all right?'

She regarded me intently for a moment.

'Of course,' she said.

32

Wednesday, February 19th 1947

For the rest of the day and all Tuesday I did very little except brood over Brian Ogilvy's duplicity. I had even given the man Sydney Stanley's name and business card …

I passed the time going to the pictures, sitting in a tearoom or a pub, and the evenings at home listening to the radio. I still wasn't convinced I was not being watched, particularly now I knew Ogilvy had been running Wolff's case. Jacob Elias had muddied the waters, although I was pretty certain he had not been the man in the Mountview and I wasn't yet ready to give them the benefit of the doubt. I even deliberately refrained from calling Magdalena in case they had gone as far as tapping our phones.

If they *were* watching me, though, I saw no sign of it and by Wednesday morning was ready for a change of routine.

****

I got to the Pimlico flats early in the hope of catching Hooper before he left for work. As it was, he wasn't even dressed.

When he opened the door his shoulders slumped. He pulled his dressing gown closer against the draught whistling along the corridor.

'You know what time it is?' he asked.

I slid my foot in front of the door.

'Did you get any flak from the office about not having followed Wolff to the hotel?'

'No, not a word.'

'Don't you think that's odd?'

Hooper shrugged. 'Wolff's dead. Obviously it didn't matter.'

'There was something else though, wasn't there?'

He eyed me warily. 'What do you mean?'

'Did something happen on the train? Or was it after you got off?'

Hooper glanced at his watch.

'I've got all day,' I told him. 'What happened?'

He put one of those white spidery hands to the bridge of his nose and squeezed it between his fingers, closing his eyes.

He stepped aside and I walked past him, down his hall and into the kitchen. A cup of tea stood on his table. He sat in front of it. I pulled out a chair.

'The woman at the refugee home told me Wolff was agitated,' I said. 'He wasn't making any sense when he talked to her. Was he agitated on the train?'

Hooper picked up his cup. The tea had that nasty discoloured look it gets when it goes cold. He drank it anyway.

'Not that I noticed,' he said.

'So whatever happened, happened after he got off the train? Is that what you're saying? Before he reached the refugee home.'

'Must have,' he said.

'That's a ten-minute walk.'

Our eyes met across the table. There seemed less warmth in Hooper's than there'd been in his tea.

'All right,' he sighed. 'If you must know, I think he recognised me.'

'What, realised he was being watched?'

'No,' Hooper said. 'He recognised *me.*'

'How could he do that?'

'Because I'd been detailed to watch him about ten days earlier. I know,' he said before I could ask why the same man had been sent to follow Wolff twice, 'but the man who was supposed to do the job was down with the flu. I drew some extra shifts at the last minute and someone must have buggered up the paperwork because I was put on Wolff again.'

'Didn't you tell them?'

I thought Hooper was about to laugh.

'You know we were short-handed. Everyone was running round trying to keep everything covered. Besides, I didn't know it was Wolff again till I got to Oxford to take over. The man there had the paperwork and when I realised it was Wolff, he told me it was too late to make other arrangements.'

'So what happened?'

'I kept out of his way as best I could, at the station and on the train. But when we changed at Norwich there was hardly anyone else going to Riseborough. I think he saw me on the platform but I can't be sure. Then once on the train I knew he had. He stared straight at me. I didn't let on I knew, of course, and when we got to Riseborough I made a point of walking in the other direction. He had to be going to the hotel so I thought it best if I kept my head down. After all, you were waiting for him and he hadn't seen you before, had he?'

'You told me you didn't want to miss your train back,' I said.

'Better than admitting I'd been spotted.'

'And you think that's what agitated him?'

'I don't know about agitated,' said Hooper. 'Angry, more like. I thought for a minute he was going to challenge me when we got off at Riseborough. That's why I went off in the other direction.

'So where was it you followed him before Christmas?' I asked.

'Another bloody dreary seaside town. On the south coast. Barton-on-sea, this one was.'

'What did he do there?'

'Went to visit someone. Big house on the sea front. He was there about an hour and a half. I don't know what it was about but he looked pretty grim when he came out. Certainly different from the way he was when he went in.'

'Who did he see? Did you get a name?'

'The house belonged to a Major Fairfax. I got it from the postman when he delivered the second post that afternoon.'

'And all this was in your first report, I suppose?'

'Of course,' he said, sounding indignant as if I was accusing him of withholding information.

Hooper gave me the address of the house in Barton-on-sea and all the other details he could remember, watching suspiciously as I wrote them down in my notebook.

'So what now?' he asked when I'd finished.

'Nothing now,' I said.

'It wasn't my fault,' he insisted. 'They should've put someone else on him in Riseborough. But you try to tell them that.'

****

At the flat I reread Konstantin Berezin's translation of Oksana Janowski's letter to her sister. Major Fairfax, she had written to Katja, was the officer in charge of security at Butterwick Camp and Samuel Wolff's commanding officer.

I looked out my old road atlas of Great Britain and found Barton-on-sea lay on Hampshire's coast, west of Southampton Water and midway between Lymington and Bournemouth. According to an old pre-war Bradshaw I could have taken a train from Waterloo that afternoon. That would have got me to a town called New Milton, and which wouldn't leave me too far short of my destination. But if I was in Barton more than a couple of hours it would leave only one connection back that evening. Given the current state of the railways, I didn't want to risk getting stuck overnight. The Bradshaw assured me there was an express through Southampton in the morning which would get me there by eleven.

I knew nothing much was like it had been before the war – even Bradshaw. But I trusted that if I got to Waterloo early enough I'd find something going my way.

After all, little had so far.

Something had to change soon.

33

Thursday, February 20th 1947

Sitting in my compartment on the train, wondering if the heating was going to start working any time soon, I recalled that it hadn't been much more than six months since I'd travelled south through Hampshire with my second-in-command at the war crimes unit. It had been summer then and we'd visited a POW camp in the New Forest. We'd gone to interview a young SS prisoner whose testimony had tied up the loose ends of an investigation on which we had been engaged. We had finally got to the bottom of the business even if it hadn't quite ended there – not for me personally, nor well.

Now, this current affair was also promising not to turn out well either. Listening to Bryce on Monday one might have thought he was shining a light into corners of the concern that had a bearing on why Wolff was being watched and why he drowned himself. Perhaps he had, but I hadn't been sharp enough to see it. What he had wanted to tell me was just enough to slake my curiosity, of course; enough to make me fall into line. But he hadn't told me anything I didn't know. Not beyond the fact that Wolff's wartime work involved codes and that his family had been Russian in origin. It was possible either – or perhaps both – had a bearing on events although as yet I didn't see how.

****

I had left London reasonably early although not early enough to avoid bumping into Muriel downstairs in the hall. I was about to ask if I could have my spare key back now their plumbing had been fixed when she glared at me in that way she had.

'You know we had the police round, don't you.'

It wasn't so much a question as statement of a fact universally accepted.

'Here?' I asked innocently. 'What did they want?'

'Not *here*. At Solly's office. Asking questions and turning everything upside down. They took Solly in for questioning.'

'What for?' I tried to sound surprised.

'Simply because he is Jewish. Your name was mentioned.'

'My name?'

'They were asking about that friend of yours. Elizabeth Lazarus? Remember her? They wanted to know where she lived and how well Solly and Miriam knew her. Miriam had one of her attacks.'

I said I wasn't aware Miriam had attacks.

'Anxiety attacks.'

'I'm sorry,' I said. 'How is she?'

'Better now. No thanks to you.'

'It's really nothing to do with me, Muriel,' I said, but she had already stormed out, slamming the door behind her and rattling the glass.

I might have gone down to the basement to see if Carol or Frances could tell me more, but there wasn't time if I was going to catch my train.

Not that I needed to worry. By the time I got to the station I found that all the trains were running late due to frozen tracks. Waiting on the equally freezing platform, I knew how they felt. It did give me the opportunity to consider the lack of subtlety employed by Special Branch when following up confidential leads, though. Had circumstances been different I might have complained to Gifford about his methods. Given that he and Bryce were currently complaining about mine, though, I thought best not to muddy the waters.

When the train finally arrived I found the compartment little warmer than the platform. I sat in the corner by the window, wrapped in my greatcoat and waiting for my blood to start flowing again. I hadn't brought anything with which to pass the time except that morning's paper and there wasn't much in that to warm the cockles of one's heart. Like everyone else, the newspapers were preoccupied with the weather, so I stared out the window as the city gave way to suburbs. After a while the country opened out into farmland and copse, lying under its blanket of snow, and I eventually closed my eyes and listened to the hypnotic rattle of the wheels as they ran over the rails.

I was thinking of pleasanter things. Of Magdalena, for one. I tried to picture her but unwanted obstacles kept appearing between us. Hurdles I had to jump. And the more I strove to reach her, the higher the hurdles became, until I stumbled into the last and fell on my face. Magdalena watched me impassively for a moment before turning away.

The jolt of the carriage woke me as we pulled into Southampton. It was only another half-an-hour to my destination so I gathered my coat a little tighter around me and tried to stay awake for the rest of the journey.

There wasn't much to recommend New Milton station – two platforms spanned by a bridge, a ticket office and waiting room – and there was no one to take my ticket at the gate. I walked out to the small car park that stood between the station buildings and a railway siding. A couple of coal tenders and an old carriage advertised a coal merchant's office and a man was bent over a pile of the coal, shovelling the lumps into sacks. He watched me approach, coal dust smearing his broad face and coating his leather apron.

'Barton-on-sea,' I asked. 'Marine Drive?'

He leaned on his shovel. 'Two miles. There'll be a bus. Be quicker to walk.'

He gave me directions, down Station Road to the end of the town, then right at the cinema for a mile. Marine Drive ran along the cliff top.

The town itself seemed an odd amalgam: shops on the one side of Station Road; and large houses half-hidden behind tall, snow-covered pines on the other. The cinema stood at the far end, past a pub and after the shops petered out into a few pre-war bungalows. The Waverly, as the picture-house was called, was only a small place but grand enough to boast a flight of steps up into the foyer. Glass panels either side of the steps displayed stills from the feature playing and what was showing next week. Directly opposite, I saw Barton Court Avenue, the road that led down to the coastal village and the sea.

An air of heavy somnolence hung over the place – much to do with the covering of snow, perhaps – but there was no traffic and no pedestrians once I had left the town behind. Large detached houses lined either side of Barton Court Avenue, isolated on their driveways and quiet behind curtained windows. At a crossroads I found a small parade of shops, a garage and a small café. Then the houses got bigger and gloomier, the trees that sheltered them taller, like frozen obelisks.

Marine Drive ran along the cliff front. Beyond it, the English Channel looked grey with white-edged waves. Out across the Solent the chalk cliffs and snow-covered upland of the Isle of Wight loomed out of a shrouding mist.

Standing on Marine Drive, the road appeared to stretch for several hundred yards in either direction. Hooper had given me the name of the house but as they didn't seem to go in for street numbers in this locality I saw myself having to trawl up and down until I located the place. Then I spotted a grocery delivery boy, weaving precariously over ridges of ice on his bicycle. I waved my hand and he wobbled to a halt.

'Barton Grange?' I asked.

He squinted at me, looked back over his shoulder and waved a hand to the left. 'Big place,' he said. 'Can't miss it.'

I thanked him and started towards the far end of Marine Drive. They were all big places, as far as I could see, some mathematical progression being at work, perhaps – size increasing with proximity to the sea. Value too, no doubt, although I didn't suppose it was the sort of problem Wolff would have bothered himself about. He was there to visit his brother's commanding officer and the reason was, I suspected, because after two years he had somehow discovered that the account he had been given of Samuel's death had not been the truth.

I wondered how he had felt. Barton-on-Sea might as well have been a thousand miles from Oxford and its colleges. Hooper had said it was an odd place – even odder than Riseborough. Somewhere that those who had had enough of the world might come to retire; a quiet corner where they could live in peace and die undisturbed.

Barton Grange fitted the bill. Large and dark with steep gables and deep eaves, the house hid behind heavily curtained, diamond-leaded windows. An arched oak door within a porch sat square on to the gravel drive with a deeply recessed bell-pull that gave the impression it was likely to take off the hand of anyone impertinent enough to pull it. I scowled at the thing and gave it a yank.

Somewhere deep inside I heard it toll as if it was time for vespers, but still had to wait for some time before a heavy latch was lifted and the door creaked open. I don't know what I expected –Mrs Danvers from *Rebecca* perhaps, or even Baron Frankenstein's assistant, Fritz. What I got was a small, inoffensive-looking woman in a housecoat, wiping her hands on her apron as if that was her default reaction to visitors.

'I'd like to see Major Fairfax if it's possible,' I told her.

She peered up at me as if I were a species of coastal fauna she hadn't encountered before.

'Your name, sir? And the nature of your business?'

'Captain Tennant,' I said briskly, in the hope that rank might go down well with a man who had kept the use of his own after the army. 'It's a rather sensitive matter and concerns a man formerly under the Major's command,' I added, having found that a little mystery never hurt in getting one's foot in the door.

'Very well,' she said. 'If you'll wait I'll see if the Major is in.'

He already was, of course, although rather disappointingly, instead of having me wait in the library as she might have done in *Rebecca*, the woman shut the door in my face.

Cold as well as disappointing.

I kicked my heels in the porch, trying to suppress the urge for a cigarette while waiting for Fairfax to decide whether he wanted to see me or not. Back up the drive a partial view of the Solent showed a bleak sky meeting a gray sea on an indistinct horizon.

After a minute or so the door creaked open again and the housekeeper stepped aside and allowed me in.

'This way,' she said, as if I was liable to wander off through the house on my own.

I followed her across a cavernous hallway, through a door into what was obviously Fairfax's study.

He'd spent time in Africa to judge by the artefacts that decorated his walls. I counted a mouldering cowhide shield or two hanging beside an array of ugly tribal masks that looked as if they'd take a bite out of you if you strayed too close.

On first glance Fairfax wasn't much more attractive than his masks. A big man, he wore a heavy moustache balanced by a pair of heavy eyebrows that topped-and-toed two suspicious eyes. Dressed in heavy tweeds, he was standing with his back to a fireplace. I got a glimpse of glowing coal and a lick of flame and felt like sidling up to him and turning my back on it, too. But his eyes had locked on mine and I decided to settle for just getting a foot in the door to start.

'Captain Tennant, is it?' he declaimed as if he was opening the first act at the Shaftsbury Playhouse. 'I don't know who you represent but—'

I didn't say anything. I had my Service ID to hand, thankful that Bryce hadn't thought to take the thing off me.

'Ah,' Fairfax said. 'This will be about Captain Wolff again, will it?'

He didn't sound too pleased by the fact.

'I was under the impression I had satisfied the other fellow about this business when you were here last.'

I inclined my head a little, hoping to display regret.

'I'm aware you've already been interviewed concerning Captain Wolff, Major ...' not quite the truth although it was a fair supposition that after Hooper had reported Joseph Wolff's visit B Branch would have sent someone down to find out what it was Wolff had wanted, '... but I'm afraid there are a few loose ends we'd like to tie up.'

'Loose ends?' The major's voice lifted a decibel or two, rattling the shields on the wall. 'It's been two months since the other chap was here! And it seems a bit rich having been told not to discuss the matter to find someone else altogether sent down to "tie up the loose ends" ...'

'My colleague couldn't come in person ...' I began to explain.

But Fairfax hadn't finished.

'The other fellow stressed the security implications. As if I was in the habit of talking to all and sundry about military affairs. And,' he went on, glowering at me as if I'd been the one to suggest careless talk cost lives, 'I can tell you I do not take kindly to threats from whatever quarter they issue. Any more of that and I will take up the matter with my member of parliament. Colonel Crosthwaite-Eyre is a personal friend—'

'Threats?' I managed to slip in as he drew breath. 'I can assure you, Major, there are—'

'In fact,' he interrupted, 'to be quite frank, I didn't care much for the fellow's attitude at all. Obviously not army. Desk wallah. Ogilvy his name, was it?'

'Yes Major,' I said, 'Ogilvy. And you can be assured I'll be having a word with him concerning his manner when I get back to London.' I was disproportionately pleased with myself to be speaking impertinently about Ogilvy in his absence.

Fairfax sniffed noisily, but I could tell he was now mollified having got the complaint off his chest.

'Well,' he said. 'I suppose you'd better sit down, Tennant, and state your business.'

He crossed the room and jerked a bell cord.

'You'll take coffee, I daresay? You need something to warm you up in this damnable weather. No end to it.'

'Thank you,' I said, pleased once he'd moved to get another glimpse of the fire.

Apart from Fairfax's desk chair, there was only one rather Spartan upright ladder-back in the room, discounting a single comfortable-looking armchair. I took the self-effacing option and sat in the ladder-back while Fairfax dropped into the chair behind his desk.

The housekeeper reappeared and Fairfax asked if she could bring us some coffee. Then he enquired into my war service while we waited. I gave him the potted version, ending up with my stint in war crimes before joining the Service.

'Is that what all this is about?' he asked peremptorily. 'War crimes? Rather late to be thinking about that, isn't it? Eden should have considered the possibility before committing the government to a policy of appeasement. I would have thought our dealings with Hitler before the war might have demonstrated where appeasement gets one. Besides, how do you plan to bring the Russians to book? Or is this just an exercise in sabre-rattling?'

I had no idea what he was talking about, although the last thing I wanted was for him to realise the fact.

'We're still in the process of gathering evidence,' I said vaguely. 'What will be done with it is a matter for my superiors.'

Fairfax glowered again.

'It's a matter of diplomacy,' I added, since he seemed to think the Russians were involved.

'Diplomacy?' he thundered. 'It was diplomacy that led to this deplorable policy in the first place.'

'Perhaps we can get back to Butterwick Camp and Samuel Wolff,' I suggested.

'Captain Wolff was responsible for his own actions. I made that clear to Ogilvy, although he seemed more concerned about what I had told Wolff's brother.'

'Quite so,' I said. 'We'll get to that in a moment if we may. You were in charge of the camp, I believe.'

Fairfax's bushy eyebrows knotted over the bridge of his nose.

'Security, Tennant. Only security. Look here—'

At that moment the housekeeper returned, knocking on the door and walking straight in with a tray. Fairfax swallowed whatever he was going to say and watched as she poured the coffee.

'Perhaps I should explain,' I said as soon as the door had closed behind her and before Fairfax could resume. 'Two weeks after Joseph Wolff talked to you he committed suicide.'

That made him pause and he stayed silent long enough to pick up his cup and drink his coffee.

'I don't know if his brother, Samuel, told you anything about Joseph Wolff's work,' I said, 'but he was a mathematician. I can't say any more than that he was involved in government work during the war. The manner of his death – and that of the death of his brother Samuel – means we have to conduct an enquiry.'

'Captain Wolff told me his brother was an Oxford academic, nothing more.'

I nodded, as if that were no more than I would have expected.

'Given the circumstances,' I went on, 'perhaps you'll excuse me if I cover some of the same ground you covered with Ogilvy.'

'Of course,' Fairfax said. 'Go ahead.'

'Captain Wolff was your second-in-command at Butterwick Camp,' I believe.'

'Yes.'

'And the men held in the camp were mainly Russians?'

'Russians initially. Later we were sent other nationalities well.'

'Ukrainians such as Oksana Janowski?' I suggested.

'Yes, although Mrs Janowski came up with the first detachment of detainees to arrive. They'd been captured shortly after the Normandy invasion. They were mainly workers who had been conscripted into the Todt Organisation to work on the Atlantic Wall. Mrs Janowski's husband had been the doctor attached to this particular Todt battalion. She'd had some nursing experience and after her husband died she remained with the group when the Germans retreated. Until they came to us they had been held in Kempton Park in Surrey. Russians by and large, as I say – some civilians as well as soldiers. Even a few children.'

'And Mrs Janowski acted as the camp interpreter, is that correct?'

'One of the interpreters. She spoke her native Ukrainian and also Russian. She had assisted in liaising between the authorities and the detainees at Kempton although she was not a detainee herself. My understanding is that she volunteered to remain with the Todt workers when they were transferred to Butterwick.'

'And her liaison duties meant she worked closely with Captain Wolff?'

'Once the camp began to fill up, yes. After that first detachment from Kempton Park all sorts were sent up to Butterwick. Before long we had Poles, Georgians, Ukrainians … Tartars … Even some tribesmen from further east, although God only knows what they were doing there. The point is, they were classified as Soviet citizens which was one reason they ended up at Butterwick. That's really when the trouble began.'

Fairfax paused to offer me more coffee and refill his own cup.

'Most of the new arrivals, you see, had been taken after we pushed down through Normandy. They were ROA.'

'ROA?'

I saw his brows knot.

'Russian Army of Liberation, Tennant,' he said as though I should have known. 'Those who chose to join the German army voluntarily to fight the Russians.'

'Of course,' I said. 'ROA. We find the acronyms used often differ …'

He grunted and picked up his coffee again.

'I say joined voluntarily but it was rarely as clear-cut as that. Many of those had been taken prisoner during the German invasion of Russian-occupied Poland, overrun in most cases without even time to defend themselves. The majority of their officers deserted. A great number of the rank and file were only too happy to be out of the Red Army. It was their subsequent treatment that initially persuaded most of them to join the Todt Organisation. That is assuming they had a choice, of course. Many were simply recruited as slave labour. There were others, though, and not just Russians but Poles and Ukrainians, who had no love for Stalin and took the opportunity to join the ROA. Caught between the Red Army and the Nazis, I imagine they did what they could merely to survive.'

'Tell me about the camp,' I prompted. 'You said there was trouble.'

Fairfax finished his coffee and reached for a cigarette box. He offered me one and a light from a desk lighter.

'Once other detachments began to arrive,' he said, exhaling a cloud of smoke, 'they were polled on their willingness to return to their homeland. Be it Russia or wherever. Some were unwilling although many professed to want the opportunity to resume the fight against the Nazis. Of course, one had to take this with a pinch of salt.'

'Why?'

'Those that hadn't joined the ROA,' Fairfax said, 'wanted the opportunity to display their loyalty to Russia. If only in a poll. They were worried, of course, that they'd be lumped in with the ROA men and regarded as traitors.'

'Even though they'd been forcibly conscripted into Todt?'

'Certainly. The War Office – in its wisdom – made no differentiation. They were all classified as POWs and every camp inmate was required to wear POW uniforms, regardless of their status when captured. When they got to Butterwick and saw they were all to be treated the same, many refused to put the uniforms on. The camp commander decided to take a hard line and struck their tents. He put them on bread and water, expecting them to fall in line.'

'They didn't?'

Fairfax smiled grimly. 'After what they had been through in German POW camps and under Todt, a little matter of sleeping in the open and eating bread and water was no hardship at all.'

'But the dispute was resolved?'

'When a number of the detainees expressed a wish to have their case heard by a representative of the Soviet government, the Foreign Office arranged to have General Vasiliev from the Soviet Military Mission in London to visit the camp. He had been tasked to tour other POW camps in the country to report on the conditions in which Russian nationals were being held. The Soviets were apparently accusing the Allies of mistreating detainees. Ironic, don't you think?'

'In what way do you mean?'

Fairfax stubbed his cigarette out. 'Until then Stalin hadn't given a fig for the Russian prisoners in German hands. He denied the Germans held Russian prisoners of war. Any Russian nationals subsequently found working for the Nazis he could therefore regard as traitors to the Socialist State.'

'But that's nonsense,' I said. 'Hundreds of thousands of men surrendered at Stalingrad alone.'

'Stalin never publicly accepted the fact,' Fairfax said. 'The consequence, of course, was that Russians in German hands received no help from their own government. In contravention of the Geneva Convention, I might add. But as Stalin had never signed the accord, he saw no contradiction. The German riposte was simple: if Stalin wasn't prepared to feed the POWs, they saw no reason why they should. The result was the Russian POWs suffered appalling neglect. Under these circumstances it's hardly any wonder some of them were happy to join the ROA. Those that didn't were doomed to become either slave labour in the Todt Organisation or simply starve to death.'

'And what, exactly, was Oksana Janowski's status?'

'Her husband had been a doctor and, as such, had been conscripted into the Todt Organisation. After he died she remained in her capacity as a nurse.'

'It was at Butterwick she met Captain Wolff?'

'That's correct. Part of Wolff's duties were to relay any orders I or the camp commander issued concerning the security of the camp and of the detainees. Also to address any concerns that might arise between the camp guards and the detainees which could be prejudicial to military discipline. Wolff didn't speak Russian or any of the other languages of the detainees held in the camp. Mrs Janowski proved useful to the commandant in some cases where a translator was needed, and it was only natural that Captain Wolff came to depend upon her in that regard.'

'I understand they formed an attachment,' I said. 'A romantic attachment, I mean.'

'So I believe,' Fairfax replied gruffly.

'You didn't approve?'

'I thought it neither suitable nor advisable. Wolff should have known better.' Then, to my surprise, his features relaxed. 'These things, though, are not always within our control.'

'What was your opinion of Mrs Janowski, Major?'

He shifted in his chair. 'My opinion? I found her to be a decent woman. Dependable as far as any matters of liaison between the camp officers and the detainees went … Always willing to do the best for the men in her charge. And she was popular among them. Respected. I would have to add that she was still an attractive woman. Despite what she had been through. That's neither here nor there, of course, but it might go some way to explain Captain Wolff's behaviour. Having said that,' he added after a pause, 'it was Mrs Janowski's character one came to admire most. She had opportunities to leave the camp but chose to stay in order to help those men who had been in her husband's charge. I believe she saw them as victims rather than as belligerents. Not a view universally shared, I might add.'

'Did the trouble in the camp subside once this Russian general visited the prisoners?'

'Not entirely,' said Fairfax. 'Although it was generally believed the men had requested a visit from the Soviet Military Mission, I think it was more a case that certain agitators had called most loudly for it. And, of course, the Foreign Office was eager to scotch the rumours of ill-treatment the Russians had put about.'

'Do you mean Soviet agitators?'

'In the main. Many of the captured Red Army detainees certainly had no love for Stalin, although there was also an element of old White Russians. Men rounded up by the German army after Hitler overran the continent. Their objective was to establish that they had been neither Todt workers nor ROA men, even if some of the older men from the ROA had been in the White armies during the civil war. None of these groups were as prevalent as General Vasiliev would have liked us to believe, but they were there nonetheless.'

'And you expected the situation to calm down once the detainees had seen General Vasiliev?'

'There had been rumours circulating for some time – not only at Butterwick but at some of the other camps – that all detainees were to be repatriated regardless of their status. We had been told that Vasiliev would determine who among the detainees wished to return to Russia and who did not. At the time this seemed a reasonable way to proceed. We were told that General Vasiliev would be able to give assurances as to what would happen to those among them who were apprehensive about returning.'

'What happened after General Vasiliev's visit?'

'The men were visibly cowed. Although Vasiliev didn't admit as much to us, I believe he had explained precisely what would happen to those men suspected of disloyalty once they were returned to Russia.'

'And there was no doubt in anyone's mind that that was what was going to happen?'

'On our part, none whatsoever. I wasn't aware of the details of the arrangement at the time, you understand. Other than that the Foreign Office had acceded to Stalin's demands regarding Russian nationals being returned. The only matter in dispute concerned who was a Russian national and who was not. Stalin, it turned out, wanted them all – Poles, Ukrainians, Balts … anyone, in short, who had formerly lived in the territory now under Soviet control.'

'Even though they might have left before the Soviets took control?'

'Vasiliev wasn't troubled over such niceties,' Fairfax replied.

'How did your detainees take the visit?'

'As I said, they were cowed. And not only the ROA men. They knew exactly what sort of reception they were likely to receive once they were back on Russian soil. It was those who had fallen into German hands but had done nothing to assist the Nazi war effort who began to fear the worst.

There was further unrest following the visit, a few attempts at escape and more than one suicide.'

'And then the repatriation began?'

'Vasiliev had lists of the men he regarded as Russian nationals and who he expected to be returned to Russia. When we were able to examine them, we found there were very few detainees at Butterwick who weren't on his list. One of the names on it was that of Oksana Janowski.'

'Even though she was Ukrainian and not a Russian citizen?'

'Stalin didn't recognise the distinction. She had been taken prisoner in Normandy along with the Todt workers and they expected her to be returned. She was far from being the only one. I know of camps that had similar cases. People of arguable nationality who had been caught up in the sweep.'

'The sweep?'

To judge from Fairfax's reaction, I suspected he not only regarded me as ill-prepared for the interview but had come to the conclusion that I was virtually ignorant of the matter under discussion.

I could hardly blame him. The interpreter, Berezin, had told me that Russian Todt workers had been repatriated from Butterwick although, at the time, I didn't see that the fact had any bearing on Joseph Wolff. Now, having been told by Fairfax that Oksana's name had been on General Vasiliev's list of those to be sent back to Russia, it was starting to look as if it had.

'Major,' I said before Fairfax could start asking any more awkward questions, 'I have to admit that I know very little about the repatriation of Russian prisoners. My enquiries were meant initially to attempt to establish any reason Joseph Wolff might have had to commit suicide. Russian repatriation is not something about which my department has any specific knowledge.'

'That isn't the impression I received from Ogilvy,' he countered.

'Ogilvy is on the Russian desk,' I said, trusting the terminology sounded authentic. 'And,' I added for good measure, 'operating beyond his remit.'

Fairfax grunted. I went on before he could think of anything else to say.

'It seems obvious to me now that what happened at Butterwick, specifically as it concerned Joseph Wolff's brother, had a significant bearing on his action.'

'Had I known he was likely to kill himself,' Fairfax assured me. 'I'd never have spoken to the man.'

I pulled my packet of cigarettes out. 'May I?'

Fairfax declined my offer but I lit up.

'I find it hard to believe,' I said, 'that whatever you told Wolff was the sole reason for his suicide. There must have been other factors. Am I right in saying he suspected the circumstances of his brother's death were not those he had been led to believe?'

'In part,' said Fairfax. 'He had been told his brother had been lost at sea.'

'That was the official version?'

'Yes.'

'But that's not what happened?'

'Not if my understanding is correct.'

'Am I to assume Joseph Wolff knew nothing about the repatriations either?'

'No, you're wrong there,' said Fairfax. 'He not only knew about the repatriations from Butterwick and the other detainee camps, but had been told the repatriation programme was still continuing.'

'Still? You mean there are still camps here sending Russian detainees back?'

'Not here.' He reached absently for his cigarette box. 'From camps in northern Italy and Austria. Germany, too, I believe. In the main, though, these are Cossack regiments the Nazis had organised specifically to fight the Russians. It has to be said they never opposed our men, and made a point of surrendering to the British Army when their situation appeared hopeless. Wolff maintained he had evidence that they are still in the process of being sent back to Russia.'

'Is it possible he learned this from his brother?'

'No,' Fairfax said flatly. 'I'm not saying that Captain Wolff wouldn't have given his brother some indication of who it was we were holding in Butterwick. Anything further, though, would have been a breach of security. And there is no way Captain Wolff would have been privy to information about what was happening on the continent. In any case, the repatriation of Cossacks didn't start until after Butterwick had been cleared.'

'Could he have learned anything of what was likely to happen from the detainees in Butterwick themselves?'

'That is most unlikely. The camp was always rife with rumours, it's true. But the men could never have known what was going on in Europe, or what was likely to happen. Not in the kind of detail Wolff gave me when he was here. And,' he added, flicking ash from his cigarette towards the ashtray on his desk, 'these were not rumours. Despite the deliberate attempts at obfuscation by the Foreign Office, from what I gather from Colonel Crosthwaite-Eyre, Wolff was substantially correct.'

'Under the circumstances,' I suggested, 'before we discuss exactly what it was you and Joseph Wolff spoke about, it might be helpful if you could brief me on exactly what happened at Butterwick when the repatriations began.'

Fairfax gave a small shrug.

'As you wish, although there isn't a great deal I can tell you beyond the logistics of the thing. We had some trouble getting the men on the lorries when we began clearing the camp. Regrettably some duplicity was attempted in an effort to convince them they were not about to be shipped back but it wasn't very successful. Neither was it the sort of operation on which one could keep a lid. Particularly as our detainees were some of the first to be repatriated and we had sent a number of men and women who had been held at the London Reception Centre to join them. Among these, it transpired, were a good number of expatriate Russians who had been living here since the 1920s and who had been rounded up in order to be shipped back. I imagine Stalin couldn't believe his luck.'

I remembered how Miss Patterson in Riseborough had told me of the men who had come one day for her Russian refugees. To "re-home" them, they had told her.

'Are you saying there were Russian nationals sent back regardless of who they were or how long they had been here? What on earth for?'

'Simply because Stalin asked for them,' Fairfax said. 'The vast majority would have been of no interest to him whatsoever, of course. But there were among them, no doubt, the odd Tsarist officer or aristocrat he might have had a grudge against.'

'But surely the Foreign Office hadn't agreed to send these people back?'

Fairfax stared at me long and hard.

'As I told you earlier, Tennant. The Foreign Office had agreed to *all* Stalin's demands. Joseph Wolff informed me that Anthony Eden had attended a conference in Moscow in 1944 where he had given the Russians all they had asked for. It was confirmed the following year at the Yalta conference. The ostensible motive for agreeing to Russian demands was an apparent concern for Allied personnel who had fallen into Soviet hands. The Red Army had taken many German POW camps as they had advanced west. Eden and the Foreign Office maintained Stalin might not facilitate their return unless we acceded to his demands.'

'From what I've heard,' I said, 'the Russians did very little "facilitating" at all. They opened the prisoner of war camps and expected the prisoners to fend for themselves.'

I had met a few of these men passing through Berlin in 1945, ragged and hungry from having to walk from camps further east. By then they were indistinguishable from the general mass of displaced persons washing to and fro across Europe.

'So I understand,' said Fairfax. 'But that didn't cut much ice with the Foreign Office. Eden had given Stalin his assurances and we were expected to comply. As far as those at the sharp end were concerned – the men housing and guarding the detainees – we were expected to obey our orders.'

I was acutely aware that of late, that phrase had assumed a hollow ring.

'And the change of government at the election made no difference?' I asked. 'After all Eden was no longer Foreign Secretary.'

'Not according to Joseph Wolff. I can't be sure but I suspect he may have received his information from a source within the Labour Party. The Foreign Office had given their word, though, and the new Foreign Secretary was prevailed upon to honour the agreement.'

That was Ernie Bevin, who I'd always regarded as a decent chap. As far as politicians went. Then, I supposed politicians only went as far as the next pragmatic decision.

'The Foreign Office was well aware,' said Fairfax, 'that some of the men held in the camps might resist being returned and issued orders that we were to provide armed escorts to prevent any escapes. Our brigadier wasn't keen and suggested that General Vasiliev should supply his own men for guard duty. In the end we provided the escort from the camp to the port of embarkation alongside Vasiliev's men.'

'How did Captain Wolff take the fact that Oksana Janowski was on the list for repatriation?'

'Not well,' Fairfax said. 'We went through channels, naturally. The commander of the camp relayed his concern to his superior officer. The fact that Mrs Janowski was a Ukrainian married to a Pole seemed sound ground for petitioning the Foreign Office. Unfortunately the petition was dismissed. It was understood that everyone on General Vasiliev's list was to be put aboard the transport ship and that there were to be no exceptions.

The ships were available and waiting and it was made plain there was no time for argument.'

'So she was taken with the others?'

'We entrained for Liverpool at the end of October along with Russian representatives from the military mission. It was then it became clear to us that there had been a small number of NKVD among the detainees.'

'Secret police?'

'Yes. Somehow it had been arranged to have them planted in Butterwick in advance of Vasiliev's tour of inspection. In that way they knew who they wanted returned before he even arrived. What I don't believe they expected was that the Foreign Office was willing to give them everyone they asked for. As soon as they realised that, or course, they simply asked for everyone.'

'None of this is common knowledge is it, Major?'

'That our government kowtowed to the Russians and gave into every demand Stalin made of us? No, it is not. Nor do the Foreign Office want it to become so. They feared public opinion would be against it at the time and rightly so. This country has always had a reputation as a safe haven for the oppressed and persecuted. Orders were issued that the operation was to be conducted with as much secrecy as possible. Given what we heard later about what happened to the people we sent back, it comes as no surprise that they wanted to keep it quiet.'

'The ship was the *Scythia*, wasn't it?'

'That's correct. Once at Liverpool and the men embarked, our responsibility was supposed to be at an end. Vasiliev's men were to take over.'

'But Captain Wolff was aboard the *Scythia*?'

'A request was made on behalf of the *Scythia*'s captain that a small detachment of our men accompany the ship to Murmansk. He was concerned about security. He didn't trust either the detainees or the Russians from the Military Mission who were guarding them. Captain Wolff volunteered to command the detachment.

'Needless to say,' Fairfax added, 'had I any idea of what he was going to do, I would never have allowed him to board.'

34

Friday, February 21st 1947

It came as no surprise when, back at the station, I was told my return train was delayed. I should have been grateful it was running at all. Many of the lines in the north were still blocked by snow. But gratitude was the last thing on my mind as I got back to Broadley Street. The place was an icehouse. I lit the fire and put the kettle on to boil, subconsciously still missing those telltale signs that one of the girls from the basement had been up to use the bath – the trace of scent or of face cream in the air; condensation beading the windows … the shade of a wraith having passed through leaving nothing behind but its aura.

Over a cup of tea, I sat munching stale biscuits still going over what Major Fairfax had told me of the *Scythia*'s arrival in Murmansk. He had had the story from the men in Samuel Wolff's detachment and from what they had gathered from crewmembers of the *Scythia*.

After being disembarked, the detainees had been stripped of all the new clothing and supplies issued them in Butterwick. Once everything they brought with them had been piled on the quayside, they were ordered to put on the few inadequate rags that were waiting for them. Then they stood in ranks while the names on Vasiliev's lists were called, separated into groups and marched to a nearby collection of sheds and warehouses.

A few minutes later machine gun fire was heard. The NKVD men who had escorted the men on the *Scythia* then returned to sort through the clothing and supplies left on the quay.

'I won't give you the names of the men from whom I got the story,' Fairfax had told me. 'As far as your office is concerned, anything you have learned, you learned from me. The Foreign Office obviously wishes to keep this business quiet. Especially in light of the fact, as I learned from Captain Wolff's brother, that the repatriations are still ongoing.'

I hadn't argued with him. I wasn't sure how much sympathy I had with Cossacks who had joined the Nazi cause. And, the way things were going, very soon I doubted I'd be in any position to use the Service's resources even if I had wanted to track down demobbed FSS personnel or members of the Merchant Marine.

I didn't really need their testimony. The jigsaw was falling into place, even if I still didn't know exactly what had happened to Samuel Wolff.

But then, neither did Fairfax.

No one on the *Scythia* had seen the FSS captain get off the ship, but neither did they find him on it. When they had made a search of the *Scythia* the second lieutenant with whom Wolff shared a small cabin found his uniform in a locker, neatly folded with everything present except his army revolver.

As I listened to Fairfax, I couldn't help remembering Samuel's brother's clothes as I had found them on the stony beach at Riseborough – jacket and coat, trousers and shirt tidily folded; those good Oxford brogues left neatly side by side, the toes pointing like a clue at the cold North Sea.

But Samuel had left no clues. In the confusion of their arrival and disembarkation and the forming-up of the *Scythia*'s human cargo on the quay, no one had noticed his absence. It wasn't until the machine gun fire alerted the *Scythia*'s captain and the FSS men that something untoward was happening that anyone noticed that Captain Wolff was missing. A quick search of the ship was conducted and representation made to the port authorities. They maintained they knew nothing. The NKVD who had been in charge of the disembarkation and were on the point of entraining out of the city those remaining detainees who were ever going to leave Murmansk, listened but would not allow the FSS detachment to search the port. They took a cursory look around themselves and came to the conclusion that Captain Wolff could not have left the ship. And if he wasn't on the *Scythia*, they could only suggest that he must have jumped off before it reached Murmansk.

The evidence of his uniform in his cabin may have suggested suicide although the second lieutenant with whom he shared would not accept that explanation. Oksana Janowski had been seen on the quay earlier, lined up with the Butterwick men, and he thought Wolff might have gone ashore with her in a uniform borrowed from one of the detainees. If unable to protect her, he suggested, then ready to share her fate.

But there was no proof to substantiate the speculation. No detainee was found on board whose place Wolff might have taken in the lines of disembarking men. The captain of the *Scythia* protested again, consulted with the Allied Naval Mission in Murmansk and then, reluctantly, had been forced to sail.

By the time the *Scythia* reached Liverpool, Wolff had been entered in the ship's log as lost at sea.

A ship-board accident and the story his brother Joseph had been given.

****

It was too late in the evening to telephone Magdalena so I turned on the radio. I'd missed the serialisation of *Beau Geste* they were running earlier in the evening and the Home Service was now broadcasting excerpts of Lupino Lane in *Sweetheart Mine*. I wasn't in the mood for musical comedy, though, and tuned to the Light Programme instead. This turned out to be *By Gaslight and Hansom*, songs from a Victorian London that no longer existed.

On Friday evenings, I usually listened to Ernest Dudley's *Armchair Detective*, a programme that previewed crime and mystery fiction, dramatising small excerpts in the hope, I suppose, of hooking the audience. But this was Thursday evening and I had my own mystery with a plot that made Dudley's offerings seem no more than pale puzzles by comparison. So I went to bed, Fairfax's story and the puzzle of what had happened to the Wolff brothers still rattling around in my head.

The piece of the jigsaw with which I was left, that of Joseph Wolff's reaction to what he'd learned about his brother's fate, still didn't fit neatly with what Hooper had told me. I lay thinking about it until I finally fell asleep, finding in the morning that, unlike Ernest Dudley's characters, the solution hadn't conveniently come to me while I slept.

I almost telephoned Magdalena, to catch her before she left for the office. With the creeping pre-dawn light, though, I felt a sense of paranoia steal over me as well. I'd always been suspicious of how much Bryce and Gifford might be capable. Now that I knew of Ogilvy's involvement and understood from Fairfax the lengths to which the Foreign Office would go to keep the general public in ignorance of the Russian repatriations – particularly as, according to Fairfax, they were still happening – I looked on every telephone as a source of a potential tap. Perhaps it was simply the nature of the work Magdalena and I had been doing, or the fact that I'd been followed and some Irgun gunman had tried to kill me, but I had a sense there were very few people I could trust.

Magdalena was in the habit of catching a number 16 or 36 from Edgware Road if she took the bus. On the assumption she was still following

Bryce's stricture to take public transport rather than walk across the park, after a quick wash I swallowed a cup of tea and hurried off in the hope of catching her.

The streets were still slick with ice from the overnight frost and the few people who had to be up and around were trudging along like the dispirited workers in Fritz Lang's *Metropolis*. By the time I reached the bus stop there was already a queue, one man bundled in coat and hat clapping his hands and stamping his feet like some demented Cossack dancer the Foreign Office had overlooked.

Magdalena wasn't there so I got in line and waited as the different buses edged their way along the road, pulled carefully to a halt and waited while their frozen passengers climbed aboard.

I couldn't remember the last time the temperature had climbed above freezing. According to the forecast, it wasn't likely to do so any time soon. Lost in my thoughts I didn't see Magdalena until she appeared beside me.

'What are you doing here? You should have telephoned.'

'I wanted to see you,' I said. 'Besides, I wasn't sure about the telephone … Just in case.'

'Silly. You needn't have said anything.'

'I know. But as far as they know we're just colleagues.'

'And are we more?' she asked, slipping her arm through mine.

I looked into her face, pale and pinched with cold.

'I'd like to think so.'

She squeezed my arm. A number 16 bus came and we shuffled in behind those boarding. We took the stairs on to the top deck. It wasn't any warmer up there but it seemed more private. We sat side by side and I took her gloved hand between my own, rubbing it to get the numbness out of her fingers.

'So what have you been doing?' she asked.

I didn't want to go into it on the bus so I just said I'd been to see Samuel Wolff's commanding officer at Butterwick.

'What did he tell you?'

'He doesn't know what happened to Wolff but it doesn't look as if he went overboard.'

'What do you think happened to him then?'

'Not here,' I said. 'Can you get away lunchtime?'

'I'll try. Where do you want to meet?'

'What about the Lyons tearoom on Kensington High Street?'

The bus turned into Park Lane. We were sitting near the front and I looked over my shoulder at the passengers sitting behind us. They were just ordinary people with ordinary faces, staring out the misted windows at the street below. I couldn't help wondering, though, if any had been on my train the previous day. Or waiting with me on platforms.

'Who are you looking for?' Magdalena asked. 'You don't still think you're being followed, do you?'

'I don't know,' I said.

'You're getting paranoid, Harry.' Her gloved fingers stroked my cheek. 'The man in Kensington Gardens was a Jewish terrorist. He's hardly likely to try again. Not now we know who he is.'

'No, you're right,' I said. 'It's just that talking to Fairfax has made me jumpy.'

'Who's Fairfax?'

'The man I went to see. Wolff's commanding officer.'

'What did he say?'

'That Ogilvy had been to see him.'

'*Ogilvy*?'

The couple in the seat opposite turned our way.

'Sorry,' she said, whispering. 'Why did Ogilvy go to see him?'

'I'll tell you all about it at lunchtime,' I said and changed the subject. I asked how things were in the office.

'We're even busier now,' she said. 'There's been a lot of traffic this week and Abel Bryce keeps popping in to see what we're turning up.'

'Are you sure it's only that? Has he mentioned me?'

'No, not a word.'

'What about Ogilvy?'

'What about him?'

'He hasn't been in, has he? He knows about the Lazarus girl. I thought he might turn up to stick his tuppenny-worth in.'

'The *Lazarus* girl?' Magdalena repeated wryly.

'Lizzie, then,' I said, uncomfortable talking about her with Magdalena. 'Have you got any more help yet?' I asked.

Magdalena smiled at my discomfort. 'Geraldine is helping me with the intercepts. She's a quick learner. I've got one of the other girls to work with Lily.'

We were almost at Magdalena's stop on Piccadilly, by Hyde Park Corner. She had to change for Kensington Road.

'I won't come any further,' I told her. 'I'll see you at lunchtime.'

She stood up and I followed her down the stairs. I took a seat on the lower deck as she stepped off, watching those who had come down behind us.

Magdalena had already started walking away when a man who had followed us down from the upper deck hesitated before getting off. For a second our eyes met. He looked away quickly and stepped off the bus, taking the opposite direction to Magdalena. As the bus pulled past him, I looked down. He was walking quickly, head bent. He didn't look up.

****

I bought some groceries on the way back to the flat and made myself something to eat. After I cleared away, I picked up Oksana's letter to her sister and Berezin's translation and slipped them both into my pocket.

I took the Tube back to Kensington and walked around for a while, ostensibly looking in shop windows while trying to catch the reflection of anyone I thought might be tailing me. The only conclusion I came to was that there was a gap in the market for window cleaners.

It was still early when I got to the Lyons tearooms and found it was now one of the new self-service shops. Something else the Yanks had left behind for us when they'd decamped back to Butte Montana or Tallahassee, or wherever else they'd come from. I queued with my tray at the counter and bought a cup of tea and nursed it until Magdalena arrived.

She was uncharacteristically late and looked flustered. 'Sorry,' she said. 'A bit of a flap on for some reason. Bryce was there again going back over some of this week's intercepts.'

'Has something happened?'

'No. Not that we've been told.' She smiled. 'It can't be anything to do with you, Harry. You're too suspicious.'

I asked if she wanted anything to eat.

'I don't have time. Just tea, please.'

The self-service queue had grown and it was five minutes before I got back to the table with a fresh pot and two slices of sponge cake.

'Tell me about yesterday,' Magdalena said as soon as I sat down.

I outlined what had happened as she poured the tea. I told her I had got Fairfax's address from Hooper; how Joseph Wolff had recognised him in Riseborough because Hooper had been assigned to watch him when Wolff visited Fairfax.

'Well,' she said, 'that at least rules out the fact that whatever this Major Fairfax told Wolff, it could not have been the reason he was followed to Riseborough. Not if Hooper had already been assigned to watch him.'

'No, you're right. Wolff must have already aroused someone's interest. And if I'm right, I think I know what it might have been.'

'Because they thought his brother had defected?'

'I think he did, although not in the sense you mean. I don't know what Bryce and Ogilvy believed, but someone was certainly concerned about Joseph Wolff.'

'Isn't that what you said Bryce told you in the first place?'

'Yes,' I said, 'it was. Although I'm not sure if Bryce meant it in the way I understood. Whichever, I got hold of the wrong end of the stick.'

'What are you going to do now?'

'I'm not sure. Before I do anything, though, I'm going back to see Konstantin Berezin.'

'The translator?'

'I got the impression he knew more about what was happening at Butterwick than he wanted to tell me. Not just Butterwick but the other camps, too. I keep remembering what he said to me as I left. "The big secret," he said. I didn't understand then. I'm beginning to now.'

Magdalena stood up. 'Sorry, but I'll have to fly. If Bryce is still around he might wonder where I've got to and start putting two and two together.'

I started to get up but she reached across the table and laid her hand on my arm.

'We'd better not leave together,' she said, then smiled again. 'Now you've got me half-believing it.'

I watched Magdalena as she walked out the door and finished the tea in the pot to give her plenty of time to reach the bus stop. I was pretty sure no one had been on my tail that morning but it crossed my mind that someone might think it clever to follow Magdalena instead.

I studied the people leaving the tearoom. After five minutes when I hadn't see anyone I thought fitted the bill, I relaxed. Then I realised there wouldn't be much point in following her *out*. They would assume she was going back to the office anyway.

I glanced around casually and wondered if Magdalena wasn't right and that I *was* paranoid. People had been coming and going all morning and the place was busier now than it had been when I arrived. Most of the customers were couples or larger parties. Except for me and a few single women. The only man I could see on his own was sitting at a table at the back of the room. He had a pot of tea in front of him and a notebook on the table in which he was writing. So I wouldn't have to turn around to see him, I tried to catch his reflection in the mirror above the self-service counter. But the angle was wrong and I lost patience.

'Paranoia,' I muttered to myself. I stood up and dropped a threepenny-bit by the teapot as a tip for the girl who cleared the table.

I left the tearoom and stepped out on to the freezing pavement. I wrapped my greatcoat closer round me and turned up the collar.

I thought how Joseph Wolff might have had cause to be paranoid. He was being followed and realised it when he recognised Hooper in Riseborough. Wolff had been regarded as a threat, but what sort of threat was I? Even Jacob Elias's attempt to kill me hadn't been because of any danger I posed. That had been no more than an act of terror. Besides, if Bryce or Ogilvy wanted to know how much *I* knew they could pick me up anytime and sweat it out of me.

Paranoia? Who did I think I was?

****

The afternoon light was fading by the time I came out of the Tube station at Dollis Hill. I turned into Randall Avenue, past the bombsites. They were barely noticeable anymore, so used to them had we all become. Like lost memories, even the gaps left between the buildings seemed to be healing over. Filled by rubbish and softened under snow, detritus was beginning to mask the missing.

The old house where Berezin had his rooms appeared gloomier than ever. Gaunt and forbidding, it resembled a mental depression sculpted in brick and mortar. There were no lights at any of the windows and from the street those in the attic flat were out of sight. I assumed Berezin would still be at work but I climbed up the dark stairs to the top of the house anyway. There was no bulb under the grimy shade on the upper landing and I almost had to feel my way to Berezin's door. The house was silent below me and my knock reverberated in the vacuum like an unwanted intrusion. I waited until the house swallowed the sound then knocked again.

In the deep gloom I saw the door had no cylinder lock, only a handle and tenon lock. I might have knocked again but instead tried the handle. The door opened.

I called Berezin's name but the flat was as silent as the rest of the house. I closed the door softly behind me and flicked on the light switch. I half expected the aroma of incense again but there was nothing more than the faint smell of an old meal clinging to the freezing air. I peered into Berezin's sitting room and bedroom, then into his kitchen. The meal I could smell, some kind of porridge, still stood in a bowl on the table, half-eaten. The chair in front of it was lying on its side. I set it straight and touched my hand against the bowl.

It was as cold as I felt.

A pot of tea and a half-filled mug stood beside it, both ice cold. In the sink a dinner plate and cutlery lay in water gone grey and greasy. I looked around the kitchen again then went back to Berezin's bedroom. The bed had been made and was tidy although the door to a wardrobe lay ajar. The few clothes hanging on the rail and in a drawer beneath had the look of having been sorted through. Nothing else seemed out of place.

The sitting room was as it had been when I was there last. With the absent exception of the vodka bottle. Back in the kitchen I looked into Berezin's bin and found a few small bones and a lump of gristle, the discarded scrapings of a meal. I pulled the dinner plate out of the sink and examined it. A smear of what might once had been stew still ringed the rim.

It had been a long time since I had last looked around a crime scene. And then it had only been on sufferance, allowed to voice unlikely surmises for the amusement of the investigating detective. But I'd picked up the rudiments and I'd have laid an each-way bet that the unwashed dinner plate had held Berezin's evening meal; that the half-eaten porridge on the table had been the following morning's breakfast.

He had been interrupted, that was plain enough, and had been allowed neither to finish his meal nor to return. How long he had been gone I could only guess. If it had been summer, flies and their maggots might have pointed the way. But it was the coldest winter in living memory and flies with any sense had flown south for the sun long ago.

For a second, the sudden thought that earlier that morning I had told Magdalena I was going to see Berezin stopped me cold. I froze on the spot, then immediately felt ashamed of myself.

Berezin had been gone for a couple of days, at least, I thought. Even, perhaps, as much as a week.

I turned out the light and closed the door behind me. Berezin had no neighbours in the attic I might ask, and I imagined those on the floor below would have seen little and profess to know less.

I looked at my watch as I let myself out of the house. It had just gone five o'clock. Walking back to the station at Dollis Hill, I squeezed myself into the first telephone box I came to. I dialled the number of our office, gave my name to the girl on the switchboard and asked for our extension and to be put through to Magdalena Marshall.

It was a risk but Bryce had only told me to take the rest of the week off. As far as I knew, that would be all the girls on the switchboard would know, too.

'Mr Tennant,' Magdalena said, in that detached way she had at work; the way it had taken me some while to get past. 'This is Magdalena Marshall. What can I do for you?'

'It's just an administrative matter, Miss Marshall,' I replied, playing the game. 'The fellow I spoke to you about recently. A matter of language if you recall ...?'

'I think so,' said Magdalena. 'Is there a problem?'

'It's probably nothing. But you couldn't check his file for me, could you? His present status and such ...?'

'Of course. Shall I ring you back?'

'No,' I said. 'No need. Next time we speak.'

I replaced the receiver, pressed button B out of habit and got nothing back. Which was my usual habit. I pushed my way out of the kiosk, hunched my shoulders against the cold and thrust my hands deeper into the pockets of my greatcoat.

A risk, yes, but somehow I doubted I'd get the opportunity to examine the Service personnel files again. And even if the girl on the switchboard had been listening she would not have been surprised by the arcane nature of the conversation. Precaution was our bread and butter and, while using an outside line, circumspection was a method constantly hammered into us by circulated memoranda, wall posters and incessant word of mouth.

****

I had two hours to kill. Back at Dollis Hill station I took the Tube to Oxford Circus and began walking. Under the intermittent lighting and away from the shops, there was little to dispel the darkness. Like an opaque fog, the gloom had also begun to worm its way inside my head. Walking, I found, would often clear it, but this time the shadows refused to part. Nor was I sure I wanted to see past them if they did.

I believed I had finally come to understand why Joseph Wolff had killed himself.

It hadn't been the death of his brother. He had lived with that knowledge for more than two years, even if the circumstances of Samuel's death had not been those he had been led to believe. He had discovered the truth from Fairfax – at least as much of it as Fairfax knew – but I believed Wolff still might have lived with those new facts had he not attempted to do something about them.

Any evidence of what he had already done had, I assumed, been removed by the time I looked over his Oxford rooms. I couldn't be sure, but thought it likely that his brother Samuel had written him from Butterwick Camp telling him something of what was happening there; and certainly – as evidenced by his letter to Katja Tereshchenko – Samuel had written about his relationship with Oksana Janowski. What I couldn't be certain about was whether it was Samuel who had first raised Wolff's concerns about the Russian repatriations.

Whatever the answer to the question was, it was clear he had already been making waves – and waves sufficiently large to warrant Ogilvy, or whoever controlled him, having Wolff watched by the time he visited Fairfax.

These concerns, I suspected, tipped into anger when, on the train to Riseborough, he discovered he was being followed. But it was only after he arrived and spoke to Miss Patterson that his anger became shock. Shock and an overwhelming sense of betrayal.

He had begun to say as much in the unfinished note he had left in his hotel room.

It was something I now knew with a certainty I couldn't dismiss. I had witnessed the detached, listless way Wolff had behaved at the hotel. But mostly I knew how Wolff had felt because some small part of that sense of Wolff's desolation had begun to descend upon myself.

I recalled what I had been thinking on those cliffs at Riseborough. How, if the day ever came when I would want to put an end to myself, I would not choose freezing water. How I would just as soon take the bite of the razor. Well, had I been a man of Wolff's sensibilities, that day might now have come. But, walking those dark pavements, snow and ice and frozen faces unseen all around me, I realised I was not that man.

I had done what he had, only with less excuse. Wolff had asked questions and put wheels in motion without ever comprehending the result. I should have known better. The clues were there, I just hadn't read them correctly.

So, in the end, as with Wolff so with me. We were both culpable. Only Wolff's culpability lay in innocence; I was culpable through negligence.

****

I had been hanging around the entrance to Archery Close for the best part of an hour trying not to look furtive before I saw Magdalena turn the corner. She faltered when she saw me skulking in the shadows then must have recognised me. She quickened her pace and I went to meet her.

'You look frozen,' she said. 'I thought you might telephone again.'

I took her arm and we crossed the road towards her house.

'I didn't want to risk it,' I said. 'I thought it best to meet you.'

She peered at me, her face pale under the dim streetlight. 'Still paranoid?'

'That's what I told myself earlier. Now I'm beginning to think there's a reason to be.'

'What's happened?'

'Did you look at Berezin's file?'

'They've let him go,' she said.

I thought how innocuous that sounded. Almost as if Berezin had be detained against his will and now justice had been served by his release.

'What you mean,' I said, 'is that he doesn't work for us anymore.'

She pressed against me. 'I suppose so. "Employment terminated" had been stamped on his file.'

'I hope it was just his employment,' I said. 'Any severance pay?'

'I didn't look at his pay.'

'I don't suppose it matters. He won't be needing money where he's going.'

'Where is he going?'

We reached her door and she took her key from her bag.

'His flat is empty. He left in a hurry.'

'Why would he do that?'

'I don't think he had any choice,' I said.

Magdalena closed the door behind us. I saw the table at one end of the sitting room had been laid for two, wine glasses and napkins standing by empty plates.

'Expecting company?'

'Jane Archer,' Magdalena said, pulling off her gloves. 'I asked her round for supper. Do you mind?'

She stood by the table with her coat on, still looking pinched and cold but now worried as well.

'Why should I mind?'

'It won't be much but I can stretch it for three if you want to stay.'

I smiled at her gently, despite everything still able to feel touched.

'Better not,' I said. 'I know she's your friend and you trust her ... Even so, I think we ought not to tell her what's happening.'

'What *is* happening?'

'When are you expecting her?'

Magdalena glanced at the clock on her mantle. 'Not for another half hour.'

'Then give me a drink. I'll leave before she arrives.'

Magdalena took off her coat and mixed the drinks while I lit the fire that had already been laid in the grate. The kindling crackled as the paper flared. As it caught, I placed a lump of coal in the heart of the flames. Magdalena passed me my drink and we stood together watching the fire grow. She preferred a gin and tonic water to rum when she got in from work, I had discovered. I was past caring what was in my glass, as long as it was strong.

She took my hand and drew me down on to the settee. 'Tell me what's happened, Harry.'

I sat beside her, watching the reflection of the fire dance in my glass before I spoke.

'I told you Wolff went to see his brother's commanding officer at Butterwick Camp. Major Fairfax. I don't know how much Wolff knew before he spoke to Fairfax but he must have known there was something wrong with the story he'd been given about his brother's death. I suspect his brother had written from Butterwick hinting about what was going to happen. Samuel couldn't have told him what he was going to do, though. Whatever Major Fairfax told him came as a surprise. Then he got the letter from Katja, delayed because it had been badly addressed and – I suspect – because it had been intercepted. They must have been reading his mail by then or they wouldn't have known anything about Katja. Wolff replied and said he would come to Riseborough after Christmas.'

'If they were already having him watched and were worried about who he was seeing,' Magdalena asked, 'why did they deliver Katja's letter? If Wolff had never got it, he'd be none the wiser about Oksana having a sister in England.'

'No, but it's like the postal intercepts we deal with,' I said. 'They're opened and copied then sent on as quickly as they can be. Those that do the copying aren't authorised to pick and choose which should be delivered. Gaps in correspondence can soon start to look suspicious.'

'And it was Hooper again who followed Wolff to Riseborough?'

'Because B6 were short-handed. Which was why I was there. Only this time Wolff recognised Hooper on the train from his visit to Fairfax. Perhaps Wolff was already getting suspicious, I don't know, but it was the kind of world he worked in during the war. He knew only too well how Intelligence Services work. And Hooper was sure he'd been spotted. It's why he didn't follow Wolff all the way to the refugee home. Hooper said Wolff appeared angry. To find out he was being spied on, on top of what he'd learned from Fairfax, must have infuriated him. He must have already been on the edge. What he found out from Miss Patterson was enough to tip him over.'

'What did he find out?'

'You have to remember he already knew we were forcibly repatriating Russian prisoners of war from Butterwick—'

'Forcibly?'

'Certainly. Most of them didn't want to go back. They knew Stalin saw them as traitors to the motherland. Several had already killed themselves rather than be sent back.'

'But why traitors? The Germans had used them as slave labour. It's not as though they had any choice.'

'That's not how Stalin looks at it,' I said. 'He holds the same view that Hitler had – soldiers don't surrender or allow themselves to be captured. Anyone who does is regarded as a traitor. Those Russians who volunteered to fight in Hitler's Russian Army of Liberation knew full well they'd be shot out of hand as soon as they returned. The Todt workers thought they'd either suffer the same fate or be sent to some Arctic labour camp. Whichever way, they were still going to die. Only in the camps it would take a little longer and be more painful.'

'What about Wolff's brother?'

'He'd fallen in love with Katja Tereshchenko's sister, Oksana. But her name was on the list of those to be repatriated so we sent her back, too. Even though she wasn't Russian and hadn't been a Todt worker. She'd been a nurse. But whoever made the decisions in the Foreign Office didn't care. Stalin had demanded we send him everyone he claimed as a Russian citizen and that included as many Ukrainians and anyone else he could lay his hands on. We didn't argue. Anthony Eden and the rest of the gutless wonders at the Foreign Office agreed to whatever he wanted.'

'And Samuel Wolff?'

'I can't be sure,' I said. 'Perhaps he thought it was some bureaucratic mix-up and they wouldn't go through with it. Otherwise why wouldn't he try to get her away from Butterwick? Maybe by the time he realised his mistake it was too late. I think he either changed places with one of the Russians or just joined the queue as they filed off the ship. Just so he could be with Oksana. What happened to them afterwards is anyone's guess.'

Magdalena shivered and I put my arm around her.

'I don't know when we started watching Joseph Wolff. Perhaps after he'd been told about the repatriations he started asking questions about his brother. Someone who knew what was happening must have given him information. Someone in the Labour government, perhaps. After all, Wolff had done important work during the war. He must have had contacts. What he didn't know – or perhaps didn't care about – was that the Foreign Office was trying to keep the whole operation secret. They were scared of what the British public might think of them doing Stalin's dirty work for him. I suppose it's one thing having those who guard the camp inmates knowing what's going on. They're soldiers and subject to military discipline. They have to follow orders. It's quite another to have a man like Wolff asking awkward questions and perhaps alerting influential people.

'I suppose they started watching Wolff to find out how much he knew. Particularly when he started asking questions about his brother's death. Wolff was just the sort of man to make a fuss and go public. If he found out that we were assisting a ruthless dictator murder tens of thousands of innocent people ... Shooting some and shipping the rest off to labour camps to be worked to death? It all has a rather familiar ring to it, doesn't it?'

'Yes,' Magdalena replied sombrely. 'It does.'

'Wolff had spent his war doing what he could to defeat the Nazi machine. Hitler had enslaved those he could squeeze a few months' work out of before they died, and shot or gassed those he couldn't. Especially if they were Jews like Wolff himself. Imagine how he felt when he discovered our government – the government he'd worked for – was helping Stalin do precisely the same thing to Russian ex-prisoners of war. And not only POWs but probably to Wolff's own brother. Simply because

Sam had followed the woman he loved into captivity. I think he must have felt betrayed. He left an unfinished note saying as much.'

'But he didn't publicise it, did he? He went to Riseborough and killed himself.'

'I don't think that was his intention. Not until he spoke to Miss Patterson at the refugee home. When he finally got the letter from Katja Tereshchenko that had been delayed because she'd used a vague address for him, he decided to go to Riseborough to see her. He wanted to tell her what had happened to her sister. Then he recognised Hooper and became aware he was being followed. Being watched by the secret police, just the way they used to do in Germany, and are still doing in Russia ... being treated like a man who wasn't trusted – treated as if he was a traitor. A traitor to the very country he'd served during the war.'

The room had begun to warm but I hadn't taken my coat off. I still felt chilled to the bone.

'Perhaps he'd wanted to find out more about Oksana,' I said. 'Perhaps he was gathering as many facts as he could before he did anything about it. I don't know. They knew he was going to Riseborough to see Katja Tereshchenko, of course, because we were intercepting his mail. It's what we do, after all. What Wolff didn't know was that they'd taken Katja before he got there. Poor sick Katja who was probably going to die anyway, and they took her away and sent her to Russia the way they'd already sent tens of thousands of others before her. And are still sending if Fairfax is right. Shipping them back to Stalin and his waiting NKVD. Feeding them to his goons. Perhaps Katja was lucky and died before she got there.'

I went to take another mouthful of my drink and found I'd already finished it.

'I think *that's* why Wolff killed himself,' I told Magdalena. 'He'd discovered his own government – the people he'd worked for to defeat a monstrous dictatorship – were hand-in-glove with another monster. One just as brutal and just as ruthless. But I think what really killed him – just as certainly as walking into the North Sea did – was his realisation that it had been his decision to visit Katja Tereshchenko that had persuaded them to take her.

'She was only a Ukrainian refugee, after all. It must have seemed an easy solution to them – have her shipped back like the rest of the flotsam they'd herded into camps. Just to avoid Wolff meeting her. And of course when

Wolff found out, he knew better than most what it meant. That it was a death sentence for her. She had died because he was going to meet her. *That*, I think, was the last straw. The final blow. I don't suppose by then he was thinking too clearly. He certainly looked like a man in a daze when I saw him. He must have felt a sense of guilt. Perhaps he was afraid that anyone he approached would suffer the same fate. Because of him.'

'Are you sure?' Magdalena asked. 'Are you sure that's what happened? Do you really believe our own people are capable of doing something like that?'

I didn't doubt that for a minute. That's what having the power of life and death does – it gives people the desire to use it.

'I think they're capable of it,' I said. 'Those that made the policy – Eden and the rest of the Foreign Office lackeys – they make their decisions in their comfortable offices, holding their comfortable assumptions. Most of the time they have one eye on their own position, their advancement. They don't care to see the damage they do on the human scale. Like Pontius Pilate they can wash their hands of it if it gets messy. They get their minions to do the dirty work. That way they can still sleep at night.'

Minions like us in our not-so-comfortable offices, I thought. Men like Ogilvy and Bryce. And me. But I didn't say it. Not to Magdalena. She had to work beside them.

I stood up.

'What are you going to do?' she asked.

'I've no idea,' I said truthfully. 'They've been one step ahead of me all the way. They've done to me what they did to Wolff.'

'What do you mean?'

'Don't you see? They got rid of Berezin. I involved him and they got rid of him. If he's not dead now he will be soon … a few weeks … a few months. Once he's back in Russia. It doesn't matter to them that he left the place shortly after the Revolution. After all, he's not the only one they've sent back who had nothing to do with the war, who has been here for years. And Stalin doesn't care. He's got a long memory and anyone who left Russia rather than suffer the Bolshevik's tender mercies is fodder for his labour camps. He wants them all. He'll take Berezin and be glad to get his hands on him. And that means Berezin is a dead man. Dead because of me.'

'Surely not,' Magdalena said. 'Would we send him back to Russia knowing what he knows about us? He's worked for us for years.'

It was something I'd already considered during that long walk to Archery Close. I doubted it had made any difference.

'What does he know?' I asked her. 'Privy to some disjointed translations? Can remember a few names? It's not as if he's got any documents to give them. And can you imagine how many of those poor devils facing a bullet or the labour camps try to save their lives with stories about what they supposedly know? I doubt the NKVD even bother to listen.'

Magdalena was looking at me with alarm. But I couldn't stop myself from twisting the knife.

'Or maybe you're right,' I said coldly. 'We won't send him back. Maybe we'll shoot him ourselves and save Stalin the bullet.'

Her expression turned from alarm to desolation and I hated myself for bringing pain back into those eyes.

'Stay and talk to Jane,' she said. 'Jane will know what to do.'

'I can't involve her,' I said. 'I'll have to work it out for myself.'

What I meant was: Jane Archer was one of them and I couldn't trust her any more than I could trust Bryce or Ogilvy.

'Can you meet me tomorrow?' I asked.

'Of course.' She put her arms around me and pulled me close. We kissed. 'Here?' she asked.

'No. I don't want them to see us together. Not out of the office anyway. And don't tell me I'm paranoid. Not now. They are the paranoid ones. Terrified that people will discover their dirty little secrets.'

'Don't, Harry. Let's meet tomorrow. Somewhere where it's light and there are people around us who don't know anything about it. What about the Mountview again?'

'Is this a date?' I asked, trying to smile.

'Why not?' she said. 'Tea? Four o'clock?'

I kissed her, wishing Jane Archer wasn't about to arrive.

'Tomorrow,' I said then slipped out of the front door.

Crossing the street past the bombed-out shell of the terrace, I saw someone at the corner. Jane Archer, I thought. Or one of Gifford's men detailed to watch Magdalena's house.

I pulled my collar up and, head down, walked swiftly past on the other side of the road.

35

Saturday, February 22nd 1947

I suppose we had all got used to the weather by then. The traffic on Oxford Street might still be skidding and slithering about like oversize curling stones but we'd all learned not to step off the kerb if there was anything within fifty feet of us.

We were used to ice and slush and frozen pipes and accustomed to even the prettiest of girls looking like pixies with their red noses and pinched faces. But none of it seemed to stop people going out.

I found the Mountview already crowded. The windows were steamed up and the trapped moist air inside was redolent of tea and cake. Most of the tables were already taken and it took me a few minutes to find a vacant one.

It was almost four and since Magdalena was always as prompt as a doctor's bill, I ordered a pot of tea and some cakes before she arrived. I'd recently been considering doctors and the fact that their bills would soon be a thing of the past. We were to have a National Health Service and all medical treatment was to be free. I wasn't sure I completely believed it – in my experience nothing came free. One way or another we were going to pay for it although, to listen to the complaints of some doctors, you'd think they were the ones expected to foot the bill.

No doubt Aneurin Bevan planned to squeeze the money out of the wealthy and the privileged classes and I wished him luck. My father-in-law would have had plenty to say on the subject. The thought of it would probably have brought on a fit of apoplexy if a heart attack hadn't already killed him. I almost wished he was still around just so I might witness his reaction. But that would have been vindictive and one mustn't think ill of the dead, apparently, so instead I took some vicarious pleasure in imagining what Brian Ogilvy thought of the matter. Another cudgel to berate the Labour Government with, no doubt.

Deep in meditation I didn't see Magdalena until she was standing over the table. Her arrival coincided with the tea and cakes so we got straight to it.

'You've ordered,' she said as the waiter held her chair and she sat down. 'Hungry?'

'Rather. I didn't have lunch.'

She had taken off her hat and coat and unwound her scarf and was working on her gloves, finger by finger. The temperature outside had given her cheeks a healthy glow and I was struck again at how beautiful she was. Even those doleful eyes now seem to hold a spark. Expectation, was it? I hoped it had something to do with me. How could I have ever found her intimidating?

'What?' she said. 'What are you smiling at?'

'Am I? I was just thinking how you used to scare me to death.'

She laughed and put her hand on mine. 'Ridiculous. It's good to see you're in a brighter frame of mind today.' She turned in her chair and looked round the room. 'Who's watching us today?'

'You're cruel,' I said, refraining from telling her I hadn't spotted him yet. 'How did your supper with Jane Archer go?'

'Fine,' Magdalena said, pouring the tea. 'And I didn't tell her anything, in case you're wondering. She heard what happened after we left her last Saturday, of course. She wanted to know all about it.'

I helped myself to a cake. 'You told her?'

'I could hardly pretend it was a secret, could I? Not with Jane.'

'I suppose not. What did she make of it?'

'Much the same as Superintendent Gifford. That this Jacob Elias wanted to kill you because of the work we're doing. I didn't mention your involvement with the Lazarus girl, naturally.'

'Decent of you,' I said, po-faced.

She stared at me a second as if I meant it. Then she laughed.

'Stop it.'

'I don't suppose Mrs Archer swallowed it, did she? I'm not important enough to warrant my own assassin.'

'You're too modest.'

'Hardly. My light's so deep under the bushel we're back in the blackout.'

'Self-effacement doesn't suit you, Harry.'

'Now you're beginning to sound like my mother,' I said.

She threw me an inquiring look. 'I'm assuming you don't mean that.'

I put some cake in my mouth to stop myself asking her what *she* meant. I was determined not to rush things. I didn't want to do anything precipitate that might offend Magdalena's sensibilities. The problem was I had no idea what sensibilities Magdalena possessed. It had taken some time but I'd finally understood what I could and could not say to my wife, Penny. Even if, in the end the lesson hadn't mattered. In many ways Penny had a far shallower personality than Magdalena. I wasn't demeaning Penny in thinking this – it wasn't any particular defect in Penny's character, rather an appreciation that there was more depth to Magdalena's nature. Of what it consisted, I didn't exactly know. The scars of having lost a man she loved at the beginning of the war were there, but how deep their effects ran I couldn't guess. Nor the sense of inadequacy she had felt in having been found wanting by SOE. Whatever it was, while I had always felt that a blunder committed with Penny was never beyond repair, I suspected an affront against Magdalena would be irrevocable.

We talked inconsequentially for a while and she asked when I was coming back to the office.

'Monday, I suppose. Bryce said take the week off, not don't come back. No doubt he'll want to give me another talking to. In his rather bashful way, that is. Ogilvy, too, I shouldn't wonder.'

'Do you think so?'

'I'm almost sure of it. I've been interfering in his operation. He was the one behind Wolff being watched. And it was Ogilvy who went to see Fairfax after Wolff visited him. And tried to scare him off with the Official Secrets Act. Luckily Fairfax doesn't scare easily. I suppose he was only acting under someone else's orders but it must have been Ogilvy who organised the men who came for Katja. Berezin, too, probably.'

'I've always thought there was something unpleasant about Brian Ogilvy,' Magdalena said.

'That's just your natural good taste,' I assured her. 'Has anyone said anything to suggest I might not be coming back?'

'Not to me. But I'm wondering if I ought to ask for a transfer to another office.'

'Why? I thought we were getting on rather well.'

'That just it. Is it wise to work together if we get involved'

'Are we involved?'

'Aren't we?'

'One of us ought to make up our mind,' I said. 'I hope that's what's happening.'

I wanted to be alone with her but felt apprehensive about suggesting she come back to my flat.

When we finished our tea I signalled the waiter for the bill. It was still too early for a drink but the cinemas were open and I suggested a film. It was always dark enough there to pretend it was just the two of you alone together.

Odd Man Out with James Mason was playing at the Odeon Leicester Square, with Mason as an IRA gunman, which brought back a few memories I'd rather have forgotten. But Magdalena wanted to see it and the film wasn't really the point. We climbed the vertiginous steps to the back of the circle and sat together in the dark, shoulder to shoulder and holding hands like a pair of adolescents. Below us on the screen Mason and Robert Newton played through their scenes, inhabiting not the usual glossily sophisticated world of film where everyone knew that everything would turn out all right by the end of the last reel, but a world peopled by terrorists and security agents and police informers. An altogether greyer and grittier world and one closer to the world we ourselves inhabited.

After it had finished and we were back on the street, instead of the usual sense of buoyancy that seeing a film gave – that feeling that, at bottom, all was fundamentally well with the world – I felt the gloom descend upon me again.

Like Mason – I felt trapped in a world I no longer believed in, cornered by people I no longer trusted.

Magdalena sensed my mood and suggested we stop for a drink.

'You're a mind-reader,' I told her and we found a pub off Oxford Street where we could get out of the cold.

Magdalena squeezed herself into the corner of a settle and asked for a rum.

'Your father wasn't once a chaplain to the navy by any chance?' I asked when I came back with the drinks. 'Did he sit in the Lords?'

'Why do you ask?'

'I like to know the kind of circles I'm moving in.'

'No, you're safe enough,' she said. 'My father had no interest in politics.'

'Other-worldly?'

'I wouldn't say that,' she replied, sipping at her rum and giving me a sideways glance. 'Are you thinking about me?'

'I'm always thinking about you,' I said.

'I slept with my fiancé, if that's what you were wondering.'

It was although I would never have admitted it.

'We wanted to and it seemed pointless to wait,' she said. 'Things being what they were. I'm glad of it, the ways things turned out.'

'And since?' I asked, although it was none of my business.

'There have been a couple of men. After Tony died. That was his name, Anthony Sheffield. They were more a reaction to Tony's death than because I cared anything for them. I prefer not to think of them now.'

'And where on the spectrum might I fall?' I dared to ask.

She smiled at me. 'You're still a moving target.'

'Perhaps you'll let me know when I come to rest,' I said.

'I will,' she said, finishing her drink. 'I'll have another, then perhaps you'll take me home.'

'Archery Close?'

'I was thinking more of your home,' she replied holding out her empty glass. 'After all, I can see no reason to wait. Things being what they are. Can you?'

****

Any lingering warmth left in the flat from earlier had long since dissipated. I lit the gas fire and nervously tidied the kitchen while Magdalena looked around. There were a few books on my shelf but most of my reading material lay in the pile of newspapers and magazines stacked by my chair. Beyond these and the mess the kitchen, it occurred to me there was nothing of much relevance to *my* character. There were no photographs or pictures on the walls; no possessions that spoke overtly of me. I'd owned a few things before the war that had either got lost or wound up with Penny and my mother in the west country. I had acquired very little since. My old flat in Cowcross Street had not been the sort of place one was predisposed to make homely. I thought how my bedroom must look much the same as my sitting room. My clothes had an air of things picked up in a shop run by the St Vincent de Paul Society, their only connection to me being their lack of care and general nondescript appearance.

I was acutely conscious of all this because the bedroom was where I found Magdalena after I had finished messing around in the kitchen.

She had turned on the light and drawn the curtains.

I stood in the doorway. 'The sheets are clean,' I said stupidly.

'You're the mind-reader,' she said.

Then everything seemed to happen so naturally. We came together, not in any animal rush but with care, undressing slowly as if every moment was to be savoured. I watched as Magdalena slipped out of her skirt and unbuttoned her blouse. She glanced at me a little shyly and I turned out the light so that she became a shadowy figure moving in the reflection of the gas fire in the sitting room.

In bed she flinched under my cold hands. Her skin to me felt like fire. I muttered something and smothered her reply with my lips as she came to me.

****

Like so many other times before I didn't hear the key turn in the door.

It was the light springing on that startled me.

Magdalena stiffened beneath me and as I turned I was blinded by a flash of light.

I experienced an unthinking moment of *déjà vu*. Though it wasn't Bryce photographing a body on the floor as it had been the previous summer.

It was someone else altogether.

I rolled off Magdalena, got tangled in the sheet and blankets and fell out of the narrow bed. Magdalena, with the bedclothes having been pulled off her, was sitting up trying to shield her nakedness.

The flashlight popped again as I struggled free of the blankets and stood up. The someone else by the door with a camera in his hand was the man who had watched Magdalena and I from another table in the Mountview on her birthday. He was the man on the bus; someone I'd begun to see everywhere.

The oddest thing though, unaccountable to me at that moment, was that Muriel was standing beside him.

There was a look of triumph on her face that disappeared as the flashbulb popped a third time and I saw nothing except a sunburst on my retinas.

Blind and cursing, I struggled across the room. I could see enough to smash my fist into his mouth then winced with pain as he tried to protect himself with his camera. Skinning my knuckles on the thing, it skidded from his grip on to the floor.

Then I had him by the hair, ramming his head against the wall. When he finally stopped struggling I punched him as hard as I could in the stomach.

Someone screamed – Muriel or Magdalena – but I didn't care. The man went down and I kicked him. But I was naked, without shoes, and I felt my toe break as it connected.

I might have kicked him again regardless, had Magdalena not pulled me off. Just as naked as I was, she was pulling and shouting my name, if with a different imperative to the one she'd been using only moments before.

Muriel scuttled away and the man on the floor moaned a bit. He got on to his knees and wiped the blood from his mouth.

'No need for this ...' he was saying through his swelling lips, 'I'm just doin' m'job ...'

I was breathing hard but the rage had passed. I didn't know where it had come from. Lying in abeyance the last few days, waiting for an outlet I supposed.

The outlet was on his feet now, glancing at me warily. He bent down and picked up his camera.

'Just a job,' he said again.

And now, spent, I knew that's all my paranoia had added up to: just a job. I hadn't been watched and followed because I'd been getting too close to some shameful state secret; he was there because of my own procrastination over hiring him – or someone like him ...

Penny had got tired of waiting and had done it herself. She wanted a divorce and needed evidence. Now she had it, only it was Magdalena on the bed in the photo with me, not some convenient tart for hire who'd do the job for ten bob and not worry about her reputation.

I turned aghast to Magdalena but she was already dressed and moving towards the door. Stark naked I watched as she and the private detective struggled through it together then came up short as Muriel appeared again, this time with a policeman in tow.

Since the saying goes "you can never find one when you want one", I suppose the converse must be true, although where she had found him at such short notice I had no idea. Sheltering from the wind in a doorway, probably. *I* may not have wanted him but he looked glad to be inside out of the cold and I could tell he meant to make the most of the situation.

I turned away and pulled on my shirt and trousers. By the time I looked back it was just the copper, Muriel and the detective. Magdalena had gone.

36

Sunday, February 23rd 1947

I spent Saturday night in the cells.

It wouldn't have happened if I hadn't had another go at the detective. I wanted him arrested for breaking and entering, but since nothing was broken except my toe and he'd entered with the key I'd never got back from Muriel and the girls in the basement, there wasn't much of a case to be made. He countered with a charge of assault and battery – easier to prove given his mouth and my knuckles – and, after a shouting match in which I tried to fatten his other lip, I was frog-marched down to the local nick.

They let me telephone Gifford. He listened patiently on the other end of the line and assured me he'd sort everything out. I suppose he did as they released me in the morning. He had taken his time, though, and it occurred to me he'd probably thought it fun to let them keep me overnight.

He dropped by the flat Sunday afternoon and I limped painfully round the kitchen making tea while he watched lugubriously from the table.

'Still sore?'

'I think it's broken.'

'Not much you can do with a broken toe,' he said. 'Tape it up.'

'I asked to see a doctor,' I said.

'On a Sunday?'

'It was Saturday night.'

'Well,' Gifford said, 'you remember what it's like. Saturday night you get the drunks and the brawls ...'

I put the pot on the table between us, gave it a stir and let it brew.

'What did you tell them?'

He looked mildly surprised. 'Tell them? I didn't tell them anything. Just to let you out.'

'What about the detective?'

'I'll let your lot handle him,' he said. 'I don't suppose you'll hear any more once he finds out who he's dealing with.'

'What about the photos?'

'That's up to you,' he said.

After he left I taped my toes together and went down to the basement. Frances answered the door, grinned knowingly and stepped aside without a word. Muriel and Carol were in the sitting room huddled over their fire.

'What do you want?' Muriel demanded.

'My key for one thing,' I told her.

'I'll get it,' said Frances who was watching from the doorway. 'And don't blame Harry,' she called back over her shoulder. 'I don't suppose it was his fault.'

'What was my fault?'

'You don't even know, do you?' said Muriel.

'Please, Mu,' said Carol.

'Know what? All I know is you set a private detective on me.'

'Me?' Muriel said. 'That was your wife. I'm talking about those men who raided Solly's office.'

'What's that got to do with me?' I asked as if I didn't know the answer.

I assumed Gifford's men had been their usual ham-fisted selves.

Muriel glowered at me. 'Because they were asking about that tart you brought to Miriam's party. Now they've raided Miriam's flat. Just because she's Jewish ...'

She put a protective arm around Carol who, for some reason I didn't understand had begun to sob.

Frances came back with my key. 'Thanks for letting us use your water, Harry. Some of us appreciate it.'

Muriel scowled at her sister who just shook her head. 'Get over it, Mu,' she said. Then turned to me. 'Miriam flew into one of her rages and sacked Carol.'

'What for?'

'Because it was Carol who asked you and your friend to her party.'

'That's hardly Carol's fault,' I said, adding, as if it made any difference, 'We were only there an hour or two. Why would they bother Miriam?'

Frances looked at her sister again. 'You want to tell him or shall I, Mu?' Muriel just glared at her. 'Miriam had a fling with her,' Frances explained. 'Your girlfriend, I mean. Sorry if you didn't know, Harry, but that's Miriam all over. Ever the opportunist. The way she takes advantage of some of those girls ... She deserves all she gets.'

Down the corridor the doorbell rang.

'That'll be Bertram,' Frances said. 'Thank God my taste runs to men.' She gave me that sardonic look of hers, said, 'Bye, Harry,' and left with a wave.

I turned back to the two sitting on the settee; the sobbing, unemployed Carol and the disgruntled Muriel. Then I followed Frances out. I might have stayed and asked Muriel how the detective had got on to her, but it was easy enough to work out. He'd been watching me, and they lived in the basement flat. I'd have made their acquaintance if it had been me on the job. And given Muriel's dislike of me, it didn't take too much imagination to suppose that, after the raid on Solly's office and Miriam's flat, Muriel was only too eager to help him.

Back upstairs I dithered for a while between telephoning Magdalena or calling round to see her.

In the end I did neither.

37

Monday, February 24th 1947

All Bryce had said was take the week off, so on Monday morning I saw no reason not to go into the office. I was feeling a little apprehensive about facing Magdalena and wished I'd telephoned her on Sunday. I imagined she had been embarrassed by what had happened – even humiliated given the man had taken photographs – although I didn't think that being caught *in flagrante delicto* was too outlandish a situation to get over for a girl who had trained under SOE. After all, it didn't compare with being half-drowned in a tub of filthy water, having her fingernails pulled, or any of the other tricks the Gestapo had been known for.

But I hadn't called her and she hadn't called me and when I finally hobbled into the office at my usual time I found she wasn't there. Instead Geraldine was sitting at Magdalena's desk and Lily at mine. Their expressions gave nothing away beyond a mild surprise at my appearance. Although, as neither enquired as to why I was limping, or asked how my week off had gone, I was inclined to suspect that word of what had happened had got out. Lily stood up, smiled sweetly and began clearing her papers. Magdalena, she said, had been called over to the St James's HQ. Geraldine, already at work on the weekend's intercepts, had barely paused to say good morning.

Lily ran through some of the relevant developments from the previous week for me then retired to her own office. There had still been no trace of Menachem Begin although at that moment he wasn't uppermost in my mind. I sat down and shuffled a few papers around and, ignoring Geraldine, smoked until half an hour later the telephone rang in Lily's office and she put her head round the door.

I was needed for a meeting upstairs at noon sharp.

****

I assumed they'd send Bryce over to tear another strip off me and prepared myself to swallow one more lecture from him. It would be unpalatable although, given his diffident way of doing things, not entirely indigestible, so I was as sharp as Lily suggested I should be and ready to take my medicine.

But it wasn't Bryce. It was Brian Ogilvy.

And he wasn't sharp at all. By the time he finally arrived at twelve-thirty, I'd filled the ashtray with cigarette butts and familiarised myself with the view of a snowy Hyde Park through the one window.

'Well,' he began without preamble, 'this is all a bit of a mess.'

As it didn't sound like a question and I wasn't sure which mess he was referring to, I didn't reply.

He sat at the desk and motioned me into the chair opposite. Taking out his gold cigarette case, he tamped the end of a cigarette before lighting up, then eyed me through the resultant smoke.

Not for the first time, I noticed the distinctive aroma of the brand Ogilvy smoked – something Sherlock Holmes could have identified in a heartbeat, no doubt, giving the region where the crop had been grown as well as the Christian name of the farmer who had harvested it, probably. I wasn't that good, nor that interested. So I merely breathed the stuff second-hand until he was ready to continue.

'Henry Gifford tells me you were attacked in the park by one of the Irgun rabble last week. They got on to you through some little Jewish tart you've been seeing? Magdalena Marshall was with you, he said. And now it seems you've got her involved in another scandal.'

So far as I could see there was only the one scandal and I said, stretching a point: 'Gifford told me he'd keep the matter quiet.'

Ogilvy raised a supercilious eyebrow.

'The man had been hired by your wife, I'm told. Perhaps you should have done the decent thing and given her a divorce when she first asked for one. Instead of letting her set that fellow on you?'

'I assume you're not talking about the Irgun still.'

It didn't surprise me in the least that Ogilvy knew all about my private affairs. But it didn't stop me resenting the fact.

The eyebrow lost its supercilious air and joined its companion in a scowl.

'Special Branch wasn't formed to pull your fat out of the fire, Harry.'

'I was thinking more of Magdalena than myself,' I said.

'A bit late for gallantry, isn't it?'

'There were some photographs.'

Ogilvy smiled unpleasantly. 'You don't have to worry about the photographs. That's been taken care of.'

'You've destroyed them?'

But Ogilvy didn't choose to answer. He sucked on his cigarette again and opened a file he'd brought with him.

'Another matter,' he said. 'You found a letter that Joseph Wolff wrote to the Ukrainian woman, Katja Tereshchenko. Would you care to tell me why you didn't share this piece of information with us?'

I wondered how he knew that. I'd not told Bryce or Gifford. Berezin knew and I supposed they must have sweated it out of him.

'Bryce told me the case on Wolff was closed,' I said. 'That since he was dead our interest in him had ceased.'

'But not yours apparently,' he replied pithily. 'It didn't occur to you that the letter might have been relevant whether Wolff was dead or not?'

I shrugged. 'As no one thought fit to tell me anything much about Wolff, I was hardly in a position to judge its relevance.'

Ogilvy let a stream of smoke drift between us in the chill air, regarding me just as coldly.

'Judging its relevance was not your concern. And what makes you suppose you should have been told more than you were?'

'I was put on the case,' I said.

'You were told to watch the man. Nothing more.'

'Which is what I did.'

'And yet you didn't mention the letter.'

'I didn't have it then.'

'No. Apparently you went back to Riseborough. Without orders. Not only that, you took your Jewish tart with you. Compromising our operations.'

'Lizzie Lazarus may be many things,' I said, 'but she's not a tart.'

'A terrorist?'

'An accomplice of one it seems,' I agreed.

Ogilvy cleared his throat with obvious dissatisfaction.

'It didn't occur to you the girl was a plant?'

'No.'

'Rather naïve of you, wouldn't you say?'

'I think I'd already been that,' I said. 'Telling you I couldn't find Wolff's file. You had it all the time, I assume.'

'It was none of your business,' he said. 'You should have dropped it then. As it is, you've meddled in one operation that is none of your concern and compromised another for which you are responsible.'

That seemed a fair summary. He'd obviously got everything about my going back to Riseborough from Gifford or Bryce and that I'd used Berezin to translate Katja's letter from Oksana. I wasn't sure he knew I'd been to see Hooper again, though. Or Fairfax, and that Fairfax had told me what had happened to Wolff's brother.

I didn't suppose Ogilvy could arrange to dispose of Fairfax with the ease with which he had got rid of Katja and Berezin, but I wasn't going to give him the opportunity to try. Or a motive for sacking Hooper.

'It's probably only fair to warn you that I think it was Sydney Stanley who put Lizzie Lazarus on me,' I said. 'You remember Stanley? I gave you his card when you asked me about those government leaks. Did you speak to him at all?'

I must have touched a nerve because Ogilvy's expression turned as black as a coal cellar.

'What are you suggesting?'

'Nothing at all,' I said. 'By the way, what happened to Konstantin Berezin?'

'Who?'

'Berezin. The translator. Did you arrange to have him sacked? Is he on his way back to Russia like Katja Tereshchenko? Or did she die before you could get her out the country?'

Ogilvy's eyes narrowed. 'You're out of your depth, Tennant.'

'They were harmless,' I said. 'I suppose Wolff could have made things awkward for you if he told anyone what he knew about the deportations from Butterwick. But what could a sick Ukrainian girl and a Russian émigré do?'

'You're meddling in political decisions and government policy that has nothing to do with you,' Ogilvy snapped. 'The Security Service is a non-political organisation.'

'Unless you can find something it can pin on Manny Shinwell?' I suggested.

For a moment I thought I had pushed him too far. But Ogilvy wasn't the kind who lost his self-possession. At least, not in front of the likes of me.

'Do you think you can coerce me, Tennant? You know nothing.'

'I know the repatriation of men to Russia is still going on,' I said. 'It doesn't bother you what happens to the people you're helping to send back?'

Ogilvy looked genuinely perplexed.

'Why on earth should it bother me? These were men who collaborated with the Germans. After what we've been through why should any of us care what happens to them?'

'And those innocent of any collaboration? The ones who've been caught up in your net. Like Katja Tereshchenko and her sister? Like Berezin who's been here for twenty-five years and working for us?'

Ogilvy waved a hand as if swatting at a fly.

'What do they matter? There are bigger things at stake than the fate of a few refugees. Open your eyes, Tennant. We've got Russia breathing down our necks now. We don't have the luxury of standing on our principles. We have to come to an accommodation with Stalin or risk another war. Do you think the Americans baulked at sending back Russian nationals?'

I didn't know anything about the Americans repatriating Russian nationals – whether they had baulked at it or had complied as willingly as Anthony Eden had. All I knew was that the Foreign Office and the rest of our former government hadn't baulked. Any more than out present Labour government was *baulking*. I wondered why the whole thing stank so badly to me when it didn't seem to offend anyone else's nostrils any more than Ogilvy's brand of cigarettes did.

'So what happens now?' I asked. 'Do I get shipped east, too?'

'Don't be so melodramatic. You don't know enough to be a problem. You'll resign. In fact your resignation has already been accepted. With immediate effect. Personal circumstances will be the reason given and you're to have a month's salary in lieu. But you will cease to have any contact with Service personnel forthwith. If you try to contact anyone, Gifford has been given instructions on how to deal with you. Any questions?'

'Those photographs?' I said again, concerned what Ogilvy might do having that sort of thing in his possession.

'They are safe,' Ogilvy assured me, a little of his former superciliousness returning. 'You won't have to worry about them, Tennant.'

He closed the file and stood up. 'I'll save you the embarrassment of being escorted from the building. But don't take too long about collecting your effects, there's a good chap.'

38

Friday, June 6th 1947

I don't know if anyone has ever thought of drawing up a profit and loss account of our having the Yanks here during the war. I don't mean their part in winning it, but more the social effect. I had heard there'd been a lot of disgruntled talk between 1942 and June of 1944 when most of them had shipped out across the channel. Sour grapes, probably, from men who saw the heads of girls they had always taken for granted as their own – girls from humdrum towns like Barnsley and Bolton and Bideford – turned by the exotic strangers hailing from outlandishly named places like Dallas and Detroit and Des Moines. All those faraway places they had only heard of at the pictures. And then there was all that wonderful food from the PX and the chocolate and the nylons …

I hadn't been around to experience it, of course. I knew nothing of the PX and wouldn't have had a lot of use for a pair of nylons in North Africa. Although the odd bar of chocolate wouldn't have gone amiss.

On the profit side there would be the things they had left behind. Their slang, for example, even if a lot of it had already become common currency through those same movies. I only mention it now because it was one warm day in June, the third anniversary of the D-Day landings as it happens, and three months after I walked away from Ogilvy and the Prince's Gate office, when – in the Yanks' parlance – the shit hit the fan.

****

I was about to leave for work when there was a knock at my door. I was working for Jack, because I had needed a job and because Jack was the only person ready to offer me one. The generous "month in lieu" Ogilvy told me I would get from the Service, I soon found, had started from the day Bryce had told me to go home. I spent a week or so after that considering whether I ought to apply for the police again, but I was already in my thirties and had never got beyond uniformed constable the first time. I'd been commissioned in the army, of course, but was hardly alone in that – walk into any suburban golf club and you can find ex-officers still clinging to their rank like it was the last lifeboat on the *Titanic*.

"Meeting and greeting", Jack called the work – taking care of those clients he thought might appreciate dealing with someone from the "officer class". Jack's phrase, not mine. And, if they did appreciate it, I suspected it was only so they might persuade themselves that Jack's business wasn't quite as shady as we all knew it really was.

Opening the door I wasn't hugely surprised to find Henry Gifford and Abel Bryce standing in the corridor. I hadn't seen either since I'd been sacked from the Security Service although I had rather expected I might. Ever since Ogilvy's murder the previous March.

'Hello, Harry,' said Bryce, blinking like an owl who'd woken up prematurely and found it was still daylight.

Gifford remained expressionless – if one didn't count the usual look he wore of having seen it all before.

I gave them a grin. It rarely works in awkward situations but usually makes me feel better.

'I always thought the secret police knocked on doors before dawn,' I said. 'Do I need to call a solicitor?'

'That depends what you've been doing,' said Gifford.

I let them in and took them into the kitchen.

'As a matter of fact,' I said, 'I was just off to work.'

Gifford glanced at his watch. 'For Jack Hibbert? I'd save myself the journey if I was you. My men are raiding his premises just about now.'

I stared at him but I could tell he was serious. I took a deep breath and dropped into a chair. Bryce and Gifford looked down at me curiously as if I were an exhibit in a glass case, then each pulled out a chair of their own.

'We're not after your old corporal,' Gifford explained. 'Just putting a little pressure on someone else. Herding him in the direction we want, you might say. Although it wouldn't hurt to let Hibbert know he's been sailing a little too close to the wind lately.'

'You know he'll think I arranged the raid,' I said.

Gifford nodded. 'Probably.'

I felt another door close on me. Or gate, perhaps, herding *me* so that the avenues that remained open only led somewhere I had no wish to go.

Like cattle to the slaughterhouse, I thought.

But things weren't that bad. Not yet. I was just feeling morose and not a little guilty about Jack.

It was a pity. Some might have found it humiliating working for a former subordinate although I didn't mind. It made a change from working in an office and I got to get out and travel around a bit. And for once it looked as if we were going to get a decent summer. Then, after the winter we'd just been through, I suppose any weather that didn't involve snow and ice looked decent. Nor had I anything better to do when Jack offered me the job.

I had finally made arrangements for my divorce, even if it would still be a year before the decree was granted. A weekend away in Brighton had nailed down all the messy details – the very things I had been avoiding but finally handed over to a private detective whose bread and butter was arranging that sort of thing. He found the hotel room and the girl – even provided a pack of playing cards and cribbage board for us to pass the time until the appointed hour when the maid let the detective in along with a photographer to capture the moment for posterity. We put the cards and crib board out of sight and posed for a couple of candid shots, then I put my hand in my pocket and paid all concerned.

If it had a ring of familiarity about it, it lacked the spontaneity of my first appearance in the part. Nor was the girl Magdalena, or the maid Muriel. The detective, needless to say, hadn't been the one who'd been dogging my footsteps back in February.

'So,' I finally asked Gifford, 'who are you after if it's not Jack? Or is that sort of information only for the cognoscenti?'

I had assumed it was me, of course. A feeling reinforced when Gifford glanced at Bryce who smiled ruefully and said: 'Well that's why we're here, Harry.'

I had read the previous March about Ogilvy's murder in the newspaper and assumed it would only be a matter of time before someone would think of me. Robbery, the papers had said, and although none of the reports had gone into detail – his position in the Security Service probably limiting what they were able to print – Ogilvy being who he was did result in one paper devoting an opinion piece to the upward trend in criminal violence and the rise in gun crime. It was all blamed on the war, naturally – everyone's favourite scapegoat for anything they didn't care about in Britain's new post-conflict situation. And, as far as I was concerned in this case, not without some justification.

In a rather Machiavellian way.

The newspapers preferred to put all our woes down to austerity; to the general lack of respect for authority these days, not to mention the proliferation of guns on the street. Everything, in fact, except continued rationing. And they probably only left that out due to the ongoing shortage of paper.

As far as I was aware no one had yet been arrested for the murder and since Ogilvy and I had parted on bad terms I had been expecting the usual urgency to solve the crime would mean they'd think of me sooner or later.

After all, it wasn't any secret that I blamed Ogilvy for what had happened to Katja Tereshchenko and Konstantin Berezin. And while not exactly a strong motive for murder, my time in the police had taught me that desperation had a tendency to make criminals of more people than just criminals.

As it was, Bryce surprised me.

'Sydney Stanley,' he said. 'Remember him?'

'Of course,' I said. 'He's the one who put the Lazarus girl on to me. What about him? I'd have thought you'd have nailed him for something by now.'

'He's too fly for that,' said Gifford. 'He's got friends in high places. Government connections.'

'So he told me when we met. I thought it was all hot air at the time. Is this why you're raiding Jack Hibbert's place?'

'Not exactly,' said Gifford. 'Although the pressure helps. This is less to do with Stanley's business dealings than with the connections he has to the terrorists. We might finally have a chance to bring him down.'

'I'm glad to hear it. Should you be telling *me*, though? Since I don't work for you anymore?'

'You signed the Official Secrets Act,' Bryce said. 'Just because you have left doesn't alter that.'

'Right,' I said. 'Anyway, as far as I know Jack's not done any business with him for months. So what have you got on him? Don't tell me he had something to do with Ogilvy's murder?'

'Brian Ogilvy?' said Bryce. 'What makes you say that?'

'Because he knew Stanley.'

They both looked surprised.

'Didn't you know?' I said. 'Ogilvy was worried about information leaking from the government. He asked me if we had picked anything like that up while we were monitoring the Jewish intercepts.' I looked around as if trying to remember. 'This must have been last January. I gave him Stanley's name as Stanley had been boasting about his government contacts. I suggested to Ogilvy that if Stanley wasn't the one catching the leaks he was the sort of man who might be able to find out who was. Actually,' I added, looking at Bryce innocently, 'he particularly asked me not to mention it to you for some reason. Of course,' I went on while that was sinking in, 'that was before I realised Stanley had set me up with Lizzie. I certainly wouldn't have passed his name on otherwise. And at that time, you remember, I didn't know what Ogilvy was up to.'

'Up to?' Gifford repeated, nose twitching like a dog's on a scent.

'How he had it in for Manny Shinwell,' I said. 'Magdalena told me. Then I realised he was looking for a way to bring Shinwell down.'

I was gratified to see Bryce and Gifford exchange a glance, as if I had inadvertently touched on something sensitive.

'As a matter of fact,' Bryce admitted, 'Shinwell's name has come up in connection with Stanley. Nothing incriminating, but it's there nonetheless.'

'I did wonder at the time,' I said, throwing another spanner in the works, 'if one of your lot hadn't taken him out.'

'Are you serious?' Gifford asked.

'Or that maybe he committed suicide.'

'Suicide?' Bryce said. 'What on earth would make you think that?'

I shrugged. 'The papers said it was a robbery but didn't go into any detail … About how he died, I mean. And since he worked for the Security Service … Well, you know, wheels within wheels? Besides, Stanley's name happened to come up the last time I saw him.'

Bryce perked up. 'In what context?'

'You remember he was none too pleased when he found out about me and Lizzie Lazarus? He said I'd compromised our operations by getting involved with her. He had a point, of course, and I thought it only fair to tell him of her connection to Stanley. If he didn't already know about it, that is.'

'And?' Gifford prompted when I didn't go on.

I tried to look mystified. 'Well, I wasn't going to say anything, but Ogilvy all but accused me of trying to put pressure on him because I knew he knew Stanley.'

'He thought you were trying to blackmail him?'

'He didn't exactly use the word.'

'How far *had* things gone between Ogilvy and Stanley?' Bryce asked.

I shrugged again. 'I've no idea how far he took it. I merely passed him Stanley's name. To be honest I didn't know much about either of them at the time.'

'But you suspect Ogilvy contacted Stanley?'

'He said he would. I know he hated Shinwell,' I added. 'Something to do with the family estate? Magdalena told me about it. He seemed pretty well set against the Labour government but how far he might have taken things I can't say. I have to admit that when I read about his death it crossed my mind that perhaps he'd taken things too far ... couldn't see his way out, if you see what I mean ...'

I thought I'd made a pretty good case. Considering it was on the spur of the moment and I'd had no time to study the brief. But I hadn't convinced Gifford. He looked too relaxed. He even pulled out that pipe of his, quite happy to stink up my kitchen with his smoke even though it wasn't yet nine o'clock.

'No, won't wash,' he said, tamping down the tobacco with his thumb and looking pointedly at me as he said it. 'Not Ogilvy. He may have held a grudge but he was too smart to allow himself to be compromised in any way.'

'Was it a robbery then?'

'His safe was open when we arrived.'

'He might have left it open himself,' I suggested. 'Getting rid of anything incriminating, perhaps. Or was it forced?'

'Wouldn't have to be,' Gifford replied, lighting the pipe. 'A man will usually do as he's told with a gun to his head.'

'Still ...' I persisted.

'Can't see it,' said Gifford, beginning to puff like a traction engine at harvest time. 'Besides, Ogilvy was shot in the temple yet no gun was found at the scene. Good trick for a suicide.'

'I didn't know that,' I said.

Gifford puttered a moment on the pipe. 'Interesting bullet though, once we dug it out.'

'Oh? In what way?'

'Quite distinctive, according to ballistics. Most likely came from a Russian gun.'

'Russian?' I said. 'So you think it might be connected to the office after all?'

'We're still working on it,' Gifford said.

'If it's not his connection to Ogilvy, then what is it you think you can get on Stanley?'

'That's why we've come to see you,' said Bryce.

He eyed me in that rather vacuous way of his, like something out of P G Wodehouse.

'We've arrested Elizabeth Lazarus,' he said.

That did surprise me.

'Lizzie?'

'She's been going under the name of Betty Knouth. Sometimes Gilberte Knut. A few weeks ago there was an attempted bombing at the Colonial Office. Luckily the device failed to go off.'

I'd read about it. The newspapers had suggested that one of the Jewish terrorist organisations had been involved. Going through the story had afforded me a moment of nostalgia. For Magdalena mostly, not for the work.

'Some members of the Lehi group were picked up in Paris a couple of days ago,' Bryce went on. 'They were carrying explosives. Shortly afterwards Betty Knouth and an accomplice were stopped crossing the border into Belgium. Envelopes addressed to a lot of prominent people in Britain were found in their possession.'

'Letter bombs?'

'That's the way it looks.'

Gifford took the pipe out of his mouth. 'The man she was travelling with turned out to be Yaacov Levstein. He was still travelling under the name of Jacob Elias. You remember Elias, I suppose?'

I wasn't likely to forget. The last time I'd seen Lizzie was in early February not long before she stood me up at the ABC tearooms. The last time I'd seen Elias was just after he tried to shoot me in Kensington Gardens and I'd hit him with a lump of wood. It seemed a long time ago now.

'Are they talking?'

'No, nothing useful,' Bryce admitted. 'We've enough for a conviction. We were already familiar with Levstein. His fingerprints link him to the murder of several policemen in Palestine. The attempted assassination of the British High Commissioner, as well.'

'Had we known when he had a go at you in Kensington Gardens that Elias was Levstein,' Gifford said, 'we might have been able to pick him up earlier. He'll hang now, of course, and his cooperation won't alter that even if he was inclined to talk.'

'And Lizzie Lazarus?' I asked.

'All we have on the Lazarus girl are the envelopes, and you know how it'll go … all a pretty girl has to do is bat her eyelids at a jury. They'll imagine themselves spanking her bottom and telling her to be a good girl in future and as likely as not let her off altogether.'

I sympathised with the jury.

'We need to put some pressure on her,' Gifford said. 'But she won't talk to us.'

'Mislaid your rubber truncheon?'

Gifford stared at me gloomily.

'That's why we thought of you,' Bryce said. 'We thought you might be able to get something out of her.'

'I thought I was *persona non grata.*'

Bryce gave one of his diffident smiles. 'Ogilvy was set against you, I'm afraid. He had Guy Liddell's ear and once it reached the DG … There wasn't much I could do, Harry.'

'Are you're offering me my job back?'

He temporised but he wasn't going to go that far.

'What do you expect me to do?'

'Just talk to her. She might be surprised to see you. Given what … you know, your—'

'Friendship?' I suggested.

'Yes … she might feel better disposed to you than the rest of us.'

Having filled the kitchen with pipe smoke, Gifford knocked the thing out and slipped it back into his pocket. 'She's a tough one,' he announced.

I didn't remember there being too many tough bits to Lizzie, but then she'd only given me the parts she'd chosen to offer.

'I don't see why she shouldn't expect to see me,' I said. 'She knows I worked for you. Presumably she doesn't know what's happened since. I don't mind trying, though.'

Not least because I was intrigued to see her again.

39

Lizzie was being held in Holloway. It was a Saturday and as I drove over with Bryce I saw a queue at the gate waiting to get in.

'Visiting day,' said Bryce, swinging the car into a side street towards another entrance. Gifford was waiting for us and although his greeting was cordial enough I could see he thought he was wasting his time.

'We'll be recording what she says,' he told me as he showed his badge at successive doors and we walked deeper into the labyrinth that was Holloway Prison. 'Try being friendly and lead her into an indiscretion,' he suggested. 'Failing that, bait her. Make her lose her temper.'

Waiting alone in an interview room while they brought Lizzie up from the cells, I was thinking that I couldn't remember Lizzie ever losing her temper. She'd expressed irritation often enough, although in hindsight that was usually when she'd been unable to get information out of me.

Ironic, when I thought about it, that now our roles were reversed.

On the drive over Bryce had said unexpectedly, 'I didn't want to say anything in front of Henry, but one thing you might like to know is that the repatriations have stopped.'

'Oh?' I replied neutrally.

'Last month. The Americans were having their doubts and it wasn't sitting well here with some of those that knew either.'

'Suddenly found they had a conscience?'

Bryce ignored the sarcasm. 'The thing is, when the Labour government took over in '45, Bevin was doubtful about the policy. He only agreed to continue with it because he was assured that no force would be used. That all the detainees went voluntarily.'

'You know that wasn't the case,' I said.

'No,' he said hesitantly. 'I'm very much afraid they lied to him.'

'To Bevin? Who lied?'

'Some of the Foreign Office officials.' He paused. 'They lied to their minister.'

Listening to Bryce, every word he said coming out of his mouth as reluctantly as pulled teeth, I got the impression that in his eyes this had been the real outrage: officials lying to their minister.

'I thought you'd like to know, Harry,' he finally said. 'In case it helps.'

I supposed it helped someone. Any Russian still knocking around who had so far eluded Stalin. But not me. Nor the thousands of poor buggers who they'd already shipped back to the waiting NKVD thugs.

Bryce didn't dwell on the subject. He began talking faster and filled me in on some background information they had turned up on Lizzie.

After the war, he told me, she had been given the Croix de Guerre by the French for her work with the Resistance. She had always maintained as much, although I had never believed her. She'd also worked as a war correspondent, been given the rank of lieutenant by the Americans, and had been awarded a Silver Star. General Patton had pinned it on her himself, which I guessed both he and Lizzie would have enjoyed.

I'd have thought that that might have been enough for any girl, but Bryce said she'd also lived in America for a while and saved the biggest surprise for last. While there she had married a Yank and had three children.

I didn't believe him at first. I'd seen no sign of it on her body, although I have to admit I'm no expert in the field. I'd never been one for young mothers and married women. And Lizzie had always kept herself in trim.

That's how she looked when the wardress escorted her into the room. Lizzie hadn't been told it was me she was seeing and Bryce was right, the surprise was plain on her face. It only lasted a moment, though.

'Hello, Harry,' she said, regaining her composure in a heartbeat. 'You are not looking so good.'

I couldn't say the same about her. I might have had a few ups and downs in the past few months but nothing, I suspected, to hers. Yet despite the prison garb and even without the benefit of makeup she was still a looker. The coquettish pout remained in place but I was trying to picture the body beneath, as if some wishful x-ray vision could pick up what I had missed – stretch marks and whatever other signs are left on women's bodies after they've given birth.

Oddly though, all I could picture was Lizzie in her fur at Miriam's party, and the little black dress she had worn beneath.

I smiled at her. 'Do you know how long I waited for you at the ABC tearoom that evening?'

'That was not very nice of me, was it Harry?' she said. 'But I met a man who offered me a film part and he wanted me to read for him that evening. Would you want me to pass up such an opportunity, Harry?'

'It was one thing to stand me up, Lizzie, but putting Yaacov Levstein on my back wasn't very friendly of you.'

She batted those long black lashes of hers, practising for the jury I imagine, and looked back at me as if she had no idea what I was talking about.

'And you never got back in touch.'

'I felt so guilty.'

'I can imagine.'

She pouted. 'We had some fun, Harry. Nothing lasts forever.'

I considered asking about her husband and children and if she'd stood them up for a film part too. But I thought I might save them for later.

'So what are you doing here?' I asked.

'It is a misunderstanding.' She shrugged. 'A silly mistake.'

To listen to her one might have thought she'd been caught leaving Derry and Toms without paying for a dress.

'And the envelopes?'

'The envelopes were not mine. They belonged to someone else.'

'Jacob Elias?'

'Who?'

'The man you were picked up with? Otherwise known as Yaacov Levstein.'

'Him? I do not know him, Harry. Truthfully. We had only just met. If you saw him you would know he is not my type.'

'We did meet once,' I reminded her. 'Very briefly. I suppose the envelopes were his?'

She shrugged in that Gallic way that says so much more than mere words. I knew then I could stay there all day and not get anywhere with Lizzie Lazarus ... or Betty Knouth ... or Gilberte Knut, or whatever she was calling herself this season.

We carried on in the same fashion for another half hour, Lizzie making eyes at me and managing to convey the impression that if the stone-faced wardress wasn't there watching us she'd be up for a tryst over the interview table. I might have considered it myself if Gifford wasn't taping the encounter.

And watching it too for all I knew.

In a last attempt to get under her skin, I asked about her husband and children back in America. She just frowned at me a little distractedly, as one might if trying to remember whether or not they'd turned off the gas before coming out.

So in the end I wound up the interview. Lizzie watched as I stood up. An amused smile was playing on those full lips and I might have been tempted to give her a peck on the cheek in farewell if the Medusa hadn't been standing at the door.

'You know they're going to hang Levstein,' I said as a passing shot. 'I'd be sorry to see them stretch that pretty neck of yours, Lizzie.'

She pouted at me for the last time. 'The fascists shot my mother, Harry. Do you think I am scared if they threaten to hang me?'

****

Bryce and Gifford were none too pleased at my failure to get anything out of Lizzie, of course. Gifford didn't come right out and say it, but I got the impression he would have let me give evidence against her if he could come up with a few malleable facts that might be bent to fit the case. It was all nods and winks and innuendo as you'd expect – nothing you could pin down. But I'd never done that when I was a policeman and wasn't inclined to start now.

To give him his due he did his best. I spent the next couple of days on the wrong end of an interview myself while he and Bryce tried to dredge up anything of consequence that Lizzie and I might have inadvertently shared while having our affair.

I couldn't blame them. I even offered to testify against Yaacov Levstein if needed. With his fingerprints, however, they'd been given enough rope to hang him and he wouldn't have to trouble my conscience.

Lizzie wasn't going to hang, though, and if she charmed the jury the chances were she wouldn't even get much of a sentence. And she was still young – hardly much over twenty. I couldn't help wondering what else she might pack into an already eventful life before she was done.

40

Bryce and Gifford dropped me back at the flat and as I got out of the car and said goodbye, I couldn't help but hope I would never meet them again. Watching them drive away it occurred to me that, as they had now queered the pitch with Jack for me, I was back where I had been four months earlier: out of work and out of prospects, and with an ever-narrowing circle of acquaintances.

Some things were different though. Back then my frame of mind had been as bleak as that winter had been. I had lost my job and almost certainly lost Magdalena.

Despite Ogilvy's stricture about not contacting Service personnel, after a few days of indecision I did finally go to see her in Archery Close. I might have telephoned first, but what I had to say had to be said face to face.

She opened the door, but if she was surprised to see me she hid it well.

'You shouldn't be here,' she said.

'They told you, too?'

'That I wasn't to speak to you.'

'I didn't resign,' I said. 'They sacked me, whatever they told you.'

'Well,' she said, 'you knew the risks.'

Perhaps everything that had happened had made me over-sensitive. But somehow that seemed an abrogation of responsibility; as if once having wanted to be part of what I was doing, now it had all gone wrong, she was letting me know I was on my own. Perhaps I was too sensitive, but she wasn't looking me in the eye.

'About what happened ...' I began.

'Best not talk about it,' she said.

I was still on the doorstep and it seemed that was as far as I was going to get.

'That man ...' I tried again.

'The detective?'

'Yes. The photographs ...'

She gazed down at my feet.

'You really shouldn't be here,' she said once more.

'When I saw Ogilvy—'

'I can't talk about it,' she interrupted.

'No, but I—'

'Please!'

'They're not following me anymore,' I said after a moment.

This time she did look me in the eye.

'They never were, Harry.'

Neither of us spoke.

'Well,' I said at last, 'I just wanted to say I was sorry. For how things turned out. Have you seen Ogilvy?'

'Don't,' she said abruptly. 'Don't talk about it.'

We looked at each other. There was so much to say although at that moment I couldn't think what it might be.

'I'll call you,' I said eventually.

She regarded me with those doleful eyes for a moment longer and didn't reply. I couldn't tell what she was thinking. Perhaps SOE had trained her not to give anything away if she fell into the wrong hands. Well, she'd fallen into mine briefly, but any futile attempts I made now wouldn't get her to tell me what I wanted to know.

****

I went back to my empty flat and tried not to think about her. Sometimes it worked but when it did it left only one other thing to think about. So, when not thinking about Magdalena, my mind returned to all that had happened and I was haunted with thoughts of Joseph Wolff's suicide.

I knew by then, of course, that what he had done had been prompted by a combination of circumstances. To a man who was perhaps as sensitive to such things as was Wolff, each, it seemed to me, had been sufficient to demonstrate to him the helplessness of the individual when faced by the monolith that was the state.

Wolff's grief for his lost brother and for Oksana had gone unexplained by those who knew the truth. And when he discovered what had happened to them, I imagined he must have felt a sense of betrayal – betrayal by those whom he had served. He'd started to say as much in the note he had begun in his hotel room, the note he'd never finished.

Perhaps what weighed most heavily upon him, though, had been the sense of guilt he must have felt at his own responsibility for the fate that had befallen Katja Tereshchenko. A guilt that should have been borne by those who had formulated a policy which they had neither the courage to make public, nor the decency to acknowledge.

And, I suspected, it was this last sense of guilt – this final blow – that pushed Wolff's already fragile state of mind into accepting that an act of self-destruction was the only avenue left open to him.

An act that now underscored my own responsibility for the fate of Konstantin Berezin.

****

It is never easy to look back and see oneself at any given point in one's past. We may know what we did at a particular moment, and even still feel a trace of what we had once felt. But circumstances – feelings and perspective – change, and the person at whom we are looking becomes hardly more than a cipher. That past representation of our old self is just a shade, a ghostly apparition we can no longer bring into focus. Too much has happened between and we have since become different people.

This is probably why, in June, I found it difficult to follow the reasoning I had followed in March. Perhaps the intervening months had inured me to all that had happened; perhaps, as the symptoms I felt then didn't kill me, I had been inoculated against feeling that same way again. It is impossible to say.

What was left though, what remained the same, was that I felt no sense of regret.

****

After my sacking, but mostly after Magdalena, I subsided into a pool of self-pity. I might have stayed there and wallowed in it had Jack not pulled me out and given me something to do.

Having to deal with his clients kept me busy and meant I needed not only a thorough knowledge of those items he could lay his hands on, but also such stock as he kept on-hand in his lock-ups.

That is how I first became aware of the store of guns and ammunition he held.

It was kept in a secure basement, separate from his other run-of-the-mill stock and safe under several locks and keys. My first impression on seeing the place was that he had gone into the gun-running business.

'Do the police know what you've got down here?' I asked the first time he showed me around.

'I've got licences for it all,' he insisted.

I had my doubts. Alongside the kind of stuff you might have expected – British and German arms, some French and American – there was also a few items that were out of the ordinary: Czech pistols and a Russian Nagant.

I picked up the revolver.

'What sort of licences have you got for this?' I asked him.

'Ah,' Jack said evasively, 'something like that doesn't exactly come under the Act ...' He looked sideways at me. 'Given its provenance,' he added.

I'd heard Jack's shilly-shallying before.

'Well that's all right then,' I said.

I turned the piece over in my hand. A Russian star and the date 1941 had been stamped in the metal by the grip. A serial number had been etched just forward of the chamber. Not that a serial number would be of much use to anyone – the Russians were hardly likely to cooperate should anyone want it traced.

'I've only got one load for it,' Jack said, taking the piece off me and wrapping it back in its oily rag. 'So it ain't worth much. It's a .38 but they're gas-sealed cartridges. Not easy to get hold of. Shame, really. Handy little weapon since it takes a suppressor.'

In retrospect I suppose that was the moment I made the decision. I had had the will for some time. The intent, as any prosecution barrister would no doubt have argued. Until that moment, though, it had been no more than a vague notion.

Jack laid the gun and its grubby rag back on the shelf.

'I suppose you've got the suppressor as well?'

'Yeah,' he replied, off-hand. 'It's in the box there. Bloke I got it from said it came off an NKVD man. God only knows what poor sods he used it on.'

And the remark came as a sort of benediction. A blessing that clothed my intent with a kind of virtuous aptness. One that closed the circle.

All the same, I didn't rush things.

I left it a week or two until the next time I happened to be in Jack's basement. I went back to the shelf and slipped the Nagant, its suppressor and the meagre stock of shells into my pocket.

I didn't say anything to Jack, of course. What one doesn't know can't hurt one.

At least, that's supposed to be the way things work.

****

It was a foggy night towards the end of March when I climbed the steps up to the street from the Tube station. According to the Met Office, the thaw had finally set in although we'd have to put up with a lot of fog until a decent wind turned up to blow the stuff away. Not that the lack of visibility was ever a problem for Londoners – during the war they'd got used to finding their way blind around blacked-out streets. The heavy fog, though, mixed with coal smoke from the city's chimneys was another matter. The combination tended to leave the air as thick with tar and grit as the old Capstan cigarettes I used to smoke.

They called it smog and it was killing hundreds of people every day.

It tended to keep people off the streets, though. And those few I did pass hurried by with handkerchiefs pressed to their faces, like inept bandits who hadn't quite learned the trick of tying a knot.

I was doing the same. As anonymous as the rest.

I walked the few streets between the Tube station and the house. Ahead of me, the pale light of the streetlamps were haloed in yellow, as if the very air was jaundiced. The names on the street signs, fixed high on the walls, were lost in the opaque haze.

But that didn't matter. I knew where I was.

Back in Belgravia and, as it happened, not far from the house of my ex-wife's aunt, Julia. Penny and I had lived with her for a while when we were first married and as I walked I recalled that one of Julia's chief complaints had been that my presence had disturbed the calm of her household. This particular evening though, I wasn't expecting to make enough noise to disturb Julia's calm. The Nagant in my pocket, equipped with its suppressor, wouldn't trouble the tranquil quiet of complacent Belgravia in the slightest.

I knew the house as soon as I reached it. I had already spent an evening watching the place and had made a few discreet enquiries about the married couple who lived in – the housekeeper and cook, and her husband, the general factotum. Once a week – on this very night – they were in the habit of spending an evening playing cards at a social club in Soho. They never returned before midnight.

Even as I climbed the steps to the door and rang the bell I was conscious of still having time to change my mind. It lasted only a moment, but time enough for the events of the past months to condense into a stream that played like a silent newsreel in front of my sightless eyes: Riseborough and

Wolff, Samuel and Oksana, Hooper and Fairfax ... I saw Lizzie, Magdalena and the detective ... his camera ... those photographs ...

The scenes flickered by in the fog, each swirling around the single character who lay like a spider at the centre of a web.

It was said we had just been through the coldest winter in living memory and yet, despite the thaw, standing on the doorstep that foggy evening I couldn't remember ever having felt colder.

The sound of movement and of a key turning in the lock broke the spell. My hand closed on the Nagant in my pocket.

Ogilvy answered the door himself.

Printed in Great Britain
by Amazon